BETWEEN
FROST AND FURY

CHANI LYNN FEENER

BETWEEN
FROST AND
FURY

SWOON READS

NEW YORK

A SWOON READS BOOK

An imprint of Feiwel and Friends and Macmillan Publishing Group, LLC
175 Fifth Avenue, New York, NY 10010

Our books may be purchased in bulk for promotional, educational, or business use. Please
contact your local bookseller or the Macmillan Corporate and Premium Sales Department
at (800) 221-7945 ext. 5442 or by e-mail at MacmillanSpecialMarkets@macmillan.com.

Library of Congress Cataloging-in-Publication Data is available.
ISBN 978-1-250-12378-7 (hardcover) / ISBN 978-1-250-12377-0 (ebook)

Book design by Liz Dresner

First edition, 2018

10 9 8 7 6 5 4 3 2 1

swoonreads.com

FOR MOM AND DAD

PROLOGUE

Delaney?!" Ruckus gripped the phone tighter in his hand. Fear was threatening to cloud his judgment, and he forced himself to still in the center of the living room. Inhale slowly until he stopped seeing black spots.

There'd been an odd note in Delaney's tone when she'd picked up a few minutes ago, a hint that something was already wrong before he'd told her about the Basileus's murder. Considering her plan had been to spend the day at the beach with her best friend, Mariana, there was no reason he could see for her to be nervous.

She'd been in the process of saying his name, which meant something had to have happened. There were any number of things that could mean—most of them bad—but until he got more information, he couldn't panic. Panicking meant making mistakes, and he couldn't afford any, no matter what was going on.

Ruckus hung up and dialed again, setting the phone on speaker and putting it aside while it rang, retrieving the clear device he'd left on the kitchen counter. He cursed when Delaney's voicemail started.

Ended the call.

Tried again.

The forgotten device in his other hand made a beeping sound suddenly, a row of tiny yellow lights flickering at the top. He drew his attention away from the phone long enough to tap the center button. A second later Fawna's face filled the palm-sized screen, the concern in her eyes apparent.

"We might have a problem."

"Something's happened to Delaney," he said, that tightening feeling in his chest getting worse when her phone went to voicemail yet again.

"There's a Kint ship," Fawna told him, momentarily glancing away to use the control panel in her own craft. He couldn't see it from the small screen, but the sound of her clicking keys gave it away. "I don't know how long it's been here. It was doing a very good job cloaking its presence. Could be they arrived before me."

His stomach bottomed out and he gripped the edge of the counter to keep himself from visibly swaying.

He and Fawna had only just ended their conversation moments before he'd phoned Delaney to fill her in. Because Xenith and Earth were in different galaxies, communications were limited to a certain range. Fawna had come all the way to tell him about the political unrest in Vakar, which meant she was still directly outside Earth's orbit.

And apparently she wasn't alone.

"Whose ship?" Ruckus asked, though he was already rushing down the hall toward Mariana's bedroom, where he'd last seen the car keys. He'd drive down to the beach and find out what was going on.

Because he was being paranoid, and there was no possible way what he feared was happening really was. No possible—

"I believe it's the Zane's," Fawna confirmed, basically shattering any remaining hope he had left. "Wait." She paused then added, "It looks like a smaller craft is about to board. Ruckus . . . it's coming from Earth."

Without stopping, he swiveled on his heel, adjusting his course of trajectory. He snatched the phone off the counter just in case, and quickly checked to make sure his fritz was turned on as he headed toward the front door.

"Come get me," he ordered, holding the screen up so Fawna could see the moment he got outside. "Now."

"We don't know she's been taken . . . ," Fawna began, though he could tell she was already preparing to do as he'd said. The console before her began to whir, and a digital voice announced preparations to approach the planet.

"She's on that ship," he stated, moving past the driveway and around to the back of the apartment building. There was more space in the yard. "Just get here."

He disconnected the device before she could respond, shoving it into his back pocket so he could try dialing Delaney one last time, already knowing it was useless. There was only one reason for the Zane's personal ship to be hovering outside of Earth.

Ruckus struggled against the mixture of anger and terror that warred within him, trying to keep his mind clear enough to run the calculations. If they'd just taken her, Delaney wasn't too far ahead. He could board Fawna's ship and be close behind, arrive shortly after.

And then?

The sound of an engine roared above him and he tipped his head back in time to see the smaller craft drop its camouflage, seemingly appearing out of thin air. A small hatch at the bottom opened, and a metal bar dropped down into his already waiting hand.

And then he'd do whatever he had to do to get Delaney back safely.

CHAPTER 1

She felt like she was dying.

Delaney came to with a piercing pain, like an ice pick was being lodged in her brain. For a moment she stayed still, waiting for the spinning sensation to dissipate and her muscles to stop quivering.

The solid surface cradled her body awkwardly, causing her to wince when she shifted. The feeling was oddly familiar, and her mind struggled to comprehend what was going on. She'd yet to open her eyes, and inhaled slowly before reaching out blindly to feel her surroundings.

She stretched her arm over her head and met with a solid, cool surface. It was clearly metallic, and beneath it she could feel a steady thrum. Her eyes snapped open, but she had to wait for the black spots to clear before she could make out the familiar walls.

She was on a spaceship. Again.

"You have got to be kidding." She pressed both hands to her forehead and tried to recall how she'd gotten here.

The first time she'd been abducted by aliens and dragged unconscious onto a spaceship, she'd been completely terrified. Now, while there was a steady seed of panic at the center of her chest, it was manageable. Staying calm was always the best course of action when it came to dealing with Xenith.

It'd been a couple of months since her first encounter with the Vakar and the Kints, when she'd been mistaken for an alien princess and ripped from her home world. On Xenith, she'd managed to evade assassination and form a couple of strong bonds with members of the royal staff. Whatever was going on here, she could count on her friends. Though it would have been nice to have gotten a heads-up this time around.

"Why does this keep happening to me?" she groaned.

"That's an interesting question."

Delaney bolted upright and turned toward the voice so fast, she got whiplash. Instinctively she tucked herself against the corner of the wall, gripping the edge of the cot hard enough that her knuckles turned white.

Suddenly it hit her: the beach, Mariana, seeing *him* in the reflection of the car window.

"Trystan," she said breathlessly, instantly recalling how easy it was for him to make someone feel off-center. He hadn't done anything yet, and her heart was already pounding.

Delaney tried—and failed—not to be so obvious, but her gaze trailed over him, noting subtle differences and similarities before she could stop herself.

His blond hair was still perfectly styled, but there were hints of dark circles beneath his eyes. He was leaning back in a white chair, the only other piece of furniture aside from the cot. When she'd spotted him on Earth, he'd been dressed like a human, but now he was wearing his traditional outfit. The sleeveless blue shirt with the inch-high collar brought back memories of being constantly on edge, of pretending.

There was a band wrapped around his right wrist and her eyes locked on to it, recognizing the weapon as one that most soldiers—or *Tellers*, to use their word—carried. All he had to do was wave his middle finger over the bottom of it to turn the band into a gun.

Delaney had one as well, and because it looked so harmless, she'd kept it on her. It'd been a slight comfort, knowing that she'd had a means of protecting herself even when there'd been no cause for alarm. She barely resisted the urge to glance down at her own wrist, knowing already that there was no way he'd left her armed.

She should have turned and run the other way when she'd realized who he was back on the street. Or shot him.

He was watching her through those eerie eyes of his, cornflower blue with a ring of crimson around the outside of the iris. All aliens from Xenith had two-toned eyes, but his were by far the creepiest she'd ever encountered.

A long silence stretched between them before he took the initiative, dropping his leg so both feet were flat on the ground. He rested his elbows on his thighs.

"Hello, Lissa," he purred, but he didn't smile. His expression remained blank in that intense way only he could pull off. He had the best poker face she'd ever seen, and after posing as an alien princess for a month, she thought herself a good judge of such things.

She swallowed the lump in her throat and forced herself to pull her shoulders back, straightening her spine to appear more offended than afraid. There was only one reason she could think of to explain why she was here: He still thought she was Olena.

An alien device that somehow affected brain waves had been behind her initial kidnapping. The Vakar princess—or Lissa, as they called her—Olena Ond had used it on Delaney as part of her plan to escape an arranged marriage to Trystan. Because of that device, Delaney had been forced to pretend to be Olena, spending weeks undercover on the planet Xenith among the Vakar people until the real Lissa was found.

Once Olena had been discovered and they'd been able to swap places, another device had been used to reverse the effects of the first. Ruckus had finally been able to see the real her, and she'd gone back to her life. Which meant it had worked.

So what was wrong now? Was there a chance the correctional device's effect had worn off? And even if it had, how had Trystan found her? Why?

"Care to explain what's going on right now?" she asked, latching on to the thread of anger she felt. She'd done everything that the Vakar had asked of her, with the agreement that, once finished, she'd be left alone. The dream had been to never see Trystan again, let alone be kidnapped by him.

Did Ruckus know where she was? They'd been talking on the phone when Trystan had knocked her unconscious. As a trained commander, Ruckus should have been able to figure out what had happened.

He'd find her, she trusted that.

"I'm curious," Trystan finally spoke, completely ignoring her question, "how you thought you could get away from this? You had to know you were already in too deep."

Great, what the hell had Olena done now? Delaney let her head drop back against the wall with a resounding clank. The two times she'd met Olena she'd disliked her almost as much as everyone else seemed to. During her stay with the Vakar, she hadn't heard a single good thing about her.

"This is a mistake," she mumbled.

"The only mistake," he sneered, finally letting some of his true feelings slip through, "was letting you fly away on that ship."

It wasn't hard to catch his anger now. She had to tread lightly. There were about a million different ways this could go, and not many boded well for her. If he'd been anyone else, pretending she was Olena again would more than likely be a good thing. Unfortunately, Trystan's hatred for his betrothed was well-known, and if he thought she'd run again . . .

That had to be it. Olena had run again, and without Ruckus there to hunt her down, Trystan had gone after her himself. It didn't really explain why he'd bother, considering he'd hated the idea of being betrothed to the Lissa, but Delaney couldn't think up any other reason for him being on Earth.

Except, what had Ruckus said on the phone before she'd been injected with whatever sleep agent Trystan had used? Something about the Basileus being dead? If Olena's dad, the Vakar king, was dead, that changed everything.

Didn't it?

"Okay"—she held out both hands, opting to try negotiation— "clearly we need to work a few things out—"

"I've already worked everything out for us," he remarked.

Frustrated, she ran a hand through her hair. When his gaze homed in on the motion, his mask wavered, but she couldn't make out what he was feeling.

"Why do you keep staring at me like that?!"

She'd never been able to read him very well; he had more facets than anyone she'd ever met. It was that very thing that always put everyone around him on edge. As the Kint prince, or Zane, it was a good thing.

For him.

For everyone else, it seriously blew.

"Your hair." It was little more than a whisper.

"It's longer." She reached up and fiddled with a strand. In the five weeks since she'd last been to Xenith, her hair had grown to a little past her shoulders.

"It's red."

For a split second the world tipped on its axis. She hadn't misheard him. He could see her, the real her, which meant the device hadn't malfunctioned and she didn't look like Olena at all.

Momentarily forgetting her earlier plan to remain calm, she scrambled up from the cot, searching the small area. Her initial perusal of the room had been accurate, however; there was nothing aside from the chair where he sat and the cot currently pressed to the backs of her knees.

Frantically, she groped her back pocket, letting out a relieved sound when she felt the heavy press of her cell phone. She almost dropped it in her haste to get it out, fumbling a little before activating the camera app.

The face staring back at her from the small screen was unequivocally her own. Her bright red hair was mussed around her face, and a bit of color stained her otherwise pale cheeks—color she'd gotten from spending the day at the beach with Mariana. Between the hair and the vibrant green of her eyes, there wasn't a single similarity she shared with Olena. No physical reason anyone, let alone someone who'd known the Lissa for years, would have to mix them up.

The relief she'd been feeling at seeing herself began to fade as the reality of her situation came into focus. She frowned, a new wave of suspicion rising.

"This isn't right," she said, even though she knew that Trystan wasn't the type to make mistakes. She forced herself to lift her gaze to his. "How about we turn this ship around, and you can drop me off in the nearest heavily populated city? Doesn't even have to be where you found me."

He eyed her for a moment, that blank mask back in place, before slowly easing to his feet to stand over her with his six-five height.

"You're smarter than that," he stated. "I didn't travel all the way to that primitive planet for just anyone, and I certainly didn't go for Olena or Ruckus. There was no mistake. I took who I meant to take, Delaney."

"You know who I am." She was too unnerved to be embarrassed by the way her voice shook. Obviously he did; proof of that had literally just been staring back at her in the mirror. Still, she'd hoped . . .

she didn't know what. Just that there was another explanation. *Any* other explanation.

"For a while now, yes."

"I don't understand."

"You had me fooled for a long time." He took a step closer. "It was suspicious, but I truly believed that her time on Earth had changed her. That perhaps I had misjudged Olena. It's too bad she wasn't as good at playing herself as you were."

"I did what I had to do to protect my people," she said. "You would have done the same."

"It's all I ever do," he agreed.

"Then you understand why I did it." She wasn't stupid enough to allow herself to feel hope a second time. He wouldn't have gone through all this trouble if he didn't intend to enact revenge. Trystan wasn't the type of guy you pissed off and lived to tell the tale.

"I understand why you lied to me, yes." He was close now, less than a foot away, and he paused there for a deceiving moment. Baiting people was his specialty. He knew all the right buttons to press, the right things to say, the right spaces to crowd. "I never once lied to you."

That, unfortunately, was true. He'd taken great pleasure in telling her how much he hated Olena, and telling her often. It was still a bit of a shocker that he was supposedly loved by his people, where Olena was disliked at best. He was just as big a jerk as she was, spoiled and pompous and entitled.

"Why bother with all this?" Delaney waved a hand to indicate the ship, unable to hold back the anger this time. "Why not just kill me on Earth? Too easy?"

He quirked a brow, the corner of his mouth just barely turning up. "Are you asking if I intend to torture you?"

"Did you murder the Basileus?" she blurted, admitting to herself that she was being a coward for doing so. Fact of the matter was, she didn't think she was ready to find out what she was doing here. If he did plan on making an example of her for lying. He had to be feeling like a fool for believing she was Olena, and it wouldn't matter to him that that hadn't been her intention.

"I happened to be there," he said, not really answering the question at all. "The Basilissa narrowly escaped the same fate, and her daughter's life still hangs in the balance."

It was hard to breathe, even harder to think coherently, with him so near.

"Of course we were going to retaliate once we discovered the truth, Delaney," he continued. "My father has his limits, and being manipulated the way that he was crossed a line. Peace was over the second you stepped foot on that ship with the Ander."

So the Rex, the king of the Kints, had ordered an attack on Vakar, even after everything she had gone through to prevent it. Guilt and frustration assaulted her, and she struggled to maintain an even tone when she spoke.

"How does killing Magnus Ond and taking his family hostage help you?"

She hadn't exactly been fond of the Basileus, but he hadn't deserved to die, either. Everything he'd done, he'd done for the same reasons that Delaney herself had. He'd been trying to protect his people.

"The Kints have taken temporary control—" he began, but she cut him off with a shake of her head.

"No, I'm not asking how it helps the Kints, Trystan." She licked her lips, bracing herself. "I'm asking how it helps *you*?" Because there was no good reason for her to be here if there wasn't some hidden agenda that benefited him specifically.

"*I've* taken temporary control of Vakar," he said, not even bothering to hide the partial smirk now. "It took some convincing, but my father, who wanted to destroy the entire Ond family outright, saw my reasoning. We don't need to annihilate the Vakar when we can add them to our forces instead. Soon the control I hold over them will be official and permanent. All I have to do is marry the Uprisen heir to the Vakar throne."

It was the ease with which he said it that had her hackles rising. He'd always spoken about his and Olena's joining with derision. Just now there'd been something else in his tone.

"The Basilissa would do anything to spare her daughter's life." He eased even closer, sliding his arms against the wall to trap her head between them. "Including agree to all my terms. Amazing, really, that there was even a single person alive who cared enough about Olena to make sacrifices for her. And Tilda made many sacrifices, not just for herself."

Delaney gulped. "That's how you found out my name."

She waited, but he didn't elaborate. Maybe he wouldn't lie, but he certainly didn't have a problem withholding.

"The Uprising is an extremely traditional ceremony," he said. "It has determined the next in line for both the Vakar and Kint thrones almost since the beginning of our civilization. The law clearly states that only someone Uprisen can succeed the previous ruler."

Delaney still wasn't following, until he lifted her right arm, pinning it next to her head. When he motioned with his chin, she glanced over and her breath caught.

The dime-sized tattoo, a small, glittery green *V* on her forearm at the curve of her elbow, winked back at her in the overhead lights. She may have looked like Olena to everyone during the actual ceremony, but it had been Delaney's body going through the process. She'd been the one branded.

She'd always intended to get rid of it, cover it up, but she'd been so distracted acclimating to life with Ruckus, she'd put it off.

"No." The word shot out before she even realized she'd spoken.

"Yes." There was no room for argument in his eyes, but of course she did anyway.

"I'm not from Xenith. And I went through the ceremony for Olena, *as* Olena! The oath—"

"Did not require you to speak a name," he interrupted. "Yours or hers." He was right about that, too. "*You* said the oath. *You* were the one Uprisen. As for the fact that you're from Earth, in your speech you proclaimed yourself a member of the Vakar people, and a citizen of Xenith."

"This is insane," she said. "Do the ceremony again! Uprise Olena. She's the one who's supposed to take the throne. She's the Vakar Lissa!"

"Yet you are the Uprisen heir. Vakar takes that very seriously. Their people value tradition above all else. Not even their Basilissa can go around breaking customs easily," he said, putting his face dangerously close to hers.

"You can't do this," she whispered, forcing away the tears that threatened to choke her.

"I'm not the one who did this," he declared. "You took the oath. I had no part in that."

The air stuttered out of her lungs. Delaney had gone through with that ceremony only to protect her cover; no one could honestly expect her to have taken that oath seriously. Could they?

The hold on her anger snapped, and it must have surprised him just as much as it did her, because when she shoved him, he actually moved away. The renewed space between them helped her push through the fog of fear.

"You're going to turn this ship around," she hissed, "and take me back. Now."

"Am I?" There was a dark note to his voice, which she ignored.

"Yes, you are." Her hands fisted at her sides, and his eyes trailed down to them, his expression tightening with annoyance. The fact that he so clearly saw her as a non-threat pissed her off even more.

"I knew you were arrogant," she snapped, "but I didn't take you for a kidnapper. You can't just expect people to agree to do whatever you say. The world doesn't work like that, Trystan!"

He lifted a brow, and she let out a frustrated growl before she could stop it. She'd be damned before she rolled over and went along with his asinine plans.

"*My* world doesn't work that way," she corrected. "I am sick of you aliens and your complexes, thinking you can just swoop in whenever you like and uproot people's lives. *My* life! You have no right to—"

"I don't need rights. You are not the one who gives orders here, Delaney." He said her name like it was an accusation. In a lot of ways, it was.

"I'm not doing this," she stressed.

"You should have thought of that before you allowed your friends to convince you to take part in a traditional ceremony. Especially one you knew so little about."

"There has to be a way around that," she murmured. "If you want someone to replace Olena, fine, but that's not me."

"I'm hardly the only one who wants another option," he said. "The Tars went through a lot of trouble to attempt to achieve that goal themselves, if you recall."

When Delaney had been to Xenith last, a rogue group known as the Tars had repeatedly attacked her. Their hope had been to kill Olena, claiming that she would not only make a terrible partner for Trystan, but also a horrible ruler.

"An entire organization dedicated itself to keeping her off the throne," Trystan continued, watching her closely. "It can't be too surprising that people are more willing to stick to tradition and choose the Uprisen girl over the Lissa they hate."

Delaney couldn't immediately come up with an argument for that logic, but she was certain she would eventually. She had to.

"I'm curious—did you ever meet her?" The look on her face must have been answer enough. "Interesting. How many times?"

"Twice," she replied. "Technically."

He made an accusatory sound in the back of his throat, but when he spoke, he sounded conversational. "Once is usually enough, but of course you'd have to be different. Difficult."

"I'm assuming there's a point?"

"You left me with Olena Ond." A hint of anger sparked in his eyes. "That is the point."

CHAPTER 2

Delaney waited, expecting more, and when he didn't continue, she crossed her arms. "Seriously? So this is about your ego? I bruised it by not wanting to stick around on a foreign planet, and that somehow justifies you punishing me?"

"This isn't a punishment," he objected. "It's about doing what's best for my people. Now, would you like me to tell you what to expect, or would you prefer to go into this blind?"

She opened her mouth to argue further, but his expression darkened. Yelling at him was getting her nowhere. Her only real option was to stall and trust that Ruckus was on his way. He'd have a plan.

"I'm not agreeing to any of this," she said, but waved a hand, indicating he could continue.

"Xenith is in a higher state of unrest since you left," he said. "While we're in Vakar, it's crucial you do exactly what I tell you. Their Basilissa has already announced you as her successor, but you'll be expected to make a public appearance, accept the position in person."

"And the Vakar are just going along with this? Because of a mark on my arm?" She highly doubted it.

"There's slight resistance," he confirmed, "which is to be expected. But nothing I can't handle. You needn't worry about that."

"Trystan." She took a breath, already regretting what she was about to say, but she had no other moves. "Please."

"Don't beg, Delaney. It's unbecoming."

Punching him momentarily came to mind before she tamped down that suicidal notion.

He smoothed the hem of his shirt and reached back to tap a panel on the wall. "I meant it earlier. I never lied to you before, Delaney," he said evenly. "I'm not going to start now. It might not be in the way that you initially thought, but you are going to pay with your life."

The door opened and a woman dressed in Kint colors stepped into view. Her hands were clasped before her, a fritz bracelet on each wrist. Her hair was pulled back in a tight ponytail that made up one single massive curl, and she kept her gaze locked on Trystan.

"This is Teller Sanzie. She'll be keeping an eye on you when I'm not around to do so," he said, not sparing the soldier so much as a glance. "If you need anything, there's an intercom on the door panel that connects to the hall where she'll be standing guard."

"It's an honor to meet you, Lissa Delaney." Sanzie bowed her head.

Delaney flinched at the title.

"We'll be arriving in a few hours," Trystan said. "Try not to cause any trouble."

He left before she could even think about how to respond.

DELANEY'S EMOTIONS WERE all over the place; one second she was angry, the next scared or sad. During her first kidnapping, she'd had Ruckus to soothe her. He'd been the tether that had grounded her through all the new crazy alien experiences.

But now she was alone.

The only friends she had on Xenith were Vakar, and she doubted Trystan would allow one of them near her. He was too smart for that; he would predict that someone close to Ruckus would attempt to make contact. And she knew they would, too. Ruckus was as well loved as the Zane; they just happened to garner the favor of different people.

The Teller, Sanzie, had brought her food a couple of hours ago, but Delaney had barely touched it. Her legs were aching from all the pacing by the time the door opened again.

Trystan motioned to her from out in the hall and, when she didn't budge, let out an annoyed sigh.

"We're on planet," he declared. "There's nowhere you could go even if you somehow managed to get past me and the five dozen guards stationed around the hangar. That's not even counting those covering the castle grounds. Think this through."

She was trapped on a ship that was now parked on Xenith. It was either stay in this room as long as she could, or get all this over with. With Trystan's patience running thin, she didn't know how plausible staying was, which really only left her one choice.

"Where are we exactly?" she asked as she moved toward him.

"The Vakar palace." He'd hinted to as much earlier while talking about the Basilissa, but Delaney wanted to be sure.

There was a small relief at being somewhere she was at least partially familiar with.

"Act like you want to be here when we exit the ship," Trystan said, warning her in a low voice so that the guards they passed as they moved through the halls couldn't overhear.

"Like hell."

"Don't do it for me, Delaney," he said. "I told you, there are still some who don't like the idea of you on the throne. Any sign of weakness will only prompt them to attack sooner. I would like to avoid a bloody battle on your first day back, wouldn't you?"

Honestly? Not really. But she wasn't too keen on getting caught in the cross fire, and she remembered all too well how good the soldiers of this world were. If it hadn't been for Ruckus—and, she was loathe to admit, Trystan—she would have been killed. It sucked, but for now she'd need him to help protect her.

Using him to keep herself safe until there was an opening for escape was as good a plan as any at this point.

They came to a stop at the side of the ship, and he made a motion before the door sensor. When it whooshed open, it exposed the hangar and the sixty or so Tellers who were waiting for them.

"Five dozen strong, huh?" She bobbed her head, slipping into that good, old-fashioned security blanket called humor. "You must be so proud."

Without a word he stepped out, not bothering to wait and see if she followed, which of course she did.

All the Tellers were dressed in Kint colors, navy blue with silver trimmings. There were three times as many Tellers in the castle than when she'd been there before, but that didn't surprise her. Trystan had taken Vakar by force and twisted the law to suit his own needs. Even with the queen backing his story, there were people here who would rebel against him. It wasn't just Delaney who had to worry about being attacked.

"You know," she said, casually waving a hand, "this seems like a lot of hassle. Convincing me to go along with your plan, which isn't going to happen. You're not really the type who enjoys trivial arguments."

He lifted a single golden brow as they passed under the arch that would lead them into the castle proper. The hallway was white, and lined with even more Tellers. At the end, the color scheme changed to match Vakar tradition, with fake-wood-paneled walls that were really metal, and deep forest-green carpeting and curtains.

"You believe your freedom to be trivial, do you?" he asked, obviously finding the possibility amusing.

Her eyes narrowed. "Of course not. But you do."

They traveled up a familiar flight of stairs, and across another section of the castle toward a room Delaney had only entered twice during her last visit. There was a set of Kint guards flanking the office, both men bowing their heads low at their approach.

Trystan didn't bother knocking, swinging the door open and stepping through without hesitation.

A fire roared in the hearth to the right, the orange and purple flames flickering wildly. The sweet smell of burning wood—more sugary here than it would have smelled on Earth—tickled Delaney's nose as she entered.

The Basilissa came into view then, seated behind the large desk positioned in the center of the room. She stood and held her chin up, her hands clasped before her. Her normally warm eyes, golden-brown surrounded by a rim of violet, went cold when she set them on Trystan.

Her hair was long, past her elbows, and so blond that it appeared as though she'd been standing in the sun for days. Her dress was formal, a deep forest green made of silk and sheer material that didn't leave much to the imagination.

"You swore to give me news of my daughter." When Tilda spoke, her lyrical voice was firm, far harsher than Delaney remembered it.

"That's why I'm here," he replied. All of a sudden Trystan cocked his head, looking to the ceiling.

Delaney knew that look. She and Ruckus still spoke telepathically all the time, especially during Mariana's lengthy stories about her most recent crush.

Everyone of importance on Xenith went through a process called a fitting, where a tiny computer-type device was inserted at the base of their skull. It worked a lot like a radio, giving off and receiving frequencies. To communicate with another person who'd been fitted, their specific frequency had to have been imprinted onto the receiver's device. Sort of like a password to access the brain.

Clearly, the message Trystan was receiving was a lengthy one, because he remained silent for so long, Delaney began to grow antsy.

He finally shook his head and took a deliberate step back. "Something has come up, if you'll excuse me for a moment." He held Delaney's gaze. "I won't be long."

She gave him a mock salute. "Got it."

He clenched his jaw, clearly wanting to say something, but changed his mind. Without another word he spun on his heel and exited the way they'd come.

She waited until he was gone before turning back to the Basilissa.

Tilda gave her a once-over. "Shorts and a T-shirt. That's not really the look of a Lissa, Miss Grace."

"Probably because I'm not a Lissa," she snapped.

Tilda glanced away, guilt flashing over her perfect features. There was a single couch positioned in front of the fire and she motioned to it, waiting for Delaney to come around and take a seat before following suit. They kept a good foot of empty space between them.

"For what it's worth," Tilda began in a low voice, "I regret your being here. Again. You did my family a great service, protected us and our daughter, and this is not the way you should be repaid."

"From the sounds of it, neither of us was given much of a choice in my being here."

Tilda nodded, then hesitated, biting down on her lower lip and wringing her hands in her lap. Finally she eased herself closer, dropping her voice to a mere whisper despite the fact that they were alone.

"Do what he says," she urged.

"We don't really know each other," Delaney said, "but I think you know me well enough to know that's not going to happen."

"I'm not saying don't fight," she replied. "I'm telling you to pick your battles. Whether we like it or not, you are going to be the next ruler of Vakar. So much has been asked of you already, but I fear I must insist on asking more." Tilda shifted again so that their shoulders bumped, the smell of sweet wildflowers drifting off her lithe body. "Take care of my people, Delaney. Please."

If it hadn't been clear before that the Basilissa had completely given up, it was now. Pushing down the twinge of annoyance she felt, Delaney covered Tilda's clasped hands with one of her own.

"Fine. Whatever. But this whole thing is semantics," she said. "Trystan is only using me to legally get the crown. Once he's got it, there won't be any need for me, and I certainly won't have any real say in the goings-on here. I'm sorry, but if I was what you were relying on, you bet on the wrong horse."

Tilda frowned for a second, obviously trying to recall what a horse was before it hit her. "You weren't here to see the lengths he's gone to in order to make this happen." She grabbed on to Delaney's hand, shaking slightly. "Initially he planned on killing me as well, and Olena. With us out of the way, he could have taken Vakar."

"He's avoiding resistance," Delaney pointed out. "Say what you will about him, but he cares about his people, too. He thinks he can save lives this way."

"That's—"

The door opened and Tilda pulled back, quickly tucking herself into the other side of the couch.

Trystan stopped, his hand still on the knob, glancing suspiciously between the two of them.

"What?" Delaney flashed a fabricated grin, putting maximum effort into the illusion of not giving a shit. "Expected to see flames, didn't you?"

In retrospect, lighting a fire wouldn't have been an entirely awful idea. It would have forced the guards at the door to come put it out, and the two of them might have been able to slip away. Of course, there would have then been the hundreds of other guards patrolling the castle to deal with.

Half-baked schemes were nice for passing the time but awful for reality.

Besides, it didn't seem like Tilda would go for something like that anyway. She wasn't exactly chained up in a dungeon right now. Seemed more like she was free to go about her business as usual, so long as she kept Kint guards around.

Trystan's expression tightened but he didn't respond, turning to glare at the Basilissa instead. "I'm giving you five minutes."

Tilda stood, folding her hands in front of her, probably to hide the shaking that Delaney had caught. There was a single screen attached to the opposite wall, and she turned toward it, waiting.

Trystan removed a square device from his back pocket and hit a few buttons.

The screen flickered then filled with the image of a pale, exhausted-looking girl. Her inky black hair was limp around her face, and there were dirt smears under her eyes. The wall at her back was dark gray, and there was nothing to indicate where she was.

"Olena." Tilda inhaled sharply, scanning her daughter. The image only showed an inch or so past her shoulders, so there wasn't much to see.

Delaney was staring herself. She'd known Olena had been taken captive, but the girl before her looked nothing like the Lissa she recalled. It appeared as though she hadn't slept in days.

"This is how you take care of royal prisoners?" Tilda snapped, voicing Delaney's thoughts. She glared at Trystan.

"Mother." Olena's voice shook through the screen.

"It's going to be okay," Tilda said, starting forward, only to stop abruptly when Trystan shook his head.

"Don't make promises you can't keep," he warned.

"I have done everything you've asked." She jabbed a finger at the screen. "And this is how you treat her?!"

"As you can clearly see," he said, "I'm standing right here, nowhere near where your daughter is currently being kept."

"You are not innocent in this, Zane Trystan," she snarled.

"I'm not claiming to be," he stated. "Merely pointing out that once she was delivered to Carnage, she became my father's concern. Not mine. Keep doing as you're told, and I'll try to petition for better treatment."

"Mother," Olena repeated. She was scowling, and seemed impatient as ever. "Mother, I want to come home."

"You will," Tilda assured her, clearly ignoring Trystan's suggestion about promises. "Soon. Just do as they tell you, and we'll put an end to this."

Olena glanced over the Basilissa's shoulder, spotting Delaney for the first time. She frowned, then leaned closer to the camera as if to get a better view.

"What is *she* doing there?" Her words were rushed, forced past her lips in a breathy burst. "Why is she there? This is her fault. It is. Trystan—" Frantically, she searched her side of the screen, but from where he stood he couldn't see him. "She's the one who tricked you! She made you look like a fool!"

"Olena." Tilda's voice was pleading, but her daughter either didn't pick up on it or didn't care.

"She should be in this hellhole, not me! This is what she deserves," she insisted. "I did us both a favor, Trystan, but she . . . she deceived you. She's the one who messed with your head!"

Something caught Olena's attention behind the camera where she was and she steeled herself indignantly. When she spoke next, it was obvious she was addressing whoever was there with her.

"Put her here!" She pointed a finger at Delaney through the screen. "She's the one who should be locked up! I can—"

The screen went black, the only sound now the crackling of the fire at their backs and a slight hum coming from the device on the wall. Trystan hadn't touched the smaller one in his hand, so he hadn't been the one to end the connection.

"What. The. Hell." Delaney stared at Trystan, her shock no doubt painted across her face.

Tilda dropped back down onto the couch.

"Agreed," Trystan said, catching her gaze and holding it. "I didn't expect her to so quickly place all the blame on you. That was a miscalculation on my part."

"Seriously?" Delaney's mouth dropped open. "She's being tortured."

"Hardly," he grunted. "She's merely being kept in a room without a four-poster bed and silk sheets. I assure you, no one's laid a hand on her. She's being dramatic."

"You just got done telling Tilda you aren't there," she pointed out, "so how can you possibly know that for certain?"

"Fine." Trystan glowered. "As far as I know, orders were not to harm her. And besides, whatever is being done, did you miss the part where she offered you up in her stead? Trust me, she wouldn't lose an ounce of sleep if you were the one being held in that room. *That's* who you left me with." He set a heated glare on the Basilissa. "That's who my father and Magnus Ond attempted to tie me to."

"What did you do to the Basileus?" Delaney demanded.

He tilted his head, eyes narrowing almost imperceptibly.

"I assume *you* murdered him," she continued, pressing her luck and not caring. He hadn't wanted to tell her on the ship, but she wanted answers. "Did you try to blow him up, too?"

If he was affected by her reference to his attempt on her own life, he didn't show it.

"What did you do? She's giving up everything." She glanced momentarily at Tilda, frowning. "So it had to be horrible. Whatever you did, it had to have been bad enough to get her to relent within a few weeks' time."

"He was executed privately," Trystan finally revealed, his words cutting across the room, "and quickly, under my father's orders. I happened to be present, but no, I didn't do the actual slaying."

Delaney opened her mouth but was swiftly cut off.

"They're ready for us in the ceremony room," he said, giving Tilda his attention. "I trust what you just saw hasn't dismayed you from continuing as planned?"

Silently, Tilda stood and regally glided toward the door.

CHAPTER 3

"Where are we going?" Delaney asked a few minutes later.

Five Tellers had fallen into step at their backs, herding in the Basilissa so that she was trapped between them. Not that she looked like she was even considering running.

Reaching a point where the hallway branched off in two directions, Trystan stopped and faced Tilda, blatantly ignoring Delaney's question.

"The Tellers will take you to the main room while I prepare Delaney for the ceremony. Once this is finished, you'll get to see your daughter again. I might not be there to watch you myself"—he took a threatening step closer, his Tellers doing the same to cage Tilda in even more—"but remember the agreement."

"I've given my word," she stated tersely. Trystan flicked his fingers to the left, indicating the corridor, and five Tellers began moving in that direction, forcing Tilda into motion. She glared over her shoulder at Trystan for a moment before gliding smoothly forward.

Without waiting for them to reach the end of the hall, Trystan turned and led Delaney down the original path.

Questions burned the back of her throat, but she was afraid to ask them. The answers would no doubt be even more terrifying than the unknown, and she wasn't sure she was prepared to hear them just yet.

She was putting on a brave front because she had to—it was the only way she knew to get through this—but on the inside she was shaking.

Trystan pulled a clear square device from his back pocket and hit a button. A door at the end of the hall emitted a sharp click before it opened on its own.

The room beyond was large, and decorated in various shades of green and gold. There was a main sitting area, with three other rooms branching off. A wall of windows to her left showcased a darkening turquoise sky, and there was a small circular table next to it.

"This isn't Olena's room." That was where Delaney had spent most of her time before, and she'd sort of assumed that was where she'd be sleeping now.

"No, because you aren't Olena. I had this room converted."

"I don't see anything special here," she said.

"The changes aren't visible. I recalled the way you were constantly slipping out of your room the last time you were here. That's how we met in the library, wasn't it? I doubt you were meant to be there."

No, she definitely hadn't been. Ruckus had left Pettus on the door, and she'd given the poor guy the slip.

Trystan motioned toward the electrical panel to the right of the door. "This emits a force field, preventing anyone with human DNA from exiting the room without first typing a passcode. It also prevents anyone without specific DNA from entering. You'll be much safer here. No one can get in aside from Sanzie and me."

She crossed her arms, glaring. "What if there's a fire? Or the building starts to collapse?"

"Trust that I'll come retrieve you," he said absently, moving toward the bedroom. The motion-censored lights flicked on to bathe him in a warm glow, and standing there beneath it, he could easily be mistaken for Adonis.

Or Lucifer.

She heard the slide of the zipper on his shirt before she registered what he was doing, and her cheeks stained red.

"I had your clothes brought here," he told her, removing his shirt completely and tossing it carelessly onto the olive-green bedspread.

"Olena's clothes," she said, regretting that her tone lacked the firmness it should have had. His half-naked state was putting her on edge, and when he reached for the top of his pants, she took a step in retreat.

"*Your* clothes. I had new ones made for you."

Trystan had gotten her a new wardrobe? That was . . . unsettling.

He turned around, his bare chest suddenly in view. He was just as fit as Ruckus, with well-defined muscles he clearly used. His torso was a little longer, tapering down to narrow hips. There was only one thing wrong with the perfect image: a small scar the size of a nickel right beneath his right pectoral.

"That's where I took the zee," Trystan said, realizing what she was staring at. "For you."

He'd saved her life that day. She wasn't complaining about that, but she didn't want to feel like she owed him something. He'd just uprooted her from her home, on purpose. Surely he couldn't imagine that was a fair trade for what he'd done during the Uprising.

"I thought with your advancements in medicine you could avoid scars?"

"It took too long to get me to the medical wing," he said with a shrug, continuing to unfasten his pants.

Delaney spun around. She moved closer to the window, pretending to take interest in the darkening sky.

All it did, however, was let a sadness sweep over her, a feeling she'd been fighting against since waking up on the ship. Thoughts of Ruckus assaulted her, and she caught her breath and counted to ten in a poor attempt to regain control. If she let him in now, she'd never recover, and she needed to stay on her toes with Trystan so near.

"Okay." Delaney took a deep breath, noticing from the corner of her eye that Trystan was busy putting on a different pair of pants. "So, how'd you get the Vakar to get along with the Kints in this place?"

"I asked them nicely," he said sarcastically. Then: "The same way I get your government to consistently do what I say. Threats. Kint tech is better than Vakar, as it is Earth's. Our advanced technology is the only thing keeping your increased numbers from standing a chance against us. If we chose to invade, you'd hold your ground for a while, but ultimately our weapons would cut down legions of your Tellers, whereas you'd only manage to take out a few of ours."

"Soldiers," she corrected, still not risking a full glance in his direction. "We call them soldiers."

"Same thing."

She jumped when the sound of his voice came from directly behind her, and she spun around to face him. It was at least a relief to find he was fully clothed again.

"People will be watching, Delaney," he reminded. "You can't tremble in fear every time I'm near. This ceremony is important."

"It's not fear, asshole." She stepped around him so she had more space. "I'm pissed off."

"Understood." He canted his head. "But that changes nothing. This ceremony—"

"All your stupid alien ceremonies are important," she snapped.

"This would be so much easier if you just listened and did what you were told." His mouth thinned. "There's no speech, but you must clearly agree to everything the Illust asks. Simple, even more so than the last ceremony you took part in."

"Oh?" She crossed her arms and glared pointedly at the spot where his scar was hidden by his shirt. "You mean the one where you got shot?"

"You don't need to make excuses to look at my chest." He gave her that half smirk, the one that reminded her of a snake trying to beguile a mouse.

"Nice try," she drawled, feeling her cheeks heat despite her flippant tone.

Trystan sighed, losing some of that hard edge. "I've already taken a zee for you once. I protected you then; I'll do so again."

"Or maybe you've realized the error of your ways." Even as she said it, she knew she didn't believe it. Her eyes trailed back down to the scar. They hadn't gotten him medical help soon enough to prevent it from forming, and that was also because he'd been trying to keep her safe. Even after he'd been shot, he'd refused to move until Ruckus had confirmed the threat was over. He'd settled himself over Delaney like a shield, already prepared to take more bullets for her.

"I wouldn't need protecting if you hadn't brought me here," she pointed out before he could say anything. "You do know that, right?"

"Of course," he replied softly.

"If anything happens to me during this ceremony, Trystan—"

"Nothing will."

She blew out a breath, crossing her arms protectively. "This doesn't mean I'm conceding."

No, all it meant was that she knew how to pick her battles. Ruckus needed more time to get here, and even though taking part in the last ceremony had clearly been a massive mistake, she couldn't see a way out of this one.

The blue of Trystan's eyes darkened, but he merely motioned at her. "You need to change. You can't very well attend this wearing *that*."

"You are such a snob."

"I've laid out what you're to wear." He motioned toward the bedroom, ignoring her comment. "I trust you can manage yourself?"

"How do you think these clothes got on?" It was the wrong thing to say, made even more obvious by the way his body tightened. She moved past him and made her way toward the bedroom, silently cursing herself.

"Delaney," he said, stopping her right before she made it to the open door.

She couldn't bring herself to look at him, so she kept staring straight ahead. Unfortunately that was where the king-sized bed was.

"If you don't come out within ten minutes, I'm coming in."

"I hate you." She slammed the bedroom door behind her. It didn't take long to figure out there was no lock, and she cursed, giving him the finger through the wood. Sure, he couldn't see the small act of defiance, but it made her feel better.

Until she spotted the dress he'd hung over the floor-length mirror. She was tempted to tear the thing to shreds, but then what?

She pulled the flimsy material off the mirror. After dropping it onto the bed, she made quick work of her shirt and shorts. Stepping into the dress, she turned to check out her reflection.

When Trystan had said he'd gotten her new clothes, she'd hoped they'd be a bit less revealing than Olena's or Tilda's. Of course that'd been wishful thinking on her part. The dress was gold and made of thousands of tiny beads. The neckline was low, a sharp V that dipped so far down, it exposed the space between her breasts. The straps were about an inch thick. The front only went halfway down her thighs, while the material in the back touched behind her knees. It was surprisingly heavy, and when she reached for the zipper in the back, she cursed again.

She could only get it an inch of the way up on her own, which meant—

As if reading her mind, Trystan chose that moment to knock. He entered without waiting, easing the door open in a purposefully taunting manner. When he spotted her, something unnerving flashed in his blue-and-crimson eyes, and her gaze immediately shifted to the only exit.

He shut the door and came forward, covering the hand she had on the zipper with his own. She let go and he slowly slid the zipper up, catching her gaze in the mirror, holding it unblinkingly. He stepped back and went to the nightstand once it was done, and she let out a shaky breath.

He wasn't away nearly long enough, coming back a second later holding three pieces of gold jewelry. A golden band was attached to her left bicep, a twist of three different circles crisscrossing together. The second piece was similar, though smaller, this one covering her right wrist.

The last was a necklace, and she watched as he secured it around her neck. There were three Xs—one gold, one silver, and one bronze—two side by side, and the third directly below them in a weird upside-down pyramid shape. At the center of each X was a small gem the size of a water droplet. The one in the center was bloodred, with a sapphire to its right and an emerald to its left.

He ran the pad of his finger over the red gem, staring at it in the mirror before raising his eyes to meet hers.

"Don't screw this up, Delaney," he said by her ear. "People will get hurt if you do."

She didn't know how to respond to that, so she kept her mouth shut. He seemed satisfied to take her silence as agreement, and moved away again.

"The ruby signifies Earth," he said. "Red and bronze. Those are your colors. You may be taking the Vakar throne, but you're still an Earthling. You have a claim on that planet."

She did not like the sound of that, but in typical fashion, he changed the subject before she could dive deeper.

"You'll go through a similar process to the one you did when you received this." He lightly cupped her elbow, turning it so that the glittering *V* tattoo was staring up at her.

Then he presented her with his opposite arm, where there was a glittering capital *K* imprinted into his skin, an *X* just beneath that. Between the left arm and leg of the last letter there was a small blue gem, similar to the one on the necklace.

"It might sting a little," he confessed. "I suggest you don't let that show. We value strength."

She nodded, and he dropped their arms.

Getting the first tattoo hadn't been so bad; she could certainly stand up there unflinching and do it again. Part of her felt sickened by the idea that she'd be even more tied to this place, but if everything he'd told her was true, so long as she had the original mark, getting more wouldn't matter.

He was standing by the edge of the bed now, and waved a hand at it. "Sit down. The shoes are on the side."

The second she got her hand on a fritz, she was really going to enjoy shooting his bossy self.

Delaney sat and reached over the edge, frowning as she picked up one of the shoes. It was a high heel with at least eight long straps attached to the top. She picked at one, tried to figure out what to do with it, and then shook her head.

"Yeah"—she waved it at him—"I'm thinking not. How does this thing even work?" Why did all their fashion have to be so overly complex?

Trystan caught her eye and hesitated. When she tilted her head in silent question, he seemed to resolve himself of something.

She sucked in a breath when he dropped to his knees in front of her, and was even more shocked when he plucked the shoe from her hand.

He avoided eye contact as he slipped her foot into it and began adjusting the straps with immense concentration.

Her foot now resting on his thigh, she watched as he twisted the alternating straps of navy and forest green all the way up to the bottom of her knee. The base of the shoe was the same shade of gold as her dress. The second shoe went on the same way.

Once finished, Trystan moved, grabbing a shirt from another drawer. His pants were a blinding white tucked into shiny black boots. The shirt was similar in style to the traditional one he'd been wearing before, only now the front was navy blue and the back was green. Gold trim crossed over the tops of his shoulders, separating the two colors, and in the front where it zipped, another gold stripe folded over to conceal the metal.

A pair of black fingerless gloves were the final touch, and after he had the straps secured, he paused before her.

She was grateful for the silence during that time. Her heart was racing and her skin felt too tight. The nervousness she was feeling had escalated to the point of near terror. The only other alien ceremony she'd had to do she'd had days to prepare for.

This time? She didn't even know what the hell it was for.

She watched him, fear getting the best of her, blocking out anything clever she may have otherwise been able to pull off. The fact that they'd just changed in the same room together had her skin buzzing uncomfortably. It was too intimate, too familiar.

"Would you like an atteta to help with your makeup?" he asked her softly. "I have one waiting in the hall."

Her previous experience with maids hadn't gone all that well, a fact he was aware of. Was he asking her in an attempt to be . . . thoughtful? Somehow that made all of this worse.

"Trystan, this ceremony . . . It's not . . ." Crap. Now she was turning into a blubbering idiot. She took a deep breath and was about to try again, but he stopped her.

"It's not our binding ceremony," he said. "No. It's a Positioning."

"A what now?" She frowned.

"It is when a person in a position of high authority publicly backs a legitimate successor. Tilda already announced that you'll be taking her position weeks ago. Tonight is about you officially agreeing to do so, in front of the people."

It really was a lot like last time. All she had to do was stand up there and make promises to them she had no intention of keeping. Awesome.

"Afterward," he continued, "we can go over the steps that need to be taken before our binding ceremony. That process takes two months."

"So, two months from today . . ."

The corner of his mouth turned up. "*Will* be our binding ceremony. Yes. Which you will not be wearing gold to, I can assure you."

He spoke about it like it was set in stone. Like he didn't expect her to fight it. Or maybe he just didn't expect her fighting to make a difference. And, really, why should he? She was a lone human on a planet surrounded by odd customs and strange languages and people.

"I can handle my makeup on my own," she finally answered. "The color scheme seems obvious." She stood and went to the bathroom door, pausing with her hand on the silver handle.

Delaney left and was relieved to find that the bathroom did have a lock. She clicked it and turned to the sink. It was a single marble slab set against the wall, with a mirror on top. Just like in Olena's room, when she waved her hand underneath the lip, a drawer sprang open. She stepped back to give it space to slide all the way out, exposing rows of different-colored products.

The rebellious part of her wanted to select some of the pinks or purples just to spite him, but she refrained. She'd been here long enough the first time to know the basics, and was able to apply the Vakar equivalent of gold eye shadow. She lined her bottom lid with a deep blue liner, and dabbed a bit of emerald green at the outer and inner corners of her top eyelids.

She took a moment to inspect herself, weirdly pleased with what she saw. Her red hair really popped against the metallic color, the hints of blue and green making her eyes appear larger. Hopefully looking like she belonged would help her sell it.

Aside from the passing comment he'd made about her hair, Trystan had yet to say anything about her outer appearance. In fact, it was a bit weird how easily he seemed to fall back into their banter, one moment insulting her, the next being sweet. Or, at least as sweet as she suspected he was capable of being.

A light rap on the door told her she'd been in there too long, and she gave herself one last long look, not really seeing herself. She could do this.

Trystan was standing directly outside, arms crossed over his broad chest. He took in her makeup and nodded. As if she needed his approval before he'd allow anyone else to see her.

She rolled her eyes and pushed past him. "I should have punched that bitch Olena when I had the chance."

CHAPTER 4

here were so many people, way more than she'd expected. More than had been at Olena's—aka her—Uprising. It made sense when she took the time to think about it, with both Vakar and Kint now in attendance.

She could tell them apart in the crowd now, the missing Vakar Tellers from before mingling with the Kints, their green uniforms singling them out among what had once been their enemy.

The room was the same massive ballroom, large enough to fit two football fields at least, with a golden balcony stretched against three of the walls. The final wall held floor-to-ceiling windows.

Tilda was already standing on the stage, looking out over the masses. When Delaney and Trystan appeared at the back of the dais, Tilda met his gaze with a hard one of her own.

Delaney wasn't quite sure what to do; she remained still until Trystan motioned her forward. He stepped down to join the Tellers at the front, leaving Delaney and the Basilissa together for the crowd to see. Trystan remained close enough that he could react if she tried anything, but far enough to make an obvious statement.

An older man moved before her, the same one who'd conducted her Uprising. His hair was short and chestnut brown. A few gray hairs could be made out, but he didn't appear much older than forty. There were crinkles at the corners of his hazel-and-green-rimmed eyes, and a distinct look of pity on his face.

"Lissa Delaney Grace"—the older man indicated she should step forward—"during your Uprising you swore an oath to accept the responsibilities and sacrifices that come with being Vakar royalty. Do you recall such an oath?"

The crowd's eyes were like lasers burrowing into her, making a thin sheen of sweat break out over her skin. She was completely unprepared for this, had no clue what she was doing, and they were all watching like she did.

In her panic she turned to the only person she could, given her horrible circumstances, catching Trystan's gaze pleadingly. He bobbed his head once.

"Yes," she stated in a firm voice, hoping that was what he'd meant. He'd told her to agree to whatever the Illust said, and this man conducting the ceremony must be him.

The older guy—who she really needed to learn the name of—nodded at her approvingly.

Then she spotted a familiar face in the crowd and almost ran off the stage.

Pettus pressed a finger frantically to his lips. He was dressed in his Teller uniform, blending in with the rest of the crowd. It was good knowing he was safe; he'd helped her get off Xenith the last time. Seeing him was a lot like seeing an old childhood friend you thought you never would again.

Had Ruckus sent him? Ruckus wasn't there; if he had been, he would have contacted her through her fitting so . . . just Pettus, then.

She tried not to stare at him, afraid she'd tip Trystan off if she did.

"And are you now prepared to uphold your vow"—the Illust drew her attention back his way—"to protect and defend your people, no matter the cost? To rule them with honor, respect, and their best interests in mind?"

"Yes." If that was all she had to say, this might not be as bad as she'd feared.

He held up his right hand for hers, the familiar metal device clutched in his left.

She placed her right arm in the Illust's grasp, the device positioned at the tip of her green *V* tattoo, and then he pressed down. The burning sensation it brought wasn't so bad, and she barely had to clench her jaw to fight back the pain. It was quick, and the cool air stung when the device was removed, exposing the now raw flesh beneath.

Below the *V* was another brand, this one of an *X* about the same size. Before she could be glad it was over, he brought the device back, angling it slightly. This time there was a slight prick, and she bit her tongue to keep from outwardly flinching. A small green gem was added between the right arms of the letter. He pressed it again lower, inserting a small red gem between the bottom legs.

She braced for a fourth time, momentarily caught off guard when he turned to hand the device off to a nearby Teller. It was easy enough to guess that the final mark, the blue circle that would symbolize Kint, would be added after or during her binding ceremony to Trystan.

The one she never intended to happen.

"It is done," the man's voice boomed out once more, and he bowed to her. "Allow me to present Delaney Grace of Earth, the Lissa of Vakar and heir to the throne."

The crowd burst into cheers. She stared out at them, shocked by their reaction and more confused than she'd ever been. Back home, no way would an alien swooping in and claiming their crown be considered a good thing. She could see it now, a Kint soldier showing up at the White House, saying they were taking over.

Yeah. Right.

She searched for Pettus, but the mass had shifted, and try as she might, she couldn't spot him anywhere. She doubted he was here on anything other than reconnaissance, as badly as she wished otherwise.

But she had to trust there was a plan. Her friends wouldn't just leave her here like this.

Ruckus wouldn't leave her.

The feeling of being alone returned, and her chest ached right along with the fresh marks on her arm.

Then Trystan was there, easing her toward the single golden throne positioned at the stage's center. She sat without fuss, still too dazed to consider fighting him. He stood tall at her side, more like a sentry than her betrothed. Tilda stepped up to Delaney's other side, resting a hand firmly on her shoulder.

"They're going to greet you," Tilda informed her from the corner of her mouth. "All you have to do is nod and smile. All right?"

Delaney gritted her teeth and nodded.

Tilda motioned for the first line to move forward, keeping her hand on Delaney the entire time. Every once in a while, a person would step forward and her grip would tighten. There were a few faces that contained curiosity, but they moved on quickly, probably not wanting to risk the Zane's wrath.

After a while reality started weighing on her. Holding herself together earlier had been easier due to adrenaline, which she could feel seeping out of her with every passing second. Curling into a ball and sleeping for a week was starting to sound like the best plan ever.

She was about to lean over and demand Trystan put an end to this—or rather, ask him politely considering all the people currently eyeing her every move—when a commotion in line disrupted her train of thought.

A large Teller was shoving his way unapologetically through. He was burly, with sandy hair, and twice the height of most of those around him. His uniform was distinctly Vakar, the forest-green jacket decorated in numerous gold pieces shaped like octagons. Delaney assumed that, like on Earth, the medals signified station, but she'd never bothered to ask before.

It took her a moment to recognize him as the general she'd met in Tilda's hospital room after the shooting at the Uprising. If she recalled correctly, at the time he'd been polite, cordial even. That was not the vibe he was currently giving off.

"Fendus," Tilda said. "What is the meaning of this?"

"Forgive me, Basilissa." Fendus stopped at the foot of the dais. His eyes were hard, and Delaney noted that his right hand was twitching. "But this is a travesty."

"Excuse me?" Tilda's mouth thinned.

"You are making a mockery of our laws and traditions by announcing this human as our next ruler." He jabbed a stubby thumb toward Delaney.

Part of her was actually a bit relieved by his statement. For one, his anger made a hell of a lot more sense than the acceptance the rest of the room had shown thus far. For two, it stirred back that dying ember of hope. Maybe this wasn't set in stone after all.

Both Vakar and Kint began to whisper among themselves. A few took steps back; others began nodding in agreement.

"It is exactly because of tradition that I'm doing so. She was the one Uprisen; she is the new heir. That's been our way for centuries," Tilda announced, addressing the entire room with how she threw her voice, despite the fact that she kept her gaze locked on Fendus. "My decision was final when I gave it two weeks ago. If you'd had a problem with it then—"

"You refused to hear me out," he interrupted with a growl. "You've refused to hear any of us! This is a disgrace! Not just to Vakar, but to Kint as well! To all the people of Xenith!"

The sounds of agreement increased, voices rising in the crowd. Bodies shifted closer, at first moving slowly, then with more determination, forcing themselves forward so that they swarmed the edge of the dais.

"He's right!" one of the Vakar Tellers cried out, with others quickly joining in.

The mass surged closer, a ring of loyal Tellers, surprisingly a mix of Kint and Vakar, keeping them at bay. They held the crowd off, aiming their weapons at the most vocal of the bunch.

It wasn't everyone; a good many people hung back, shaking their heads. Delaney searched for Pettus again but still couldn't find him.

One of the angry Vakar leaped forward, almost making it through the barrier of Tellers. Acting on instinct, Delaney's hand shot out, grabbing Trystan's arm tightly. She felt him shifting closer, his hand settling down over hers, but she didn't risk tearing her gaze away from the swarming threat.

Fendus was still at the forefront, but he seemed just as caught off guard as Delaney. Before she could read too much into that, he looked to Tilda. A second later his expression firmed, and his voice rose over the rest once more.

"We will not let this stand! To place a human child on one of *our* thrones—"

A loud popping sound went off, silencing the room. No one moved. A slightly salty smell filled the air, mixed with a hint of burnt rubber.

Delaney didn't immediately understand what had happened. She was about to seek out Trystan's gaze when a small trickle of red coming from Fendus's mouth caught her eye.

It was so subtle at first, she thought she might be seeing things, but then the trail of blood dripped lower. He coughed, the sudden movement breaking the spell over the room as everyone turned to stare at him in shock. Fendus lifted a fist to his chest, and Delaney realized there was a fresh wound there.

His body tumbled to the ground with a loud crash. No one approached, though many watched, still in shock, as he bled out on the floor.

Her first instinct was to blame Trystan. After all, she'd seen him shoot many a person in the past. But when she glanced at him, it was to find his hand still over hers, the other empty at his side. His expression was blank. Like nothing had even happened.

She turned toward Tilda next, and couldn't help the short gasp that escaped her when she did. She hadn't even noticed the metal armband on the Basilissa's wrist. It certainly hadn't been there earlier when Trystan had left the two of them alone.

Tilda lowered her arm, keeping the weapon activated so that it was visible to all. Her left hand, amazingly, was still resting on Delaney's shoulder.

"Illust Victus," Tilda called, and the older gentleman who'd led the ceremony stepped forward, his shoulders stiff.

"Basilissa?" He angled his head down in a bow.

"It seems my people need a reminder of the law," she stated. "Is a member of the royal family allowed to be questioned in an open function?"

"No, Basilissa."

"Or in front of esteemed guests?" She held a hand out toward Trystan, obviously indicating the immense Kint presence currently in the room.

Even though everyone here knew the truth, that the Kints weren't guests so much as they were taking over, the Vakar Tellers in attendance all straightened their spines as if being scolded for real misconduct.

Delaney couldn't help her burst of shock; the Basilissa had always seemed the meeker of the regents. She'd assumed Magnus had completely run the show and Tilda had merely been along for the ride. It was becoming clear, however, that the Basilissa could certainly hold her own.

Though, murdering one of your top councilors in cold blood . . . Kind of scary, and not in the good way.

"Some of you obviously believe that Zane Trystan's arrival indicates

I no longer have a say in the governing of my own lands. I assure you, this is not the case. The decision to make Delaney Grace the heir was mine, and mine alone, and it will be treated as such from here on out. Those of you who do not heed this warning will suffer the same fate as Fendus Rynd. I don't care how high a position you hold, or how long our supposed friendship has stretched. Any more attempts to undermine my authority will be considered treason. Am I understood?"

The resounding agreement was so loud, the room shook.

DELANEY BARELY REGISTERED that they were moving, didn't realize they were entering the room from earlier until she was already standing in the center of the sitting area.

She paced in circles, moving easily in her anger despite the heeled shoes, ignoring the way the heavy material of her dress tugged every time she turned too quickly. She felt sick to her stomach.

Trystan was the one who wanted this. And yet Tilda was going along with it to protect her daughter. She'd willingly just killed one of her own to do it. How was that right?

If anything, tonight merely proved that this wasn't going to be all sunshine and rainbows like both Trystan and Tilda suspected. Of course there was going to be outrage. How could they expect anything less?

Delaney stilled. They wouldn't. At least, Trystan wouldn't. He was too smart to leave it to chance. It'd literally only been the three of them up on that stage, the nearest guards a good ten or so feet away.

She braced herself before she turned to him. "You set it up, didn't you?"

His expression remained blank, which only stoked the anger rising in her chest.

"How much of it?" she asked. "Did you just arm her? Give Tilda the gun in case, hoping that something would happen and she would have to use it?" She paused and shook her head. "No. No, you wouldn't do that. You'd have a plan. You knew Fendus was going to make a scene. How? Your spies find out for you?"

His continued stoicism was answer enough.

"You put him up to it." The realization brought a fresh wave of fear, and she struggled to bury it. "Did he know he was going to die?"

"I'm not sure," he finally replied, cool and casual. "That wasn't part of the original plan. He volunteered to help stir up the crowd so that Tilda could reprimand him in front of them all. It should have been enough. Why they chose to take it further, I can only speculate."

"You honestly expect me to believe that?"

"It's the truth." Finally a note of anger entered his tone.

Delaney wasn't sure why, but she believed him. Which meant Tilda had decided to kill one of her oldest friends on her own.

"You're monsters," she growled. "You're all monsters!"

He stepped toward her.

"You're sick!" she snapped at him. "You're all disgusting and I want no part in this!" Her hand was at her arm, nails already digging into her flesh to claw out the two tiny gems.

He was on her so fast, she didn't have time to blink, let alone get out of the way. Snatching her hands, he twisted their bodies, bringing her up against the cool surface of the window. Holding her was as easy for him as she imagined holding a mall mannequin would be, but that didn't stop her wild attempts to free herself.

"Let me go!" She twisted against him, not caring that she was turning her arms at painful angles.

"You're going to hurt yourself," he scoffed. "Stop it. Right now."

"I'm *going* to hurt you!" she promised. "You don't even care that he's dead, do you? It doesn't matter to you."

They'd just witnessed a murder, and he was as calm as ever.

"My plan will go accordingly no matter who lives or dies." His expression tightened to the point that it was painful to look at. "I promise you that, Delaney. We will be ruling Xenith. Together. Since the moment I decided I was going to bind you to me, your life became the only life that I cared about and I will not apologize for that. Ever."

She felt the blood drain from her body, muscles suddenly going lax. That was too much. Hearing him say stuff like that sucked the last bit of energy right out of her.

It terrified her.

He caught her, cradling her as if she hadn't just been all but threatening to kill him. Moving to the bedroom, he placed her on the bed with more tenderness than she expected. Then he sat next to her, combing his fingers through her hair.

"I've finally done it," he said quietly.

She couldn't muster enough energy to speak, but the question was clear in her eyes.

"I've finally frightened you to the point you've lost the ability to use your tongue as a weapon."

She managed a half grunt, forcing emotion she didn't feel. "Never gonna happen."

He smiled at her, then got up and went back to the main room. She heard the sound of clinking glass, and when he came back, he was holding two glasses, similar to champagne flutes, filled with dark gold liquor. Trystan held one out to her, waiting patiently for her to push herself into a sitting position.

She was exhausted and needed the backboard of the bed to help hold her up. Taking the flute from him, she watched cautiously. He was so mercurial, there was no way for her to ever know which version of him she was going to get.

"To the soon-to-be new Basilissa." He raised the glass and then sipped. When she didn't immediately follow suit, he quirked a brow. "It's bergozy."

She recognized the teasing lilt in his tone. Was he trying to reminisce?

Done with the power plays, at least for tonight, she purposefully set the glass down on the end table and turned back to him.

"That was not what you promised me." She was pleased to find her voice didn't quaver nearly as much as she'd feared it would.

He glanced away, but not before she saw a flash of regret in his eyes. When he looked back, however, there was nothing but anger, making her feel like maybe she'd been mistaken. His fingers flexed around the delicate glass; it was a wonder he didn't shatter it.

"The rest of them joining in," she said, "that wasn't part of the plan either."

"No," he conceded. "It was not." He sighed and leaned forward, setting his drink down next to hers. She didn't like being this close to him when he was so furious. "Trystan, don't do anything rash."

He stilled, his perch on the edge of the bed instantly less casual. "I don't do anything without carefully thinking it through, Delaney. Remember that."

She bristled but said nothing.

His eyes momentarily glazed over and he angled his head, indicating he was getting a call through his fitting. Whoever it was with, their conversation didn't last long. He got to his feet and paused, seeming to struggle with what to say next.

"Stay here," he told her. "Sleep. Teller Sanzie will be at the door. You can trust her."

"Coming from you, that's not exactly a glowing recommendation." She just couldn't help herself.

Trystan clenched his jaw. Without another word, he spun on his heel and left, and Delaney heard the main door in the other room slamming shut. Then there was nothing but quiet.

CHAPTER 5

Delaney woke with a start. Trystan hadn't come back last night, and within a few hours she'd amazingly fallen asleep. Probably due to the adrenaline crash.

She sat up and tossed her legs over the side of the bed, squeezing her eyes shut against the rush of dizziness. Seemed like the few hours of sleep she'd gotten hadn't been enough, but there was no way she was staying here, no matter how tired she was.

With nothing else to do, Delaney headed for the main room without bothering to check it first. She jolted when she glanced up to find she wasn't as alone as she'd believed.

Trystan ignored her reaction, casually leaning back in his chair at the circular glass table. She noticed that he'd changed into more comfortable wear. His pants were still white, but made of a softer material, and though his shirt was an unsurprisingly cerulean blue, it was more a T-shirt than anything.

There were two mugs set out, steam wafting from both to flick and twist in the air. The smell was rich and a bit chocolaty.

"How long was I asleep for?" she asked, noting that the sun was now shining through the windows. Outside, a view of rolling green hills and a pale, almost gray sky, met her. Unfortunately, nothing she'd seen outside of the castle gave any indication what the rest of the planet was like.

Not that she planned on sticking around to find out. First chance she got, she was gone. But there were stories Ruckus had told her of beautiful places that she wouldn't mind getting a peek at. If circumstances were different.

"Not as long as you should have been." Trystan's gaze swept over her disapprovingly. What he saw that was such a disappointment wasn't clear.

He motioned her to the only other seat at the table, directly across from him, and let out an annoyed growl when she didn't budge. "I've been busy dealing with what took place at the ceremony."

"So you didn't sleep at all?" There was hardly any sign of it. When all he did was continue to stare, she sighed. "Did you at least find out anything useful?"

"Such as?"

"Whether or not I have to worry about Vakar Tellers attacking me in the halls, perhaps?" That hadn't been a concern the first time she was here, but then, Ruckus had been in charge, and she hadn't been viewed as the human trying to steal the throne.

"It's been dealt with. After witnessing Tilda kill Fendus, the rest of the Vakar have dutifully fallen in line."

"Do they know that, despite their tradition, I don't want to be here?" Not that she believed their knowing would be much help. Tilda knew, and that didn't make a difference.

"Delaney," he growled, "enough."

"Why do I get the feeling you're not telling me something?" she said. Rehashing everything wrong with this scenario wasn't exactly helpful anyway.

"Probably because you don't trust me," he replied.

She grunted. "What reasons do I have to trust you? You're controlling, hotheaded, and egotistical."

"Has it occurred to you that now might not be the best time to bait me, considering I've currently got you so vastly outmaneuvered?" He held up his arm to indicate where they were and the impossibility of it all.

She opened her mouth, but had nothing.

When he eyed the empty chair once more, she shut the bedroom door and leaned back against it. It was childish, sure, but right now she'd take her licks any way she could get them, and judging by the clenching of his jaw, she'd succeeded.

Trystan stood, leaning over the expanse of the table to reach for the steaming mug farthest from him. Bringing it over, he held it out to her.

Delaney glanced at it, then settled more comfortably against the door. She realized he needed her generally unharmed, but that didn't mean he was above knocking her unconscious again.

"I don't feel like waking up on another ship. Unless it's headed back to Earth."

"It isn't drugged," he said tersely. "Now you're just being ridiculous." Holding her gaze, he lifted the rim to his pale lips and sipped. His point made, he offered it a second time. Once she'd taken it, he returned to his chair, angling it so he was facing her.

"You can cut it out," she said. "This whole casual act you've got going? I'm not buying it."

He cocked his head, amused. "You think I'm rigid all the time? You know better, Delaney. You've seen me relax before. Should I remind you of that time in the bunker? Or out on the balcony?"

"You mean"—she lifted a hand and began ticking off fingers—"that time directly after I was almost strangled, and that other time when I was almost poisoned with acid? Those times?"

His gaze hardened. "I had nothing to do with either of those events. In fact, I was the one who helped you evade both deaths."

"You killed people." She clutched the warm mug in her hands, relishing the modicum of comfort it gave. The smell, so much like hot chocolate, reminded her of autumn and drinking out on the porch in the afternoon. Watching the leaves fall. Did they even have that season here?

"And I'd do it again. When it comes to protecting Kint, I have no limits." He canted his head. "Don't think I didn't notice Pettus in the crowd last night."

She blanched.

"You made a valiant effort, trying not to stare at him too long, but I picked up on your initial reaction. We're searching for him now. He can't stay hidden for much longer."

Was that what he'd actually spent all night doing? Hunting down her friend? She barely resisted the urge to splash the hot drink in his face.

Pettus knew this castle better than any of Trystan's men possibly could. She had to trust he could evade getting caught.

Still, part of her wanted to ask what would happen if he was caught, though she feared the answer. Fortunately, he changed the subject and she didn't have to dwell on all the horrible possibilities.

"I don't want to hurt you, Delaney."

"Just use me to take over the world," she mused.

He seemed disappointed in her response, dropping back against the chair with a sigh. After a moment he asked, "Do you remember what we spoke about in the bunker that night?"

How could she forget? It was hard to hold back a shiver. There'd been a lot of threats made, of both the verbal and physical kind. Tars had been bombing the grounds. Fortunately, it hadn't lasted long because Ruckus had been able to stop them.

"There was a lot of talk about how much you disliked me, and didn't accept me, blah, blah, blah. Oh, and then there was that little gem about how I was passably attractive. That one was great." She realized her slip too late. That made it sound like she actually cared about his opinion.

Trystan grinned. "I was talking about how much I hated Olena. You may have been the unfortunate recipient, but I didn't know at the time that you were you. It's her I don't accept. You're here because I feel the opposite in regard to our betrothal."

"We are so not betrothed."

"Except we are," he insisted. "The whole world, as you put it, knows it. It's just taking you a little longer to catch up. As for that other thing . . ." He slowly uncurled from the chair. "To say I was pleased when I was finally presented with a photo of the real you would be an understatement. You're gorgeous, Delaney. But I was referring to the part where we spoke about being responsible for each other's people. Remember?"

She nodded mutely.

"That's what these are." He tapped the mark on his arm, the glittering capital *K* and *X* sparkling in the sunlight spilling through the window. "They signify kingdoms."

His finger pressed the single blue gem.

"The green and red will be added after our binding, to signify that your people will then be my people. I don't just mean the Vakar, Delaney; I also mean Earthlings. Once I'm Rex, they'll be safe from any further threats of war."

The Kints had wanted to invade Earth for decades, held back only by their own fight on their home planet. When the shaky treaty had been built on the betrothal of both rulers' children, the Kint had agreed to put those threats aside.

"The Kints want to control Earth," she said. "They think we're weaker beings, that we're beneath them."

"They do," he agreed with a nod. "I don't."

"That's a lie."

"All right," he admitted. "I don't think *you* are. Is that better?"

It was more believable, anyway.

"The fact of the matter is," he went on, "I'll protect them as if they were my own because they will *be* my own. As you will be. We can keep each other's people safe. Our binding will avert two wars."

The unspoken question hung in the air above her like a guillotine. She was smart enough to decipher the true purpose of his little speech. If her marrying him would save countless lives, how could she say no? But there had to be another way.

Her internal debate must have shown on her face.

"There's nothing to think about," Trystan said, losing some of his patience. "I'm not asking."

"You never do," she countered.

He was silent for a moment, and she grew uncomfortable under his stare.

"Would it have made a difference?" he asked softly.

"What?" Even knowing that going down this road couldn't be good, she took the bait. She couldn't help it. Trystan was a mystery, and she hated those.

"If I'd shown up on Earth and requested you return with me," he explained, "would you have had a different reaction?"

"You mean, if you'd arrived and told me point-blank that you planned on attacking the planet unless I came along, would I have done so willingly?"

"All right," he said, "that is more than likely how it would have gone, so, yes. My point, however, is that if I had asked you, Delaney, would I have gotten what I wanted? Or would you have hated me then as much as you hate me now?"

She didn't want to answer because she'd walked right into that one. Instead she latched on to the end of his statement and hoped she could distract him.

"You don't sound all that bent out of shape about my hating you," she stated. "Probably means that you're not as invested as you believe you are. Tell you what: Let's just call this now, save us both the future trouble, and—"

"Are we still playing this game?" Any of the ease he'd been feeling a moment prior vanished. "Do you really think you can manipulate me into letting you go?"

"Of course not." She barely resisted the urge to roll her eyes.

"Then why do you insist—"

This time she was the one to cut him off.

"Because!" She shoved off the wall so quickly that some of the liquid from the mug sloshed over the rim and onto her hand. She only partially registered the heat. "I'm trying to cope here! You can't just take someone to another planet, tell them you're going to force them to marry you, and call it a day! I am freaking out!"

The air rushed out of her all at once, and she finally dropped down into the empty chair across from him. She set the mug on the table to keep from spilling it further, and then closed her eyes to try to get ahold on her racing heart.

Having a meltdown in front of him had not been on the agenda. It'd been easier before, when she'd been pretending to be Olena, because at least when she'd screwed up, she could blame it on the Lissa. Now?

She was here on this planet as *herself*. There was nothing to hide behind. No false face, or false identity.

"You've been here before," Trystan said after a moment. "Xenith is hardly unknown to you."

"Ruckus brought me here by accident," she reminded him. "It was a mistake, and he spent the whole time trying to fix it. You kidnapped me on purpose. You knowingly took me from my home, away from my friends. I. Hate. You. And you don't even care."

Trystan slowly got to his feet, carefully placing his mug back on the table. When he turned again, his expression was stony.

"You're afraid of me," he said calmly. "Fear and hatred are not the same emotion. You can get over the first, and you will."

"Wow." There really wasn't more she could say than that.

His big comeback was that she would get over it. Like she'd been stood up on a blind date or someone had spilled punch down the front of her prom dress.

"I'm not afraid of you," she told him, holding up a finger when he opened his mouth to argue. "I'm not. I'm afraid of the things you might do, yes. But of you personally? What's to be afraid of? Is it the scared little boy who'd rather steal someone else's toy than fix his own broken one?"

She'd totally just referred to herself as a toy, but she didn't bother backtracking. She was on a roll, safety be damned.

"Taking away someone's free will so you can avoid an unwanted marriage? Sounds familiar, doesn't it? Tell me, what is up with you egotistical alien princes and princesses? You don't like the fact that Mommy and Daddy set you up to be married, so you have to go and screw up everyone else's lives? You are just like Olena. Worse, in fact, because you did this to me already knowing what she put me through!"

His jaw tightened, but then he cocked his head to listen to a communication through his fitting. Less than a heartbeat later he took a deliberate step back and met her gaze with a smoldering glare.

"We'll finish talking about this later," he said.

Trystan headed across the room without a second glance, reaching for the door.

Delaney opened her mouth to call him back but caught herself. What exactly would she say? *Please don't leave me here?* She certainly wouldn't apologize for the things she'd said, no matter how stupid it'd been for her to say them.

People hated Olena because she was vapid and self-centered. But those traits made her the less dangerous of the two royals, and Delaney had allowed herself to forget that.

Trystan? His intelligence made him deadly.

Delaney groaned and dropped her head into her hands. The sound of her sobs echoing throughout the spacious room should have made her snap out of it and try to maintain some dignity.

It only made her cry harder.

CHAPTER 6

It didn't matter what she thought about him. Thoughts changed. Why let it put him in a bad mood?

With a quiet curse, Trystan stormed down the long hallway toward one of the conference rooms. He'd set a few of them up around the palace as soon as he'd taken over. It made conversations with home easier, not that he was particularly looking forward to speaking with his father. Just the idea made him grind his teeth.

If it'd been anyone else, he could have put it off, using what had happened at the ceremony as an excuse. Unfortunately, the only person in the entire universe capable of yanking his chain was the one to interrupt him and Delaney. Though, in some ways that may have been a good thing.

She thought he was like Olena? Impossible. Olena Ond was a moron, and while Trystan had been called many things in the past, *moron* had never been one of them.

He shook his head, slamming both palms flat against the double doors leading to the conference room. They slapped against the inner walls, rebounding with a loud clatter that he hardly noticed.

There were five Tellers in the room already, all Kint, and without needing him to say a word, they scattered. They bowed as they passed, but Trystan was already turning his attention toward the large screen on the wall.

He checked his clothing, cursing under his breath when he remembered he wasn't in uniform. He ran a hand over his hair to smooth down any unruly strands. He was painfully aware of the dark circles still under his eyes—a result of the constant meetings his father had been calling lately—but there was nothing to be done about it now.

Just as he was going to bend down and flick a speck of dust from the toe of his boot, the screen emitted a low chime. A second later his father's face filled half the wall before him.

Of course, the Rex looked impeccable, and Trystan clasped his hands behind his back to hide the fact that he was making tight fists. To the End family, appearance was everything, and if his father wasn't reminding him of this verbally, he was always sure to do so physically.

His father got straight to the point. "I hear there were complications at the Positioning."

"Nothing I couldn't handle," Trystan said.

"It's my understanding that Basilissa Tilda handled it," the Rex stated. "Smart, to renew fear of their Basilissa in the Vakar. But was an all-out riot part of your brilliant plan as well?"

"It hardly got that far."

Damn his father's spies for making it sound otherwise. Usually he carefully screened the Tellers he had around him, made sure none of them had overtly strong ties to the Rex. Taking over the Vakar palace had been too big a play, however, and Trystan had been forced to accept whatever troops he'd had to send.

"From the sound of it, even your human was worried."

It took all Trystan's strength to keep from snarling. To anyone else, it may have sounded like a mere statement, but he knew the truth. Despite his agreement to move forward, the Rex didn't completely approve of Delaney.

"I've got everything under control," he said.

"Good." The Rex waved his hand absently. "I don't need to know the details. I trust you'll handle it."

What he really meant was that he didn't want to be linked back if it *hadn't* all been handled. Trystan might have been insulted, but he understood where his father was coming from. As the Rex, it was far more important that he appear above reproach. Ordering his son to take care of the things he couldn't be caught doing himself helped with that.

It was always Trystan who was seen doing the dirty work. Trystan who was seen as the conniving and scheming one of the two.

The Rex was sitting in his office, a wall of black shelves at his back housing neat rows of leather-bound volumes that Trystan was positive his father had never actually read.

"Speaking of the human, when do you intend to bring her to Carnage?"

Trystan should have known this call wasn't a congratulatory one.

"It makes more sense to keep her here," he said, having already rehearsed this argument in his mind a dozen times. "She was seen publicly for the first time last night. I think it's important she remains here, for a while longer anyway, so that she can be seen again. A visual reminder to the Vakar. Despite Tilda's announcement, there is still unrest among some of the Vakar council."

Regular citizens were easier to control; the council took more effort.

"It's not just the Vakar you should be worried about, son." In typical fashion, his father didn't elaborate. "But fine. You'll remain there for now, just long enough to bash her presence over the heads of those foolish Vakar idiots. For this to work, we need them on our side. For now. We can't risk losing support."

The fact that it was a "we" sent Trystan's blood pressure soaring, but he kept himself outwardly in check.

"We won't," he said evenly.

"Hmm." His father gave him another once-over and then tapped his fingers against the solid surface of his desk. "How are you? Now that she's here, I expected your mood to improve, yet it still appears as though you haven't gotten any sleep."

"I've been busy, that's all. Once things settle—"

"You lost control last night," he added. "What have I always told you? Actions have consequences. We cannot afford to make mistakes, especially not ones as public as the Positioning."

"It was an error in judgment," Trystan admitted, knowing that it was what the Rex was waiting for. "I underestimated the Vakars' disapproval, or overestimated their loyalty to tradition and the Basilissa. It won't happen again."

"The Tars are growing in numbers every day," the Rex reminded him. "You need to get control of the people you can before they defect and join the rebels."

"If the Tars become an actual threat, I'll take care of them."

"Your arrogance is amusing, boy, but it'll hardly get that human of yours on the throne." He shook his head. "I'm sending the coordinator tomorrow. You convince her, and perhaps you'll be able to pull off convincing the rest of the planet."

"What?" Trystan went stock-still, muscles tensing. "Father, that's not—"

"Oh, I believe it's entirely necessary," the Rex said snidely. He was enjoying this. "If you're as serious as you claim, you should be pleased. Having a coordinator verify your compatibility will help ease unrest in both kingdoms. Surely you can see that?"

"Of course, Father." His words came out calm, the exact opposite of what he felt.

The coordinator was an obstacle Trystan had been hoping to avoid, and now he inwardly cursed himself for being foolish enough to think the Rex would let him get away with that. Whoever his father was going to send, they weren't going to be coached into passing him and Delaney. Which meant they were actually going to have to take the time and go through the entire tedious process.

"You are aware that should you fail with the coordinator, something must be done about the girl, correct?"

His heart squeezed, but Trystan ignored it.

"She can't simply be allowed back to Earth, now can she? Not after everything she's witnessed here."

"She doesn't know anything." Trystan hadn't so much as mentioned his father to her other than in passing for that very reason. To keep her from discovering the Rex's true motives. "Her planet knows enough about us that taking such extreme actions shouldn't be necessary regardless."

"Those are not risks I am willing to take." The Rex's eyes narrowed into thin, judgmental slits. "If you're so opposed to it coming to that, I suggest you make sure the two of you pass. As I've said, I'll send the coordinator to you tomorrow. See that you don't look like that when she arrives. She might find it suspicious."

"And you'd find a problem with that?" Trystan spoke through gritted teeth, knowing he should just bite his tongue. The threat toward Delaney had done something to him, clouded his judgment, but he couldn't very well take the words back. So he waited silently for his father's retaliation.

His father sighed and rubbed at the spot between his brows as if a headache were forming. "Trystan, you're the one who came to me with this ridiculous plan. Do you expect me to be pleased with your choice of bondmate? She's human, and her being here complicates things. However"—he held up a hand to stop any interruptions—"I agreed taking her as your betrothed made the most political sense, and I haven't changed my stance."

That was good, considering it was all but done already. Delaney was here, and she'd been officially announced as the heir to the Vakar throne. Although, Trystan knew his father wasn't just referring to Vakar. His intended reach stretched much further than that.

"It would be simpler if we skipped the testing ceremonies," Trystan said, making one last attempt at changing his father's mind. "If we rushed the binding, no one could argue it." They couldn't challenge something that was unchangeable.

"The Vakar aren't the only ones voicing their disapproval of this merger. This process is imperative. If you can't get her to successfully pass, the council will make their distaste public, and it won't just be the Tars you'll have to worry about."

Trystan was the Zane, and he hated the idea of having his decisions ruled by anyone on his father's council. But he would agree to go through all the traditions if it meant appeasing the Rex.

The sound of a door clicking open somewhere offscreen distracted the Rex for a split second. He nodded at whoever was now in the room with him, and then motioned to Trystan. "We'll discuss this further after you've had more time to assess the situation. Now that it's become a reality, you might find things don't always work out the way you planned."

It was another barb about his broken betrothal to Olena, but Trystan barely felt it. The fact that he was free from tying his life force to that whiney monstrosity made all the disappointment his father could throw at him worth it.

"Until again, Father." Trystan bowed his head.

DELANEY SWORE SHE was done crying. She'd given herself a good hour of sobbing like a child, and now it was out of her system. It had to be.

Suddenly the door to the main room swung open, revealing Trystan standing there. He didn't move forward, his body filling the exit so that each shoulder almost brushed against the door frame on either side. His mouth was twisted in frustration, and there was a crease between his blond brows.

Wherever he'd just been, being there hadn't helped any with his mood.

Delaney had spent a good amount of time in the bathroom, making sure any signs of the tears she'd shed weren't visible. Still, she braced when he ran his gaze over her.

"Are you hungry?" he asked, breaking the silence.

"Yes." She hadn't realized until now, but she was starving. She couldn't recall the last real meal she'd had. He held up an arm toward the door, indicating she should exit the room, waiting for her to comply.

Delaney couldn't see a reason not to, and as soon as she was in the hall, he steered them to the right and began leading the way. They moved at an even pace and fell into a steady silence.

They'd gone down a few corridors and made one last turn to find a Kint Teller standing in front of a single door. He twisted the handle before they'd even come to a full stop before it.

"Why didn't we just eat in your room?" she asked as Trystan tugged her beneath the archway after him.

"Because then I wouldn't have been able to surprise you," he said, stepping to the side so she could see their surroundings. "With this."

Delaney scanned the area, taking in the flat stage that stretched wall to wall at the far end, and the rows of built-in chairs in front of it. The rows were set in levels, leading downward. There were two seats separated from the rest at the very center, a small table between them, with two silver trays and a set of glasses already filled.

"What is this?"

"Did you get a chance to watch one of our movies during your previous stay?" Trystan asked, leading her to the seat on the left, and took the place next to her.

No, she hadn't. Ruckus had told her he'd show her, but he'd never gotten the chance.

Somehow already knowing the answer, Trystan continued. "The one about to play is my favorite. I used to watch it a lot as a child. I thought we could try it while we eat. See if you enjoy them as much as you do your Earth films."

There was a warm calculation behind his blue-and-crimson eyes. It was different from the way he usually looked at her before pulling something. Was he trying a fresh approach, perhaps?

"You're trying to get me to relax," she accused him. Her stomach chose that second to growl, loudly enough that there was no way he hadn't heard.

He grinned and then reached across the small table, lifting the lid off the plate nearest her. A far too confident look crossed his face.

There was a cheeseburger and fries on her plate, and a glance over when he took the lid off his own lunch showed he had the same. She inspected the dark liquid in the two glasses, a wave of déjà vu hitting her.

"Clever." It was out before she could stop it.

"You remember."

"It was probably the most nerve-racking meal of my entire life," she said. "I'll never forget it. Don't take that as a compliment. It wasn't one. I was terrified and confused and not entirely convinced you weren't going to stab me sometime during the meal."

"The thought only crossed my mind for a second or two," he told her, chuckling darkly when she blanched a little. "That was then, Delaney. Calm down—you've got nothing to fear now."

"That's a lie," she said. "You promised you wouldn't do that."

"Is it?"

She grunted.

"You are impossible to please, Delaney Grace."

"Nope." She snatched her own glass from the table, needing

something to distract herself with. "Pretty easy to, actually. Just send me home, never bother me again, and I'll be pleased as punch. Pinky promise."

His eyes narrowed. "Setting aside the fact that I only partially understood the meaning of all that—what do punches and fingers have to do with anything?—I thought I made myself clear. You aren't going back to Earth, period, so put those hopes aside."

Showed what he knew. Ruckus was coming and he was going to get her out of this mess.

Trystan curled his fingers at the glass she was holding, and without a word she handed it over. His thumb brushed against her knuckles in the process, and she ended up pulling back too quickly. The glimmer in his eyes proved he'd noticed her reaction, but he sipped her drink without saying anything and then held it back out to her.

Delaney hesitated, and then felt stupid for doing so. It wasn't like they'd never touched before. Steeling herself against it, she carefully took the glass back, trying to avoid skin-to-skin contact without making it obvious she was doing so.

She failed, but at least she'd tried.

"Bergozy." She'd expected as much, yet she still enjoyed the burst of grapefruit and lemon flavors when she finally drank.

"Just like before," he said with a smirk, then leaned closer across the table. "And, if you're good, I've even got dessert."

"That's just evil." If that was also the same, which she was sure it was, that meant he'd gotten her pumpkin pie, her favorite. For some reason, it was even better on this planet than it was back home, so there was no way she was giving up a chance to eat some.

"You're lucky I really like that pie," she told him, shifting in her seat.

Fortunately, he got the hint, and talking ceased. Without having to lift so much as a finger, the stage began to buzz, a series of dim lights flicking across the floor. They formed patterns, and then suddenly the walls boxing in the stage changed, taking on the appearance of mountains. It was like actually being there.

Before she could ask Trystan any questions about how they did it, the scene zoomed in on a cabin tucked against the side of one of the mountains. Two men stepped out and began talking.

For the next two hours she was completely engrossed in the movie, so much so, she hardly noticed Trystan's constant stares.

It was toward the end, when one of the hover cars—aliens had perfected the flying car—flipped and headed straight at them that she remembered he was sitting next to her. Mostly because her hand shot out and gripped his wrist tightly before she realized what she was doing.

Of course, the car stopped a good ten feet from them, still on the stage. There'd been no actual danger, despite how real it all appeared. Her heart rate accelerated, and she felt her cheeks flush as she quickly pulled her hand back, tucking it beneath her thigh.

He was probably silently laughing at her, but she couldn't bring herself to look at him to find out. Instead she kept her focus straight ahead, pretending like nothing had happened. It'd been a mistake.

Guilt stabbed at her and she winced. Because she'd been enjoying this, and this was something she was supposed to do with—

"Delaney?"

She froze at the familiar voice in her head, scared that she was hearing things.

"Delaney?" It started out as a question, seemingly getting closer and closer so that the volume of his voice went up. *"Delaney, are you here? Delaney?"*

"Ruckus?" She sent her thought outward and held her breath, waiting.

Having him in her head had become as common as breathing since she'd gotten her fitting months ago in Gibus's lab. Ruckus was the only one who could telepathically communicate with her, and back on Earth few people even knew the tech existed.

"Thank the stars," he said.

"You found me." She closed her eyes and exhaled, then quickly composed herself. Out of the corner of her eye, she saw Trystan shift closer, but his gaze was locked on the stage. As long as she didn't give them away, he shouldn't have any idea she was conversing with Ruckus.

"Of course I did," Ruckus said. *"It took me a while to find a way onto the planet. The Rex has the airspace on lockdown; Fawna had to sneak us in through a couple of back channels even I wasn't aware of."*

The more friends she had on this planet, the better. She had a feeling that even with Ruckus here, things weren't going to get much easier. At least, not right away.

"You're not inside, are you?" she guessed, deflating some. No, of course he wasn't. He would have shown himself.

Trystan had a mixture of both Kint and Vakar soldiers surrounding the place. And he was smart. He wouldn't leave any of the latter unattended by the first.

"I'm working on it. Trust me?"

"Always." She smiled to herself at the familiar words.

Whenever she wanted him to try something new, something distinctly *Earth*, she'd pose that very question. His response never changed, just the one word, *always*, and he'd be ready to do whatever crazy thing she'd suggested. Like trying tofu for the first time, or petting a stingray at the aquarium.

"Are you okay?" he asked.

"I'm fine," she said. *"He won't hurt me."*

There was a slight pause before his response came. *"If he does, I'll kill him."*

Sometime during their conversation, Trystan had shifted even closer so that his arm was propped on the table between them. It brought his shoulder almost right up against hers, and she tried not to think of the fact that he was three times her size and would be seriously pissed if he knew what was currently going on in her head.

"Trystan is looking for Pettus."

"I know." Ruckus sighed. *"Don't worry—he's with me."*

"Is there a plan?"

"Yes. Come and get you."

"Doesn't sound like much of a plan," she said.

"I'm coming, I promise. I just need a little more time." He grew silent for a moment, and just when she was about to panic, he said hurriedly, *"My position's been compromised. I have to go before I'm spotted. I'll let you know as soon as I'm close. Be ready."*

She felt the connection sever before she could say anything else, and disappointment settled over her shoulders like a heavy blanket. Ruckus was finally here, but she was back at square one. Waiting.

CHAPTER 7

Trystan had walked her back to her rooms after the movie last night, but she only partially recalled what they'd talked about. She'd tried holding up her end of the conversation, yet she was positive she'd failed. He must have realized how distracted she was, though he didn't call her out on it.

She'd spent the night hoping to hear from Ruckus again. But there'd been no word from him, and with every passing minute, she drew closer to panic. Which was stupid, because if anyone could take care of themselves, he could.

Delaney had already been up and pacing for an hour when the main door finally opened. She watched a woman push a metal clothes rack into the room, a variety of colors stuffed from one end of the rack to the other. Too many for any one garment to be discernible from another.

Without a word, the woman parked the cart next to the table and spun on her heel back toward the door. She passed Trystan on his way in, and angled her head in a low bow.

Ignoring Delaney, he moved to the rack and thumbed through a few different items, swishing hangers across the center rod. Every so often, he made a subtle negative or positive facial expression.

Delaney crossed her arms and cocked a hip, waiting. It was childish, but she knew he wanted her to be the first to speak, and she was loath to give him what he wanted. Could be he was annoyed with her for not showing enough interest after the movie. A concept that frustrated her more, because why should she reward him for doing one nice thing among a slew of awful?

A minute later he finally looked over, eyes scanning her from head to toe. He removed a dress from the rack and held it out, lining it up with her body. Clearly not satisfied with the look, he set it back and selected another, repeating the process.

"Oh, for the love of . . ." Delaney took a deep breath. "Fine. I'll bite. What are you doing?"

"I'm trying to dress you in something that will impress the coordinator." He glanced at her. "Obviously."

"Like I know what a coordinator is," she countered. When all he did was return to the clothing, she sighed. "What is a coordinator, Trystan?"

"I'm glad you asked." He turned back toward her, this time with a dress far too see-through to ever be considered appropriate for anyone.

"Absolutely not."

He pretended to think it over and then pursed his lips in agreement. "Though the better question is, *who* is the coordinator. The answer being, of course, the woman you need to convince."

"I can't convince this coordinator of anything if you don't explain to me exactly what it is you want me to sell," she pointed out, hating the way the corner of his mouth turned up in self-satisfaction.

"The coordinator's job is to ensure that the bonding ceremony isn't done in haste. She'll meet with us and determine based off our chemistry whether our claim to each other is legitimate."

Delaney waited a moment for him to continue, but when he kept his attention on the dresses, she let out a humorless chuckle. "You're kidding me, right?"

He paused with a hanger halfway off the rack and glared at her.

"Let's just assume from now on that I am never joking with you, shall we?" He set the dress back and selected another. "I'm perfectly aware how difficult this is going to be—for the both of us. Believe it or not, our sessions with the coordinator were not my idea. I'd prefer to avoid them just as much as you would."

"I somehow doubt that."

"You have a tendency to say foolish things," he told her, "and then I predictably react to them. We can't do that in front of the coordinator. Everything we say and do has to be flawless. She must be convinced that we're sufficiently satisfied with this bonding."

"You sound like a sleazy business tycoon." At his questioning look, she shook her head. "It's not a good thing."

"And that right there is what I'm talking about." He grabbed two dresses and took a step closer. "None of that when we meet with her. You will act the way a proper Lissa should."

"You mean meek and a kiss-ass."

"You'll manage."

"Will I now?" she said dryly.

"Yes." He held up both dresses, and then brought up the one in his right hand a second time. He glanced between it and her another three times before adding in a satisfied tone, "And you'll do so in this."

After draping the garment over his arm, he replaced the rejected dress and walked toward her.

"Here."

Knowing that he wouldn't give her space until she took it, she obliged, making sure to add more force in the grab than was necessary. When he didn't immediately step back, she clutched the dress closer to her chest and stared at him.

"I'm not changing in front of you."

He smirked and motioned toward the door to his right. "You can change in the bathroom."

Delaney pushed her way into the bathroom, not wanting to give him the opportunity to disagree.

"This is just like last time," she mumbled as she quickly slipped into the dress. "Same game, different set of rules, that's all. Instead of pretending to be Olena, you're going to pretend to like Trystan." If only it was as simple as it sounded.

On autopilot, Delaney pressed a finger against the curved bottom of the countertop. When the hidden drawer popped open, she absently selected a few different beauty products while her mind twisted around what he wanted her to do and why it was important.

He'd said that it wasn't his idea, and there was only one person on the entire planet with the power to force the Zane to do something. But why was the Rex insisting they go through with this? Surely he knew how Delaney felt about his son, that she was merely being used to avoid his binding to Olena. Unless he didn't?

She paused while adding eye shadow, thinking on it. She certainly wouldn't put it past Trystan to keep something like that from his father.

Still, wouldn't it be in the Rex's best interest to speed this process up? If their roles had been reversed, and Delaney were the domineering Rex, she'd want to force Trystan to marry as fast as possible. Before he was able to find yet another loophole and avoid the whole thing entirely.

She slicked on a final layer of lipstick and then stepped back to inspect herself in the mirror. She hadn't paid much attention to the dress, aside from the coloring, to match her eye shadow, but now she was forced to admit that it was gorgeous.

Damn, Trystan had good taste in clothing.

It was a deep navy blue, which she would have thought too Kint for a Vakar princess, if not for the fact it'd been paired with vibrant gold lace. The gold embroidery formed vines and flowers that draped over both shoulders, the ends sewn into the high waist of the skirt.

There were a few inches of blue material left between her breasts, so that it was clear the design was cohesive.

Gold was one of Vakar's colors, while the blue was distinctly Kint. The pairing of the two was an interesting way of declaring her supposed mutual loyalties.

Delaney headed back to the main room, not wanting to give Trystan any reason to seek her out. He was standing by the table, pouring a dark liquid from a silver carafe, and she paused, watching as he gently set the cup aside and began filling a second.

"See something you like?" His voice snapped her out of it and she glanced up to find him watching her. "You were staring."

"I didn't think you did anything gently," she said before she realized how stupid it sounded. To buy herself some time, she closed the bathroom door, keeping her back to him as long as possible.

"This is for you," he said, placing one of the cups at the end nearest her.

Just as she was about to reach for it, he held up a hand. With a frown, she watched as he lifted the cup to his lips and sipped.

"In case you thought it might be poisoned," he explained, setting the cup back down.

"You going to do that every time now?" Was he . . . teasing her?

His response was a single shrug.

The beverage was similar to coffee, and one that she'd grown quite fond of her first visit here. She greedily sucked down the cup's contents and was reaching across the table for the carafe when he brought out the shoes.

"These were delivered while you were changing," he said, putting the sparkly gold heels down on the empty seat between them.

They fit perfectly, like the ceremony ones had the other night. Of course he knew her shoe size. "I don't usually care about clothing—"

"A fact made apparent by your Earth-wear," he mumbled, the corner of his mouth curling up when he received an annoyed glare.

She pretended he hadn't spoken. "But I have to admit this is a very nice dress."

He lowered the cup and angled his head, taking her in. Just as it was starting to make her uncomfortable, he said, "You wear it well."

Delaney didn't know what to say to that, so she changed the subject. "We going to do this thing or what?"

"RELAX," TRYSTAN ORDERED. He was leading them through the palace, her hand tucked neatly at the crook of his left arm. It was a compromise against her having to hold his hand.

"Yeah, right," she said under her breath, trying to count how many Tellers they passed. She finally gave up at fifty-something. "There are a lot of Vakar guards."

He lifted a brow. "We're in Vakar, Delaney. This is where they tend to coagulate."

"You aren't worried they'll turn on you?"

"I trust they're all intelligent enough to avoid making that kind of mistake." Trystan shrugged. "Besides, I have you with me, and as their future Basilissa, they're sworn to ensure your safety. I am your betrothed, therefore that is also my duty. What cause could they have for attacking me when we now share the same task?"

He sounded far too sure of himself for her liking.

"And the Tars?" If they hadn't liked the thought of Olena ruling, how did they feel about having a human rule? "There's no way they're as okay with this as everyone else seems to be. I doubt they're as interested in tradition as the rest."

And all the Vakar they passed did seem to be taking it well enough. There was no obvious animosity toward her anyway.

"Delaney." He paused in front of a set of tall golden double doors, turning to face her. "I won't let anything happen to you."

The words were so identical to the ones Ruckus had spoken to her months ago that she actually flinched. Her slip must have given Trystan the wrong idea, because his mouth thinned.

"Do you honestly think I'd bring you all the way here just to let you get murdered?"

"No," she said, then licked her lips and added, "at least not until after the bonding ceremony."

His eyes narrowed and his arm turned to stone beneath her hand. She would have pulled away, but the sound of the doors shifting from the other side prevented her from doing so.

Trystan swiveled back around as the doors opened up to a large domed room. The walls and ceiling where made of thick glass, and sunlight spilled in through the top, lighting the lush greens and vibrant colors of surrounding plants. There was a single path made of white stone with gold flecks leading straight ahead, and at the center sat a glass table designed to seat four.

There was a woman waiting for them, and she slowly got to her feet as they approached, bowing her head first to Trystan and then to Delaney.

She was tall and lean, in a tight dress the color of wine. Her hair was nearly to her elbows, the burnt-umber strands loose and straight. She held her palm out toward the two empty chairs across from her.

Trystan pulled Delaney's out first and waited for her to be seated, then settled down at her right.

"Let me start by saying," the woman said, her voice smooth and confident, "how honored I am to have been selected as your coordinator, Zane Trystan. I assure you, your trust in me will not be misplaced."

"My father and I wanted the best," Trystan replied matter-of-factly. "There can be no argument by the end of this that the Lissa and I are a good bond-match."

"Of course." She bowed her head, clasping her hands in her lap. "I feel that I must inform you of the Rex's wishes, however."

"He doesn't want you to fix the exercises." Trystan nodded. "Neither do I. I want this to be a legitimate process, Co Gailie. There can be no mistakes. No one is to be given any opportunity, no matter how small, to question our commitment to each other, or each other's people."

"Of course." She looked to Delaney. "Lissa, do you have anything you'd like to ask? I'm aware of your upbringing, that you are from Earth. I imagine this is all a tad confusing for you, so if there's anything, anything at all, you'd like to ask me before we begin, I welcome it."

Resisting the urge to glance to Trystan for permission, Delaney attempted to keep her expression impassive. Truth was, there were a million questions swirling around her head, but she was clinging to the hope that none of them would matter. Ruckus had a plan, after all.

Still, not asking anything might be suspicious, so she blurted the first thing that came to mind.

"Trystan mentioned something about sessions, plural," she said. "How many will there be, exactly?"

The corner of the woman's lips tipped upward in a way clearly meant to instill a sense of camaraderie. However, the coordinator worked for Trystan. Delaney had no doubt that she'd do everything she could to ensure her Zane got what he wanted.

"You didn't tell her?" Co Gailie clucked her tongue at Trystan in mock disapproval, surprising Delaney with her boldness. "Our Zane isn't one for explanation, so I'll do the best that I can. Our bindings have traditions that must be followed. They're set in place to ensure no one rushes into a binding, as our people can only procreate with one partner during our lifetimes."

That wasn't news to Delaney. It was one of the reasons she'd actually felt bad for both Trystan and Olena. She hadn't thought it was right to force them into something so . . . definitive.

"These steps, which we refer to as exercises or testing ceremonies, help coordinators assess whether a pair wishing to be bound is truly right for each other. Better to know beforehand, agreed?"

Delaney nodded.

"Good. Now, this is our first exercise, and it also happens to be the simplest. All we're going to do today is get to know one another. More specifically, I am going to get to know the two of you. I must insist that you both be one hundred percent honest with me, as any lie, no matter how small or seemingly insignificant, could greatly affect the results."

Why did Delaney suddenly feel like she was being interviewed by immigration to see if she was trying to get away with staying in the country through marriage?

"Tell me: How did the two of you meet?"

Trystan settled back in his chair and crossed his legs. The move, which would have appeared casual on anyone else, was a clear tactic. "You already know the answer to that one, Co Gailie. As important as this is, I'm afraid the Lissa and I are on a schedule."

"I'll stick to the questions I don't already know the answers to," she said, forcing that smile back in place. "I'm aware you're here mostly because you were the one Uprisen, Delaney. However, it's written here you decided to come back due to your feelings for Trystan. It's very romantic, if you don't mind my saying so. The two of you discovering each other amid such complex circumstances."

Was *that* how he was spinning it? She glanced at Trystan, but he was focused on the coordinator. It was a little less suspicious that everyone here seemed so resigned to accepting her if they believed it was because the two of them had legitimately fallen in love. It made sense, in a twisted sort of way. It at least explained why they thought she'd agreed to give up her life on Earth and move to another planet.

"When did the two of you realize there was more between you, romantically?"

"When he took a zee for me," Delaney said, forced to play along and thinking up the first logical thing she could.

Co Gailie asked them a few more questions, all easy to fabricate responses to. She finished another note on her device and then motioned between them with a thin finger.

"I'll need to interview you both separately now. How would you like to go about this?"

"I won't leave her alone in the room," Trystan said, rising to his feet and smoothing out his uniform. "I can wait on the other side, out of hearing range. But I won't let her out of my sight."

"Yes," Co Gailie said, "that will be fine, Zane. Thank you."

Delaney watched Trystan circle the table and then cross the room, continuing on the path that led to the other side of the dome where there was a single bench. He settled onto it, throwing one arm over the back, the other in his lap. Another faux casual move; she wondered who he was trying to convince.

"Your last name is Grace, Lissa?" Co Gailie drew her attention back, typing when she got a nod in response. "Do you have a middle name?"

For the next fifteen minutes, Delaney answered a slew of seemingly random questions. Not once was she asked anything about Trystan, which she found odd. After her time was up, she was sent to switch places with him, and she couldn't help but frown as she moved across the stone path.

Trystan met her halfway, momentarily blocking her. "Problems, Delaney?"

"Was that supposed to be all about me?" she asked.

He laughed, and when it was obvious she didn't get the joke, shook his head. "Everything is about you."

He brushed past her and retook his spot across from the coordinator.

With nothing else to do, Delaney took the vacated bench and waited.

And waited.

Maybe it was because she wasn't engaged in anything this time around, but it felt like Trystan's questioning was taking three times as long as hers had. Perhaps there was just more to ask him, like things that she wouldn't have been able to answer because she was from a different planet. Aside from tandem games and 3-D movies, Delaney didn't know much about the kinds of activities that took place on Xenith.

Ruckus had tried explaining a few to her while they'd been on Earth, but he'd get distracted by something and she'd forget all about whatever he'd been going to tell her. Watching him get excited over mundane things that she'd taken for granted, like seagulls and salt-water taffy, always thrilled her.

She wrung her hands in her lap, wishing she had a clock. How much longer until Ruckus could come get her? Would Fawna really be able to keep the spaceship hidden long enough to get them off the planet? So many things could go wrong, and none of them were factors she could control.

An annoyed growl traveled up the back of her throat, and she was grateful the others were too far away to hear it. Something told her that kind of reaction in front of the coordinator, for any reason, wouldn't go over very well.

Finally Trystan and Co Gailie stood, the latter bowing to the first before turning to direct a similar move to Delaney.

Delaney waited until the coordinator had left the room before walking back to the table. She stopped, keeping it between them, and tried searching Trystan's face for any clues as to what the two of them had been talking about.

He had his hands tucked into the front pockets of his white pants, head angled slightly while he stared back at her. His silence made it clear he had no intention of telling her what had just been discussed, which wasn't all that surprising. He hadn't asked her what she'd talked about with the coordinator, so either he already knew—which was likely—or he didn't care.

"That wasn't so bad," she said, just to break the silence between them.

He grunted. "Give it time."

"Kind of seems like you're overreacting."

With a hand at her elbow, he turned her so that she was facing the door, and began easing her toward it while he spoke. "This is a dated tradition that I had hoped not to bother with."

"And now that we are—"

"We have to be careful to come across as the perfect match," he finished for her. It didn't take long for them to reach her room, but almost as soon as they did, he received another telepathic communication. "I'll be back soon," he told her briskly, stepping away. It was obvious he didn't want to go.

"I'll be here," she said pointedly, but if he heard her, he didn't show it.

CHAPTER 8

Delaney?"

She stilled in her seat at the table. Hearing Ruckus's voice enter her mind immediately calmed some of her nerves.

"You're okay." She'd known he would be, but proof was always preferable. *"Where are you?"*

"Close," he replied. *"You?"*

"I'm in my room. Alone," she told him. *"For now. Trystan will be back soon."*

He'd said he wouldn't be long, but it felt like a couple of hours had passed.

"I'll come for you tonight," Ruckus said.

She glanced at the window, trying to gauge how long from now that would be. *"You have to be careful. There are guards everywhere."*

"I can handle them."

"We've been through worse," she said, hoping the teasing light in her voice carried over, wanting to ease some of the tension. *"Wouldn't you say?"*

"I don't think Mariana's yelling about wet towels on the floor counts, sweetheart."

"Really?" She clucked her tongue. *"I'll be sure to tell her that next time we see her."*

"On second thought . . ." His sentence faded out, but when he spoke again, the firmness was back. *"Wait for my signal. I love you."*

She was about to repeat it, but the connection dropped and she ended up letting out a frustrated groan instead.

"You're prettier when you don't make weird noises like that," a small voice said, making her jump.

Pressing a hand to her heart, she turned to glare at the speaker, blinking when she spotted him. He was just a boy, maybe six or seven, with thick sandy hair and sharp gray eyes rimmed in silver. His small uniform resembled that of a Kint soldier, though in the same way a child's Halloween costume might resemble a police officer's uniform.

"Wow, you move quietly." She'd been so caught up with Ruckus, she hadn't heard the boy come in.

"I'm not supposed to be here," the boy confessed. "Uncle Trystan might get angry with me."

Uncle Trystan? But he was an only child; Ruckus had told her as much. Perhaps *uncle* didn't mean the same thing here as it did back on Earth? She'd been implanted with a device that translated their language into English, but sometimes words didn't carry over properly.

"He gets angry with me all the time," Delaney said a moment later.

"I know," the boy told her, sounding proud of that fact.

"You do?"

"Uh-huh."

"Did he tell you that?"

"He tells me lots of things."

"Is that so?" She took a step closer. "What kind of things?"

"All kinds. Like that the word *asomatous* means to have no body, and xanapers are herbivores. There's a hidden forest in Carnage that only worthy people are allowed to enter; Xenith's three moons are Ambrite, Armite, and Agite; *and* your favorite flower is the stellaperier!"

Information overload. Delaney hadn't known any of that, aside from the last bit, which twisted her heart painfully.

Ruckus had been the one to show her the flowers, star-shaped blooms in white and pale yellow that emitted a neon glow at night. Their name loosely translated to "star climber," and there was a whole mythology to them about how they were once fallen stars trying to return to the sky.

"Why did Trystan tell you my favorite flower?" More important, she realized with a frown, how did he even know it in the first place? She certainly had never shared that information with him.

"I asked." The boy shrugged. "I ask him things all the time. Uncle Trystan swore he would never lie to me."

"Ah." She nodded conspiratorially. "So you take advantage of that."

"No." He pursed his lips. "I do not. He doesn't have to answer. He doesn't have to answer to anyone."

"Bet he told you that, too, huh?" she said dryly.

He breezed past her comment, rocking on the balls of his feet. "Why is the stellaperier your favorite? Is it because they glow? I like that they do that, too, but they're not my favorite. I like gorganatias, because they're my mother's favorite. Have you ever seen one?"

Delaney shook her head, but her response didn't seem to deter him.

"Mother used to have a whole garden full of them, taller than me." He lifted his hand high over his head then dropped it with another shrug. "That's why I like them, anyway. So, is it because of the glow?"

It took Delaney a second to follow, then she crossed her arms and moved closer, easing down into one of the glass chairs.

"No," she admitted, inhaling to keep the catch from entering her voice a second time. "I like them because they remind me of myself."

He scrunched up his nose and eyed her up and down. "Do you glow?"

She smiled and shook her head. "Unfortunately, no. I meant, their story is all about how the stellaperier are trying to go home. They're trying so hard that they're constantly climbing upward, and at night they light up, hoping that their friends will realize where they are and come to rescue them. I feel a little like that, I guess."

The boy continued to stare at her for a moment. Then, like a switch had been flipped, his rocking restarted.

"You miss where you come from," he concluded, far wiser than she'd expected him to be. "I miss my home, too. But Uncle Trystan says that things happen sometimes that are out of our control, and the best thing we can do is adapt so that we aren't swept away by our emotions."

"He's paraphrasing."

At the sound of Trystan's voice, Delaney shot out of the chair so fast, the legs clattered against the floor. The boy laughed at her, but she didn't look at him.

Trystan had been standing in the doorway across the room, unnoticed—there was no telling how long he'd been there. Now he made his way inside, eyes set on the boy with his hands in his pockets.

"What are you doing here, Dominan?" he asked, stopping a few feet from him.

"You wouldn't let me go to the Positioning," Dominan said with just a hint of complaint in his tone. "And I wanted to see her." He leaned in closer to the older Kint. "Uncle Trystan, is that really the color of her hair?"

"It is."

"How?"

"I told you," he said, sighing, "she's not from around here. Where she comes from hair like that is perfectly natural."

"Apparently you tell him a lot of things," Delaney drawled.

"And it is supposed to be under the agreement that he not repeat any of them," Trystan said, directing his words to Dominan.

"Apologies," the boy murmured, hanging his head.

"How did you get away from your security detail, Dom?" Trystan asked.

"I led them to the kitchen and let the cook distract them."

If she hadn't been watching so closely, she would have missed the slight twist to Trystan's mouth.

"They're out in the hallway now." Trystan angled his body toward the door pointedly. "You're to go with them and stay with them. Understand?"

"Yes, Uncle Trystan." Dominan went to step away and then hesitated, glancing quickly at Delaney one last time. "It was nice to meet you, Lissa Delaney."

Still not used to the title attached to her own name, it took her a moment to return the sentiment. Once she had, Dominan skipped off like he hadn't a care in the world. She watched him go, immediately wishing him back when she realized his departure meant she would be alone with Trystan.

"So, you going to show me your pet next?" she said as soon as the doors shut behind Dominan.

"What?" Trystan frowned at her.

"You know." She waved a hand in the air. "Your cute, adorable, irresistible pet. The one that's going to make me realize you've got a heart made of cotton candy and you're just really, *really* misunderstood."

She watched as his cheeks flushed with anger and his gaze hardened. It was a miracle he couldn't use that stare to shoot laser beams at people—that was how intense it was.

"You think I set this up?" His voice was low, dangerous. "I'm sorry to disappoint you, Delaney, but even I have my limits. I would never use Dom for anything, let alone to manipulate you."

Before she could react to that last part—or freak out about it—he was talking again.

"He likes to wander, break the rules. I'm sure being around me his entire life is partially to blame for forming that habit. No doubt that's also why he was so curious about you."

"You talk to him about me." She wasn't sure how she felt about that.

"I just got back from speaking with my father," he said, and even though she knew it was a diversion tactic, she went along with it.

"What about?" She'd never met the Rex and, in truth, always hoped she never would. Dealing with Magnus, the Vakar king, had been hard enough, and he was supposedly the more lenient of the two.

"It seems we both did well with the coordinator today." It should have been a good thing, but the way he said it showed he was anything but pleased.

"Your dad found out about that already?"

"He received a full report before we even made it back to this room," he said. "Typical. He's never been one for waiting. For anything."

"You didn't get your patience from him, then." Trystan had patience in spades. It would even have been an attractive quality if not for . . . everything else about him.

"No, I did not." His uniform was impeccable, as ever, but there was a dull shade to his usually vibrant eyes, and his hair was mussed, as if he'd recently been combing his fingers through it.

"You seem tired, Trystan."

"Do I?" The corner of his mouth turned up, but even that was lackluster in comparison to his usual half grins.

She was still wearing the dress, and now she tapped the lacy flowers on her shoulder. "How did you know the stellaperier is my favorite flower?"

He feigned sudden interest in his right sleeve, adjusting it even though it was perfectly straight.

She took his silence as meaning he wasn't willing to discuss the topic, so she shelved it. For now.

"Maybe you should get some rest," she suggested, and he let out a sharp, humorless laugh.

"Concerned for my well-being, Delaney?" He looked up and latched on to her gaze. "Or are you merely trying to get rid of me?"

She forced herself not to react. "Don't be ridiculous. Why would I bother?"

"Hmm." He stood there a moment longer, like he was either waiting for her to say something more, or he was trying to find the right words to voice a thought of his own. He ended up not doing either, and stepping away instead.

"Going to bed?" The sky was finally starting to darken outside. A tingle of anticipation ran down her spine.

"I'm much too busy for that," he said over his shoulder. Just as he was about to leave, he hesitated, turning back to face her. "You did well today, Delaney."

She opened her mouth—to say what, she wasn't sure—but he wasn't finished.

"You're a very good actress."

CHAPTER 9

When she finally heard from Ruckus, the sky was almost pitch-black and it'd been forever since Trystan had left her for the night.

"Delaney." Ruckus's voice was low, like he was whispering into her head.

It was somehow more intimate, and she took a second to breathe past the adrenaline and hope, needing to calm herself enough to focus. They had one chance for this to work, and she certainly wasn't going to be the one to screw it up by being overexcited to see him.

"You're here. Are you all right?" she asked.

"I'm fine, sweetheart," he said. *"I'll be with you shortly, but I have to cut communication in order to focus. I know where you are. I'm coming."*

She felt the connection sever before she could respond, and her shoulders slumped. If anything, she was more nervous now than she'd been prior to hearing from him. Having found a way inside didn't guarantee he'd actually make it through the palace.

Delaney left the bedroom, pausing as soon as she entered the sitting area when she heard a muffled thump. With a slight frown, she angled her head, trying to get a better listen. For the most part it was quiet, but less than a minute later the sound came again, closer this time, accompanied by a light tapping sound. A seemingly endless moment passed where nothing happened, and she held her breath. But then the door eased slowly inward and a Kint walked in.

Before Delaney could feel panic, recognition dawned. The uniform had thrown her off, but now it was clear who was actually there. "Ruckus."

He'd slid between the gap in the doorway, and was followed closely by Pettus and Gibus. The latter quickly moved to the electrical panel, while Pettus angled himself so that he could peer out into the hall.

She let out the breath she'd been holding, and flung herself at Ruckus, not caring how damsel in distress the move made her look. Despite the seriousness of their situation, she closed her eyes and allowed herself a second to just relish the feel of his warmth around her.

"Gibus is working on the passcode so we can get you through the door," he said.

"How did you guys manage to get in?" The door was meant to keep people out as well, yet here they were.

"Who do you think designed this system?" Gibus said without turning from the panel.

Pettus sent him a look. "And who helped you hack it?"

"I would have eventually figured out—"

"Thank you," Delaney interrupted, smiling when they both grew silent and nodded at her.

"How much longer, Gibus?" Ruckus asked, also not wanting to give them time to argue.

"Soon," he replied.

"Until then, all we can do is stay quiet." Ruckus eased closer to her so their sides were practically pressed together. "The guards outside have been taken care of. But if anyone walks by, they'll know what's going on."

"If that happens?" She was not a huge fan of this plan so far. Waiting around seemed dangerous. "Aren't you all committing treason by doing this?"

"Technically." He shrugged a single shoulder. "They might even claim we're kidnapping you."

"Ironic."

He smoothed a large palm up her back. It hadn't been that long since she'd last seen him, and yet now that he was next to her, it felt like a lifetime had passed. She scanned his features, checking for differences, filing away the curve of his jaw and the sharp angle of his nose. The only thing out of place about him was the fact that he was dressed in Kint colors.

She'd been so focused on keeping herself together, she hadn't allowed herself to feel just how much she'd truly missed him.

"Is it totally lame if I mention how much I hate when we're apart?" she asked, smiling when his arms tightened comfortingly.

"Only if it's lame for me to agree with you," he whispered, then leaned down to kiss her.

"Not the time," Pettus reminded them, glancing over. Doing so caused him to look away from the corridor.

His split second of distraction cost them.

The door slammed open with enough force to send the Teller backward. Before Pettus could regain his footing, it was too late. The lights flicked on, sudden and bright enough to momentarily stun them all.

"Well." Trystan's smooth drawl cut across the expanse. "Isn't this interesting?"

Delaney blinked as her eyes adjusted. At her side, Ruckus tensed, his whole body curling around hers protectively.

Trystan propped himself against the door frame, arms over his chest, ankles crossed before him. There were at least five guards visible over his shoulder, though they remained in the hall.

Pettus and Gibus both moved back, putting distance between themselves and the Zane.

Ruckus's hand twitched; he was clearly debating whether activating the weapon around his wrist was worth it.

The move instantly drew Trystan's gaze, and his eyes narrowed, that dangerous half smirk never leaving his lips. "I wouldn't."

Another tense moment passed, then Ruckus's hand went lax.

"You should probably step away from him, Lissa."

Trystan was blocking the only exit, and he'd brought along reinforcements. How had he known? The lack of surprise on his face when he regarded Ruckus was telling.

"Delaney, now."

Before she could decide what to do, Ruckus thrust her behind him. She let out a startled cry, struggling to reverse their positions. Trystan wouldn't hurt her, but he definitely didn't have any qualms about shooting Ruckus.

She glanced over to see the Zane uncurl from the door frame, cocky smirk gone. He didn't immediately draw a weapon, which could be either a good or bad sign. There was really no telling.

"I'm really going to have to insist you do as I say," Trystan warned her. "Back away from him."

Ruckus tried to rush forward, but she caught his arm, using all her strength to tug him back. He was so angry, she could feel his muscles shaking beneath his heated skin.

"I'm not going to let you hurt him," she told Trystan.

"And yet," he growled, "the longer you stand there, the more hurt I'm going to deliver."

This was bad. Really, really bad. She couldn't think of a way to get them out of this. At least, not a way to get them all out unscathed.

But maybe she could make sure Ruckus and the others were safe.

She took a step forward, and this time Ruckus was the one to reach out and stop her. Even though she wanted to glance over at him, she didn't, keeping her gaze locked on the Zane's, her body angled in front of the Ander.

"I want assurances they aren't going to be harmed," she said, glad when her voice came out strong and authoritative.

"You aren't exactly in a position to ask for favors," Trystan replied, though some of the tension eased from his shoulders. He was being smug, and she hated him for it. "I could have my Tellers come in here and remove you all by force."

She swallowed a biting retort. Despite the satisfaction sparkling in his eyes, she could still see the note of anger burning beneath. Honestly, she was a bit surprised that he hadn't just shot Ruckus already.

"I'm going to walk over there," Delaney said. "But first, you're going to promise me that you will not shoot my friends when I do."

"And you'll take that?" He canted his head. "You'll be satisfied with my word alone?"

"You never lie to me, right?" she said. "So don't lie to me now."

"Delaney," Ruckus growled, but he didn't attempt to drag her back again.

"Do you see another way?" she asked through their fittings.

His silence was reply enough. There was no other obvious way out, and Trystan was close to losing patience. They could only delay this so long, and it wasn't like anyone else was coming to help.

With all four of them trapped, that was it. Delaney was going to have to do what the Zane wanted. The only thing more terrifying than that was the idea of Ruckus being injured because of her.

"All right, Delaney," the Zane conceded calmly. "I won't shoot—or let anyone else shoot—the Ander or the other two once you come to me. I promise."

She could read between the lines; that left a lot of other horrible possibilities on the table.

"That's not—"

"Don't get greedy, Lissa," he cut her off. "That's all I'm willing to offer you. Take it or leave it."

Ruckus's fingers flexed around her arm. He was strong and solid at her side, the familiar smell of burning firewood drifting to her. If anything, it just drove home how important this was to her, how badly she needed to keep him safe.

"It's my turn to play hero," she joked, aware that the hint of humor she'd attempted to put in her tone sounded forced. *"Besides, how can you get us out of this later if you're dead?"*

"I don't like this."

"Well, yeah. Neither do I."

"If he hurts you—"

"He won't." She didn't mention that she was well aware that Trystan's calm was all for show. *"He won't hurt me."*

Afraid that if she waited any longer she'd somehow lose her nerve, Delaney pulled away. With each step toward the Zane, her heart pounded louder in her chest, the crescendo drowning out everything else.

She felt more than saw Ruckus reach for her at the last second, but Trystan was faster, stepping swiftly between them. As soon as he had, the group of guards in the hall filed in, and she tried to watch as they moved toward her friends, but she was forced out of the room.

Delaney started to turn back, wanting to make sure Ruckus and the others were okay. The sight of the hallway caused her to stop in surprise instead.

A line of bodies trailed all the way down to the end where the corridor branched off. A pair of booted feet poked out from the side, indicating there were more fallen soldiers around the corner. She thought they were probably unconscious and not dead—she hadn't heard any shots—but there were still a lot of them, at least two dozen, all unmoving.

"Did you do this?" She sent the question to Ruckus telepathically without thinking, then let out a startled sound when Trystan rested a hand at her elbow.

Once he had her attention, he let go, tilting his head down the opposite end of the hall. Without a word, he started walking away, expecting her to follow. He moved confidently enough, though his spine was stiff.

"Focus on staying safe, Delaney," Ruckus told her before the connection ended.

The guards had completely blocked her view from within the room. Seeing no other choice, she risked one last glance at the Tellers who Ruckus and her friends had knocked out, then quickly went after Trystan. Even once she'd reached him, she had to practically jog to keep up.

"What are they going to do with Ruckus?" she asked when he didn't acknowledge her. "If you've—"

"Let's keep the threats to a minimum, shall we?" he said, a hint of irritation slipping through. "The Ander is fine. For now."

She faltered, almost falling. Strong arms caught her before she could face-plant, hauling her up against a wall of muscle.

"Thanks," she growled, "but I think I would have preferred the floor."

Trystan instantly let go and turned away, continuing to stride down the hall before she could catch sight of his expression.

Why had she done that? Inwardly, she cursed her stupidity. He had Ruckus, and yet here she was taunting him. Again. While he was furious with her.

They reached the hangar, and she slowed when he stopped in front of a large aircraft she'd never seen before. It was sleek and white, with silver trimmings around the curved wings. It vaguely resembled spaceships she'd seen in the past, only with all rounded angles. And it was twice the size of the one Ruckus owned.

Without a word, Trystan started up the narrow steps that led to the wide opening at the side of the ship.

She hesitated, all her instincts screaming to turn and run the other way, but she scoffed at them. It wasn't like she'd never been in an enclosed space with the Zane before. She'd survived it then; she'd do so now.

The loading dock she entered was dark, the only lights the ones that lined the walls at their base. The stairs retracted immediately behind her, and resealed against the side of the ship a few seconds before the engine thrummed to life and she felt them lifting.

She scanned the room, jumping a little when she realized Trystan was standing with his back toward her on the other side. In the dark, it was impossible to make anything out other than his large outline.

"How did you know?" She needed to stay focused on that, on the logistics of it all. Trystan had not only discovered them, he'd timed it perfectly.

"You told me." His answer was sharp, to the point.

She froze. "That's a lie."

"It isn't," he said. Only, not out loud.

His words entered her mind like a cold breeze, making her shiver. The fact that he could speak to her telepathically meant only one thing, and she felt sick to her stomach.

"You hacked my fitting," she said, though she couldn't get the strength to return to her voice. "When? Do you know how invasive that is?"

"We're going to be bonded, Delaney," he said, like that should excuse everything. "And I did it on our way to Xenith, while you were still sleeping."

"I was unconscious!" she snarled.

The lights flickered around them and then burst to life again, the sharp white glow momentarily disorienting her. She blinked past the pain, not wanting to let him out of her sight.

When she was able to see again, Trystan merely tilted his head. The arrogance written across his devilish face made her curse herself for ever believing getting away could be so simple.

Of *course* he'd hacked her fitting. Why hadn't she thought of that possibility herself?

"Where is he?" she asked. In the same instant, a side door swooshed open with a gust of warm air.

Sanzie stood in the newly exposed hall, her hands clasped before her, a fritz bracelet on either wrist. She kept her gaze steady on Trystan.

"Zane," she said curtly, "D-Sub is approaching now. It's been confirmed they have the cargo. Shall I direct them to Carnage?"

Trystan eyed Delaney before answering. "No, have them follow us to Inkwell. Tell the pilot to maintain a thirty-five-yard distance at all times, and have him dock at the west-side entrance."

The Teller's jaw clenched. "Yes, Zane." Then she departed as quickly as she'd come.

"She didn't seem to agree with your orders," Delaney said, staring at the still-open door.

"Teller Sanzie doesn't approve of keeping the Ander. They have history." He motioned her closer with two fingers before she could ponder that last statement. "Follow me."

THEY WENT ALL the way to the back of the ship through a network of twists and turns impossible to keep up with. Trystan stopped her at another doorway. "Here."

The room was empty aside from a small cot attached to the right wall and a table with two chairs in the left corner. A single window rested in the center of the wall, exposing a view of the teal sky and the front of another ship.

"There's your Ander," he said, tapping a finger against the glass to indicate the other craft.

Even though there was no way she'd actually be able to see Ruckus from where she was, she rushed over to get a better look.

"Where's Inkwell?" What she really wanted to know was if it was some kind of torture facility, if that was why he was bringing Ruckus along, but of course he didn't answer.

"I'll be back in less than a minute. Don't try anything foolish." He headed toward the door, pausing. "I really am doing this for my people." Trystan rested a hand on the door frame, one foot already in the hall. "It doesn't seem that way to you right now, and I understand your reasoning. But I hope, one day, you'll see it the way I do. I may not be good, but I'm not the bad guy, either."

She turned away and, after a moment, heard him leave.

He wasn't gone long.

This time when he entered, the door slid shut behind him, and he went to the small table to set down a metal tray. It held a plate of triangular biscuits and two steaming white mugs. She was beginning to note he had a strange obsession with that one chocolate drink.

He caught her watching, which ruined any plans she had for ignoring him, and motioned her toward one of the empty chairs. When she silently refused, he shook his head and sat down, reaching for one of the biscuits. He'd slipped into a long jacket the same shade of red as his eyes, and had another in white draped over his left arm.

"It's going to get cold," he said. "You really should put this on."

"I think I'd prefer to freeze to death."

"Really?" He settled back in his chair. "Have you come close to freezing before? I have. It's a special kind of suffering, starting with a numbness that's more irritating than anything. Then there's the muscle clenching, and the shivering. In the end, you feel like you're on fire. But the disorientation is my least favorite part. Somewhere between the start and finish you begin losing your mind. I hallucinated that I was sitting with my mother in her reading room."

Delaney frowned at the way he stared off, distracted all of a sudden. There was an air of sadness settling around him, a dimness to his eyes.

His mother, the Regina, had died when he was a child. She'd never considered how Trystan still felt about it.

"When did this happen?" she asked, mostly to get him to snap out of it. She didn't want to feel sorry for him, not after everything he'd done and was going to do.

"A few years ago," he said, then cleared his throat. "When the war was still going on. My ship was shot down over Morray in the middle of winter. Out of twenty-seven of us Kints, only three survived. Two of my men and I." He met her gaze, his momentary distraction over. "Brighton was one of them."

"If you want me to say I'm sorry you had to kill him, you're out of luck." His right hand had been leading the Tars. Not a single part of her was upset he was dead.

"I don't." He held up the jacket, and she realized she was shivering.

"Don't you have a heating system in this thing?" she grumbled, moving over to snatch the jacket out of his grasp. The material of the white coat was velvety soft, and she wanted to rub her face against the gold trim.

Now that she was here, she figured she might as well sit and warm herself with the hot drink. She selected one of the biscuits as well, practically moaning when the sugar hit her tongue. She was starving.

"I must remember to feed you more regularly," he said to himself. "I procured this ship very last minute, actually, so no, the heating system is broken. The one I usually use was sent on ahead this morning, with the coordinator."

"So you've known this entire time Ruckus was coming?" She took another biscuit. "Why put on the production? If you knew what we were going to do, why didn't you say something during the movie?"

"I was curious to see how you acted with the Ander when you thought no one else was there to bear witness," he said. "This way I was able to capture him *and* his accomplices. If I hadn't, he would have simply tried again. We can't afford distractions like that right now. Neither of us wants to be looking over our shoulders every five seconds."

"Love how you're lumping us together there," she drawled. "Almost like you actually believe you and I want the same things."

"We do." He leaned forward, propping an arm against the edge of the table. "You want your people to be safe, and so do I."

"The only thing we have in common," she said, "is that we both want to be free. Difference is, you getting your wish means ensuring I don't get mine. The Vakar aren't my people. Why should I give a damn about them?"

His mouth twitched. "You aren't callous, Delaney. Don't bother pretending to be. I know you better than that."

"You don't know me at all."

"Don't I?" He quirked a blond brow.

"Hacking into my fitting doesn't allow you to read my mind." All it did was give him access to thoughts she broadcasted, and generally only if she did so to him specifically. Of course, because she hadn't known there was anyone else tapped in to her frequency, she hadn't bothered shielding herself mentally during her conversation with Ruckus.

"I don't need to read your mind to understand your inner workings," Trystan told her. "Even as Olena, you wore your personality like a cloak. It was nearly impossible not to get to know you. And I did try, trust me. I was controlling, abrasive—"

"Domineering, gruff, creepy, intrusive, a complete and total asshole, et cetera, et cetera."

"I'm almost positive those first two things hold the same meaning as the two I started with," he said, not the least bit affected by her insults.

"Basically you're saying I did a crap job pretending to be the Lissa. Great. Now that we've got that cleared up, I'd like to point out you're virtually telling me to do the same thing. You want me to act like I like you, but I don't, and you already have firsthand experience with how shitty of an actress I am, so . . ." She pretended to be heavily invested in her drink when she didn't get a reaction.

"You're taking this rather well," he said once she'd placed her cup back down and could meet his gaze again.

"You expected me to cry? Throw a tantrum?" She lifted a mocking brow. "Thought you knew me better than that."

"Touché." He cleared his throat. "By capturing your only friends here on Xenith, I've just stopped your escape plan and ensured there's no chance of your ever coming up with another, yet you're calm."

"I'm panicking, actually," she said, crunching down on her fifth biscuit. "You should know when people are covering up their emotions. You're so good at it."

"Am I?"

"You aren't humble, Trystan. Don't bother pretending to be," she parroted, keeping her voice serious. "I know you better than that."

"You're mocking me."

"I do so frequently," she said. "You just don't seem to notice very often."

"That's good. I like it."

"You do?" She wasn't expecting that.

"If your instincts are to tease me, it means we're making progress."

She wanted to argue with his reasoning, but before she got the chance, he canted his head and got that familiar far-off look.

A moment later he grunted and rose from his chair carefully, adjusting his jacket to smooth any wrinkles. He took his cup, which was still pretty full, and sipped it while she watched him.

"I'm needed elsewhere," he said.

"You so often are."

It appeared as though he had a comeback to that, but he opted not to give it. Instead he smiled and continued, "We've only a couple of hours before we reach our destination. I'll leave Sanzie here to keep you company."

Trystan didn't wait for a reply, going straight to the door. He also didn't bother leaving Sanzie with instructions; he merely passed her in the hall and disappeared around the corner.

Despite his choice of words, the Teller wasn't here so Delaney had someone to talk to, but why waste an opportunity?

"The last time I was alone with one of Trystan's Tellers, he tried to kill me," Delaney said.

Sanzie frowned, genuinely perplexed by her statement. "Harming you would be committing treason, Lissa."

"You don't have to pretend. You probably don't like me."

"My approval doesn't matter. It's not my job to have an opinion about you, your station, or how you got it," Sanzie replied.

With a sigh, Delaney reached down and yanked the zipper up on her jacket, and glanced longingly at her now empty cup.

"I can have another cup of squa brought, if you'd like," Sanzie offered, noticing where Delaney was gazing.

"So that's what it's called." She'd been referring to it as faux hot chocolate in her mind. "I can probably wait until we get there. How cold is it? Where we're going, I mean?"

The thickness of the jacket she was wearing indicated *cold*.

"It's the middle of winter in Kint right now," Sanzie answered. "The temperatures can quickly turn deadly."

Her stomach tightened. She'd never been to Kint before, and she definitely had no desire to visit now.

"I'd suggest keeping indoors if you're not one for snow and ice."

"Noted." Could that be why Trystan was relocating her here? To keep her from wandering off? If so, it was going to work. Getting herself lost in a frozen tundra did not sound appealing.

"Trystan mentioned you know Ruckus?" Delaney certainly wanted more details about that.

"I did," Sanzie confirmed, that impassive mask on her face slipping marginally to reveal either guilt or sadness. "A long time ago."

"How?"

"I was part of the Vakar guard."

Delaney blinked. "I'm sorry, what? But aren't you Kint?"

"I am now," she said, her voice proud. "Vakar was where I was born, however, so that's where I began my initial training. The Ander and I were part of the same squad for a while."

She licked her lips. "So, you grew up together?"

"We did."

"How did you turn Kint?" Delaney hadn't been aware that was even an option for people.

Sanzie smiled lightly. "What you mean is, how did I get the Zane to trust me, considering where I come from?"

Okay, yeah. That was what she meant.

"I'm loyal, Lissa," she said. "I hope that you'll see that, and realize that that loyalty now extends to you."

"Because I'm betrothed to Trystan?" she snapped.

"In part. But also because as I just told you"—she met Delaney's gaze—"I was once Vakar, too."

CHAPTER 10

He despised the smell. That dank, musty hint to the chilled air mixed with cleaning solution. The first was a byproduct of the dungeons being part of the original structure, the second created in a poor attempt to mask the first.

When he'd taken over the castle at Inkwell, he'd thought it quite brilliant leaving the lower levels with the holding cells as they were. Not that he'd intended to hold prisoners here, but he liked to plan ahead, and in the off chance one day he would have someone worth holding, he wanted to ensure there was a proper place to put them. And a properly uncomfortable place at that.

Aside from a few technological updates—like electrified walls and reinforced doors—he'd kept it all the same, right down to the circular stone stairwell that was meant to draw out a prisoner's misery by giving their imagination more time to play out the coming horrors.

It seemed like a complete and utter waste now, however, when he was the one in a rush to reach the bottom.

Something was always pulling him away from Delaney right when he wanted to be near her most. They'd stepped off the ship less than fifteen minutes ago, and he was curious how she'd react to the rooms he'd had her escorted to.

Which was foolish, because it didn't matter whether she liked them; she was staying there either way.

The sound of his boots clicking down the stone steps echoed off the walls and he schooled his features, trying to mask his ire and impatience. He didn't need the Ander to know how much of an inconvenience this was going to be. Killing him, and the others, would be the easiest course of action, not to mention the most satisfying. Unfortunately, the conversation he'd had with Delaney had been accurate. Ruckus was worth more to him alive.

For now.

After what felt like an eternity, Trystan finally reached the foot of the stairs, ignoring the silent greetings of the two sentries there. He turned the left corner, adjusting his jacket, and headed toward the far cell, where he'd ordered Delaney's friends be placed.

He had to admit, if only to himself, that he admired them for their attempt to help her. It was a rare occurrence to find someone, let alone some*ones*, truly willing to do anything and everything for a friend. There'd only been four of them, and yet their plan might have worked if Trystan hadn't thought ahead and tapped into Delaney's fitting.

The conversation between Delaney and Ruckus he'd overheard ran through his mind, further darkening his mood. He'd been partially curious about how they would speak with each other in private, it was true, but more than that, he'd hoped to glean some understanding of how comfortable the two of them were physically. It was one thing to compete with a man who Delaney viewed as her savior and ally, another to try to get between her and someone she thought of as lover and friend.

He knew it was already too late to prevent the last, but the first . . .

Trystan shook his head and inwardly cursed himself. This entire line of thinking was a waste of time. What did it matter how close to the Ander she'd gotten on Earth?

He arrived at the end of the cell block, and moved so that he was standing in the wide center of the hall.

There were six cells in this section of the dungeon, three on each side, all connected by thick white stone walls. The bars had been replaced with electronic shields that would leave second-degree burns on a person if they touched it. The shield was a sheer light blue, easy enough to see through, but still a clear visible barrier to keep prisoners from getting any ideas.

He'd ordered the others into a separate cell, directly across from the one he'd placed the Ander in. The three of them were badly bruised, and the Teller—Pettus, if Trystan recalled correctly—was favoring his left arm.

There were five Tellers, all Kint, stationed around the box-shaped room, and he jutted out his chin to dismiss them. Whatever was said between him and the Ander, he wanted it to remain private.

"How's the eye?" Trystan asked, slipping with ease into the role of arrogant Zane.

One of his men had landed a decent punch back at the palace, and Ruckus's right eye was swollen three sizes too big, already coloring purplish blue. Navy, like the Kints' official color, which gave Trystan a sick twist of pleasure. He would have pointed it out if there weren't other matters to discuss.

"I'll return the favor," Ruckus said gruffly. "Trust me."

"Bold, coming from someone currently out of moves." Trystan pointedly ran his gaze over the edges of the cell wall, where the blue hue was darkest.

"You can't actually believe people are going to accept a human on the throne," he growled. "You're not that naive."

Trystan merely stared at him.

"No," he said, seeming to realize, "you're just that arrogant."

"You know something of arrogance, Ander. You did just attempt to steal *my* betrothed."

"It eats you up inside, doesn't it?" Ruckus growled. "Going through all this trouble for someone who's never going to want you back? I didn't come to steal anyone. I came to rescue *my* girlfriend from the delusional bastard who actually thinks this is going to end in his favor."

"Clearly," he drawled, forcing composure, "you've been taking lessons from the silver-tongued Delaney. Is that how you spent your Earth days? Her training you how to properly deliver a verbal barb?"

"We did other things with our tongues, actually," Ruckus said.

Before he knew it, Trystan was standing close enough to the cell wall to feel heat radiate from it. This side wasn't dangerous to touch, but the heat signature was an added level of precaution to remind people that the force field was activated. He let it brush against his skin for a moment, sucking it up until he was uncomfortably hot and had something outward to focus on.

"This isn't just about avoiding Olena," Ruckus murmured, though it was clear it was more to himself. "I knew it."

"Care to share?" Trystan asked, glad when his voice came out deadpan.

"You're in love with her."

He grunted, ignoring the strange buzzing sensation that flittered over his body. "Hardly."

"You are." For a second it was obvious the Ander couldn't decide whether he felt cocky at being right, or angry about it. He settled on the latter. "She's never going to love you, and if you really care about her, you'll put an end to this insanity now. We both know you're putting her in danger by keeping her here."

"I'll say it once, and only once." He took a deliberate step back from the wall. "This is about what's best for Kint, and while I admit it also benefits me in the sense that I no longer have to tie myself to Olena, any connections I have toward Delaney are sheer byproducts of circumstance. I am no more in love with her than I am with you, Ander Ruckus. Feelings, especially those of the heart, are fleeting and fragile.

"My interest in Delaney is born of curiosity and necessity. She has a purpose, and once she's completed that task, I'll have no further use for her." Even as he said that last part, he knew it was a lie.

Trystan needed time to go over that in private, figure out what exactly he was going to do with her once they'd taken crowns, if not dispose of her. Keeping her around would probably cause more problems than not, especially once his father announced his plans for Earth. But getting rid of her . . .

"I don't buy it," Ruckus insisted, unaware of how close he was to getting shot in the head by pushing the issue. "I remember the look on your face when you took the zee for her during her Uprising. How quickly you threw yourself in front of it, no hesitation. You were falling for her then and didn't even know it. How does it feel, Zane? To be oblivious? To not have control over something?"

"You are still Vakar," Trystan stated. "And I am still Zane of Kint. I hold all the cards here, Ander."

Ruckus grunted a second time and crossed his arms. "No, Delaney does. You're too stubborn to see it, that's all. She's the only reason I'm alive." He motioned to the cell across from him. "Why we're alive. Admit it: I'd be dead by now if you didn't think you could somehow use me to bend her to your will."

Trystan didn't bother responding to that. He didn't have to explain himself. The things he did and the reasoning behind them were his and his alone.

Ruckus lowered his voice. "Think about this."

Trystan was curious enough about where this was going to allow the Ander to continue.

"It isn't any better than being with Olena if you have to manipulate Delaney. The Basilissa had already agreed to tie the two royal houses; you're going to get the crown either way. You don't need Delaney to do it."

Trystan rolled his eyes, glad that he didn't have to fake his amusement this time. "You should have taken more lessons. That was hardly convincing, and now I'm bored."

The guards had moved to the far end of the hall, out of earshot, and he motioned them back with a few curls of his fingers. He'd come to confront the Ander, and he had.

"She has nothing to do with this," Ruckus said, trying one last time, a hint of desperation slipping through. "She doesn't belong here!"

Trystan headed away without bothering to glance over at him. He didn't need to see the Ander's face to know that he was losing his cool. Disappointing, to say the least. "She has nothing to do with this!" Ruckus yelled a second time.

Trystan held up a hand and couldn't resist throwing over his shoulder, "You're the one who got her involved, Ander. And thank you for that."

THE END OF their conversation had returned him to his good mood, but it hadn't lasted long. Now that Trystan was standing outside Delaney's door, he found himself hesitating, the Ander's accusations playing on a loop.

Love? It was a ridiculous notion, and obviously a ploy to disarm him somehow. The only thing was, he couldn't figure out the how. What could Ruckus hope to gain by making such an accusation?

Annoyed that he'd allowed the Ander to get to him for even a second, he forwent knocking and threw the door open.

He'd placed her in a series of rooms, with the main door opening to a sitting area complete with a fireplace, glass table, and two large plush chairs. Two doors on opposite sides of this room led to the bathroom and bedroom, respectfully, and he'd already turned to the right, expecting to find her in the last, when he realized with a start that she was actually in the room with him.

She was sitting in one of the chairs in front of the fire, which was lit and flickering, casting in a golden light from behind and a bright one from the sun filtering through the windows. Her body was angled so that she was facing him, and she was watching unblinkingly, with a stillness that masked what she was thinking.

Which he hated.

It shouldn't matter to him what was going on in her head, yet it did. Even so, seeing her, knowing she was near, instantly eased the tension he'd carried with him from the dungeon.

With that hesitation he'd felt outside her door a vague memory, he made his way over, ignoring the urge to touch to her. Instead he took the seat opposite, perching on the edge so that he could lean forward with his arms rested on his knees. It wasn't as close as he wanted to get, but it would do for now.

Delaney surprised him by breaking the silence: "What are you thinking about?" She was still watching him, a mixture of curiosity and caution in her eyes. If she was worried—and he was positive she was—she hid it well. Very well.

She should have taught the Ander how to better mask his emotions. He almost wondered aloud how the man had ever gotten such a high position with such poor acting skills, but caught himself. The longer he could put off talking about Ruckus, the better. He was smart enough to know that.

So he answered, shocking them both a little when he did so honestly.

"My father."

Her brow furrowed slightly, but that was the only indicator of her interest. "What about him?"

"It took a while for me to get him to see things my way," he said carefully.

"You mean"—she pointed to herself—"to agree to me."

"Yes." He sighed and ran a hand through his blond hair, careful not to leave any strands permanently disrupted, then settled back more comfortably in his chair. He wanted to be able to see all of her when they had this discussion, and the closer he was, the more distracted by her face he became. "Back on the ship, I mentioned the Tars."

After a brief hesitation, she mirrored his move, and even went so far as to tuck her feet beneath her. "I was told Brightan was the leader."

Was she avoiding speaking of Ruckus as well? Why else wouldn't she say his name when they both knew that he was the only one who would have kept her informed?

"He was."

"And you expect me to believe you had no idea?" Delaney gave him that look, the one he'd so often pictured while he was waiting for his father's permission to retrieve her. Her dark pink lips pursed and slightly pouty, thin left brow arched and held aloft.

He'd had to imagine what it would look like on her face instead of Olena's. It was a challenging look, and one he always felt obligated to respond to. There were a few occasions where he'd thought about it, and concluded she might be able to get him to tell her just about anything with that look alone. So soon after his unsettling conversation with the Ander, however, the possibility didn't leave him intrigued like it once had.

Now he just wanted to make the look go away before he foolishly tested his theory.

"I was aware of the identities of a few members of the group," he admitted, feeling a twinge of satisfaction when the admission had the desired effect and she scowled. "I'd met with some, in fact, to orchestrate that bombing on the tandem field."

"When you tried to lead me to my death," she added.

"We both know I could have, and chose not to. We've discussed it before—don't backtrack, Delaney." He ran his hands across the smooth leather of the armrests to give himself a moment to re-collect his thoughts, and then: "Afterward I called it off. I was told my orders had been met, so you can imagine my surprise when a few days later bombs were going off outside the palace."

He hadn't been at his best that night. For no real reason at all, he'd actually been concerned over her safety, and had hastily made his way to the bunkers to confirm that she was all right. Then he'd convinced himself it was merely to ensure that he hadn't been defied, that the Tars had, in fact, ceased any plans to kill the Lissa.

Here, sitting across from her, he could admit that he'd been lying to himself. Especially when he played back the way he'd reacted when he'd spotted her with the Ander. He'd attempted to mask his actions with superiority and protocol, but the Ander had clearly seen right through him.

And he'd just been thinking about how poor the man was at hiding his own feelings?

"How did you discover it was Brightan?" Delaney asked, forcing his thoughts back to the now.

"It was simple once he was dead. The Tars' main goal has always been aligned with mine, so I'd never had true cause to expose them before. They fought to keep Olena off the throne because they believed, as I do, she would be a terrible ruler. Given they were mostly made of Kint, they didn't want that tied to us. To them, war was a better option. Brightan was always very vocal that he agreed with this logic. It should have been a major clue that he was involved. It was childish of me not to see it sooner."

"You trusted someone you thought was a friend," she corrected. "There's nothing childish about that." She glanced away and then quickly back, having settled on something. "I know I said before that I wouldn't say I'm sorry he's dead, and I'm not, but it does suck that you had to kill a friend. It's not something anyone should have to do."

He stared at her a lengthy moment and then rushed out the first thing that came to mind. "You shouldn't say things like that."

"Because it makes me sound weak?"

"No." He shook his head. "Because it makes me like you more."

She frowned and leaned forward. "You'd rather hate me?"

"It would be simpler."

"Because it worked out so well for you and Olena?"

"Touché." He cleared his throat, wondering how he'd allowed them to get so off topic. "How much did they teach you about our geography?"

"Nothing, really." She slumped back and he immediately regretted the renewed distance.

To prove to himself he was being ridiculous, he got up and moved across the room, putting even more space between them. When there were no annoying tugs or strange sensations, he smiled smugly to himself and opened one of the drawers to the desk. After removing a pad of paper and a pen, he returned to his seat.

"Here." He twisted so that he could rest the pad on his thigh and she could get a good look. "Let's say this sheet of paper is Xenith. This"—he drew a misshapen box on the left side that took over more than half the page—"is Kint territory. And this"—he made a similar shape on the other side, noticeably smaller than the first—"is Vakar."

"Your landmass is bigger." She shrugged, but he caught the worry finally flickering behind her gaze as she watched him make more marks.

"This is the current population of Kint, roughly, of course."

"Of course," she said breathlessly, but her heart wasn't in it.

He jotted down thirty-five million, then realized her translator wouldn't work and said the number aloud for her. He repeated the process for Vakar, in part because he liked the use of the visual, but also because she was eventually going to have to learn to read their language.

"Their numbers don't even come close to ours," he said after a moment when all she did was sit there and stare. "Your Ander didn't tell you any of this, did he?"

She shook her head.

"You didn't realize how important you were when you were pretending to be Olena," he guessed. "This merger was literally the only thing keeping us from taking over, and with sheer size alone, we could easily do it. You really did avert a war."

That snapped her out of it and her eyes narrowed. "You found out Olena wasn't really there in the end anyway."

"Timing is important," he said. "If I'd known it wasn't her that first day, I would have declared war right then and there. My men were actually on the ground, awaiting my order. We would have attacked before the ship even docked. You prevented that from happening."

"Is he dead?" She blurted the question so suddenly that it caught him off guard, and at first he didn't know what to say.

"You're being nice," she explained when he still hadn't spoken. "Well, nice-ish, and the only reason I can think for that is that something happened and Ruckus is dead. Or Pettus. Or Gibus." Her face fell, and it was an obvious struggle for her to recompose herself. "Or all of them . . . ? Say something. Trystan—"

"He's not dead." He hated how relieved she looked then, how she closed her eyes and exhaled. "All three of them are fine." His usual *for now* almost passed his lips, but he caught it at the last second.

She let out another breath, and when she reopened her eyes, determination was burning brightly behind them.

"There's a reason you brought up the Tars," she said, "why you're explaining to me the differences between Kint and Vakar. What is it?"

Before launching into an explanation, he allowed himself a moment to be impressed with how quickly she bounced back.

"The Tars didn't disband. Olena might no longer be an issue, but you're an unknown factor. They have no proof you'll be a better ruler than she would have. I'm telling you this so that you have a clear picture of what you and I are up against. Vakar will follow tradition, but they won't like it, and already there are factions forming in secret that hope to discover a way around the law. We're taking care of them. You'll be safe."

"You said that about the Uprising," she reminded him, and he was forced to see her point.

"That was different," he told her, even though it hadn't been and they both knew it. "I didn't let anything happen to you then; I won't let anything happen to you now. It's why I'm showing you the numbers. Even if all of Vakar rose up against us, there's nothing they could do."

"And tradition is keeping Vakar at bay for now," she said, nodding. "Without Vakar members, the Tars won't be able to pose any true threat. But what about Kint? Tar members were originally Kint; you made it sound like your people would accept that I was Uprisen as well."

"They will, as long as we keep my father happy. Because," he said, though he hated to admit it, "my father is still Rex, meaning his word is law above my own. I told him that you developed feelings for me and would therefore be more easy to control than Olena. He believes you want this. Tell me you understand, Delaney."

She licked her lips and he followed the motion despite the fact that this was a serious conversation they were in the midst of.

"Now that we're in Kint," she began, not leaving him any time to ask how it was she knew that, "you want me to try harder. It's not just the coordinator I need to convince; it's everyone here. If I don't"—she met his gaze head-on—"you're going to hurt Ruckus and my friends. And"—she looked down—"others are going to hurt them as well."

Was it wrong of him to feel good that there was someone else for her to blame now?

"Yes," he said, "they will. If we don't convince my father that we can do this, he'll let them. I know it. If we get through this," he said, making a split-second decision, "after our binding, I'll let your friends go. Including the Ander. Agreed?"

Not having to worry about how close Ruckus was would probably be a blessing. Sending him away, far away, sounded good.

When she lifted her gaze to his, she was smiling, but there wasn't any humor in the look. "I've pretended on this planet before," she said. "Why not go again?"

"Before"—he knew he shouldn't say it even as he did—"you were playing for weeks, a handful of months at most. Now you're playing for life. Life, Delaney," he reminded her. "Because as much as you believe I'm not in this for the long game, I am."

She paled, but that was the only indicator his words had any kind of effect on her.

"You did say I was going to pay with my life," she said, feeding him back the threat he'd made on the ship.

Finally giving in to the need, he reached over to run the tips of his fingers through a few strands of her red hair. It was such a fascinating color, like melted copper and liquid fire mixed.

He was still smoothing it between his fingers when he murmured, "I did."

CHAPTER 11

She was having a minor panic attack.

It didn't help the room also made it painfully obvious she was in Kint. There were tones of blue from the pale color of the sky back home to the deep navy of the ocean, with bright bursts of silver and grays scattered about. The floor was made of some material similar to marble, and warm to the touch. Everything was clean and pristine, more like the room at a fancy five-star hotel than a place that was actually meant for living in.

At least Trystan had left her alone after the big reveal about his dad. He'd given her the rest of the day and an entire night, in fact. She already knew the Rex wasn't someone she wanted to deal with, but now she was being told she'd have to lie to him?

She shuddered, clenching and unclenching her fists in a poor attempt to calm down. Freaking out wasn't going to help anyone, especially not Ruckus. He deserved better after everything he'd done for her. The risks he'd taken simply by showing up in Vakar while it was under Trystan's control.

The sudden knock on the door had her jumping and then cursing herself. Sunlight shown through the thin curtains she'd pulled over the floor-to-ceiling wall of windows. How had morning crept up on her so quickly?

Without waiting for a response, Trystan entered confidently. He glanced at her before moving toward the bedroom, leaving her to either stand there or follow.

Deciding on the latter, she went after him, pausing by the bed to watch him enter the walk-in closet. He started shifting through different outfits hung neatly on silver racks.

"I could probably start dressing myself," she called to him. When he didn't so much as glance in her direction, she frowned. "Trystan?"

"Hmm?" He lifted a skirt from the rack and then replaced it.

"Is it really that big of a deal?" she tried, hoping to spur him into a dialogue. Quiet Trystan was always the most unsettling. "What I wear, I mean?"

Still no reaction.

Fighting against her better instincts, Delaney moved closer until she was only a few feet away from the closet door. He was so focused on selecting things—spending more time than she ever had on picking an outfit—it didn't seem like he even noticed.

"I'm pretty sure after our conversation last night," she drawled, "I'm the one who's supposed to be giving you the cold shoulder, not the other way around, Trystan."

Finally he angled his head toward her, frowning while he tried to decipher her words. Once he had, he grunted and returned to what he was doing, which, oddly, made her feel slighted.

"What's with you?" She braced herself on the door frame, the move bringing her that much closer.

"I just spoke with my father," he surprised her by admitting.

"I take it that didn't go well." When she'd initially discovered that the Rex was all but selling his son's future away by tying him to Olena—a girl he hated—Delaney had felt bad for Trystan. To her, the Rex had always made questionable choices, but then, she'd never been in a position of power like he was.

She didn't know what it was like to have every single decision affect the lives of an entire race. Trystan had rarely spoken of his father to her when she was pretending to be Olena, so Delaney had never really grasped the mechanics of their relationship before now.

"You don't like your father, do you?" she asked, though it was so obvious, she didn't really need to bother. She had a strained relationship with her own dad, and it was a struggle for her to bank any rising pity or sympathy she felt toward Trystan.

They weren't the same, and allowing her mind to make those false connections would only lead to more trouble.

"My father is the Rex," Trystan stated, and the next item of clothing he took he practically tore by yanking it off the rack. "One does not *like* their king. They obey him."

"I should probably warn you now then," she said, pushing him when she shouldn't, "that I'm not in the business of obeying kings, so if that's where you think you and I are going, think again."

That made him pause, and while it caused warning bells to go off in her head, it also brought an odd sense of relief. Anger and annoyance were familiar emotions coming from him; that weird sullen look he'd been wearing a second prior was not. He was already so unpredictable, having him in a state of mind she wasn't used to actually made her more uncomfortable.

What did that say about her, that she'd rather piss him off than let him sulk?

"You obeyed the Basileus," he reminded her.

"I didn't exactly have a choice."

"You don't have one now."

"Correction"—she settled her features into one of disinterest—"you don't. You're the one who wants to impress Daddy. I could decide this very moment to be a coldhearted bitch. My friends would die—horribly, I'm sure—but then you'd be out of leverage."

"Caution, Delaney," he said, his voice so low, she almost didn't catch it.

"What?" She painted a look of innocence on her face and then idly turned back into the bedroom. "I'm practicing."

He gritted his teeth. "I don't want you to be Olena."

It bothered her a little that she hadn't needed to further explain what she'd meant, but she shoved that feeling aside with the rest and spun back around. Dropping down to the edge of the bed, she forced herself to shrug a single shoulder.

"I'm assuming the same set of personality traits you gave me to use on the coordinator aren't the ones you want me to execute on the Rex, though, right? I've never met the man, but from what I've heard of him, he doesn't really seem like the type who respects docile."

"He doesn't like petty and disrespectful, either," he countered. "Neither do I, for that matter. Unless you want me calling your bluff, you'll refrain from lying about letting people die. Murder in your name isn't something your conscience could ever accept, Delaney, so don't joke about it."

She didn't argue with him, instead giving another shrug before motioning to the clothes he was still holding. "What will it be then?"

His eyes narrowed and he stared, a weighted silence settling over them. It was obvious he was trying to work something out—if only she could deduce what exactly that was so she could better prepare for it.

"Would you like to help me choose my new Sworn?" he offered suddenly, and the way he did it made her feel like he hadn't meant to.

Recognizing the Kint equivalent of an Ander had Delaney's throat closing up. She felt the hot sting of angry tears threaten to pool, and bit down on her tongue hard enough to draw blood in order to force them back. As badly as she wanted to, raging at him right now wouldn't be beneficial.

"Sure." Brightan had been his last Sworn, and it'd been almost two months since he'd died. "Why haven't you done it already?"

"I don't need a head of guard," he scoffed, more of who he usually was bleeding through. "I am perfectly capable of defending myself, thank you very much. Now that you're here, however, I feel that it's a necessary precaution."

She couldn't help but scowl at the implication. "I'm not letting one of your people follow me around, Trystan."

"Do you want to be allowed out of this room?" he inquired. "I've managed to push off my father's visit, as he never wanted me to bring you here in the first place, but that can't last. Eventually he'll make an appearance, and I need to be prepared for that moment's arrival. I also have responsibilities, ones that don't yet include you, which I cannot continue ignoring to babysit. So"—he moved closer, bending down so that they were at eye level—"you can let me assign a Sworn, or you can stay here. Cooped up."

"Like a chicken," she practically growled as he straightened.

"I believe that's a flightless bird. Correct?" He didn't wait for her to reply. "Then, yes, like a chicken."

"I'm pretty sure I hate you more than anyone else on any planet in the entire universe."

"That's not bad." He actually smirked at her. "Two days ago you were certain; now you're only 'pretty sure.' That's progress."

"That's not what—"

"This." He held out a dress to her, practically whipping her in the face with it. "You'll wear this. You can change in the bathroom again, like last time. Or you can put your ridiculous modesty aside and do so here."

Delaney tugged the white dress out of his hand and pointedly turned toward the door. He stopped her just as she was about to reach it, though, and when she looked back around, it was to find he was holding out a pair of leather leggings.

Forced to go back, she tried to snatch those from him as well, but he'd anticipated that, tightening his grip on them.

"Thank you," he said, and she blinked, taken aback for a moment.

"For what?"

"You goaded me on purpose. I'm in a much better mood now."

She wanted to snap and tell him that hadn't been her intention, but something held her back. She'd wanted him to shake off the quiet disposition—that was true. Had she inadvertently meant to make him happier? She didn't think so; her goal had been to piss him off . . . make him argue with her, because that was normal for them.

Normal was comfortable, though, and comfortable was certainly better than feeling melancholy after a conversation with your dad.

Shit.

"It won't happen again," she promised, hoping that her tone covered up the fact that she'd just realized he was right.

"It will," he disagreed. "You can't help yourself, Delaney. You don't like seeing others in pain."

"You're hardly in pain," she told him.

"As you've said"—his smile wavered, but only slightly—"you've never met my father."

Finally his hold on the leggings eased so that she could easily take them. When she didn't immediately move away, he lifted a pointed brow.

"We'll be late if you don't change, Delaney."

His words snapped her out of it, and she rushed from the room as quickly as she could. It didn't even matter that it looked like she was running; she just needed to get away from him as fast as possible. She slammed the bathroom door behind her for good measure, and quickly put on the new outfit.

There was no safe feeling when he was around, she thought, a bitter taste filling her mouth. It wasn't like with Ruckus, where having him near was never near enough. Trystan made her skin buzz in that way between discomfort and confusion, neither an emotion she liked.

How the hell did he expect her to live like this? Even for another week—let alone for the rest of her life.

It wouldn't come to that, though, she assured herself. Eventually,

Ruckus would get out and then they'd come up with a new solution. Maybe she would have to make it to the binding ceremony, give Trystan what he really wanted—a merger of Kint and Vakar.

Recalling his promise the other night sparked a renewed sense of hope, a plan taking form.

He said he'd let Ruckus and the others go so long as she successfully convinced the world that the two of them were a well-bonded pair. Surely if she did that and helped him join Kint and Vakar, he'd extend the same offer to her. He would no longer have any use for her, after all, and it would solve the Tar problem at the same time. They wouldn't have to worry about what kind of ruler she was—and Trystan could more than handle ruling two kingdoms on his own. All his talk about forever was just show, she was almost positive. A means to scare her into playing along.

Keeping her around for the rest of their lives? He couldn't want that. He'd be busy playing high king. After hearing more about his father, she might even understand. His need to get away from the Rex, to no longer have to worry about following his orders, it made sense. Hadn't she gone to boarding school to get away from her dad? Trystan was taking it to an entirely different extreme, but the end goal was similar.

So why not help him get what he wanted? If she agreed, and she actually tried, they could both focus on convincing his father and the rest of the world, as opposed to wasting all this energy on threats.

That option would appeal to him, wouldn't it?

And in the end, when it came time for him to let her go home, they could come up with a good lie as to why. Hell, it was a bonding in name only anyway. It didn't have to mean anything. Not really.

Ruckus wouldn't like that she'd made a deal with Trystan to stick around willingly, but he'd understand if it meant in the end they could return to their lives and not have to worry about looking over their shoulders.

Trystan needed her, and now she needed him. This could work. She merely had to make it to their bonding without blowing it. Act like she liked Trystan in front of other people, keep her friends safe by doing so, and, ultimately, get to go home.

The whole plan hinged on Trystan agreeing, but she was confident she could get him to. As a human, they didn't need to undergo the same process he would if he were marrying an alien. That meant he'd still be able to choose someone himself, someone he could spend the rest of his life with and procreate with.

With a renewed sense of hope, Delaney exited the bathroom only to find Trystan already waiting in the adjoined sitting area.

"I have stipulations," she blurted, already plotting out how she could work her way up to asking for what she really wanted.

"About?" He seemed genuinely intrigued, which was a good sign.

"This"—she twirled a finger in the air—"making this seem legit."

"I don't know what that last word means," he admitted, canting his head. "But all right. I'm curious. Proceed."

"I want regular visits with Ruckus and the others." She needed to find a way to tell him her plan. He had to be just as worried about her as she was for him. Before Trystan could immediately veto the idea, she held up a hand. "I need to be able to see for myself that they're all right. Talk to them and hear they aren't being mistreated. Which also means I want guarantees they aren't going to be mistreated."

Trystan clearly didn't like it, but he thought it over before giving a curt nod. "But only so long as your acting is convincing."

She eyed him suspiciously and he chuckled.

"Deal."

"That can't be all," he said.

"It isn't." She nibbled on her bottom lip, silently cursing herself for not being more prepared. She'd spent most of the night feeling sorry for herself and pissed at him; she hadn't thought up much more than asking to see Ruckus.

She ticked off a list in her mind of all the things he did that bothered her most. Over the past few days there'd been a few things he'd said that made her believe that he might be open to giving her more information.

"I need you to tell me, in detail, about things before they happen. No more making me walk into rooms blindly, hoping there's no one there I need to impress. Like throwing the coordinator at me fifteen minutes before my first meeting with her. Not cool, and it makes my doing this job a lot more difficult."

"I'm not very big on sharing, Delaney," Trystan said, though he was smiling. "But all right. I can agree to try my best when it comes to events that directly correlate with pretending to like me."

"Good. There's more," she quickly added, "and if you refuse, I'm out."

She held her breath, watching a play of emotions flicker over his face before he settled on cautious. Clearly, he'd just realized that her two other requests had been to ease him into what she really wanted.

He could have called her bluff—they both knew despite how angry she was by all this, she would never let anything happen to Ruckus—but he didn't. He didn't even take the opportunity to remind her that she didn't actually have an "out." Which should have been the flashing neon sign that he was teetering dangerously close to the edge.

And she was the one pushing him.

Taking his silence as a means to continue, she squared her shoulders and said, "I want you to release all of us at the end of this."

He still didn't speak, and she felt her own irritation start to claw uncomfortably at her insides.

"I'm sick of you dangling my friends and my future in my face every time I step out of line," she snapped, unable to contain it any longer. "Last night you promised that you'd let my friends go after the binding. Well, I've thought about it, and it's not good enough."

"Isn't it?"

"No, it isn't." So caught up in getting the words out, she breezed on through, completely missing the bite of iron in his tone. "And stop looking at me like that. You think you're angry? I'm angry! This is my life!" The other thing he'd said last night came to mind, and she shoved it bitterly away. "If you want me to do this, successfully do this, you've got to give me better motivation. Something other than just threats against the people I care about. I need hope that there's going to be more at the end of all this. That we'll be safe."

He watched her as she deflated in front of him, all the fight flooding out of her so quickly, it was a wonder her legs didn't fold beneath her.

Good sense was returning, making her realize that she'd gone about this all wrong. What she should have done was wait, carefully plan out exactly what she was going to say to him. Make it so there was no way he could refuse to accept her terms. She could tell, now that her own frustrations were bleeding out, that all she'd managed to do was fuel his own fury.

But that was what she'd wanted, right? Him angry instead of sullen. *Careful what you wish for*, she thought.

"Hope," he said finally, his voice cutting across the silence like a knife. "You want hope."

"Yes," she said breathlessly.

"You want me to tell you that once I get what I want, I'll let you go back to Earth? Telling you that, that'll give you hope?"

"Yes," she repeated.

She knew she should be paying more attention, trying to find some hidden meaning in his words, but she was blinded by desperation. She was so close to having an end in sight, she didn't want to jeopardize it, or the relief that possibility brought. It'd been so long since she'd felt like she could breathe, and she wanted that, even if it was just for a moment before they went off to do whatever it was he had planned for the rest of the day.

Even if he was the one inadvertently giving it to her.

"And you're certain, Delaney? That's what you need?"

"Yes."

"All right."

She blinked, sure she'd misheard him. When he didn't make any moves to take it back, or even any moves at all, her mouth dropped open. "What?"

"As soon as I've gotten what I want"—he took a deliberate step toward her—"*everything* that I want, I'll take you back to Earth."

"Really?" She barely heard, let alone cared, the way her voice cracked.

"I said it, didn't I?"

"And my friends?" She swallowed. "Ruckus?"

His mouth twisted in distaste, but his tone was even. "I'll set them free."

She'd expected more of a struggle, a fight, especially considering how angry he'd been. And still was.

"I'll release them after our binding," he said, when she took too long to speak, "like I initially promised."

He was agreeing. She was going to get to go home again, return to her life with Ruckus. With any luck, this whole ordeal could be nothing more than a horrible blip in their lives. She just needed to get through it, convince the Rex and the rest of Xenith that she wanted to be here. That she had feelings for Trystan.

Trystan, who'd somehow moved to stand directly in front of her without her noticing.

Widening her eyes, she tipped her head back so that she could see him, feeling her throat close up when their gazes met. Oh yes, he was definitely still furious, and it was being barely contained right beneath the surface. So it came as a huge shock when he lifted a hand between them.

"This is how deals are struck on your planet, are they not?" he asked when all she did was stare down at his palm.

His hand dwarfed hers, practically folding all the way over it. Surprisingly, he didn't hold on to her longer than proper social etiquette dictated. He let her go and watched as she stepped back without so much as a scowl.

"There is one thing," he mentioned. "We're about to attend a meeting with a group of extremely important people. In my defense, it was set before you made that particular stipulation."

"Who's going to be there?"

"We were supposed to attend this meeting in Vakar, at the palace, with Tilda and her council," he told her. "The Ander's interference made that impossible, so now it's going to be in our conference room. A few Kint high council members will also be joining, so it's imperative that you don't do anything to give us away."

"Don't act disdainful." She saluted him, needing to cut through the tension. "Check."

CHAPTER 12

They're going to be projected into the room," Trystan's voice filtered through Delaney's head, causing her to stop abruptly in the middle of the hallway. When he frowned down at her, she was still grinding her teeth.

"Please don't do that."

"Now that you're aware of the connection, it makes sense strategically to use it," he said. "Trust me, you're going to be grateful for it once we're in there and cannot communicate aloud."

"See, that's the thing," she said, lowering her voice as they began moving again, passing by a group of Tellers. "I don't trust you. At all. Especially not enough to willingly let you into my mind."

Though she had just trusted him ten minutes ago, hadn't she? When she'd taken him at his word that he'd eventually let them go. Smartly, neither of them brought that up.

Right now mentally preparing for this meeting was more important than fighting an impossible battle with him. She'd only ever met one member of the Kints' high council, and they hadn't directly spoken with each other. As for the Vakar, she'd dealt solely with the Basileus and Basilissa.

She was utterly unequipped for this.

"You'll do fine," Trystan told her, resting a hand over hers where she had it on his arm. "This is more about seeing you than anything. Taking you from Vakar this soon wasn't the best course of action."

"Why did you?" She'd been trying to figure that out since yesterday. "You have Ruckus in custody. What would it matter if we'd stayed at the palace?"

"He has too many friends there," he said, and he didn't sound happy about it. "Say what you will about the man, but no one can claim he wasn't good at his job. He has the respect of the Vakar forces at the palace. It wasn't worth the risk to stay and hope no one decided to try to help him."

Delaney felt a rush of pride. Ruckus was honorable, and generally cared about others.

"Don't smile," Trystan said, interrupting her thoughts. "Attempts to help him mean more Tellers I have to brand as traitors to the crown. That's why we left."

She frowned, but to him the conversation was over and he was already distracted by the double doors before them.

He opened the one closest and moved forward, slipping his arm from her grasp so that he could grab on to her hand. The room they entered was large, with a table shaped like a stretched-out octagon. Both ends had three sides, with two long ones forming the length. There was a total of twelve white leather chairs, all pulled half a foot out from the table.

Trystan went toward one end, moving the chair to his left out for her. He waited for her to seat herself, and then took the spot in the very center. There was a thin electronic screen hovering over the dark surface of the table, and he began pushing buttons on it.

The entire wall to the right was made of windows and overlooked an expanse of vibrant white. The landscape had many dips and arches, leading to a cluster of mountains in the far-off distance. They were snowcapped gray stone giants reaching up toward a sky tinted pale blue.

Even though it was toasty in the room, Delaney shivered, imagining how cold it would be out there. Trystan's warning about freezing replayed in her mind, sounding even less appealing now that she was getting a visual of the grounds.

"They're about to come online," Trystan said then, pulling her attention back to the empty room. "Try not to stare."

There was a slight buzzing in the air, followed by a flicker of neon blue and green in the chairs. Images of people formed next, some leaning forward onto the table, others already settled back in their seats. All of them had their attention turned toward Trystan and her, their eyes unblinking and intense.

Delaney didn't recognize any of them at first, too taken aback by their sudden appearance. The glow was gone, so that anyone who glanced into the room would think the occupants were actually there. The only thing that gave them away was the way their images would blur every so often, seemingly at random.

Tilda was seated directly across from them at the head of the other end of the table. Two bulky men, both old enough that their hair was graying, sat on either side of her.

Everyone to the left of Delaney wore uniforms of green and gold, while everyone on the right of the table was dressed in blue and silver. Out of them only three were women, and there was a single seat on the Vakar side that was vacant. Probably Fendus's chair.

Aside from the Basilissa, the only other person there who Delaney knew was the man now on Trystan's other side. It was the general she'd met the one time in the Basileus's office: Jackan.

Tilda was the first to speak, her voice ringing through the large space with a thick air of authority. "Zane Trystan. Lissa Delaney. I'm glad to see you arrived at your destination safely."

"There were no troubles at all," Trystan stated, his own tone formal.

"With all due respect, Zane," one of the female Vakar said, angling in her seat to better face him, "removing our Lissa from her home was very unwise."

"Zane Jager Trystan does not need approval from the likes of you," a Kint growled in response before anyone else could.

"He does when our future Basilissa is involved," argued another Vakar, this one male with slicked-back sandy-colored hair.

"You mean our future Regina," came the Kint counter-reply.

Delaney glanced at Tilda, wondering if she was going to jump in, but the Basilissa was still staring at her.

"Enough." Trystan barely lifted his palm from the tabletop, but everyone was immediately silenced. "She will be both Basilissa and Regina, let's not forget. Arguing over the matter is a waste of time."

Delaney lifted a brow and looked at him. It must be nice to put an end to a conversation merely by saying it was done. That kind of power could go to a person's head; no wonder he had ego problems.

"We're here so the royal council can clarify for themselves that the Lissa is well." He motioned to her. "As you can see, she is."

"That is debatable," Tilda said, and when all heads snapped in her direction, she forced a half smile to her red lips. "She must tell us that, is all I mean. Delaney, are you being treated fairly?"

Delaney briefly wondered what would happen if she told them the truth. There were a lot of important people here; surely, they would come get her if she said she was in trouble. Of course, by then Trystan would have killed Ruckus and the others.

Easing the tension from her shoulders, she mirrored the Basilissa's smile. "I'm very well, actually. It's beautiful here. I've never seen mountains like these before."

"We have mountains," one of the generals at Tilda's left said. "Wouldn't you prefer to be here, surrounded by your people—"

"We aren't her people," the female from earlier interrupted. "She's an Earthling, remember. We're all strangers to her."

The man sitting next to her mouthed something that looked similar to the word *careful*, but she didn't listen, rushing on without so much as an apologetic glance in the Basilissa's direction.

"I'm only voicing aloud what we're all thinking." She eyed Delaney pointedly. "She is not one of us. We'll allow her to take the throne as tradition decrees, but that doesn't mean we have to sit here and pretend she's truly Vakar."

It didn't take a psychic to see where this was going.

"This is what your father feared." Jackan had directed his comments to Trystan, but he'd spoken loud enough for the entire room to hear. "How can they be trusted to honor their word when they clearly don't stand with the Lissa?"

"A Vakar cannot be trusted," agreed one of the Kint, going so far as to slam his fist down on the table. Nothing happened—the table didn't so much as rattle, a big reminder that even though it looked like it, they weren't really there.

"*We* can't?" said the female Vakar. "You're the ones who invaded our cities!"

"Calm down, Ria," whispered the man who'd tried to get her to ease up before.

If Delaney hadn't been watching, she might not have caught it.

"I will not," Ria snapped, loudly enough for everyone. "This is why we're here, isn't it? To discuss this matter out in the open, with the girl in attendance."

"Delaney." She said her name before anyone could add anything else, waiting for everyone to stare at her once again. She kept her own gaze locked on Ria, ignoring the rest. "I have a name, and it isn't 'girl.' Actually, to you it isn't just Delaney. It's Lissa Delaney. If you're going to talk about me like I'm not here, you might as well be as respectful about it as possible."

Ria blinked and leaned forward as if she was about to retort, but Delaney moved on before she could so much as open her mouth.

"You," she addressed the guy sitting next to Ria, the one who'd tried to warn her. Also, the only one in this entire room who seemed to recall what had happened to the last person who'd spoken out against the Basilissa's decision. "What's your name?"

"Rue Corodonus, Lissa." He cleared his throat and clasped his hands on the top of the table.

Delaney had never heard the title Rue before, and was about to file it away for later when Trystan accessed her fitting and answered without her having to ask.

"Rue is a high-level soldier. Corodonus has been in the Basilissa's service for more than ten years. He's highly trusted but knows his boundaries. Unlike the young Teller Ria."

"I'd like to hear your take on this," Delaney said, pretending the Zane hadn't just been in her head.

"Lissa?" He glanced at the Basilissa before returning his questioning gaze on her.

"I am human," she elaborated, "and you have to have concerns about that, like the rest of them. I'd be surprised if you didn't, and possibly even a bit suspicious, if I'm being honest. It's okay," she urged him. "The Zane won't hurt you for being truthful right now."

She rested a hand on Trystan's shoulder, flashing the cockiest smile she had in her arsenal at the Rue. When the Zane shifted closer to her touch, she saw the entire room frown in unison.

"If the Lissa wants to hear your opinion, you're safe from both the Basilissa and me," Trystan agreed, motioning toward Tilda, who nodded.

Corodonus cleared his throat a second time and, in a blink, became a different person. He stood tall in his seat and held his chin high, speaking in a deep, unwavering tone.

"My concerns are more fact than anything. For one, our leaders are trained for the job starting at a young age, both mentally and physically. You, having grown up on Earth, lack the knowledge and skill sets we're used to finding in our Basilissas. For two, it's hard not to question where your loyalties actually lie, especially when you're so clearly tied to the Kint, who up until recently were our enemies."

Delaney inhaled slowly, pretending to think, when in reality she was gearing up for all the ways this could bite her in the ass. She probably should have remained silent and let Trystan and Tilda duke it out themselves. Too late now.

"Valid points," she said, and felt Trystan tense at her side. "I have a few of my own, however, if you don't mind?"

Corodonus was surprised she was asking, and it took him a moment to indicate with a wave of his hand for her to go ahead.

"Good. In regard to my being different from all your past Basilissas, that's true. I might not have had the same training that, say, Olena had, but then, I also didn't run away and abandon my people like she did."

Delaney felt a little bad about rubbing this in Tilda's face, but she couldn't risk not using everything in her arsenal.

"In fact, I went out of my way to protect both the Vakar and my own people"—she looked at Ria—"the humans, from war with Kint. A result of this was my being Uprisen instead of Olena, which, correct me if I'm wrong, Corodonus, also happens to be a standing tradition. Every Basilissa you've ever had was Uprisen first."

Corodonus nodded.

Delaney rested her arm across the table and turned it so that they could all see the sparkly *V* and the dermal-type gem there. "I was Uprisen, as per tradition. And I'm not completely untrained. I've been doing physical training with a high-standing Ander since before I returned to Earth."

"You continued training with him?" Trystan asked, clearly impressed.

"Of course," she told him. "Anyway, I'm obviously not as good as Olena probably is at hand-to-hand—"

"Olena was never very good," Tilda interrupted.

"Well." Delaney licked her lips to give herself a moment to get back on track. "My point is, I'm willing to learn what I don't know, and I've already proven that I'll do anything to keep my people safe. Which, thanks to this"—she flashed the marks on her arm again—"now includes all of you and the rest of Vakar."

There was silence for a long while, where everyone switched from looking at her to sharing glances with one another. After a few minutes had passed, Ria angled her body toward Delaney's end of the table.

"What about him?" She lifted her chin at Trystan. "You haven't said anything to quell our fears that he's orchestrated all of this against both your, and our Basilissa's, will."

Right. That.

"I'll admit it took some convincing . . . ," she began, hoping that sticking as close to the truth as possible would make it come off more believable when she deviated. "I mean, I was back home in Maine, and I had a life. But then Trystan showed up and explained things to me. I'd already seen the unrest between Vakar and Kint during my initial stay, so he knew I'd listen and believe him.

"Look." She rested her elbows on the edge of the table. "I'm not going to sit here and claim that I'm in love with him; none of you are stupid, and I won't insult you by insinuating otherwise. *But*"—she took a deep breath—"I care about him. Enough that when he posed the solution both he and the Basilissa had come up with—together—I took the time to consider it. And I realized he was right."

"Right about?" spoke up the Kint who'd originally argued with Ria. His eyes were narrowed and he was watching Delaney closely.

"My taking the throne," she said. "I'm sure we've all met Olena, or have at least heard the stories. Is it really such a surprise that the Basilissa, a woman who truly loves and wants the best for her people, would choose someone else as an heir? Is it unconventional? Absolutely. But if my taking Olena's place and binding to the Zane means peace between Kint, Vakar, and even Earth, isn't that worth deviating from the norm?" At their confused looks she reiterated, "Normal."

"If you're going to rule Vakar, you need to be here, on Xenith. You've come to terms with that?" Corodonus asked. "Of never going home again?"

"Who says I won't be going back to Earth?" Delaney stated. "I can still visit. It's not like Trystan would ever keep me here on this planet against my will." She linked her arm through his and grinned up at him. "Right?"

Because she was so close, she saw his jaw clench before he was able to get ahold of himself. In a heartbeat he was smiling at her, and leaned down to press a soft kiss to the center of her forehead.

"We agreed to holiday," he told the room. "It's not my ideal vacation spot, but personally checking in on Lissa Delaney's people makes the most logical sense. I will be duty bound to ensure their safety, after all."

That seemed like excellent reasoning, and she was glad that the two of them sounded like they'd actually discussed this before. If she'd heard a couple talking about vacationing, she'd certainly buy in to their relationship.

"Very true," Tilda agreed.

"The people have been restless ever since this announcement was made," Ria tried again, this time directing her comments to the Basilissa specifically. "They need to see that she's truly on their side. She can't do that from Kint territory."

"Technically," Trystan corrected her, "we're still in Vakar. Inkwell was returned at the end of the war. Basileus Magnus simply chose not to evict the Kints who currently reside here."

Delaney almost frowned, catching herself at the last second. She'd been under the impression they were in Kint, and she supposed in a roundabout way they sort of were, but it would have been nice to know the whole story.

"That should be acceptable," Tilda said, glaring at Ria, who finally seemed to take the hint. "The true purpose of this meeting was to hear from Lissa Delaney, and I believe I speak for us all when I say she has made her intentions clear. She wants to avert another war; surely, every single person at this table shares the same desire?"

Tilda set a stern, challenging look on all of them. When no one spoke against her, she returned her gaze to Trystan and Delaney.

"I recall your mentioning a meeting with your coordinator, Zane?" Tilda asked sweetly.

"That is correct, Basilissa." He nodded and tapped on the electronic screen in front of him, checking the time. "It's soon, in fact."

"We'll let the two of you go then." She waved at the rest of the room. "We should all be satisfied."

"For now," Corodonus said evenly, and the Kint sitting across from him silently agreed by bobbing his head.

"Very good. Delaney"—Tilda held her gaze—"I'll speak with you soon. Stay safe."

"You too," she said, then watched as one by one the projections winked out, leaving her alone with the Zane in a matter of seconds.

Exhaling, she slumped in her chair and rested her head back, closing her eyes against the blaring overhead lights. Pretending was exhausting. There'd been a few times she was sure they were all going to see through her bullshit, even when half of it—like the part about wanting to protect Earth—was true. Had she actually thought playing Olena had been difficult? This was way more grueling. And worse. A million times worse.

"You did very well," Trystan told her, and she felt him rest his hand on the back of her chair, jostling her slightly.

"Fantastic," she drawled, her eyes still shut. She wanted one more minute, just one, to pretend like all this was a horrible dream. "I want to see Ruckus."

When a moment passed without him responding, she sighed and opened her eyes again, angling her head to look at him. Unsurprisingly, he was watching her with a tight expression, his mouth thinned in displeasure.

"Are you going to make that face every time I bring him up?"

"Our day isn't finished yet." He unfolded from his chair so that he towered over her.

She had to bend almost completely backward just to be able to keep their gazes locked, the arm of her chair digging painfully against the center of her spine. "You didn't answer my question."

"That's because it is impossible to give an answer when you don't know it yourself," he stated tersely. Then, without waiting for her, he headed for the door.

Delaney got up to follow, wondering how she'd managed to say the right things to everyone in this room and yet still somehow screw up when it came to speaking to Trystan.

CHAPTER 13

After another lengthy meeting with the coordinator, Delaney was running on fumes. Trystan had responded to the coordinator's questions politely but in a clipped tone, making it clear from the start that he didn't want to be there any more than Delaney did.

Despite the fact that the meeting with Co Gailie had ended at least three hours ago, Delaney still hadn't seen her friends.

"You're upset." He was watching her out of his peripheral, avoiding direct eye contact. There were a decent amount of people roaming the halls, many of them not Tellers but maids and the like, and he scanned their faces as they passed. She wasn't sure if he was doing a threat assessment or if he was oddly interested in their goings-on.

"You're a genius," she retorted, already regretting that that was what she'd gone with.

Sure enough, he chuckled and turned down another hall. "I'm told that a lot."

"Is that all the coordinator is going to do?" She settled for at least questioning him about something that actually mattered. "Ask us trivial stuff about ourselves? Why?"

"There's more to it," he assured her. "Everything Co Gailie does has a purpose, but I'm not aware as to what end. I only know the basics involved. Getting bonded, especially at this point in my life, had never crossed my mind."

Delaney searched his face, not sure what she was looking for but feeling like she wasn't finding it. "What about after it was announced you were bonding with Olena? Weren't you curious about what you'd have to do?"

The corner of his mouth turned up in that wicked half grin, and he set a knowing stare on her.

"Right." She sighed. "You were too busy trying to find a way out of it."

"You would have done the same."

"I wouldn't have involved an outsider." She grunted. "Especially not an innocent one."

Trystan paused, angling his body slightly toward hers. With his hands behind his back and his chin tilted, he looked like the arrogant aristocrat he was.

"Is that how you view yourself?" he asked, and then momentarily slid his attention down the hall where a small group of Tellers passed without so much as glancing their way.

"My choices were taken from me," she pointed out. "And I made it clear that I wanted nothing to do with any of this. Not to mention, this isn't even my planet. Of course I'm innocent."

"That's not what I meant." He leaned in a little closer, almost like he wasn't aware he was doing it. "Do you think of yourself as an outsider? Is that how you feel?"

Delaney waited to see if there was more, wondering how he could ask something like that with such a straight face. Aside from the fact that she didn't want to be here, there was very little she actually knew about their culture, not nearly enough to ever make her feel like she could legitimately be part of it.

Instead of explaining, she said, "You've got the only friends I've ever made on this planet currently on lockdown, and I'm unfamiliar with literally everything you've shown me since our arrival. Of course I feel out of place, Trystan. I don't belong here. I don't even know why this place is called Inkwell," she added as an afterthought.

"It's on account of all the black water," a new voice answered, and she turned to find Dom standing a few feet away from them. "The rivers up in the mountains are filled with sediments that make them charcoal colored."

"Dominan," Trystan greeted, ignoring the half dozen guards who stood close behind the boy. "I wasn't aware you were visiting today."

"Mother wanted me to ask you to dinner," Dom explained with a bored shrug. "I told her you'd say no, but she insisted." He glanced at Delaney. "You're invited, too, Lissa. If you did come, I could show you my favorite flower. It's winter now, but Mother always keeps one potted inside. Did you know"—he turned back to Trystan—"that she's never seen a gorganatias?"

Because it so directly correlated with their conversation about how she didn't belong here, Delaney sent the Zane a satisfied stare.

"I may have overheard that somewhere," Trystan said. "Unfortunately, the Lissa and I are very busy. The next few weeks are going to be packed with preparation for our binding."

Dom's face scrunched up in distaste, and Delaney couldn't help but smile. It seemed kids were similar no matter what planet they were from. He probably thought girls had cooties.

"Tell your mother thank you for the invitation, but that you were right. We will, apologetically, have to decline."

"Can I say it just like that?" Dom asked, bouncing on the balls of his feet.

"Do so at your own risk," Trystan told him with a grin. "If you think rubbing the fact that you were right in her face is worth the indubitable amount of consequences, then do so."

Dom thought it over, hard, and then shook his head frantically as if his mom were already there, listening over his shoulder. "You have a point, Uncle Trystan."

"I often do." He motioned back down the way Dom and his group of Tellers had come. "Be on your way; you don't want to keep her." Before the boy could follow his orders, though, he added, "Stop in the kitchens first. I believe Yalla is making fruy. Maybe you'll get lucky and some will be finished."

Whatever fruy was, it excited Dominan, who bounded off with barely a wave over his shoulder. He disappeared around a corner almost as quickly as he'd arrived, leaving the two of them alone in the hall.

"Yalla?" Delaney asked the second Trystan looked at her.

"She's our cook. She's lived here since before Kint took over, when it was originally Vakar."

"You have a Vakar cook?"

"Does that surprise you because I'm Kint, and therefore I must hate all Vakar," Trystan speculated, "or because allowing someone from a territory that was once a sworn enemy of mine cook my meals seems outlandishly risky?"

Coming from him, the guy who trusted no one, *outlandish* was an apt word choice. It did seem odd that he'd have a Vakar citizen making food for him. Especially after publicly infiltrating and conquering the Vakar palace. Though there was Sanzie, who'd once been Vakar herself, to consider.

Delaney was sure there was more to that story, but she didn't feel like getting it from him so instead asked, "Aren't you worried she'll try to poison you?"

The crimson ring around his cornflower-blue eyes seemed to thicken as he watched her, and his voice lowered almost huskily. "Are you concerned for me, Delaney?"

She pulled back. "I'm appalled you'd even suggest it."

He grunted, though the sound was clearly forced to cover up a laugh. "When you say it like that, it doesn't sound believable at all. So, I'll settle your fears about my untimely death by poison now. Yalla has been with my family since before I was born. She kept me fed as a child, and even taught me a thing or two in the kitchens. Honestly, I'm more afraid of being attacked by you than I am of being harmed by her."

"Smart," Delaney said, because there was no reason to bother trying to hide that he was right. If it meant getting her and the others out of here? She'd hurt him, for certain. Still, she didn't want to give him too long to think that over.

"You brought Dom with us." She would never have guessed. "Was he on the same ship?"

"No," he said, shaking his head, "he was aboard one that left the day before, actually. Inkwell is his home. He grew up here, and his house is just down the street, about half a mile south."

"So you brought him with you to Vakar." That was also odd. "Why?"

Trystan sighed and looked away. "His mother insisted. His father was killed during the war, and having her son there to witness the takeover of the Vakar palace was her way of gaining closure. I couldn't deny her that. Her husband meant a great deal to me." He hesitated, unsure whether he wanted to continue. "Dominan means a great deal to me."

She should make fun of him for it, yet she couldn't get herself to do it.

"He's a cute kid," she said, smiling. "Why does he call you Uncle? I thought you didn't have any siblings."

"I don't." He began walking once more, and they fell into step together. "His father was my best friend. My Sworn before Brighton." His mouth twisted in displeasure. "What a poor replacement he turned out to be."

She wanted to ask more, but it was clear from his closed-off expression that he didn't want to discuss it. Honestly, she must be feeling a bit cowardly, because she wasn't too upset with having to let it go.

Trystan finally broke the silence. "I'm taking you to the Ander now, by the way."

The winding stairwell seemed to twist and turn for miles, so that the echo of their boots clacking against the solid steps felt like a never-ending rhythm. The walls were made of rough stone, making her think of dungeons from old movies set in the Dark Ages. Even though she was certain that was done on purpose, she couldn't help the scowl, or the hint of anger she felt toward Trystan for putting Ruckus and her friends down here.

Delaney clenched her hands into tight fists, allowing her short nails to dig into the tender flesh of her palms. It was a poor attempt at distraction, but it was better than acting on the urge to turn around and shove Trystan down the rest of the way.

Lights flickering at the bottom of another turn finally indicated the end, and she held her breath to prepare herself. This place was already pretty horrible, and they hadn't even reached the actual cells yet. She didn't realize she'd slowed until she felt Trystan's hand gently press against the small of her back, urging her down the last three steps.

Pulling away as quickly she could without tripping, Delaney entered a long hall, assessing the half dozen guards who lined the walls. They paid her no mind, but dropped their chins to their chests when Trystan appeared behind her.

She rolled her eyes and started forward, noting the only doorway was at the very end. A guard opened it when she was close, and she slipped inside when the gap was large enough for her, not bothering to wait for him to open it all the way. Inside was a set of cells nothing like what she'd imagined.

For one, there were no bars; instead prisoners were contained by some kind of electrical force field that glowed with a neon sheen. Her eyes rested on Pettus in the cell to the left, and she shot forward, letting out a sigh of relief. Aside from a few fading bruises on his bare arms, he appeared to be all right.

"Apologies," Pettus said, the words coming out a bit wheezy.

"We tried," Gibus added sadly from where he sat in the same cell.

His coloring was off, his skin more sallow than the golden hue she was used to seeing on him. Part of his Vakar uniform was torn at the collar, and now that she was closer, she could make out a couple scratches on the side of his neck.

"This damsel can take care of herself," she assured him. "You just focus on feeling better. You don't sound so good."

"Delaney." Ruckus spoke from behind her, and she twisted around so quickly, it took a moment for her vision to focus in on him.

He was standing as close to the electrical barrier as he could, so that the tip of his nose came dangerously close to touching it. There were dirt stains on his knees, and a smear of what looked like blood down his right arm; it was impossible to tell if it was his or someone else's. His right eye was swollen so that only a thin slit was open. She doubted he could see through it at all.

His other eye was wide and searching her from top to bottom, running the same medical assessment she was. The familiar yellow of his iris surrounded by a ring of deep green completed its search and finally rested on her. When it did and he was staring back, she felt her chest tighten.

"Bastard." She glared at Trystan, who'd settled against one of the empty cells.

"I didn't do anything," he said. "That's all collateral from when they fought their way to you back at the palace."

He'd slipped his hands into his pockets and crossed his ankles, propping himself against the wall with his left shoulder. Way too casual. Too calm. Like the fact that her friends were bruised and clearly damaged didn't matter at all.

To him it didn't, and the reminder made her sick. She'd been so focused on playing her part, she'd lost sight of what he truly was. A monster. He'd sucked her in with his daddy issues, and like an idiot, she'd allowed herself to buy into them. As if that made the things he'd done acceptable.

"The clock is ticking," Trystan told her in a silky smooth voice. "Do you want to spend your time hissing at me or making sentiments toward your boyfriend?"

Ruckus let out a growl, drawing the Zane's attention.

"I'm not leaving, Ander," he said, even though no one had even bothered suggesting it. "Anything you have to say to my betrothed can be said in front of me. If that makes you uncomfortable, either of you, feel free not to speak at all. Actually, that is my preferred outcome."

Delaney stepped closer to the barrier, wishing there was a way to make it disappear, just for a second. Now that they were together, she needed to touch him, needed physical contact to assure herself that he was really okay.

"Don't talk to me telepathically," she warned, trying to keep her voice down without making it obvious she was doing so. She didn't want to risk drawing Trystan closer to them; knowing him, he'd invade her personal space in order to eavesdrop. "He hacked my fitting."

"I figured as much," Ruckus said breathlessly. "How are you? Has he hurt you?"

"Only where you can't see," she said, before realizing it was a mistake.

His expression darkened, and she lifted a hand to keep his attention before he could say something to Trystan and bring the Zane back into their conversation.

"I'm fine," she said, correcting herself. "Honestly. He hasn't done anything to me except the obvious." She forced the corner of her mouth up. "I was really looking forward to seeing what you made for dinner."

Before she'd been knocked out and woken up on Trystan's spaceship, she and Mariana had been heading home to have dinner with Ruckus. He'd decided to try his hand at cooking again, a skill he unfortunately didn't have.

"Spaghetti," he said, mirroring her teasing half smile. "And you aren't fooling anyone, Delaney. I know you hate my cooking. I can't blame you. Before I got the call from Pettus, I'd already burned the sauce."

"Please tell me you at least used the canned stuff?"

"I attempted homemade," he admitted, sounding embarrassed despite the fact that the results were long gone by now. "I wasted all the groceries Mariana had just bought."

"Such a disappointment." She clucked her tongue.

He grimaced. "Delaney—"

"No." She shook her head before he could continue. "The fact that you'll never become an Iron Chef aside, you have never disappointed me. This isn't your fault."

"Isn't it?" His mouth thinned, and there was a flash of anger visible in his good eye.

"No," she insisted, "it isn't. Enough with the pity party. We won't be here forever."

He looked at her, clearly wanting to say something about that, but Trystan's presence forced him to rethink it. An air of defeat surrounded him, and she hated that the Zane could do that, make Ruckus feel that way without saying anything at all.

"Ruckus," she said, firming her tone, "I'm serious. We're going to be okay."

"I should be the one comforting you," he said.

"I'm not the one in the cell."

"Aren't you?"

She swallowed the lump in her throat and gave another shaky smile. "Well, my cell's bigger, anyway. You want to comfort me? Tell me something."

"What?"

"Something good."

"I bought you something." He shifted on his feet, readjusting his position, trying to be careful with his right ankle.

She wanted to ask him how badly he was hurt, who had done it and how. Instead she asked, "Oh, what is it? Is it shiny?"

"The shiniest," he agreed, then chuckled. "I'm kidding. I know you better than that. The thing is, you're going to have to wait until our vacation is over. I accidentally left it at home."

Usually she was the joker between the two of them, and this sudden role reversal had her letting out a real laugh. "I bet you left the bedroom window open, too, huh."

"I'm pretty sure the oven is still on as well," he added, grinning. The two halves of his split lip pulled apart. He didn't react, though it had to be painful.

"I know you can't say anything back," Ruckus said to her telepathically. *"Just nod to let me know that you really are okay. If he's done anything to you, Delaney, I wouldn't be able to live with myself."*

Because Trystan wasn't connected to the Ander, he wasn't able to read thoughts from his mind, or the ones he sent into Delaney's. It made it safe at least for him to tell her things privately, though if they weren't careful, the Zane would definitely pick up on what they were doing.

"None of this is your fault," she repeated. "It really is going to be all right." She wanted to tell him about the arrangement she'd made, but she knew him well enough to know he wouldn't take the same kind of comfort from it she did. She'd tell him, just not yet.

"We'll find a way." Ruckus smiled.

She tried to tell him with her eyes that she was serious, and hoped she was portraying confidence and that he would understand what it meant. There was no way of knowing for sure, however, and too quickly she heard Trystan straightening from the wall, adjusting his clothing in that annoying and frankly pompous way he did.

The fact that she could make out the slight rustling of his clothes and know what he was up to was further proof that he was ridiculous.

"It's time to go, Delaney," he said crisply, leaving no room for argument.

Her feet felt rooted to the ground, every fiber in her being screaming to resist, even though logically her mind knew it was useless. She'd only make it worse for her and Ruckus if she didn't go, and yet she hesitated, her gaze trailing across Ruckus's face.

"Hey," Ruckus said softly. "I love you."

"Delaney," Trystan growled darkly. "Now."

She took a step away from the cell and pulled herself together. Making sure her voice was loud enough for everyone to hear, she stared at Ruckus and told him, "I love you, too."

CHAPTER 14

The one good thing about being in Inkwell was that it was too cold for short dresses.

Her wardrobe was now made up entirely of outfits with pants, including the forest-green ones she was currently wearing. They were a material similar to leather, and pretty formfitting, but more comfortable than anything she'd ever had on before.

Delaney was in the process of scowling at the mirror—mentally scolding herself for actually caring about the damn pants when clothes had never mattered before—when the entrance door in the middle room opened with a heavy bang.

She jumped and rushed out to see what was going on, surprised when she was met with a fast-moving Trystan. He almost bulldozed into her, in fact, and she had to grasp on to his arms to keep her footing. Before she could send him a glare, he was gripping her wrist and tugging her out into the hall.

"What the hell—"

"We're under attack," he cut her off, swiftly moving them down the left side of the hall and into the west wing of the building.

For a second she was too shocked to respond, certain she'd misheard him. A fierce wave of déjà vu swept over her, and her earlier anger at him flared tenfold. This was all Trystan's fault. If anything happened to Ruckus and the others while they were locked down there, she'd kill him. She didn't know how exactly, but damn it, she'd find a way.

Unless . . . what if it was the Vakar? What if Tilda had changed her mind or somehow rescued Olena, and now she was coming to help Delaney?

"It's the Tars," Trystan told her then, snuffing out the seed of hope before it could fully sprout.

"How did they find us?" she demanded.

"Our location is hardly being kept secret," he said with a grunt. "My father and the Basilissa thought it politically best to keep the people informed. It's supposed to ensure they don't attempt to openly rebel."

It was meant to supply further proof that she wasn't being held hostage by the Kints, he meant. Handy. Of course they'd be using any tactics they could to keep the public in line.

The sound of gunfire ahead had them both pausing, and he swiveled and brought them down a different hall. Everything in this building was painted silver and white, with shots of light and dark blues thrown in. They were moving through the west wing so quickly, all Delaney got was a mass blur of these three colors, and it was beginning to give her whiplash.

"How many are there?" she asked, straining to hear if any of the shooters were following. When the sounds suddenly seemed to be coming from in front of them yet again, her heartbeat picked up.

Were they headed straight toward the Tars?

"Many." He pulled them tight against a wall and then quickly peered over the edge into another hallway. The sound of echoing boots hitting the floor clued her in that wasn't the right way to go.

She tugged on his arm until he gave her his attention, though it was clear by the calculating look in his eyes that he was distracted.

How close? she mouthed, then pointed around him to indicate she meant the approaching Tellers.

His only response was a curt shake of his head. Then he was back to plotting on his own.

Delaney narrowed her eyes—not that he noticed. This affected her, too. If they were here to kill *them*, her life was also on the line. She wished he'd let her keep her fritz. At least then she wouldn't be left completely defenseless.

As if reading her mind, Trystan activated the one on his own wrist, slashing his right middle finger in the air over his pulse point. An almost imperceptible hiss was emitted as the weapon unfolded and formed from the thick metal band. In less than half a minute he was holding the alien equivalent of a gun. A row of dim navy lights flickered at the side, and he tapped the top of the weapon, instantly turning the lights off.

"Stay near," he said, pushing his voice to her telepathically so that it felt like it was brushing against the inside of her skull.

Delaney shivered, but before she could decide whether it was because she was completely disgusted by the intrusion, he whipped them around the corner and started shooting.

She was tucked so close to him, and he was so large, she couldn't see around him. Not that she really wanted to. She was fine with hanging back and missing out on all the carnage, which she was positive there was a lot of because he kept firing as he walked them down the hall.

Strolled them down was more like it, as if he had all the time in the world to reach the end and wherever it was they were going. The fact that he was so collected should have played on her earlier anger, reminding her that he was a killer. Instead it was a relief.

Did that make her a hypocrite?

She hated how brutal he was, how dark he was willing to go, and yet the moment those predatory instincts were used on her behalf, she was glad.

The sound of heavy footsteps at her back pulled her away from those troubling thoughts. She twisted, catching Trystan's attention. She felt the air shift as he turned to see what she was doing, and before she could overthink it, she reached back and grabbed on to his right wrist.

She yanked as hard as she could, bringing the fritz he was still holding up to her eye level just in time to rest her finger over his on the trigger as the first Teller came into view.

He rounded the corner, two others close on his heels, their own weapons drawn and aimed. They were dressed in shades of dark blue, and even though she found this fact interesting, Delaney didn't hesitate.

She pressed her finger down on Trystan's and watched as tiny balls of what appeared to be neon-blue light shot forward. Her first shot slammed into the center of the closest Teller's chest, and he convulsed.

Her next two hit one of the others, and then the final shot slammed into the last Teller's right shoulder. Even though it wasn't as spot-on as the rest, it seemed to do the trick. The Teller started shaking and immediately dropped to the ground.

Delaney blinked, her mouth hanging slightly open. The Tellers were wiggling like they'd just been electrocuted. Even though this was hardly the time for her to stand there gaping, it was a good minute before she realized the entire hallway had gone silent. When she listened for any nearby sounds down other corridors, she was met with more silence.

Had this really been all the Tars? Trystan had made it sound like there were dozens of them. . . .

She turned, intending to finally get a look at where all the shot Tellers were, but she froze when she saw Trystan's bewildered expression. They stared at each other a moment, and then she realized she was still gripping his wrist. She dropped it, taking a single step back in the process.

"Zane?" Sanzie's voice came from behind Delaney, and when she glanced over her shoulder, she found that the Teller had appeared and was uncomfortably standing among the ones Delaney had shot.

She frowned, stepping to the side so that she could easily look at both Trystan and Sanzie with a turn of her head. Something about this situation wasn't adding up, and it wasn't just the way the female Teller was staring sheepishly at the fallen. She was too calm. They were *both* too calm for a massive attack to be happening.

"One of you is going to tell me what the hell is really going on here." At this point, Delaney didn't care which. "Or I swear I'm going to make your lives miserable any way I can."

When neither of them immediately responded, she swung around to glare at Trystan. From the corner of her eye, she saw Sanzie order a few soldiers to help her remove the bodies.

"What is this?" She waved at the Tellers currently being lifted from the ground.

"You informed the members of the high councils that you'd continued training while on Earth." He crossed his arms, the move affectively making him seem larger. "I was curious to see if this was the case."

She angled her head. "You set this all up to find out if I'd been telling the truth? That's the most ridiculous thing I've ever heard. You do realize you could have just asked me, right?"

"I wanted to see firsthand how well you could defend yourself," he countered, his eyes narrowing slightly.

"If you gave me back my fritz," she stated, "I'd show you." The threat was apparent. "Those Tellers—"

"They're fine," he answered before she could get the rest of the question out. "I set my fritz to stun this morning before coming to get you. They all knew what was in store, and they trusted I wasn't going to deliver any killing blows. Fortunately, because it was my weapon you used against them, neither did you."

She was more relieved by that than she should be—even if they weren't Tars, they were still technically her enemy.

He smirked and held out his hand.

She looked pointedly down at it and then back up at him.

"Now who is acting childish?" He wiggled his fingers and waited.

"Touching you right now really isn't an option for me," she admitted when it became clear he was willing to stand here like that all day.

"Because you're angry"—he didn't lower his arm—"about this?"

"Definitely."

He canted his head. "This is about the Ander."

"And Pettus and Gibus."

"But mostly about the Ander."

She ground her teeth and prayed for patience. "You make it sound like he's all that I care about. He isn't. I don't want any of them hurt, and yet they're currently down there all messed up. Because of you."

"Me?" He used his free hand to point to the center of his chest, and grunted. "My Tellers were told to stop any intruders from entering the palace—which is, as you well know, their job. It isn't my fault your little band fought back. They were in the process of breaking into the home of their Basilissa, which is also considered treason. If I hadn't taken custody of them, they'd be dead."

"That's bullshit," she snapped. "Tilda wouldn't do that."

"Oh, because she's so very fond of you, is that it? If we're going by your logic, if I'm to blame, she's to blame. She's the one who gave you up, after all. Even Magnus held out till the very end."

Delaney opened her mouth to retort and then quickly shut it the second she processed his words. "What?"

"There were things I couldn't understand," he continued, the small space between his brows wrinkling as he frowned. "Certain things you'd done and said that didn't add up. My suspicions got worse when Olena—the real Olena—arrived an hour or so after she'd supposedly departed on that ship with the Ander. It didn't make sense that he would abandon her now, make her return without him. And her excuse for running from me in the hangar? For boarding and flying off?"

She held her breath, already knowing she was going to hate whatever he said next. They were supposed to have prepared Olena on what to say and do. Had they not bothered, or had the Lissa just been stupid?

"She was afraid I was with the shooters." He shook his head, clearly disgusted by this notion. "I'd taken a zee for her only days before, had killed my second-in-command only hours before, and she had the audacity to claim she was afraid *I* was with those attacking her?"

Technically, he had been in the beginning, but Delaney didn't bother voicing this fact aloud.

"As the days passed, it became increasingly obvious she wasn't the same woman I'd done those things for," he said. "Little by little, it became difficult to stick to my earlier assumption that she was different because of her time on Earth. After all, if that had been true, a single trip into space wouldn't have magically reverted her back. Would you like to know what she did that first night she was here?"

Delaney was certain she did not, but he wasn't really asking, so he didn't wait for an answer.

"She screamed at a servant for bringing her bergozy." He held her gaze. "Apparently, she has tried it, and it's not to her liking."

She would have groaned and slumped against the wall if it'd been anyone else telling her this. Really, how stupid had they all been to believe Olena could pull it off? They'd thought that because it'd been her life on the line, she'd put in an effort. Obviously, they'd been wrong. According to Trystan, she hadn't even made it twenty-four hours before giving them up.

"It wasn't the drink," he said before she could say anything. "That factored in, but to be honest, I didn't even think much on that detail until later when I was alone and playing it all back. It was how she'd spoken to the servant that jarred me. The girl I'd been spending time with would never talk to someone—someone other than me, of

157

course—like that. You'd made a point to treat everyone here with respect, even Lura, after she'd attempted to poison you."

"How long?" Her throat was dry, so her voice came out rough and low. She tried to swallow, but when that didn't work, she cleared her throat. "How long did it take you to figure this out?"

What she really wanted to ask was how in the world did he correctly guess that someone had been altered with unknown alien tech? That seemed so far out of the realm of possibility, even for Xenithians, that it would have been nuts for him to suggest it, let alone think it.

"Two weeks. I mapped out all the inconsistencies, ran background checks on the few people you had shown an interest in, and eventually broke into Gibus's facilities and hacked his notes. He'd deleted all the information on how the technology had been created, but had left mention of its existence in his systems."

For a bona fide genius, he hadn't been very smart.

"You went to the Basileus with your assumptions?" Even with the Sutter's notes, that seemed risky.

"No." A hint of his good mood vanished, and if she hadn't been watching him so closely, she may have missed it. "I went to my father."

Right. Why would he involve someone else's king?

"I needed to formulate a plan, and I needed to convince him of its worth. I told him all the ways it could benefit Kint, and how it was a better solution than the one he himself had proposed when betrothing me to Olena. I raised the point that the Basileus and Basilissa had blatantly lied to us, playing both of us for fools. After that, it was a matter of honing the details, finding loopholes to ensure you would be put on their throne with little to no resistance."

"And somewhere in there, Magnus was killed." It was starting to sound like that hadn't been the plan.

"Like I said," he stated, "I knew someone had pretended to be Olena, but I didn't know who. It was the who that really mattered. You." His eyes searched hers. "Finding you was what mattered. Yet they wouldn't give you up. So my father took it further than I expected. The Basilissa didn't hesitate to talk after that."

"The Rex had just murdered her husband," Delaney hissed.

"It was his choice not to give you up. He's dead because of that choice. He didn't want to appear weak and broken by a Kint. *That* is why he refused to tell me who you were, not out of loyalty or gratitude toward you. For him, it wasn't about you at all, Delaney."

But to Trystan it had been; that was what he was not so subtly trying to convince her. Was that the whole purpose of this little talk? He wasn't big on explanations, and yet they'd been standing in this hallway for at least ten minutes now while he rambled on. There had to be a reason, but she wouldn't play into his game this time. If he wanted to tell her how important she supposedly was to him, he could man up and say it directly.

"We're wasting the day," Trystan said, putting an end to the discussion as swiftly as he'd started it. "Let's go."

He turned and headed down the hall in the direction they'd been initially going before his men had "attacked" them. All the bodies had been cleared away, leaving no sign that the shootout had even happened.

"Where are you taking me?" she asked, mostly to distract herself.

What she really wanted was to dissect the information he'd just unloaded, but she had to admit: She was a bit curious where they were heading. What was coming next?

CHAPTER 15

ot even if you paid me."

Delaney stood in the open doorway to a massive training room, scanning the walls covered in different types of gear and the many floor mats that sectioned off each corner of the room. At the very center there was a round table covered in weird electronic devices, the only recognizable one being a clear-screened computer panel.

Everything was done in white and tones of silver, which she thought highly illogical considering what this room's purpose was.

Trystan was already wrapping his hands in strips of white material, similar to how a boxer would before going a few rounds with a punching bag.

Only, in this case the punching bag was going to be Delaney. Hence her immediate refusal. Sparring with Ruckus was one thing. The idea of purposefully and willingly putting herself in Trystan's space was asinine.

"I have something better than money to motivate you with." He finished up on his second hand. When he turned around, he was flashing that wicked grin. "I have threats."

Very true . . . Blackmail, while not ideal, was a good motivator.

"Now"—he motioned her closer with a curl of his fingers, lifting the roll of white material with his other hand—"come here so we can get you ready."

"Pretty sure that's not going to help prepare me," she mumbled, loud enough that he caught it and chuckled. Knowing further argument would be useless, she made her way over to him, stopping with a good five feet still between them.

Trystan rolled his eyes and breached the space. Lifting her left hand, he slowly began wrapping the material around her palm. His touch was gentle yet firm, like he was trying hard not to spook her or give her reason to pull away.

"My Tellers were supposed to have come at you from behind, catching you off guard. Forcing you into a hand-to-hand altercation so that I could see what stage you were at. Of course, you went and changed that plan, but that's all right. It saves me from having to find a way to test your shooting abilities."

"Again," she drawled, yanking her left hand back once he'd finished, but allowing him to take up her right, "you could have just asked."

"That's boring," he said, the corner of his mouth turning up. He kept his gaze on what he was doing, giving her the rare opportunity to inspect him without him staring back.

She'd noticed the purple blotches beneath his eyes before. Had they gotten worse? His hair was carefully smoothed back like it always was, but he was sporting a five-o'clock shadow. She'd never seen him anything but clean-shaven. In fact, she'd never seen him anything but completely put together. Even when she'd visited him in the hospital after he'd taken the zee for her, his hair and demeanor had been impeccable.

"You're staring." His voice jolted her out of her thoughts, but he was still focused on wrapping her hand.

"You're going to mess up your hair," was what she mustered up as an explanation, wincing at how lame it was. It also didn't help that she'd just made it blatantly obvious that she'd noticed.

He finished his task and lifted his gaze, keeping the tips of her fingers in his a moment longer. "Sometimes things get messy."

She pictured Ruckus's face and forced herself to pull away.

If the rejection bothered him, he didn't show it. Instead he moved over toward the large mat in the far left corner. He waited until she'd followed and was standing nearby before taking position in the center.

"Come at me," he ordered, and when she merely lifted a brow, he clenched his jaw. "Do it. Show me what the Ander has supposedly taught you. I doubt it's very much."

"Okay." She held out a finger but stepped onto the thick white foam. "I see what you're doing, and I'd just like to point out that reverse psychology will not work on me. However, I have wanted to punch you for a very long time now. So . . ."

She rushed him without giving any more warning, letting out a startled sound when he dodged out of the way faster than she could blink. Dropping to her knees, she used her left leg to swipe at his ankles, annoyed further when he easily jumped over her. By the time she stood up again, he was silently laughing at her.

"This isn't funny," she stated, hating herself for feeling the need to.

"You're right," he agreed with another chuckle, holding his fists in front of him. "The fact that you're missing isn't. The fact that you're so adorable doing it is. Come on, Delaney, you have to be better than that."

She punched forward, already anticipating that he'd dodge in the opposite direction. Her other fist shot out, only to be blocked by his forearm.

"Better," he said. "Keep trying."

She ground her teeth, determined to land at least one punch before they were through.

"WE'RE GOING TO make this a routine thing," he told her an hour later while he unwrapped his hands.

She was busy panting, bent over, sweat slicked over her body and making her clothes stick uncomfortably. The asshole wasn't even close to out of breath. She tore at the bandages and dropped them to the floor, glaring at him the whole time even though he wasn't looking.

"I hate you."

"You should consider learning a new tune, Lissa," he said. "That one's getting old. And remember: You're *pretty sure* you hate me now. Backtracking is against the rules."

He reached for her then, and when his fingers unstuck a strand of hair from the side of her face, he smiled. It wasn't his usual smile though; it was close-lipped and almost . . . sweet.

"What now?" she blurted.

"We shower." At her look he held up both hands and took a deliberate retreating step. "Separately. There's a locker room straight through that door over there."

The door he indicated was set in the center of the right wall, and a quick glance on the opposite wall showed there was an identical one leading to a different room.

"I'll be in there," he confirmed, pointing to the other door. "You have fifteen minutes."

"And then you're coming in after me." She waved at him and headed away. "Yeah, yeah. Speaking of new tunes."

"I'll work on that," he said.

She hadn't been expecting him to agree, but when she turned back, he was already twisting the knob and disappearing into the adjoining room. Deciding she was reading too far into it, that his sudden good mood could have been brought on by any number of things, she continued to the locker room.

Inside she found a row of shower stalls, a wall made of cubby holes and clothing racks, and a line of benches. There was only one set of clean clothes there, so it was obvious what she was supposed to change into.

The shampoo that'd been left in each of the stalls smelled floral, but she couldn't place the scent. The body wash was similar, only with a hint of something sharp and citrusy added in. The combination of the aroma and the hot water cascading across her now aching muscles made her want to stay there forever.

Too soon she was trudging out of the stall, towel-drying off, and donning the new clothes. There was a comb over by the row of sinks, and she quickly untangled her hair.

She must have rushed more than she'd thought, for when she returned to the training room, she found it empty.

The door leading out and into the halls was still open, but she only considered sneaking out for half a second before rejecting the idea. There was nowhere for her to go, really, and as much as she hated it, being with Trystan was the safest place for her right now.

She filled the extra time by inspecting the equipment hanging on the walls. Some of it she recognized from the training rooms in the Vakar palace; others were a complete mystery. Then a particular armband caught her attention.

It was slightly thicker than the fritzes everyone wore on their wrists, with a strange pattern carved into the face of it. When she lifted it from the wall, she found it lighter than she'd expected.

"That's a fru." Trystan came up behind her and she almost dropped it.

"I didn't hear you come in," she said, going to replace the cuff. He stopped her by touching her wrist lightly, and she let him take the band.

"It's a shield," he elaborated, as if she hadn't spoken, turning the metal around in his hands. "It's activated in a similar way as a fritz, by waving the top of your hand over the censor, here." He tapped one of the symbols, and she realized it was different from the rest.

"Why don't you wear one?" she asked, checking his bare arms just to be sure. Aside from the single band on his right wrist, he didn't have anything else on.

"I do sometimes." He shrugged. "Would you like to see it in action?"

It couldn't hurt, so she agreed and he moved a few feet away. He unlatched the cuff and clicked it easily around his lower bicep, right above the curve of his elbow. The metal seemed to morph so that it fit perfectly around his body, and a single blue light flashed once to indicate it was ready for use.

Trystan waved his hand over the censor, and with a sizzling sound a giant hologram projected from the band. It was ovular, almost like a surfboard, and stretched a few inches over his head and all the way down to the tips of his toes so that it barely scraped the floor. It was wide enough that as long as his body was angled, he could easily keep himself protected, and see-through so that he didn't have to risk peering around the edge to locate the enemy.

Unsurprisingly, it was neon blue around the edges, the color fading to silver closer to the center, making it easier to see the other side.

"It's massive." She tilted her head back to see the top of it.

"The censor picks up on the height of the bearer, so it can stretch the shield the same length as the person using it. The force field is always safe to touch on my side, but I can turn the shock feature on and off on yours."

"That way if you're in close quarters with friendlies, you don't have to worry about accidentally zapping them," she guessed.

"Precisely." He smiled, this time with none of the usual filler. It was just a genuine friendly smile.

Which she hated, because they couldn't be friends. She *wouldn't* let them be after seeing Ruckus's face.

"One moment," he said, suddenly distracted. His gaze shifted off to the side, and she waited for whatever telepathic communication he was having to end. He'd showered, so his blond hair was damp and slicked back, a shade darker than it usually was. The hot water had done something for his pale pallor, adding a bit of flush to his cheeks.

He looked a thousand times better than he had prior, and she was annoyed at herself for noticing. It was because she was looking, however, that she saw the second his expression darkened.

"What's wrong?" she asked as soon as he came out of it.

He cleared his throat, shut down the fru, and reached over her head to replace it on the wall. It hadn't ever seemed like he'd needed to buy time before speaking, but it was clear that was what he was doing now.

"Apparently my father has called," he told her, and while his voice was firm, there was an underlying hint of worry. "He's onscreen in the conference room, waiting for us."

"Us?" She did not like the sound of that.

"Yes." He glanced around the room while he adjusted the hem of his shirt and smoothed down the material of his pants at his thighs.

"Trystan?" She frowned, watching him continue to search their surroundings as if there was something there he might be forgetting.

After running his hand through his hair, his fingers trailed across his jaw to the five o'clock shadow and he noticeably blanched.

She would have been certain she'd misinterpreted, if not for the fact that doubt lingered in his eyes. Finally, when he went to glance over his shoulder toward the locker room he'd showered in, she'd had enough.

"Cut it out." She tugged lightly on his forearm to get him to turn back to her. "You being self-conscious is making me self-conscious."

"You don't understand—" He seemed to realize he was saying this out loud and abruptly cut himself off. A flash of that familiar distaste morphed his expression, though it was obviously aimed at himself this time.

"Sure I do," she corrected him with a single shoulder shrug, trying to lighten the mood. "I have an overbearing dad, too. Does yours judge you for your choice in clothing, hairstyle, and just about every other decision you make about your life? Yeah? Awesome. Mine, too. Peas in a pod."

"I don't—" He stopped a second time, shook his head, and got back on track. "Our situations are different. For one, my father is a Rex."

"Blah, blah, blah." She waved a hand in the air and headed toward the exit. "So your daddy's a king, big whoop. Mine's an anesthesiologist, and since we're on the subject, my mom comes from old money to boot. You aren't the only one in this room born with a silver spoon in your mouth, and in typical spoiled-rich-kid fashion, I can complain about how unfair my parents are just as much as you can."

"You are aware," Trystan said a moment later, "you don't know where you're taking us, correct?"

During her spiel, she'd led them out of the training room and down the hall, mostly to distract them both from the upcoming meeting with his dad. Despite what she'd just said, she was terrified of meeting the Rex. Her dad was judgmental, sure, but he was still her dad. The Rex was going to be intimidating as all hell, and she really wasn't looking forward to that.

She didn't even really know anything about him, other than he somehow magically made Trystan doubt himself—which had to be a superpower.

But did he use his powers for good or evil?

It'd been the Rex who'd put an end to the war by suggesting peace through marriage. She didn't think he could be all that bad if saving lives was his main objective.

"Feel free to correct our course anytime." She waved Trystan ahead of her.

Trystan took her up on her offer, leading them down another set of corridors narrower than the previous ones.

Unlike back at the Vakar palace, there was no mixture of uniforms here. Every Teller they passed wore traditional Kint blues and silvers.

How did he expect to convince the world she was there of her own volition if he didn't even have a single one of her guards on the grounds?

"Delaney." Trystan held out an arm, blocking her from a door just as the Teller standing there began opening it. His hesitation clued her in to just how uncomfortable he actually was with all this.

Somehow, knowing that she wasn't the only one feeling anxious made it a little more manageable.

"Try not to speak if you don't have to," he said. Before she could get offended, he added, "I don't mean that as an insult. My father is . . . difficult to navigate. It's best for both of us if you hang back unless he calls on you." He paused, rethought his words. "But don't be too quiet, either. Silences bother him. He thinks it means the person he's with is too dim-witted to come up with something to say."

"You're rambling." It was impossible to miss the surprise in her tone. "We'll be fine. I know the stakes."

He breathed out a slow sigh of relief. "You always do. You're clever. We'll be fine."

"Exactly."

"Right."

"As great as seeing you finally be normal is"—she motioned toward the opened door—"we probably shouldn't keep him waiting much longer."

"Right," he repeated, then seemed to catch his mistake, and cleared his throat. He caught the Teller who was guarding the door looking at him, and straightened. "Have something to say, do you?"

"No, Zane. Apologies, Zane." The Teller dropped his gaze to the ground and kept it there.

"Wise choice." Trystan adjusted his shirt and then stepped into the room, leaving Delaney to follow.

Though she mouthed *sorry* to the Teller as she passed, she couldn't help the slight upward curve to her lips. Bossy and rude was more Trystan's speed than insecure and at a loss for words.

Of course, her smile quickly vanished when she entered the conference room and was met with the massive face of someone who could only be the Rex.

Trystan was already positioned in the center of the room, his hands clasped behind his back in a similar stance to the one his subjects used with him. He didn't so much as offer her a glance when she came over, keeping his eyes straight ahead and on his father, despite the fact that the Rex was paying him little mind.

All his attention was on Delaney.

It was easy enough to see the resemblance between the two of them, and not just because they both had blond hair. It wasn't the similar set of their jaws, either, or the narrow bridge of their noses.

It was how he was looking at her, with a mixture of self-serving interest and calculation. In that look, Delaney could picture exactly what Trystan's childhood might have been like. How he'd struggled to please his father, only to constantly fail. How he'd started imitating the man he saw, copying his mannerisms and his expressions. Honing them and imbedding them into his psyche until they became his own.

The Rex's hair was a little longer than his son's, and it curled at the ends. There was a single piercing at his right eyebrow, which somehow made him appear more dignified instead of less. A silver bar connected two navy blue gems, one at the top of his eyebrow, the other positioned directly beneath it. His eyes were brown with a ring of yellow.

"You were correct," he spoke, and his voice was strong and deep. "She is quite lovely. I haven't seen hair like yours, Lissa Delaney, since my last visit to Earth many years ago. I believe it was called the sixties then, by you Earthlings."

"A lot has changed since," she said, grateful that her voice hadn't shaken.

"Oh," he said, chuckling darkly, another similarity to his son, "I am very aware. I like to keep tabs on the goings-on of Earth, you see. Keeps me sharp."

Just in case was what he didn't add, but the implication was clear.

"What can we do for you today, Father?" Trystan drew the attention his way, and Delaney was grateful.

She'd thought the Zane was skilled at being underhanded, but she was positive the Rex had just delivered a warning, and she wasn't 100 percent certain she'd completely grasped it.

"Many things"—the Rex turned to his son—"but I'll settle for a few. I've received reports that the meeting between my council and Tilda's went well. Can you confirm?"

"Yes." Trystan nodded confidently. "It did."

"So she's a good a politician." The creases at the corners of his dark eyes crinkled when he grinned. "A woman after my own heart. I wonder, however, if you'll be able to keep it up, Lissa. There is a lot riding on this and your ability to calm both peoples into submission. If you can't do so, steps will have to be taken."

"I can do it." If it'd been Magnus she was speaking to, she would have retorted with something snappy and clever. Survival instincts kept her from doing the same with the Rex.

"Wonderful to hear." He leaned back in his chair, giving her a better view of the oddly shaped and jeweled medals plastered across the military uniform he was wearing. "I must admit, I was concerned when I heard you had removed the Lissa from the Vakar palace, Trystan. After our talk, I was under the impression you intended to remain there for some time."

"Circumstances made doing so difficult," Trystan said without skipping a beat. If the blatant accusation bothered him, he didn't show it.

"Yes, that's right. The arrival of Ander Ruckus Wux." He rested his heavy stare on Delaney a second time. "And how are you taking his confinement, Lissa? I've been assured that you're handling yourself, and any lingering emotions you might have, with the highest level of decorum. I'd heard the two of you were close. Strange, considering my son claims you have feelings for him."

"I've been assured the Ander won't be harmed. That's good enough for me," she replied.

"Is it?" He lifted his thick blond brows, but it was hard to tell if it was legitimate shock or a mere mockery of it. "You're stronger than you're given credit for, if that's truly the case. Personally, if I was aware a loved one of mine was being held against their will, I would do everything in my power to free them. Nothing, and no one, would stand in my way. Not laws, not morality." He chuckled again, though it was easier to catch that he was faking. "And certainly not my son."

Wow.

She clenched her teeth when she saw Trystan dig his fingernails into his palms. His dad's words were affecting him, even though from the front she had yet to even see him blink.

"Okay," she sent through their fitting without giving herself time to second-guess. *"You win. My dad's got nothing on yours."*

She opted to ignore the part where he'd blatantly revealed he knew about her and Ruckus.

"Delaney has her own motivations, Father," Trystan said.

"I'm sure she does." The Rex propped his elbows onto the edge of the desk he was seated at. "Now that you've removed her from Vakar, when do you plan on bringing her home, son? Inkwell and Carnage are on the same landmass. I'd very much like to meet the lovely Lissa Delaney face-to-face."

This giant screen was as close to his face as she wanted to get. Had she really been hoping he'd be better than Magnus? Yeah. Right.

"Technically, as we are still in Vakar territory, I haven't pushed things too far. I fear taking her all the way to Carnage would be a step too much for the Vakar public. They'd no doubt take it as a personal affront."

"Ah." He nodded. "Yes, yes. I believe I heard something of the like. It must have been in the notes I got on the meeting. My mistake. Soon, though? You'll bring her soon."

"The second doing so no longer bears the risk of insulting the Vakar people, of course, Father," Trystan agreed.

"Good." He glanced between the two of them for a moment and then lifted a pen and began scrawling across some papers on his desk. "I'm sending something to you, son, something important. A member of the Tars. You'll question him and inform me of any pertinent knowledge you uncover."

Had his dad just asked him to torture someone?

"Certainly, Father." Trystan bowed his head slightly.

He actually bowed his head.

Delaney realized her mouth was hanging open, and she quickly snapped it shut, glancing out of the corner of her eye over to the Rex. She almost let out a sigh of relief when she realized he was still too preoccupied with whatever he was writing to have noticed her slipup.

"I'll send a member of the high council to assist you," the Rex continued.

"That won't be necessary."

"With the Lissa here, I assume you might need to step away. What if she needs you during the interrogation? It can't simply stop because you choose to divert your attentions elsewhere."

Finally he deliberately set his pen aside and locked eyes with Trystan. "You can't honestly tell me that after weeks of moaning and moping about the entire planet, you wouldn't drop everything to spend a little extra time with your betrothed?"

Delaney wasn't sure what made her the more uncomfortable: the fact that he'd just said Trystan had all but been pining for her while she was away, or that she was pretty positive this whole thing had been a setup from the start. If the Rex showed them that paper before him, she wouldn't be surprised to find doodles and scribbles on it. There was no way it was actually anything of importance.

"While making sure Delaney is comfortable is important," Trystan said, and now a slight strain in his voice could be heard, "I can assure you she will never come between me and my duties. My allegiance is to the crown, and my position, first and foremost. The Lissa is highly aware of this fact."

"She must be," he said, nodding, "because she hardly looks surprised by your admission. I find that interesting."

"May I suggest which member of the council you send?" Without making it too obvious, Trystan moved his body closer to hers, so that the sides of their arms just barely brushed. It shouldn't have been comforting, having him close, yet it was.

"No, you may not," the Rex said absently. "You'll request Jackan, and while I may be old, I am not stupid. I know where Jackan's true loyalties lie. You'll get Rantan. Expect them by tomorrow evening, at the latest."

"Yes, Father." It was getting harder and harder for him to contain himself, and if she noticed, the Rex must see it, as well.

"Excellent." He pursed his lips and then partially lifted his gaze from the paper on his desk to look over at Trystan. "Don't you have something to attend to? The selecting of your new Sworn, perhaps?"

"I do." He forced a smile that wouldn't fool anyone within a ten-mile radius. "We should get going or we'll be late."

The Rex waved his hand, dismissing not only Trystan's words but his son and Delaney as well. "Until again."

"Until again, Father." Even though the Rex was no longer looking, Trystan bowed again, signaling with a look for Delaney to follow suit.

She did, but there was no way the Rex even noticed. By the time she'd lifted her head again, the screen in front of them was blank and she was left staring at a white wall.

CHAPTER 16

For a while Trystan pretended like she wasn't there, leading them to their next destination silently and swiftly. By the time five minutes had passed, Delaney was practically sprinting just to keep up with him.

"He gets notes on our meetings?" she asked, out of breath. She got that he was trying to put distance between himself and what had just happened, but icing her out wasn't beneficial for either of them.

"Apparently so," he replied.

"You didn't know."

"I assumed he'd have a talk with the Kint high council members who'd been in attendance," he told her.

"But he also knew you'd set up the selection process for a new Sworn," she caught on. "He's got a spy."

"It would seem so." He glanced at her quickly and then away just as fast. "Yes. I was going to tell you where we were going this afternoon in the training room. I had no idea my father would demand a conference today."

He was apologizing because of their deal, and she felt appreciative that he intended to honor his half of the bargain. Maybe if he was willing to keep his word on this, the other things he'd promised her would also be upheld.

"Does he have a reason to spy on you?" She tried to pose the question as casually as possible, but a note of curiosity slipped past.

"You're smarter than that, Delaney," he countered.

They turned into a new wing of the castle, its walls a pale sky blue. Across them depictions of towering mountains were painted in white, the image protruding slightly so that there was an embossing effect. Every ten feet or so they passed by a large window, and outside, the same snowy tundra could be seen for real.

"Tell me more about this selection process." Changing the subject seemed like the best course of action. He needed to be distracted, and frankly, so did she. All it'd taken was one conversation with the Rex to see why his son had turned out the way he had.

Her father's attempt at controlling her had molded her into a rebellious teen whose only goal had been to get far away. Unlike Trystan, she did love her parents, both of them, but as soon as she'd been able to leave and attend boarding school, she'd felt such relief.

Trystan had gone a different route. He'd chosen to mirror his dad's aloofness. To hone the skills he was being taught and use them against the people around him, including the Rex. In a way, his ultimate goal was the same as Delaney's had been. Distance from Daddy dearest.

He was just willing to go to extreme lengths to get it, and he didn't care who got hurt along the way.

"Tellers are allowed to apply for the position . . . ," he began, completely unaware of the turn her thoughts had taken. "I've had a stack of applications on my desk since Brightan's death. I've managed to narrow them down to the top twenty men and women I believe would be a good fit for the two of us. We'll review their files together and choose."

"Is this usually how it works?" It was a miracle the Rex didn't simply select for him, being that he was so clearly the controlling type.

"You're wondering why my father hasn't forced me to select a replacement already," he volunteered, seeing right through her. "As soon as I came of age, the decision was up to me. My father doesn't have a

Sworn himself. He believes true leaders need to be capable of taking care of themselves. With how well I've been trained, he thinks my having a commander head my guard is a sign of weakness."

"Zane Trystan." Sanzie was suddenly standing in front of them. "Lissa Delaney. The files have been set out for you."

"Thank you, Teller," Trystan said.

Sanzie bowed and twisted on her heel, disappearing back around the corner.

"I had them reprinted in English," he told Delaney as they entered yet another room. "Aside from a few symbols I'll have to explain, it shouldn't be a problem for you to read them."

"Awesome." Even though she'd meant it sarcastically, part of her was actually a little excited.

THE EXCITEMENT DIED down half an hour later. She rubbed at her temple, trying to quell the migraine that was beginning, and leaned her elbow on the surface of the long table they were seated at.

Spread out in front of her were a handful of open files, glossy photos of men and women staring back at her. None of them were smiling.

Most of it had been translated, like he'd said, but there were a series of symbols indicating things like rank, history, and skill sets that she was having a hard time picking up on.

"What's this again?" She pressed her finger against a black mark shaped like a hashtag balancing on its corner legs. It looked a lot like one she'd seen a few pages back on another file, though she thought for sure that one had a dot in it somewhere, and therefore couldn't be the same.

Trystan was busy perusing another file, and he absently glanced over before flipping a page. "It means she's trained in all eight fritz settings."

Delaney hadn't been aware there were eight. "That could be useful," she said. "What about this one?" She pointed to another shaped like a circle with a *W* drawn partially inside. The end of it hung outside the right of the circle.

"She fought over five years in the war," he answered. "If the symbol is upside down, it means they've served over ten. On its left side, over fifteen, and on its right, over twenty. Anything less than five doesn't get a marker at all."

"That seems harsh." They'd served either way, right?

"Not for what we're looking for it isn't," he disagreed. "I want someone with experience to take the position. Someone guaranteed to keep you safe."

"Us," she corrected. "Keep *us* safe."

"I fought alongside this one." Trystan pushed the file she'd been looking at aside and replaced it with the one he'd been holding. "He's good. Reliable and loyal. What's more, he's trained in three different forms of martial arts and has extensive weapons training."

"How intense do you expect this whole protecting thing to get?" she asked. "Ruckus never had to deal with extensive anything, and I was basically attacked on the daily. Why do you think your new Sworn has to be so highly trained?"

He grunted and, at her stare, leaned back on his armrest to better face her. "While your Ander is too young to have served the Vakar army as many years as this man, I assure you, Ruckus Wux is more qualified for this position than most of these"—he made a sweeping gesture at the files spread before them—"people are. It's unfortunate he wasn't born Kint."

Delaney waited a moment, sure there was going to be more, surprised when there wasn't.

"What?" He lifted a blond brow.

"You just complimented Ruckus," she said. "Without adding any insults."

"Don't get used to it." He readjusted himself in his seat, pointedly returning his attention to the stack of files. "I'm allowed to admire his military prowess."

She choked on a laugh and cleared her throat while he glared. "Sorry. In my culture that would have been taken way differently. Like, you-just-hit-on-Ruckus differently."

"And you find my punching him funny suddenly?" He was genuinely confused, which would have been adorable if not for the fact that he was Trystan, and therefore scary and intimidating all the time. Even with his lips pursed like that and his brow furrowed.

"No, that's not—" She took a breath to bank down another chuckle. "It's slang. It means to flirt. For instance, you might go up to him and say, 'I enjoy your military prowess. Come home with me.'"

The particular shade of red he turned was priceless. This time she was unable to hold the laughter back. She could feel tears at the corners of her eyes, and she folded her arms on the table and buried her head between them to try to keep him from seeing just how hilarious she found this.

Of course, it didn't work—probably because her entire body was shaking with it, and even her muffled sounds were obvious—and by the time she'd gotten ahold of herself and glanced back over, his embarrassment had mixed with defensiveness. She could easily pick out that familiar darkness lingering behind his eyes, and she sobered as best as she was able before resting a hand on his arm.

"It's a joke, Trystan," she assured him. "Try not to take everything so seriously."

He dropped his gaze to where she was touching him, the corners of his mouth tipping downward.

She quickly pulled away and began to shuffle through some of the files. "I can see why Earth wasn't to your liking. You probably couldn't understand a word anyone was saying."

"I have a hebi," he said, obviously affronted by her suggestion.

Apparently, it wasn't the best with slang, if Trystan's complete lack of knowledge was any indicator.

This was hardly the first time he'd been confused by something she'd said. She tried to think back on her conversations with Ruckus before they'd returned to Earth, but she couldn't recall if he'd ever had the same problem, at least to the extent the Zane did.

"Do hebis have different settings?" she wondered aloud, realizing that would explain it. "Is that why you can't figure out what I'm really saying?"

"Can you understand me when I use slang?" he rebuffed.

"You've used slang around me?" Weird. She hadn't noticed. "Pretty sure that would fall under the category of humor, which is a thing you don't do."

"I can be humorous," he stated, seeming to have forgotten he'd told her not to expect him to be when she'd first arrived.

"No." She shook her head. "You can be mean. You do that scary thing that you find funny but the rest of us find intimidating as all hell. Honestly," she said, knowing she was taking a real risk in admitting this, "if I hadn't caught you blushing just now, I would have sworn your only settings were angry and arrogant."

He was quiet for a moment, staring at her with an impossible expression on his face that she couldn't decipher. Then: "You think those are the only emotions I'm capable of?"

"Sometimes you mix them both together and do them at the same time," she said. "That's impressive."

He made an odd humming sound in the back of his throat and then pressed both palms against the table, pushing himself to standing. She watched as he adjusted the hem of his shirt, but he was no longer looking back at her.

"Excuse me." There'd been a note of something in his tone, and it took her a second to place it. But by that time, he was already halfway across the room, on his way to the door.

"Trystan." She stood fast enough that her chair legs scraped against the ground, and made her way over to him. When he acted like he hadn't heard her, she picked up the pace and reached out to latch on to his wrist. "Hey."

He stopped and twisted his body slightly so that he was angled partially her way, though he still didn't meet her gaze. It became painfully obvious he had no intention of speaking, which bothered her more than it should.

"Hey," she repeated, taking a tentative step closer. "Did I just . . ." She could barely get the words out, it seemed so ludicrous. "Did I just hurt your feelings?"

"Wasn't that your intention?" he said, his tone clipped.

"I didn't . . ." She bit her bottom lip, unable to finish her sentence a second time. She'd been about to say no, but he was right. Of course she had; it was just, she hadn't really thought it would work. For the first time she actually wondered how many times she'd hurt his feelings without even realizing.

Part of her was sickly glad, because after everything he'd put her and her friends through, didn't he deserve a little punishment in return? Another part of her, however, felt a little crappy.

"You deserve every mean thing I've said to you and more," she voiced, even knowing that doing so was more to convince herself than him. "You have done horrible things."

His gaze remained glued to a spot on the floor some feet away. He didn't react to her words at all, which only made her feel worse. She'd never seen him forlorn before, and this, now, was proving to be too much. It couldn't be guilt she was feeling, and yet, there was no other explanation for the tightness in her chest.

She cursed, loudly, dropping his arm so that she could cross hers over her chest. "Bearing in mind everything I just said is true"—she took a deep breath—"I'm sorry I indicated you were a robot. Okay? We good?"

"I do have feelings," he said quietly, only his lips moving.

"I know that." Had she? Of course. She'd just come from a meeting with his father. "But reacting to other people, having feelings for them, isn't the same as having feelings for me."

When he frowned, it was obvious she wasn't doing a good job of explaining herself. Rubbing at the growing migraine, she tried again.

"I know you need me, Trystan . . . ," she began tentatively. "Or at least that you think you do, in order to get what you want. To be king of it all. You need me to get you the Vakar crown, and once you have it, you won't need me anymore. Knowing this, can you blame me for assuming my words wouldn't affect you?

"I know we're always taking verbal jabs at each other," she continued, "but aside from getting angry, you usually don't react to any insults I throw. I agreed to do this in exchange for my friends' safety, so in the name of keeping the peace, I'm apologizing for hitting a nerve back there."

He was back to staring at her, and after a moment she heaved a frustrated sigh.

"Feel free to stop me anytime," she stated. "Otherwise, I'll keep rambling forever, and neither of us is going to enjoy that much."

Trystan took a step closer, an almost dazed look in his eyes that had her instinctively retreating a step. When he came to an abrupt stop at her movement, she saw his jaw clench and his vision clear.

Before she could be relieved that the familiar version of him was back—even if that did mean he was, yet again, pissed at her—he spun on his heel and left. The door didn't slam at his back, but that somehow made it worse.

Left standing there, completely unsure where to go or even really what had just happened, Delaney tightened her arms around herself. She stood there, watching the door, waiting for him to come back, but after a while she gave up. She turned toward the table and began sorting through the files again.

It was unclear how much time had passed, but when Sanzie arrived later, Delaney had three piles organized and sorted before her. She finished placing the last file and then slowly got up from the table and walked toward the Teller.

"Let him know the first stack are rejects, the middle are possibilities, and the last are my favorites," she told Sanzie, passing by her and into the hall, waiting for her to show her to her room.

CHAPTER 17

s there a problem, Lissa?"

Delaney, who'd been watching the door over her shoulder, turned back around in her seat and met the curious eyes of the coordinator.

"No, sorry." She sat on her hands to keep from fidgeting, and cleared her throat. This morning Sanzie had come to escort her to the next coordinator meeting. Delaney had assumed Trystan would already be here, but they'd been seated now for at least five minutes and there was still no sign of him.

"He isn't coming." The other woman wore a knowing smile. "We'll be doing this exercise on our own. After this one, in a few days, is when we would traditionally do the Tuning ceremony, where the couple have their fittings adjusted."

"Do you mean one of the steps is getting our fitting frequencies linked?" Because if that was the case, whoops. Had Trystan broken a rule?

She smiled sweetly. "I'm aware the Zane rushed this step—don't worry. That's why we're keeping you separate for the Choosing, which is the name of this exercise. It's to keep the two of you from cheating."

"I'm sorry, Co Gailie. I don't know what you mean."

"It's just Gailie," she corrected. "Co is my title, much like Lissa is yours. When it's just the two of us, feel free to address me informally.

Now, let me explain." She reached beneath the table and brought up a silver tray. "The purpose of the Choosing is to see how compatible you two are."

"I see." Delaney totally didn't.

At least a dozen brightly packaged gifts were on the tray, all different sizes and colors. They were wrapped in an assortment of metallic, patterned, and solid-colored paper. Even their shapes varied, some square or rectangular, others shaped like circles.

Gailie set the tray on the table between them and linked her fingers in front of her.

"Between you and me," she said, leaning slightly forward as if sharing a secret with a friend, "it's sort of bullshit."

"Excuse me?" Delaney's eyes widened.

"Apologies." She frowned and pulled back slightly. "Was that not the proper wording? I mean to say, it's superstition. Tradition that's been passed down for so long, people aren't willing to let it go despite knowing it has no real merit."

"Bullshit." Delaney nodded. "You had it right."

"Perfect." She lifted one of the smaller boxes, one that couldn't be bigger than a golf ball. "You are each presented with seventeen gifts, the contents of which are a mystery to you. You'll select three that you think Trystan will find the most enjoyable. Without opening them."

"That sounds complicated." How was she supposed to know what he'd like? She wasn't so sure she'd be able to do it even if she could see what was inside.

"It's not meant to be," Gailie told her, and Delaney feared she'd slipped up. "But some couples do find it more taxing than others. Those are usually the ones who put more stock in superstition. The gifts you pick are supposed to signify an aspect of your upcoming bond. Depending on what you select for each other, the items can be interpreted to mean you'll have a long and happy life, or that you'll have financial problems. Or jealousy issues. You understand?"

"I'm beginning to." She rubbed her hands together and looked over the pile of gifts. Not once did her gaze pause on anything and immediately tell her that was the one. Briefly she wondered if this would be fun if she were doing it for Ruckus, but she forced the thought away before it could get her down.

Reality was, this was for Trystan. She needed to start thinking like someone who was in love with him. At least until the end of this meeting.

"All right. So I just . . . choose at random?" She winced, already realizing her mistake and quickly corrected herself. "I didn't mean random, random. Stuff Trystan would like. I just pick?"

"That's correct." Gailie reached over and rested a hand on her forearm. "Relax, Lissa. This is meant to be fun."

"It's fake anyway," she said. "Right?"

"In the same way that you mortals read the stars for your horoscopes." At Delaney's look, she laughed. "Oh no. Don't tell me you believe in that?"

"I'm a Libra," Delaney told her. "My ruling planet is Venus."

Gailie opened her mouth, clearly about to apologize, but Delaney stopped her.

"I'm kidding."

Mariana was really into that stuff, though, and Delaney had to admit sometimes it was pretty accurate. She certainly wouldn't judge anyone for their beliefs, especially not after this experience. She understood better than anyone the need to find hope in even the most impossible-seeming outlets.

Delaney strummed her fingers against the table and returned her gaze to the wrapped gifts. She selected one at random, inspecting the purple box from all sides before placing it back. If this really wasn't taken seriously, maybe she could have fun with it. All she had to do was pick out three of them, after all. It wasn't a hard task.

She moved a circular box the size of her palm and paused when the one beneath it was revealed. It had shiny reddish-orange paper, the color sort of reminding her of her hair, and was rectangular.

Trystan did always seem fascinated by her hair. . . . All Xenithians did, actually. There was no way this could be a bad choice.

"Two more to go," Gailie said kindly when Delaney placed the first box off to the side. "Between you and me, good choice."

She was a little suspicious of the coordinator's friendliness, but at the first meeting the woman had tried so hard to suck up to Trystan. More than likely, that was all she was doing now, seeing as how getting on Delaney's good side in her mind meant staying on the Zane's.

Choosing to take that theory as a sign she was doing something right, Delaney selected another present. This one was in the shape of a diamond, and a rich warm brown that reminded her of Trystan's favorite drink. As she was thinking about how obsessed with squa he was, the corner of her mouth tipped up in a half smile. The box was heavier than any of the others she'd picked up, and she set it next to her first choice.

One left. This really wasn't difficult at all. She could choose things for Trystan without having to like him.

"He has to do this, too?" she asked, mostly to get Gailie to stop watching her so closely.

"Yes," she confirmed. "He'll be stopping by as soon as we're done. Truly, though, don't rush."

Normally she'd revel at the idea of keeping the Zane waiting, hoping that doing so would aggravate him. Thinking back on last night, however, she wanted to do the opposite.

She'd spent the whole night tossing and turning, worrying that he was going to take his anger at her out on her friends. Then she'd convinced herself it hadn't been anger in his eyes when he'd left, reminded that she'd hurt his feelings, only for the doubts to trickle back in.

"Are you all right?" Gailie was frowning at her from across the table. "You've gone pale."

"I'm fine." She forced herself to smile. "Just don't want to choose the wrong one, that's all."

"Go with your gut," was her suggestion, and it wasn't a bad one.

Wherever he'd gone yesterday, it hadn't been to torture her friends. That was what her gut was telling her. Trystan wouldn't do that, partially because he wouldn't want to risk upsetting her—she could then refuse to continue playing along—but also because he'd given her his word. They wouldn't be harmed so long as she did what she was told, and she was doing that.

She'd never have guessed she'd be willing to bet anything on trusting Trystan, let alone Ruckus's safety, and yet making that choice now was even less difficult than choosing these three gifts were.

A fact that was unsettling. After everything he'd done, how could she trust him to keep his promises? Sure, he'd always been honest with her, but that was a far cry from being fair.

One of the presents was covered in vibrant yellow paper, sunny and bright. She immediately pictured Ruckus's eyes when she saw it, the iris yellow with a rim of dark green. Even though she knew she shouldn't, guilt over her passive thoughts toward Trystan had her choosing this one as her final gift.

Carefully, she placed it with the other two and then looked to Co Gailie.

"Are you certain?" the coordinator asked, and Delaney took a moment to think it over before nodding. "Very well. Thank you for your cooperation and your time, Lissa. Your selections will be held for you, in secret and under strict guard, until the Unveiling ceremony."

Great. Another ceremony. She almost rolled her eyes.

Gailie took the three chosen and placed them in a bag at her feet, then began collecting the others onto the tray.

The sound of the door opening at her back had her swiveling in that direction. Trystan walked in, and when he looked at her, it was the same way he had on the ship when she'd woken up. Like she was a curiosity he was preparing to manipulate.

At his approach, she stood, waiting to see what he intended to do before making any other moves.

"Zane," Gailie greeted him warmly. "We've just finished."

"Brilliant." The way he said it made it obvious he didn't really care. He stopped at Delaney's left and then turned, sweeping his arm out toward the door he'd just entered. "Teller Sanzie is waiting for you outside. She'll escort you to lunch."

Delaney would have replied, but he abruptly turned again, dismissing her. She risked a glance at the coordinator, who didn't seem like she'd seen the exchange, because she was busy removing the tray of gifts.

Sanzie bowed as soon as Delaney exited the room, and the Teller left standing guard shut the door lightly at her back.

"If you'll follow me, Lissa." Sanzie canted her head down the right side of the hall, then paused when Delaney made no move after her.

"I'd rather wait here for the Zane," she said, biting the inside of her cheek at the Teller's shocked look. "It shouldn't take him long, and there are a few things we need to discuss."

"The Zane has a full day," Sanzie told her apologetically. "Unfortunately, I don't believe he'll have the time right now. Perhaps I can let him know you wish to speak with him, and he can clear his schedule for early evening."

"I'm his betrothed," she argued. "He'll make time for me. Now."

Sanzie hesitated, but only for a split second before bowing again. "Of course, Lissa."

It was her first time admitting out loud that she was his betrothed, and as soon as the Teller looked away, she shivered. She hadn't really thought about it, so focused on finding a solution to get Ruckus and the others out of this, but the plan still required her to do one thing.

The thing she swore from the start while pretending to be Olena, she would never do.

Marry Trystan.

IF SHE THOUGHT Sanzie had been surprised by her decision to stay, the look on the Zane's face was absolutely priceless.

He stepped out of the room quickly, lost in thought, and came to a sudden halt the moment his eyes caught hers. She was standing across from him, back propped against the wall while she waited, and he ran his gaze over her once to check for injuries.

The fact that she knew that was what he was doing, that his concern went instantly to making sure she wasn't still here because she was hurt, annoyed her. Being annoyed made this easier, so she welcomed it, lifting her chin defiantly at him for good measure.

"Delaney," he said, but set his questioning look on Sanzie. "What are you doing here? Weren't you hungry?"

"Starved, actually." And she was. She'd almost given up five minutes ago, her stomach was growling so loudly, but stubbornness had won out. "I thought it'd be better if we ate together."

His eyes clouded and cleared so fast, she wasn't sure she'd actually seen it happen. Then he was straightening his spine and stepping to the left. "I, unfortunately, don't have the time right now."

"That's what Sanzie said." It was Delaney's turn to glance at the Teller. "Almost exactly."

He tilted his head at her. "And what did you say?"

"That you'd make time." She stared him down, silently daring him to walk away.

It seemed like he still might, but when he turned his body, it was toward her. His physical appearance was better than it had been as of late, healthier. There were no longer any splotches beneath his eyes, and his complexion was back to a light golden hue. While she was wide-awake, freaking out, it seemed he'd managed to get his beauty rest.

"If this boldness is about yesterday, Delaney," he began, "there's no need. I've moved past our misunderstanding."

He couldn't be serious, could he? Not after storming off like he had, and how did he explain this morning? He'd sent Sanzie in his place! That was not the type of thing one did if they were no longer upset with someone.

Seeing that she wasn't so easily convinced, he gave a pointed sigh and addressed both Sanzie and the Teller guarding the door. "Dismissed."

They didn't have to be told twice.

"What's the matter now?" he said as soon as it was just the two of them in the hallway.

"You're asking me?"

"There's no one else here to ask." He pointedly glanced down both ends of the hallway.

She knew how stupid she looked, standing there, silently staring at him. But it took her a moment to come up with something to say. "You're not exactly known for being understanding."

"I said I moved past it," he told her, "not that I understood."

"Then where do we go from here?" Asking was even stupider than starting this conversation had been. She should have let it go, the same way he was claiming he'd done. Why did she care what he was currently feeling anyway? She didn't.

She couldn't.

Trystan thought it over, tilting his head so that he was forced to run his hand through the blond strands of his hair a second later to put them back in place. He slid the clear device that reminded her of a phone from his back pocket and tapped away on it, the images and words on the screen moving too quickly for her to catch anything, not that she could understand any of it even if she were able.

"I've rearranged some of my schedule," he told her a moment later, clicking one last button before returning the device to his pocket. "We'll have lunch together. Unless of course you'd prefer to rehash yesterday's events?"

Obviously not. She shook her head.

"Very well." He angled his chin to the left and began walking. "We'll need to gather a few things first. A proper covering, for one. You'll freeze if you go out like that."

"We're going outside?" They passed a window as she asked, and she got a great view of the frozen mountains and hills. "What do you have to do out there?"

"I have responsibilities," he said. "My world didn't stop turning simply because you arrived."

"Ouch."

"Hurts"—he glanced at her—"doesn't it?"

"What's that thing called?" She pointed to his pants, wanting to change the subject. "The device you're always using?"

"The Ander didn't tell you?" He grunted. "A shing. It's similar to the tablets you're used to on Earth. I can use it for communications, reprogramming, et cetera. It's the easiest way for me to keep connected with the rest of Kint while we undergo this inconvenient process with the coordinator."

"What if it gets stolen? Isn't all your information being in one place kind of risky?"

"They're genetically programmed, so no one can access it but me. In the off chance someone attempts to hack it, it's set to self-destruct. It's a harsh preventative measure, and few implement it, but it's handy."

"I suppose it would put a lot of people off trying." Why bother committing treason when the end results were so bleak?

Trystan brought them to a foreign room, leaving her in the sitting area for a moment while he disappeared through a side door. The coloring here was different, a smattering of blues in darker shades and grays instead of the typical whites. A bookshelf took up the center of the left wall, but unlike the shelves in Ruckus's room, which were stuffed with novels, these held a mixture of books and other items.

She was inspecting one of them, a silver statue of a creature that could only be described as a mixture of a horse and a swan, when she heard him return.

"Here." He draped a thick coat over her, his hands lingering on her shoulders a beat before pulling back.

The jacket was deep red, with a high collar and bronze buttons. There were small *E*s embossed on the surface of all seven of them, and she twisted one in her fingers as she turned.

"It's custom-made," he explained, slipping on a pair of white gloves. He tugged a matching pair from his right pocket and held them out for her.

"What's it doing in here?" she asked absently, taking the gloves from him, careful not to allow their fingers to touch. The material was soft and smooth, and when she slipped the gloves on, they were extremely warm.

"It only arrived this morning," he said. "I didn't have the chance to drop it off yet."

She took another glance around the sitting room, noticing how polished everything seemed. There was personality, like the odd statue of the unknown creature, but it was subtle, everything else giving off a feel of detachment. A coldness.

"These are your rooms." She felt stupid for not realizing it sooner.

"They are." He watched her for a moment, but when she refused to look back, feigning interest in the items on the shelves once more, he sighed. Another jacket in blue was folded across one of the arms of the couch and he donned it in one sweep.

She was standing too close to him and got a whiff of that cucumber-basil smell. She'd found it strange before, expecting him to smell more like gunpowder or something else overtly masculine, but now it was fitting. Everything about him was always unexpected.

"Delaney." Her name was a whisper, and though she'd heard it, it took her a second to process. He seemed closer than before when she finally looked up, his body hovering only a few inches away.

He had a gorgeous face, there was no question about that. There never had been. It was the rest of him that always made her blood boil.

"Delaney," he repeated, easing even closer.

"It's too bad you're such an asshole," she murmured.

Instead of getting offended, he canted his head, his gaze lingering on her mouth. "Would it make a difference? If I weren't?"

It took her longer than it should have to catch on, but once she had, she straightened her spine and hardened her expression. She didn't want to run him off again, but she also wasn't going to change the way she reacted to him simply because he'd finally shown a different emotion.

"No." She thought of Ruckus, and felt her heart clench.

"Because of him." It wasn't a question. His mouth thinned in a displeased line. "You're in love with him."

"Yes. Have you ever been in love, Trystan?" Delaney tried to picture it, the cold and aloof Zane letting loose with someone, smiling and laughing. The way she did with Ruckus.

His response was quick, no hesitation. "No." If her question bothered him, he didn't show it. His expression never changed, didn't soften or harden. He searched her gaze with his own and then asked, "What does it feel like?"

She lifted a brow. "Do you really want to know?"

"I should, shouldn't I?" He licked his lips. "How else will I know what it is when I feel it?"

"You just will." Still, she thought about it, about how Ruckus made her feel and how she could put it into words. "It feels like life finally makes sense. So much so, that you're baffled by the fact that you've gone so long without knowing this person. Wondering how you managed. And you'd do anything for them, willingly. Happily. You want what's best for them, whatever it might be, and you know that they want the same for you. They make you better. Stronger."

She'd liked her life before all this had happened. She'd been happy, excited for college and glad for Mariana. If anyone had asked, she would have told them she was perfectly content. Then Ruckus had decided to come back with her, and everything had changed. Suddenly she wasn't just living her life; she was building one, with him. He didn't magically make the world all good all the time, but his presence had certainly helped chase away the clouds on those days that felt endless.

"They make it worth it," she added.

"What?" He sounded sincerely interested, and when she focused on him, she saw he was hanging on her every word.

"Everything."

A small frown line formed between his brows. It was cute, in that sweet way. Proof he had no clue what she was talking about. He carried himself like he knew everything, cocky and self-assured, but not now. Now he was just like everybody else, asking about love like it was actually something that could be explained.

"What needs to be done outside?" she asked abruptly. This conversation suddenly seemed like a bad idea. Talking about her relationship with Ruckus, even as broadly as she was, couldn't lead to anything good. He was already looking at her like she was speaking a foreign language. What if he kept prying?

He blinked, and then must have come to the same conclusion. Piece by piece he rebuilt his walls, and it was like watching an actor prepare for a difficult role. His shoulders pulled back, and he stretched his spine so that he was at his full, towering height. Finally he smoothed his palms down the front of his shirt and zipped his jacket up over it.

"Let's go." His voice had firmed, all business once more.

They were quiet the rest of the way, until they'd crossed to the opposite side of the castle. When they turned the corner, Delaney's steps faltered and Trystan slowed, allowing her a moment.

Two large glass doors showcased a snow-covered patio. There was a circular table with five clear chairs around it. Even though there were plates and platters filled with various foods, the snow on the surface of the table hadn't been cleared. A picture had been painted with white and silver on the edges of the two doors, swirls of snow blowing across a frozen lake at the left, and looming mountains at the right. It made the real table, which could be viewed between them, seem like it came from another world.

Delaney would have scoffed at that thought, considering it was accurate, if she hadn't been so engrossed with the snow both on the ground and piled high in clumps surrounding the table. Back home it'd be glittery in the bright sunlight, but here the sparkle was so much more than mere gold or white. There were hints of icy blues and pale pinks. She saw sparkles of light green and bold oranges. Every time she turned her head, the sunlight hit it a different way, giving her a new burst of color. Almost like someone had dumped a vat of confetti into the snow.

"It gets better," Trystan assured her, done waiting. He pressed against the narrow of her back, urging her forward. It didn't take much prompting.

There weren't guards stationed, so he had to open the doors himself, waving her in before him. Usually he entered a room first, but she didn't hesitate, not once, even considering there could be danger on the other side.

It became clear why he'd been so sure a moment later, when she stepped beneath the arch and could finally see the rest of the room. Seven Tellers stood around the perimeter, forming a wide circle, their fronts facing inward.

The doors hadn't led outside at all. Glass walls created a bubble around the patio, encasing a good chunk of snow-covered land, blocking out the rest. There was a domed ceiling, with panels in the center that she imagined retracted to allow the snow in. They must have been closed recently, considering how much of the stuff was here. It was identical to the room back in Vakar where they'd met Gailie, only there it'd been spring and filled with greenery.

There wasn't really much to see outside except for more white. Off in the far distance she could make out a few mountains, but aside from that and the beginnings of a forest to the left, it was all sweeping snow on rolling hills.

"Delaney!" Dominan appeared from around a snow mound and leaped at her.

She braced for impact, but it was still somewhat unexpected, and he ended up pushing her back a few feet. She might have stumbled farther, except Trystan was suddenly at her back, propping her up. With Dom's arms tightly wrapped around her waist, it was impossible for her to move away from the Zane, and she felt her cheeks begin to darken.

Trystan's hands were at her shoulders, and his front was pressing against her back so that she could feel the solid weight of him. He was tall enough that she was sure if she tipped her head, their eyes would meet.

"Hello," Dominan said, finally pulling away, giving her the opportunity to do so as well.

She tried not to make it too obvious, stepping off to the side and crossing her arms. It was a forced casual stance, and she refused to look at Trystan, already knowing that he'd easily see through her. "I thought you might like to eat with Dom, and had lunch relocated," Trystan told her. He glanced at the table and quirked a brow. "Did you start without us?"

"Sort of." The boy didn't seem guilty in the least. "It was getting warm."

That piqued Delaney's interest, and she sent Trystan a look, which he easily deciphered.

"I picked foods that are best served cold," he explained. "It's why I thought of changing the venue to this room when you suggested we eat together. These"—he stepped toward the table and she moved after him, watching as he lifted something from a blue bowl—"are one of my favorites. Taste."

He pinched a small black cube between two fingers and brought it to her lips. When her eyes trailed over to Dom uncomfortably, Trystan grinned.

She opened her mouth and allowed him to place the food on her tongue, practically snapping her teeth down on his fingers faster than he could pull back. The texture of the cube was slick and grainy, the taste unidentifiable for a second before a burst of sweetness exploded.

It was chewy, but it quickly began to dissolve so that by the time she swallowed, it didn't feel like there was much left in her mouth. She couldn't compare it to anything back home, but found that she liked it a lot.

"You have a sweet tooth," she noted, recalling his favorite drink. She did a perusal of the table, a tad disappointed when she didn't see any steaming cups of squa.

Trystan motioned toward one of the Tellers with the same two fingers. He must have said something to the tall Kint through their fittings, for the guy gave a single nod and then left. Without skipping a beat, the Zane picked something else from the table.

"I thought you might want to try fruy." He held a triangular pastry out to her. "After hearing us talk about it the other day."

"That depends," she said, though she was already taking it. "Did Yalla make it?"

"Of course." He smiled, and before she could help it, she smiled back.

The pastry was flaky, and in that sense, familiar. Because of this, she expected some type of fruit flavor in the center, but the filling was more like a chocolate custard, surprising her.

"You *really* have a sweet tooth," she repeated, then polished off the dessert. Now that she was eating, the hunger from earlier was returning tenfold. "What else is good?"

"All of it." He selected a light-pink item that was as thin as a crepe and the size of his palm. Before giving it to her, he rolled it into a loose tube and then dipped it into a small bowl of yellow powder. "Try this."

He didn't hand it to her like he'd done with the fruy, instead opting to hand-feed her a second time. With all the onlookers—the Tellers weren't directly staring, but they were still witnessing everything—he knew it was impossible for her to protest. This was part of the agreement, part of the game. Convince them all that their relationship was legitimate, and this was just the type of gross, cutesy thing a real couple would do.

She almost rolled her eyes, leaning forward to take a bite, then narrowed them instead when she was close enough to him that she was sure no one else would see.

He chuckled, but the challenging air never left him.

"Seriously." She swallowed the sugary concoction and then reached out to pluck the rest of the pink roll from him. "How do you stay so fit?"

Her eyes roamed over his body, lingering on his arms and the place where his abdominal muscles were under his thick coat.

"I'm fortunate," he replied, and then stole the last bite from between her fingers, popping it into his mouth. "These are all traditional breakfast foods. I like breakfast."

"You love breakfast," she corrected him. "Don't lie." There were at least another seven foods she'd yet to try, all of them probably just as sweet as the ones she'd had. "Breakfast in Vakar was not like this."

"I recall your distaste," he grunted, and chose something else from the table.

She didn't bother to inspect it this time, opening her mouth and letting him place whatever it was on her tongue while she glanced at the other items. It started tart, with a crunchy consistency, and then shifted to salty-sweet.

"Have you ever had a salted caramel?" she asked, pointing at her mouth. "This reminds me of that."

"I'll add it to my list."

She met his gaze. "What list?"

"All the things I'll have to try when I'm on Earth." He glanced away as he said it, feigning interest in the food, rolling one of the thin pink circles for himself.

She waited while he ate half of it before asking, "You're going back to Earth?"

"It's what you told the councils," he said, still not looking at her. "We'll be going back to Earth, eventually. For a visit."

He didn't have to bother with the implication that they wouldn't be staying, but she didn't point that out. Arguing with him, while usually comforting in its familiarity, seemed like way too much effort right now. After yesterday especially, she just wanted a moment where neither of them had to worry about what the other was saying.

Considering the way he'd just put this Earth business to her, she got the feeling he was on the same page. He didn't want to upset her, so he didn't want her to take his mentioning of it the wrong way.

For some reason, she found that really nice, that he would bother to try to soften the blow at all, and was stupidly about to say so out loud when the Teller who Trystan had spoken to telepathically returned, carrying a silver tray with three glass mugs.

She immediately recognized the squa, and couldn't help but smile when Trystan took one of the mugs and sipped it first before handing it carefully to her.

His gaze met hers over the rim of his own as he drank, steam wafting around his face. How he'd known that was exactly what she'd been looking for when she'd checked out the table was beyond her, but for once he didn't seem to be gloating over it.

Thankfully Dom stopped their stare-off before it could become a moment, tossing a snowball at Trystan. The cold ball came flying, smacking into the Zane's side, catching him off guard. It didn't stick but immediately burst into a fine powder of pale glitter.

"It's rude to not pay attention to your guests, Uncle Trystan," Dom said through laughter.

Delaney waited for a reaction, expecting the Zane to brush the remaining snow residue from his jacket, maybe even readjust the collar for good measure—because god forbid he be out of sorts, fashion wise. But he didn't do either of those things.

In a move almost too fast for her to follow, he ran his right hand across the surface of the table, taking up a large handful of snow, and tossed it at Dominan. He grinned when the misshapen ball hit its mark, landing at the center of Dom's chest.

She was so shocked, she stood there dumbly as the two of them began firing more snowballs at each other. She didn't even move out of the way when a few came close to hitting her. Trystan playing with a kid was not what she expected. Ever.

Yet here he was, and he was having fun, too. The two of them were both laughing, dodging and weaving. Trystan was using the table as a shield, ducking down to its level whenever Dom lobbed one close enough to hit him.

Dom had moved back around one of the larger snow mounds, peeking over the side to toss a snowball, only to pop back behind the mound a second later. He didn't bother taking the time to aim.

Trystan was good with kids.

Compared to all the other crazy, impossible things she'd learned over the past six months, that was definitely the most insane.

A snowball slapped against her shoulder, hard enough that it jostled her. Surprised, she stared at Trystan, who'd thrown it.

He laughed at her expression, motioning with his chin to the snow in his hands in a clear warning. It was already a well-formed ball, yet he kept working it, giving her time to make a move.

Delaney shot toward a nearby snow mound, which was almost tall enough to completely block her. She let out a startled yelp when she felt the snowball smack against the center of her back, dropping around the mound a second too late. From her spot, she could see Dom hiding behind his.

He was smiling at her and silently pointing in Trystan's direction. It was obvious what he was getting at, and his smile broadened when she vigorously nodded.

She quickly scooped up some snow, forming snowballs until she had a nice little pile before her. Then she signaled Dom, who mirrored her when she slowly got to her feet. She took a breath, and they both darted around their mounds, tossing snowballs toward where Trystan had last been standing.

But of course he was no longer there.

Delaney started backing up, scanning around for him. She let out another yelp when she bumped into something, and before she could process it was Trystan, his arm banded around her waist and he was lifting and spinning her in a circle.

She sucked in a breath, about to scream, then inhaled again when she felt herself falling backward. Her body landed in the cushiony snow, and a second later he was falling over her.

He was careful not to crush her, holding out his arms at the last second so he could brace himself and keep most of his weight off her body. There was snow caked in his hair, and his cheeks were bright red from the cold. He was still laughing, causing warm puffs of air to fan across her cheeks.

She'd lifted her hands to his chest instinctually but didn't push him away. Out of the corner of her eye she could see Dom taking advantage of Trystan's momentary distraction, creating a stockpile of ammunition.

He worked fast, and it felt like only a few heartbeats had passed before another snowball was soaring straight for Trystan's head, slamming against his neck. Some of it clearly went down the collar of his jacket.

Trystan quickly rolled off of her to the side, taking up a handful of snow and tossing it at Dom all in one motion.

Delaney was already scrambling back toward where Dom was, taking up her own snowball so the two of them could gang up on Trystan as originally planned. Her gloves were starting to get damp, and the cold had seeped through her clothing. But she didn't care.

It wasn't until much later, when her teeth were visibly chattering and she could no longer feel her fingers, that she even thought about ending their fun and going back inside.

CHAPTER 18

Trystan was relieved the two of them had cleared the air, only now, when he should have been focused, he was too busy picturing the way her cold-kissed cheeks had looked. The way she'd stared at him. For the first time there hadn't been so much as a hint of distaste in her green eyes.

He would much rather be with her than here, outside Interrogation, with the Rue his father had sent to spy on him. Definitely not the time to be distracted.

The small room attached to the larger interrogation chamber exposed a view of the Tar his father had sent. They'd gotten his name easily enough, Mickan, but the rest had been harder to obtain. As a result, the man Trystan was looking at was broken, bruised, and in many places, covered in blood.

What would Delaney think if she saw him? He glanced down at his red-stained fingers, and tightened his hand into a fist to cover them. She wouldn't continue looking at him the way she had earlier, that was for sure.

Last week she'd called him a monster. If she knew what he'd just done, she'd tell him he'd proven her right. There was little doubt that she'd yell at him, throw around more insults. Back away, like she had yesterday when he'd reached for her.

She hadn't backed away today, though. He wondered over it. Did she regret it? For all he knew, she was sitting in her room right now, hating herself for enjoying time with him. More specifically, enjoying the company of a monster.

"There's more he can tell us." The Rue was glaring through the glass at the Tar.

Despite him being loyal to his father, there was little to fear from Rue Rantan. Not only could Trystan easily crush him if need be, the man was also too political to ever resort to violence. He preferred not to get his own hands dirty.

Rantan was one of the few members of the council who hadn't served in the war, and Trystan held little to no respect for men like that. Men who came out of hiding the moment the fighting was done, insisting to be part of something they had no hand in building. Demanding to be heard over those who actually deserved to speak.

As soon as he took the throne, Rantan would be out on his ass. It was a day Trystan was greatly looking forward to, yet sadly one that was still a ways off.

"I'm sure there is," he responded dryly. "But he won't spill the rest of his secrets tonight. Tomorrow we'll try again. Let him rest for now."

Rantan turned his gaze his way, but Trystan pretended not to notice.

"The Rex has asked me to asses you while I'm here, Zane. To ensure that the presence of the human isn't causing you to grow soft," he said.

Trystan gritted his teeth. "If we push him much further, he'll die, and then we'll get nothing. Allowing him time to heal also gives him a false sense of security. As soon as we take that away, he'll crack faster than he did today. It's a well-known tactic, and one you'd be familiar with if you ever did anything actually useful."

"Pardon me, Zane—" he began, clearly affronted, but Trystan swiftly cut him off.

"You are not excused. I don't know how my father expects you to behave, but here, I like competency and experience. You do not hold either quality."

"I'm useful in other ways," he said. "I assure you."

Trystan waved his hand absently. "Waste your assurances on someone who actually cares." He pointed to the Tar prisoner. "Did my father already know about the gathering in Kilma?"

Mickan had been taken from the Kint palace after a slipup had given away his position as a Tar.

"He was aware they were grouping," Rantan answered. "He did not know the location. That will be useful."

"I've already sent him the information." Trystan crossed his arms, watching a drop of blood slide down from Mickan's temple all the way to the tip of his chin.

The Tars were planning a riot, according to the bloodied man in the interrogation chamber. That was bad in a few different ways. Innocent citizens could be hurt, for one. For another, it could have the Tars' desired effect and start an all-out civil war, with one side against the royal family.

And Delaney.

"I can destroy the Tars easily enough," he said aloud.

"I'm sure the Rex will be delighted to hear it," Rantan told him. "He's found the Tars a nuisance since their forming."

"That's because they rejected his idea of peace," Trystan pointed out.

"If you can't stop them from spreading their hate for the human," Rantan tentatively began, "continuing on as planned could lead to catastrophe. No one wants a civil war."

"The human has a name," Trystan growled out warningly, "and a title. You'll refer to her with both, or, better yet, not at all. Hearing you talk about her pisses me off, and you've seen what happens when I lose control."

"Need I remind you, Zane, that I'm under your father's protection." It was snooty, and wholly arrogant.

Trystan had punished subordinates for less. Damn Rantan for being right.

"You're either very confident, or very stupid." He knew he should turn their attentions back to the Tar, where it was supposed to be, but he couldn't help delivering one more jab. "Should my father wish to send a council member to Kilma, I'll suggest you. You appear to have a particular interest in the Tars."

"In stopping them," Rantan reiterated, though he lost some of his color. "I'd be more useful to you both if I stayed on here."

"I have no use for you at all," Trystan scoffed. "I never have, and I doubt I ever will. You'll return to Carnage in the morning as planned, and report back to my father that everything is going smoothly here."

He moved past him to the exit, not wanting to waste any more time with Rantan.

Sanzie was waiting for him in the dark hall, and she crossed her arms behind her back in a respectful stance. Which meant she had bad news.

"Well." He waved her on when she remained silent. "Get it over with."

"Your father has requested that you attend the raid in Kilma," she said, keeping her chin up as she delivered the message.

That was fast. He'd only sent news to the Rex a little while ago.

"If it were truly a request, I could decline." He ran a hand through his hair, subconsciously smoothing down any strands that had shaken loose during the interrogation. "Judging by your tone, however, that is not an option."

"Refusing is a risk," Sanzie told him, one of the few people bold enough to attempt giving him advice. "Angering him could have dire results."

Yet another reminder that while he might be more powerful than practically everyone on the planet, his father still ruled him.

According to Mickan, the Tars were planning a mass gathering in two weeks. That was when they would organize the riot. Kilma was the second largest city in Kint, right after the capital, Carnage. There was more to the plan, but supposedly Mickan hadn't been a member long enough to get all the details.

Perhaps Trystan should go, just to ensure the job was properly done.

"He doubts my ability to separate duty from emotion toward her," he mumbled, mostly to himself, though obviously, because she was standing less than five feet away, Sanzie heard.

"Do you have emotions for the Lissa, Zane?" As soon as she asked, she dropped her gaze. "Apologizes. That's none of my concern."

"Forgiven." He wouldn't get mad at a good Teller like her for such a small slip. He understood what it was to be curious; hell, that was how he'd gotten so involved with Delaney in the first place.

After catching her in the library that first night, there'd been something about her he just had to uncover. Something odd and unique. At the time, he'd been hopeful, wanting a reason, any reason, to change his opinion of Olena. Despite what it seemed like, he preferred peace. He knew firsthand what war did, had lost more friends and colleagues than he could count to it.

He allowed himself a second to picture Dom's father. They'd grown up together; he'd been more his family than the Rex could ever be. And Trystan had watched as Vakar zees tore through Ustan like tissue paper. Powerless to do anything. Unable to even retrieve the body until three days later, and by then scavengers had made good work of it.

Shaking the image away, Tristan refocused on the Teller.

"Is she still awake?" he asked, knowing Sanzie would understand whom he meant without having to elaborate.

Sure enough, the Teller nodded. "I brought her a cup of squa fifteen minutes ago."

He smiled before he could help himself, taking some twisted pleasure in knowing that she enjoyed his favorite drink. It was oddly endearing. Were these usually the types of things people found cute in others? Was it normal for him to find the way she scrunched her nose after trying something disgusting adorable? Or that he found it sexy that she could throw a punch?

Exhausted after the interrogation, Trystan knew the responsible thing to do would be to go straight to bed. Instead he had this undeniable urge to see Delaney, to hear her voice, to feel her skin against his own. It wasn't a new desire—he'd been fighting against it for weeks—but he was tired of the struggle.

Couldn't there just be one thing in his life he didn't have to overthink? Some*one*, more aptly, he didn't always need to be so calculated with? With Rantan and his father, caution was imperative. Saying the wrong thing could be cataclysmic. He enjoyed his freedom with Delaney. Didn't he deserve more of that?

Without a good-bye, Trystan turned and walked away, his mind already back on Delaney.

A few minutes later he knocked on her door, but he didn't wait for a response before letting himself in. He found her tucked into the chair by the fireplace, her head already turned toward him.

She'd changed out of her clothes from earlier and into a pair of burgundy pants and a black long-sleeved shirt. The dark color made her hair and the green of her eyes pop in the semidarkness of the room, her alluring features almost stopping him in his tracks.

She didn't react when he moved toward her, or when he dropped down in the empty seat across from her and leaned as far forward as he could. He needed to be near her in a way he didn't quite understand. Another time he'd pick that need apart, but for now, for tonight, he'd accept it.

He was so tired of everything and all the responsibilities. He just wanted to breathe for a moment.

"Did you just have a talk with your father?" She watched him with a calm interest. "You have that look about you. I used to get it after arguments with my dad."

"What look is that?"

"The 'woe is me' look." She smiled when he frowned, and shook her head. "It's not an insult. You're feeling inadequate and you're struggling against it. That's all." She canted her head. "I wasn't aware you could question your self-worth."

"I'm perfectly capable of questioning everything," he said, clasping his hands before him. "I simply prefer to just know."

"Well, sure." She rolled her eyes, and while it should have been offensive, he took it as endearing. "Who doesn't? Knowing things is great, but you can't know everything, Trystan. Not right away."

He wondered what she'd been doing in here while he'd been down in the interrogation rooms. Torturing someone.

It wasn't the deed itself that made him uncomfortable. Mickan had joined a rebellion; he knew what could happen. It was picturing Delaney walking in on him while he was doing it that made his stomach tighten into knots. The possible look on her face, the things she'd say . . .

"I want to know something about you," he stated, realizing that it was the only topic he was interested in discussing at the moment. He feared she'd ask him about the interrogation—she'd been in the room when his father had mentioned it—and that he'd have to tell her honestly about all the gritty details.

Because he would be honest. He'd promised that not only to her, but also to himself. If he was able, he would tell her only truths.

"All right." She was tentative, suspicious, curling her legs up against her chest in a subconsciously protective move.

There were so many things he wanted to ask, things that confused him, amazed him. But asking those things might lead to discomfort on her part, and then frustration and disappointment on his, and he wasn't ready to drop this easy air between them.

"What was the first gift your father ever gave you?" It was a random question, but he stuck with it once he'd said it.

She quirked a brow at him, then lifted a single shoulder. "A pink teddy bear when I was born. If you mean the first gift he gave that I can remember, that would be my Power Ranger set. My Barbie dolls would marry them, and the Rangers would teach them how to fight crime so they could help defend the world."

She laughed, the sound light, open. As soon as she stopped, he wanted her to do it again.

"You have no idea what I'm talking about." She ran a hand through her hair, sending the thick red strands into disarray. It didn't seem to bother her, and she left it that way. "They're action figures. Toys. I'm not sure if you guys have anything like action figures here?"

He nodded. He understood the term, had owned one or two as a child. As soon as he'd hit seven, of course, those things had been too frivolous and childish for a Zane and they'd been taken away. If he recalled correctly, he'd cried about it in secret that first night, staring at his empty toy shelf.

"He doesn't sound that bad," Trystan said, bringing to mind the single photograph of her father he'd seen. During his research on her, he'd requested one of both of her parents. He'd wanted an idea of what they looked like, of where she'd come from.

"He isn't," she agreed. "He loves me, and I know it. It's just, he's always had such high expectations of me, goals that he's set. A picture of what my future is. That's when he can find the time to pay attention to me. He and my mom are usually pretty busy with work. I didn't see them often when I lived at home. It's why it was so easy to convince them to let me attend boarding school. They wouldn't have to worry about whether they'd left food in the fridge or enough money for me to at least order out."

He grimaced, thinking about how she'd scolded him for not feeding her in a timely fashion. Was she used to that sort of thing? Did it bring up bad memories from living at home? Feeling abandoned? Unwanted?

"Sometimes I'm certain my father would prefer me to be someone else," he confessed, expecting to feel embarrassed by it. Surprised when he didn't. "It isn't the same as with yours—my future is set and we both know it—but I've been forgotten before. Left to my own devices."

"It's lonely." She nodded. "I remember this one time, when I was really young, maybe five or six, my parents went out and forgot to call a babysitter. I should have been excited having the run of the house, but I wasn't. I was livid. How dare they forget me, you know? So I went around hiding all the things I thought they'd find the most important. Remotes, takeout menus, my mom's shoes."

Her expression grew momentarily distant, a sadness entering her glazed eyes, slipping past her defenses. Was she letting him see, or had she simply become too distracted by the memory to keep her guard up?

"When they got home the next morning, they found me asleep in the upstairs hallway, still clutching a pair of my dad's solid-gold cufflinks." She pursed her lips, inhaled, and then shook herself out of it. She shed the recollection like a too-tight coat, dropping it and coming back to herself with ease.

It was impressive, her ability to accept things. He didn't have that skill; maybe growing up would have been a little easier if he did.

"My mother died when I was eleven." He paused. That was definitely a subject he hadn't expected to bring up.

There wasn't a hint of pity in her gaze, and she didn't make a face or lean toward him and rest her hand over his. Didn't give him a false sense of comfort, which he appreciated.

He'd decided to only give her truths. It'd be nice if she only gave them to him as well.

"There isn't really much to say." And there wasn't. He only vaguely remembered her, mostly her smell, a mixture of sharp chocolate and hazelnut. Some of the things they'd done together often enough had made an impression. "A year later I was sent away. Training. All the royal children have to at that age."

"Trystan"—she waited for him to look at her—"you wouldn't have brought it up if you didn't want to talk about it. It's okay. I won't tease or judge you for anything you have to say about your mom. I know there are limits to us, lines that even we shouldn't cross."

Had they silently agreed upon these lines, or did she just know about them? It was nice that she had boundaries, personal or otherwise. That there were things she wasn't willing to do, no matter who she was arguing with.

Would she torture someone for information, like he'd just done?

Probably, he realized, searching her features for the answer. Sure, she was kind, and thoughtful, but she wasn't soft or meek. She had no qualms about standing up for herself or the people she loved. There was little doubt that if she had to, she would do anything to keep them protected. Even if it meant crossing some of those lines she'd drawn herself.

Did that mean, if pushed far enough, she'd take it back and use his mother against him after all? He wished he knew, but he didn't. His gut told him she wouldn't, that while she wasn't weak, she also wasn't cruel. But how well did he know her, really? How well did anyone know anyone else? He was well respected in Kint, but Brightan had been the closest thing he'd had to a friend since Ustan.

Everyone who'd ever known him, the real him, was dead.

"My mother and I were very close," he told her, suddenly needing her to know this part of him. "I don't remember much, don't have many actual memories, but I never forgot that. She would read to me, not just before bedtime, but all the time. At random intervals through-out the day she'd appear in the doorway of whatever room I was in, a book in hand, and start reading. Books, all kinds, excited her. I think they made up for the lack of attention given to her by my father."

Both of her parents were busy with work, but when he'd been younger, only his father had been. His mother, while highborn, was only royalty by marriage and therefore didn't know all the ins and outs of their political system. Not enough to be of legitimate use, and Trystan got the sense that his father liked it that way.

"I'm hiring you a tutor." He would not be his father, and what was more, he didn't want Delaney to be sad like his mother. She'd already expressed feeling lonely and swept aside by her family. As her new family—or at least, he was going to be after the binding—it was his responsibility to make sure she never felt that way again.

"One who can teach you the politics of both Kint and Vakar," he went on. "Perhaps one who can also refresh you on the politics of your own people as well. That will be important in the coming years, I'm sure. You'll have to know how to properly govern them, after all."

"What do you mean?" She'd gone a bit stiff, but he continued any-way, too caught up in his thoughts to really notice.

"You're their Lissa now," he said. "It's important that you stay in-volved, even if we don't visit Earth often. You'll be the bridge between our two worlds, the one who keeps the peace. Dropping their need to invade won't come easy for the Kints. There'll be demands, compro-mises with Earth's governments. You understand."

"No." She tightened her arms around her knees. "I'm not following. I thought you already said you'd protect Earth? That my binding to you automatically ensured that?"

"It automatically ensures that your people are kept safe because they'll technically be my people," he corrected. "That doesn't mean they won't be punished for rebelling, the same way the Tars are being. Our laws and Earth laws are very different; the original plan was to start phasing out yours for ours. It would certainly be simpler ruling both planets if they had the same set of rules to follow."

Delaney was still for a long moment in which he wasn't even sure she was breathing, then she slowly unfolded from the chair and stood before him. It wasn't until she spoke that he noted the heat in her eyes, the way the green of her irises had sharpened.

"You're talking about invading," she said, deadly calm. "About killing off our cultures, our traditions, and replacing them with your own. Are you completely insane, or just delusional? Did you honestly think I'd stand by and let that happen? That I was going to twiddle my thumbs on the sidelines while you *took over my planet*?"

"Honestly"—it took all his willpower not to stand himself, to not use his height and stature against her—"I hadn't thought about it. But this was all before, Delaney," he rushed on, wanting to reassure her before her anger got too far. "I'm telling you now that it's no longer the plan. Hence, the tutors. They can teach you everything you need to know about my people, and they can also teach us everything we need to know about yours. We can do this. Nothing has to change for anyone."

He wasn't sure she believed him; maybe she wasn't sure, either. The look she gave him was indecipherable, which was unsettling because he could usually read her so well.

In retrospect, he shouldn't have mentioned the original invasion plan, but he'd grown up with the idea that Earth would one day belong to Xenith. It was natural to him to discuss it and its inevitability. She, obviously, wouldn't see it as casually as he did.

These thoughts had also entered his head completely unannounced. Up until he'd spoken them aloud, he'd had no idea he'd changed his stance on taking over Earth. It was his father's goal, in truth, and that would have to somehow be dealt with as well. But Trystan was sure he could come up with some plan to stay the Rex's hand, at least long enough for Delaney and him to put together a presentation that got all three of them what they wanted.

She was still staring down at him, and there may or may not have been a sliver of fear in her eyes, gone before he could be certain. Was she thinking about their agreement instead? The one where he'd sworn to bring her home as soon as he'd gotten what he wanted?

The agreement he'd carefully worded to ensure he got to *keep* what he wanted? He'd be true to his word, would bring her back to her planet, as promised. But there was no way in hell he'd be leaving her there.

"You still want Earth," she stated, drawing him from his darkening thoughts. "You still think we're beneath you. Admit it. You told me back on the ship. You said you wanted me because I was better than Olena and I'd be able to get you not only Vakar but also Earth. You were honest about it. I guess I just thought . . . I don't know. I don't know what I thought. I was stupid. The fact that this caught me off guard is stupid.

"But"—she took a threatening step closer, bringing them almost to eye level with him still seated—"let me be crystal clear about one thing, Trystan. I will not help you enslave my planet. Ever. I'd take myself out of the equation long before I ever let that happen."

He was up so fast that she stumbled back, forcing him to catch her around the waist to stop her from completely falling. His arm banded around her slim form, tightened to hold her close, as if that would keep her words from coming true. Fear, real fear, slithered up his spine, chilling his insides. He wasn't used to feeling panic, especially not the kind he couldn't control, so this sensation was new.

He didn't like it.

"You will never say something like that again," he found himself telling her through the buzzing in his brain. His free hand reached up to cup the base of her skull, forcing her even closer to him. "I mean it, Delaney. Threats like that . . ." He swallowed the lump in his throat.

"Trystan—" She was pale and frowning again, but he didn't process that, either.

"If you—" He couldn't even say the word. His throat closed up and his world narrowed, becoming very small so that there was only her.

"Trystan," she said, softer this time, and when he didn't respond, she lifted a hand to his face.

Her fingers were a tad cold, but they felt good against his overheated flesh. They were soft as well, her skin smooth against his as she trailed them over his cheek and down his jaw. Then she ran them through the hair at the side of his head gently, carefully.

"I shouldn't have said that. I wasn't thinking," she told him afterward, her tone soothing. "I'm sorry."

"I threatened your people." He closed his eyes, tilting his head slightly into her touch as she brought her fingers back to his forehead so she could repeat the motion through his hair. "You'd do anything to protect them. I admire that."

"Because you would do the same," she guessed. Only, it came out like a certainty.

Still, he replied, "Yes."

He hadn't realized she was slowly urging him back until she'd turned them and pressed against the tops of his shoulders. He allowed her to maneuver him down, easing into the large chair she'd exited only minutes prior. A wave of disappointment washed over him when she took her hand away, but he didn't feel it long.

She perched on the left arm of the chair, swiveling so that she could place her feet on the cushion between his legs. Her right hand reached for him, starting up the same slow, hypnotic motions through his hair on the other side of his head.

They stayed like that for a moment, and it became clear she was giving him time to settle his nerves before asking what she wanted to ask.

"Trystan," she said, "how did your mother die?"

He stilled, hating himself for the reaction almost as quickly as it came. His muscles bunched in preparation as he readied to stand, but she must have predicted this, turning her knees inward so that they lightly pressed against his chest, blocking him.

He could easily move her, of course. But he didn't.

"She killed herself, didn't she?"

There was a spot right between her neck and her breasts, and he kept his gaze locked there. This was not a subject he spoke about with anyone, not even his father. In fact, they'd never discussed it, not once in all the years since it'd happened. He couldn't even recall the last time he'd heard his father say her name.

"We don't need to talk about it," Delaney added. "I'm sorry I brought it up."

Except she hadn't—he had, and she was right. He wouldn't have done so if some part of him hadn't wanted them to end up exactly where they were now.

"I was the one who found her," he whispered, barely recognizing the wispy sound of his own voice. "She hadn't meant for me to; she wasn't cruel. It was in their bedroom, and I wasn't allowed in there. She must have thought it the perfect place. I'm pretty sure she wanted it to be my father."

He never broke the rules; he'd respected her too much for that. That day had been different, though he could never remember why. He'd seen the door; it'd been closed like always, but something inside of him had insisted he open it. And he'd listened.

"I still don't know why she did it," he continued, trying not to allow the last images of his mother into his mind. "There wasn't a note, and my father would never tell me. My only guess is that she was very unhappy. That he made her that way, and she felt like there was nothing else she could do. She was the Regina. There was no out for her."

Realizing the way that must sound, he lifted his eyes to hers, silently pleading with her to understand. "I know this isn't what you wanted, but I swear, Delaney, I will never be my father. I won't lock you away like he did her. You'll have real power, a real say on how things are governed. On how your people are treated."

He didn't give her time to respond, was too afraid of what she might say. He couldn't even continue looking at her, not wanting to see her expression, and he pressed his lips to the spot between her neck and left shoulder.

"You won't be unhappy with me," he promised, dropping his forehead to that same spot he'd just kissed.

Trystan knew she might not believe him right now, but he believed it. He wouldn't have said it if he hadn't thought it was true. He had far more to give than any Ander ever could. He could make her happy.

He'd prove it.

CHAPTER 19

How are you, Lissa?"

Delaney glanced over to find Sanzie staring straight ahead. Her gaze, as per usual, was impassive, so it was impossible to know what the other girl was thinking. Or getting at.

"Fine," Delaney replied tentatively. "And you?"

"It's been a stressful past few days," she shocked her by admitting, though there was hardly any inflection in her tone.

"Let me guess," Delaney said. "Nothing I need concern myself with?"

Sanzie gave her a quick look. "You can concern yourself with whatever you'd like. You're the Lissa."

Which was probably how Delaney had managed to convince the Teller to take her where they were currently headed. Earlier, Sanzie had stopped by to announce that Trystan would be occupied the entire day.

Delaney had mumbled something about wanting to see Ruckus, already positive that it wouldn't be allowed. But Sanzie had merely nodded, said okay, and began leading the way to the dungeons.

"I'm simply not allowed to bring certain things up with you myself," Sanzie added then, catching Delaney's interest.

"Meaning if I asked you a question about something specific—"

"I would be forced to answer it," she agreed before she could finish. "Correct."

That could be useful.

"What are Trystan's secrets?" she blurted, unable to help herself.

"I can only confirm that he has them," Sanzie told her. "I can't elaborate."

"Right." That made more sense. "Which is why he's comfortable with you having to answer any of my questions: because I need the right question in order to receive anything important. Great."

It was impossible to ask someone about something she didn't know. Clever of him, really.

She switched gears. "All right, tell me about you, then. Why did you leave Vakar?"

They were getting close to the stairwell to the dungeons, and she needed a distraction. The thought of seeing Ruckus made her heart soar and her stomach plummet at the same time. A very unsettling feeling. Without Trystan around, she hoped she'd be able to tell Ruckus about the agreement the two of them had made.

The one she wasn't so sure they'd actually agreed on anymore. The way he'd spoken last night hadn't been the way one would talk about someone they'd eventually part from. He'd made it sound like they were going to have a long future together, the exact opposite of what he'd promised her.

Wasn't it?

She'd spent the entire night trying to ignore the sharp twist of dread in her gut, knowing that if she dwelled on it now, if she looked too closely and found something she didn't like, she'd crack. And none of them, not Ruckus or Pettus or Gibus or even Trystan, could afford that.

So she focused on the Teller at her side, and on the cold chill to the air as they began making their way down the winding staircase. The way the soles of her shoes made a light tapping sound against the stone, how the sharp bite of ice and cleaning solution made her nose twitch.

"My father died . . . ," Sanzie began. "He was Vakar, but my mother was Kint. After his death, there was nothing to keep her and she moved back to the kingdom she was born to. She took my younger sister with her, while I stayed behind because I'd already worked hard for my position in the Vakar army. I'd spent my childhood traveling back and forth between Vakar and Kint; I held no loyalty to one or the other, and because of my heritage, I was a citizen of both."

Delaney had never heard her say anywhere near this many words before, and was too afraid she'd stop if she asked any questions, so she kept her mouth shut.

"During the war, I was fighting in a battle, helping to shoot down enemy ships. I knew the risks, so when my craft was hit and I started to go down, I thought I was okay with it. But then I survived the crash, and I waited for my squad to come and find me." Her expression tightened, almost imperceptibly, because she'd been keeping a straight face anyway. "They never did."

Now the reason Delaney didn't say anything was because she didn't know what to say. Not that it mattered; Sanzie only paused for a split second before continuing.

"I was left there, literally freezing to death, standing by the massive, smoking remains of my craft, when I realized I was going to die for people I didn't care about. As I mentioned, I felt no true loyalty to either Vakar or Kint. No ties to anyone in particular. I loved my mother, but I'd also loved my father. The only reason I was even fighting for Vakar in the first place was because that's where I'd been when I'd decided this career path."

"They left you there to die," Delaney said.

"They did," she stated. They'd reached the bottom of the steps now, and were starting down the long hallway. "But that's not why I defected. I thought for certain I was going to die there, out in the middle of Morray. Then the Zane showed up. His ship had gone down as well. We were enemies, and I was afraid. I'd long since lost feeling in my limbs, so all I could do was lie there in the snow, shaking as he and his men approached.

"He gutted the only part of my craft that was still intact, propping it up so that it buffered us from the harsh winds. Then he and his men helped me into a sitting position, and we all huddled together in a desperate attempt to conserve heat. He didn't ask me if I'd been the one to shoot him down; he didn't care. He'd seen my ship fall, and they'd had come seeking shelter and help. If they hadn't, I would have died less than ten minutes later. If he'd done what he'd been trained to do, kill the enemy, I would have died a lot sooner than that. But he didn't."

The doorway leading to the last cellblock was before them now, and the Teller paused, turning toward her. "He saved my life. Kept us alive long enough for Kint forces to find us."

"Delaney?" Ruckus's call cut off anything she might have said to the Teller about that. He couldn't see them, but he must have heard them talking.

"When you're ready, Lissa." Sanzie bowed her head and turned so her back was to the room, guarding the door.

Delaney opened her mouth but then snapped it shut again. What was there to say?

Pettus and Gibus were curled up on the uncomfortable-looking benches in their cell, but she could see the subtle rise and fall of their chests, so she knew they were sleeping.

Ruckus, on the other hand, was pressed so closely to the barrier between them, it was a wonder he didn't get electrocuted. His bruises were healing, albeit slowly, but he could open both eyes all the way now, which was something.

"Delaney," he repeated on a sigh the moment she came into view, a well of tension seeming to drop from his shoulders. His gaze narrowed around her, his spine tensing again as he searched for Trystan.

"He isn't here," she told him. "I came with Sanzie."

"Be careful with her," he warned. "She's loyal to the Zane."

From what Delaney had just gathered, the girl had more than enough reason to be.

"Wait, you mean he actually let you down here to see me without him hovering?" Ruckus tried to make the statement light, but he was only partly successful. He was weary, and there was no way for him to hide that fact, not with the proof written all over his face. "What an idiot."

"Let's not talk about him." She brought herself up as close as she could. "I miss you."

"Is this the part where we both reach for the glass, pretending our palms can touch?" he asked. "Mariana would get a real kick out of that. I can see her face now, once we're home and we tell her."

"She'd yell about how cliché it is," Delaney agreed, smiling. "And she'd be right."

He lifted a single shoulder. "I guess it's a good thing my side of this barrier is electric then, huh? Stops us from being predictable."

"You don't have to do that. Be brave. It's okay if you're not. I want you to be real, Ruckus."

He exhaled slowly. "This is difficult. Being—"

"Trapped?" she interrupted teasingly.

"Being away from you," he corrected her, though he smiled softly. "Now who isn't being serious? We're both trying to get through this by using humor, but we can't keep it up forever, Delaney. With Fawna being the only one on the outside I can trust, I don't know how we're going to get out of this."

"Trystan and I made a deal," she confessed, forcing herself to hold his gaze while she explained. When the yellow of his iris turned a golden shade, the rim of green widening, she knew he was angry.

"Absolutely not," he hissed.

"We don't really have a choice, do we?" she said, trying to calm him down. "At least this way you and the others get to go free"—she swallowed the lump in her throat—"and I'll follow."

"You really believe that?" It was clear he did not.

She sighed, suddenly exhausted. "I have to. You're not here to help me through it this time. This, trusting Trystan will keep his word, that's what I need to keep me stable. It's the only thing that's doing it, in fact."

"It's naive, Delaney."

"I know that." And she did. "But that doesn't change anything. He gave me his word, and so long as you're safe, the rest can be worked out."

"Delaney—"

"You'll be out," she stopped him. "You and Pettus and Gibus and Fawna. That makes four. Between you all, I'm sure you can come up with a better plan, one that doesn't depend on Trystan keeping his promise."

Realization dawned on him, and he straightened slightly, searching her expression. She didn't know what he was hoping to find, but she made sure to keep the determination visible in her eyes.

She wanted to believe Trystan had told her the truth, that he was going to uphold his end of their bargain and let her go once he was guaranteed the crowns, like he wanted. But their conversation last night had really gotten to her, had made her revisit their agreement and the things they'd said.

There was something she was missing, she was sure of it, but until she figured out what that was, keeping Ruckus and herself from both going insane was the best course of action.

"Hoping that once we're out, we'll be able to come up with a plan to rescue you," Ruckus said, "isn't really a plan at all."

"I trust you."

"You trust Trystan as well, apparently."

"I'm trying here." She rubbed at her temples, feeling the beginnings of a headache coming on. This wasn't going the way she'd wanted. "You're the most important person in my life, Ruckus, and you're more capable of navigating this world than I am. But you're in there and I'm out here. I need you to trust me this time. Trust me to save us. Both of us."

"I've always trusted you," he whispered. "You know that."

When he'd realized on his ship that he'd had the wrong person, he'd trusted Delaney could convince the Zane anyway. He'd stuck by her when the Basileus and Basilissa had ordered her to continue the ruse, comforted her when she needed it, and backed off when she hadn't.

Yes, of course he'd always trusted her, even when it made no sense for him to do so, given their stranger status.

Which was why when the guilt came this time, she didn't shove it down. She let herself feel it. If Ruckus knew about the movie she'd watched with Trystan, about the snowball fight they'd only just had the other day, about all the times she'd let the Zane be sweet to her, soft . . . What would he say? Would he still trust her?

"I love you," she told him. Like she'd explained to Trystan, she loved Ruckus in a way she hadn't known existed before they'd met. *That* was what mattered, not what she had to do with Trystan to get through this. Anything that took place between the Zane and her did so *because* she was trying to protect Ruckus and the others.

The way Trystan had looked when he'd spoken of his mother flashed unbidden in her mind, and her heart clenched. In that moment he'd seemed so fragile, like he was back to being that eleven-year-old boy. No one should ever have an experience like that, let alone a child.

He'd opened up to her about it, about what had to be the most painful memory of his life. He'd let her in, and she'd reacted without thinking, holding him, needing to physically be there for him. Convincing herself she'd do it for anyone, and therefore it was okay.

Looking at Ruckus now, she thought maybe she'd been wrong. She never should have touched the Zane, let alone comforted him. Yet she couldn't be certain that if it all happened again she'd do it differently. A strong part of her feared she wouldn't, and the other part of her was relieved by the fact that she couldn't turn back time to find out.

"I love you, too," Ruckus said, and it was good to hear.

Because at least that was one thing she was certain about.

CHAPTER 20

Y ou're going to have to take these three with you."

Delaney glanced over to the older man standing across the table from her.

True to his word, Trystan had hired her a tutor, a middle-aged Kint named Lockan. He had silver hair and pale pink eyes rimmed in gold, and had spent twenty-some years on Earth, living among humans. After only one lesson, it wasn't hard to believe he was the Kints' top expert on all things Earth and, as a bonus, highly skilled with Vakar politics.

"Don't worry," Lockan said, noting her slightly panicked expression. "They're written in English." He glanced over his shoulder in the direction of the Zane.

Trystan had introduced them about two hours ago, and then had chosen a window seat across the room. There was an open book in his lap he'd seemed engrossed with, but as soon as the tutor looked his way, he gave them his attention.

"You should consider teaching her our written language as well, Zane," Lockan suggested. Then, before he could get a response, he added, "We're ready for you now."

Delaney frowned. She'd thought it odd when Trystan stuck around even though he clearly wasn't planning on participating. Was there more to this lesson than she'd originally been told? She watched as he set his book aside and rose, making his way toward the table she was seated at.

"Earth politics," he explained, easily picking up on her silent question. "I'll be studying that with you."

"It's wise for both of you to be well versed in it," Lockan agreed with a nod, shuffling through a pile of stacked pages in front of him.

Trystan took the chair closest to her, smiling softly. Then a sheet of paper slid across the table to him, and he turned away to read it. His copy was written with strange letters and symbols Delaney couldn't recognize, which was why she was relieved when she received her own and it was in familiar writing.

"This is the basic syllabus," Lockan told them. "Feel free to jump ahead in your free time if you're able."

Why did Delaney suddenly feel like she was back in high school?

Lockan ran through it with them once and then began that day's lesson.

Within five minutes it became painfully obvious Trystan actually knew more about how her government worked than she did. She'd hated Civics and Law back at Cymbeline, and had passed with a slightly tarnished C plus, after which she'd promptly forgotten everything she'd learned.

The next few hours passed in a blur, and due to information overload, Delaney barely registered it when their first lesson was over. She said good-bye to Lockan before he exited the room, and began collecting her things, making sure not to forget anything.

"I'm determined to become smarter than you," she said to Trystan while he waited for her.

Instead of replying, he took the pile of books from her arms and walked to the door, dropping them into the arms of the Teller standing guard there. He gave the man an order about bringing them to Delaney's room, and then turned back to her with a grin.

"Now that that's taken care of"—he motioned toward the hall—"shall we?"

They had another meeting with Co Gailie next, and apparently he was eager to get on with it. "When's your birthday?" she asked as they headed away from the library.

Her first lesson had been about the different and similar holidays between Kint and Vakar. The one that had most stuck out to her was the way they each chose to celebrate birthdays differently.

Back home, birthdays for her had been a big deal to her mom and dad. They'd throw a huge bash and invite the entire town. Of course, the parties had been more for them to impress the neighbors and reestablish themselves in the community, but she'd always had fun anyway.

The Vakar did not throw huge parties. Instead they returned to their childhood homes and spent the day alone with their parents. Apparently it was a way of honoring them, thanking them for their sacrifices and for helping turn the birthday person into who they were. It was sweet, but low-key.

The Kint did the exact opposite. On their birthdays they visited a new destination. That was the only traditional part. Once they got to this place they'd never been before—whether it be a city, a town, or even just part of the town they'd grown up in—they could do whatever they liked.

The whole thing had gotten her curious about Trystan, and how he might choose to spend his birthday. The types of places he'd gone to in the past, and why he'd picked them.

"It's coming up actually," he said, as if just recalling. "About a month from now."

Used to his non-answers, she let it slide. "What are you planning on doing?"

He shrugged his broad shoulders. "I hadn't thought of it. Something with you, I imagine."

Delaney looked away, keeping her gaze straight ahead as they turned down another corridor.

They hadn't spoken about the other night when he'd come to her rooms, and she was grateful.

She didn't know why she'd felt the need to comfort him. The reason didn't matter anyway; she'd done it, it was over, and there was no way for her to take it back even if she wanted to.

"Did you understand law 6B12 when Lockan was explaining it to you?" Trystan asked, thankfully pulling her mind back to her studies. A safe topic.

She nodded and began explaining it to him in her own words. When she got a part wrong, he politely corrected her, then allowed her to continue. They passed the rest of the walk this way, so when they came to the doors leading into the conference room, it felt like no time at all had gone by.

Gailie was already standing across the long table, waiting, and she bowed her head when they entered. They took their seats first and she quickly followed, a wide smile stretching across her friendly face.

"We've reached the halfway point," she began excitedly. "How are you both feeling?"

"Confident," Trystan said, placing his arms on the sides of his chair. The move caused his elbow to brush against Delaney.

"And you, Lissa?"

"Things are going well, thank you." She tried not to focus on how hot Trystan's skin was on her own.

"That's good to hear. Today, to mark the midway point, we're going to have the Giving." Gailie folded her hands on the table top before her. "Have you thought of what you want to ask of Delaney, Zane?"

"I have." His expression gave nothing away.

Delaney glanced between the two of them. "Apologies, but I'm not sure what the Giving is."

"Of course." Gailie waved at her. "I've purposefully tried not to bombard you with all the steps up front, but obviously you need to know this one now. The Giving is meant to further ensure that you and your partner are at a good place. A place where understanding, trust, and compromise exist."

Right . . . No. She schooled her features.

"You will each ask one thing from the other that has to be given. No matter what it is," Gailie finished.

"Anything?" That seemed too easy. Delaney risked glancing at Trystan out of the corner of her eye.

His were narrowed.

"Anything at all," she repeated.

If Delaney could ask for anything, that meant she could ask for this whole business to be over with. Was that the real purpose of this exercise? If someone had changed their mind, they got this easy, and discreet, out?

Of course, she'd also have to ask for her friends' release, which would make two things instead of one. Unless she only asked for them to be released . . . She nibbled at the inside of her cheek, returning her gaze to Gailie. If she did that, she'd be letting on that Trystan was holding hostages and blackmailing her into all this.

"Whenever you're ready," Gailie said to her, indicating she was to go first.

"We never selected a Sworn." A plan was formulating, and Delaney decided to go with it.

Caught off guard, Trystan stiffened in his chair. "I went over the files you selected. I just haven't found the time to make a permanent choice. I believe Sanzie was at the top of your list?"

By list, he meant the piece of blank paper she'd scrawled Sanzie's name across and stuck in the top file.

"She was." She took a breath to calm her nerves, prepared for rejection no matter the rules. "I have another person in mind now."

"Do tell?" Trystan's words were forced, and he rested his chin on the palm of one hand. In his eyes, the warning was clear.

"Sanzie should still be made Sworn," she said, "but as your main guard, not mine."

"A Sworn is more than a guard," he corrected. "It's a commander. They have far more responsibility than just trailing you around."

He was making a jab at Ruckus, and before she could help it, her expression darkened. It took her a moment to get ahold of herself, to brush the anger off and get them back on track. When she spoke again, there was a heavier note to her tone that was impossible to miss.

"I'm the Lissa of Vakar," she reminded him. "Therefore, it's only right that I also have a Vakar guarding me." She held up a hand when he opened his mouth to argue, seeing the fire in his eyes. "I want Pettus."

His mouth dropped open and he slammed it shut, blinking at her.

"Sanzie and Pettus can work together, and Pettus is already someone I trust. He'll do everything he can to keep me safe, and we both know it. Having him visibly with me will also be another indicator to both the Vakar and Kint people that we've agreed on this bonding together."

Trystan thought it over, but with the intense way Gailie was watching the two of them, he couldn't decline.

"All right," he finally conceded, though he wasn't happy about it. "I'll contact Teller Pettus and have him brought on immediately."

"Very good." Gailie clapped her hands, and asked Trystan to take his turn.

Delaney braced herself. She couldn't even begin to guess what it was he'd ask for, but she couldn't react.

"I want you to have dinner with me," Trystan surprised her by saying. "In a dress I picked out for you, eating food I've selected. I want to show you a traditional Kint meal. Will you let me?"

He was asking her on a date. They were the only ones who knew it, but that was what it was. They ate together all the time—who else did she know here to have meals with?—but tonight was different. He'd never bothered with semantics, with asking her whether she wanted to do things with him.

She wanted to pretend that it was all for show, to help convince the coordinator that he was romantic, that their relationship was full of racing hearts and little cherubs with bows and arrows. But she knew better.

Something had changed between them when he'd talked about his mother. He'd opened up to her and she'd been there for him. Supporting him. Like a real betrothed would.

If running were an option, that was what she'd be doing right now. Far and fast, and she wouldn't look back.

"Yes," she said, hating how smoky her words came out. Hoping it wasn't as noticeable to him as it was to her. "How could I say no?"

There was a flash of something in his eyes; it might have been hurt, but it was gone before she could really inspect it, replaced with steel.

"Well, then." Gailie stood, drawing their attentions away from each other. "I'll be checking back in a few days, sooner than our usual meeting, to ensure that you've both followed through on your promises to each other. That's also when we'll conduct the compatibility test. Until then, enjoy each other's company. Zane Trystan. Lissa Delaney."

Neither of them bothered saying good-bye back to her, too caught up in their own private thoughts to even notice when she packed up and left.

DELANEY EXPECTED HIM to rush dinner, and was surprised when he didn't. After they'd left the coordinator meeting, he'd said he needed time to put it together.

That had been three days ago, and neither of them had spoken about it since. She'd mentioned Pettus once, though, and had received the same line. In order to mask the fact that Trystan had the Teller locked up downstairs prior to her asking for him as a guard, he was stalling. Making it seem like they were waiting for Pettus to arrive from somewhere in Vakar.

Fortunately, she had their lessons with Lockan to distract her. He made learning enjoyable, and simple enough for her to grasp alien concepts.

After their third lesson, she could honestly say he was actually one of her favorite aliens ever. Of course, they weren't real friends—he was her teacher—but he didn't talk down to her or even treat her like a Lissa. He was always polite, but in the way a decent person would be, and shared stories with her about places and things on Earth they'd both experienced.

It was weird, but it made her feel like she'd regained a connection to home, having someone to talk to about hippopotamuses and the *Mona Lisa*. It didn't even bother her when she noticed that Trystan often took notes of their discussions, writing down interesting features and things that he'd like to see himself.

Apparently that list he'd told her about actually existed.

They also continued to visit the training rooms, frequently honing her skills in both hand-to-hand and even shooting. The Kint way of fighting had subtle differences from the Vakar, which Trystan was teaching her. Training provided a good outlet.

Plus, she got to hit him. Or at least she got to try. He was still mostly too fast for her, but every once in a while she'd land a blow she could be proud of.

"Tired, Lissa?" Sanzie asked her on their way back from a particularly grueling training session.

Delaney groaned, not bothering to cover up the fact that she was exhausted and achy. Luckily, the new Sworn took the hint, and didn't bother her with any other questions.

As they silently made their way to her rooms, all Delaney could think about was the move Trystan had been trying to teach her that day. She kept it on replay in her mind, hoping to figure out how to perfect it herself.

She was so caught up in this, she almost didn't realize she and Sanzie weren't alone when they entered the sitting room.

Pettus stood from the couch and smiled at her sheepishly. She was so excited, she forgot all about sleep, rushing to him.

Delaney wrapped her arms around his waist, giving herself a moment to bask in his company before pulling back. The bruises she'd seen on him had all healed, and though he was a bit pale from having been locked in a cell, away from the sun, he didn't look any worse for wear.

"How did you do it?" he asked, keeping his voice low. He glanced over at Sanzie, who was pretending not to listen. He'd been given a new Vakar uniform, the long forest-green sleeves intact and wrinkle free, black pants pressed.

"Upside to having to jump through binding preparation hoops," she joked, and when he didn't so much as crack a smile, she sighed. "How've you been since the last time I saw you?"

It'd only been a few days, but a lot could happen in that time, even when confined to a small space. Especially when. Their mental states had seemed fine when she'd spoken to them, though their anger levels hadn't petered at all, unsurprisingly.

"Not well," he confided. "Ruckus is going insane down there, between his worry for you and fear for Vakar."

"Getting you out was the only play I had," she said. "And even that took coercion and the presence of our coordinator. There's no way he's letting Ruckus out anytime soon."

"I assume"—Pettus took a step closer to the window, tugging her with him to put more space between them and Sanzie—"you have a plan?"

Delaney glanced toward Sanzie, to find the other woman already watching her.

"Unfortunately," Sanzie said, "I've been ordered not to leave the two of you alone. Apologies, Lissa. I would if I could—"

"I don't want to get you in trouble," Delaney stopped her.

"I was given strict instruction to tell you to check the bedroom." Sanzie angled her chin in that direction. "Dinner will be within the hour."

She somehow wasn't surprised. Of course he'd schedule it the same night he let Pettus out. Though it wasn't like it was going to be easy talking to Pettus with the new Sworn around anyway. As nice as Sanzie was being, Delaney wasn't delusional; obviously Trystan was using her as a spy.

"It's good to see you." She rested a hand on Pettus's arm, staring at him pointedly so that he understood not to argue. "Hopefully we can talk more later. I've got to get ready."

"Delaney." He grabbed her wrist when she went to pass. After a tense moment he let her go, giving a single nod. There was nothing they could do about their short reunion.

"I'm to brief you, Teller," Sanzie said to him as Delaney entered her bedroom.

She left the door open, allowing their words to filter into the room as she walked toward the bed. A dress had been laid out for her, a deep red almost the same crimson as Trystan's eyes. It was long-sleeved, though it only dropped to about her knees, and had two diamond-shaped cutouts at either side, right at the waistline.

"He is way too into fashion," she mumbled to herself, lifting the dress by the shoulders and holding it up to the light. That was when she noticed the accompanying jewelry that had been set next to it. A thick bronze chain with five dime-sized sapphires, and matching earrings.

Delaney rolled her eyes and stepped back to glance down at the shoes, a pair of brown leather high heels. She'd never wished for a pair of sweatpants more. Why couldn't the Lissa wear whatever she damn well pleased? Why did it always have to be sparkly and color-coded and high-heeled?

". . . hang back. I'll take lead," Sanzie was in the middle of a sentence when Delaney tuned back in. "You aren't allowed to touch her. And make sure to address her properly, not as friends. She's the Lissa of Vakar now."

"The Zane needs help convincing the world that Delaney—Sorry," he corrected himself, "that *Lissa* Delaney really wants to be here. With him. Even though we both know that's a lie, and your leader is insane."

"Pettus." Delaney took the dress and moved to the other side of the room, farther from the door. "Don't antagonize her. I want this to work."

There was a pause and then he called back, "As do I, Lissa. Apologies."

Delaney got dressed quickly, slipping out of her clothes and into the new ones with little preamble. She stubbornly ignored the urge to check herself in the mirror.

"Aren't my legs going to get cold?" she asked, breezing back into the room. They were bare from ankle to mid-thigh, and there was already a slight chill.

"The Zane has taken that into account, Lissa," Sanzie told her, but didn't elaborate. Instead she motioned toward the door and bowed. "If you're ready."

With a single shoulder shrug, she followed.

CHAPTER 21

She could see candlelight flickering from beyond the glass the moment they turned the corner. She'd begun to recognize their path, and had been about to confirm with Sanzie that they were headed toward the Ice Dome—which was what she called it in her head—but no longer needed to.

The sparks of orange seemed to multiply the closer they got to the transparent doors, so that her eyes were already trailing around the room as the sentry opened it.

Any trace of snow was gone, leaving behind polished white stone. The dome was closed at the top, and from the other side of the walls an inky night surrounded them. Candles had been set everywhere, circling the inner perimeter, trailing in spirals and rows across the floor and over stone benches that had been buried during her first visit. The wax was silver, and the candles had been set in bronze bases, some taller and thinner than others.

The table in the center of the room held only two place settings, a few silver trays, and a pitcher. Weaving through all these, across the expanse of the table, were vines with tiny star-shaped flowers. The glowing bursts of yellow and white trailed all the way to the stone floor.

It'd been a while since Delaney had last seen stellaperier flowers.

She paused just inside the doorway, the same wave of awe washing over her as the first time Ruckus had shown them to her.

Trystan was standing across the table, watching her silently. When she was able to snap herself out of it, she headed toward him, noticing the way he swallowed as if nervous.

"I hope it's warm enough," he said softly, taking her hand when she was close. "The floors are heated."

She was tempted to reach down and touch the ground to see for herself. "It's fine."

"Sit." He waved at the chair next to his, which was already pulled out. Once she was in it, he lowered to his own. "Pettus has met your standards, I assume?"

"If by that you mean I've noted he hasn't gotten any more bruises," she said, watching as he reached for the pitcher, "then yes. That is a thing that I saw. You aren't getting a thank-you, though, if that's what you're hoping for."

"I'm not naive," he assured her, filling the glass goblet set in front of her with a familiar light brown liquid. Steam billowed up from the top, the scent of chocolate and cinnamon following.

"Squa." She was already reaching for it before he'd even begun filling his own, but he playfully brushed her hand aside, taking his traditional first sip.

The heated drink felt wonderful, chasing away any remaining chills she felt. Cupping her hands around it to keep warm, she took in the room a second time.

"Did you do all of this?" she asked. The candles reflected in the glass around them, making it seem like there were twice as many, like the two of them were in a sea of flames.

"You like it." It wasn't a question, and he sounded all too pleased with himself.

She should have been annoyed by that, but she wasn't, because it was true. How could she not be impressed?

"What are we doing here, Trystan?" They were alone in the room, and she doubted anyone was standing outside the dome, observing them. There was no one here to convince.

"We're having dinner, Delaney," he said casually, like this wasn't an insanely romantic setting and she shouldn't be suspicious.

Yeah, right. She wanted to know his intentions, mostly so she could put a pin in them before this went any further. But he was already lifting the lid off her plate, and the food beneath it effectively distracted her.

It was shaped like an upside-down pie, though with a light green flaky crust and lines of dark purple sauce crisscrossing the top. The smell was interesting, a mixture of butter and unknown spices.

"It's green." She wondered if it was similar to green pita bread.

"You have something against the color?" He chuckled. "That would be ironic."

"Because I'm technically Vakar now." She waved at him. "Yeah, yeah. But seriously, why is it green? Is it made out of plants?"

"In a sense. They're an active ingredient while making the dough. They're broken down beforehand and added to the mixture. You can barely taste it. It's mostly for aesthetics."

She quirked a brow. "You mean you purposefully chose something this color?"

"Surprised it's not blue?" The corner of his mouth turned up in a half smile.

"Shocked."

"Just wait until you try it." He took up her knife and fork and cut a small piece off the edge. A gooey mixture oozed out. It looked cheesy, with bits of brown, white, and purple.

Delaney automatically opened her mouth when he brought the fork up, allowing him to gently ease the bite onto her tongue. It tasted a lot like it smelled, with a hint of sweetness and a savory note similar to fried turkey.

Trystan grinned, taking up another forkful, this time feeding himself. Then he placed the utensils down and lifted the covering from his own plate, exposing a different dish.

There were two of them, and they were circular with a browned crust resembling baked cinnamon sugar all around the sides. It was layered, and looked like it'd been cooked in a mug. Something like an egg had been placed on top, though the four yokes were bright red.

"What is that?" she asked as he cut off a small section and raised the fork to her mouth a second time. There was something between the layers, light like a custard.

"Just try it," he ordered, and without waiting, he pressed it against her lips so that she was forced to open them.

"It's sweet," she said as soon as the sugary flavor hit her. The egg-type thing on top tasted nothing like eggs did back home. Instead it was almost like she was eating a muffin with a strange tangy sauce. A weird combination, but not entirely bad. "I should have known."

"It's a traditional breakfast dish," he told her, clearly trying to convince her he hadn't chosen dessert for their meal.

Done with being hand-fed, she plucked the fork from between his fingers and dug back into the upside-down pie on her plate. That was definitely her preferred dish, and she was ashamed to admit it was probably one of the best things she'd ever tasted.

"You're very food oriented." Not that she was currently complaining.

He shrugged and began eating the untouched circular breakfast in front of him.

"Back home we'd call you a foodie." She angled her head at him, pretending to inspect him from chin to torso.

He used his knife to point at the pie-like thing. "I was worried I'd overcooked the bida, but you seem pleased with it."

She almost dropped her fork. "*You* made this?"

"I cooked everything we'll eat tonight." He smirked challengingly. "Why? Impressed?"

"That you enjoy cooking"—she looked at the food—"or that you're good at it?"

"Is the Ander not skilled in this department then?"

She did not want to talk about Ruckus, especially not with him, so she gave a single shake of her head and stuffed her face with another bite.

"Are you?"

Another shake.

He frowned. "How did you survive on Earth if neither of you can cook?"

"It's called eating out." She rolled her eyes for good measure. "Besides, I didn't say I can't cook; it's just that I won't be winning any awards, is all. I can certainly boil water and fry up a burger."

"Cooking relaxes me," he divulged. "It gives me control—"

"Because you need more of that."

"And time away from responsibility and duty," he continued as if she hadn't spoken. "I enjoy it very much. My mother taught me, actually. She was very good. Nothing I make even comes close to hers."

For a moment she didn't know what to say. On the one hand, his admission that someone actually did something better than he did was progress. On the other, it was about his mother, an already shaky subject that could only lead down a rocky road.

"My parents have a private chef," she said. "I don't think they've ever even used the toaster themselves."

"So this chef made all your meals as well?"

"Yup." She feigned intense interest in the food in front of her, trying not to notice how cloudy his eyes got when he thought of his mom. How human he began to look.

"I'll show you a few things in the kitchen," he decided. "Maybe next time you'll cook for me instead."

She couldn't help it—she laughed.

His gaze darkened. "Don't ruin the evening, Delaney."

"You're the one who brought it up." She inhaled and tried to think of a safe topic to talk about. "Tell me about your favorite dish. Have I tried it yet?"

"You haven't, no. It's a traditional celebratory meal, so one that can't be served at random. It has to accompany a special occasion. It's also rather large; there are many portions, as it's meant to feed a big party." He took a sip from his cup. "I ordered it for our binding."

She almost choked on the bite she was chewing, gulping down half the contents of her glass to stop it. Their binding was definitely another topic she did not want to discuss with him. Ever. She'd resigned herself to being here, in this overly romantic setting, sharing food with him. But talk of the future was pushing it too far.

"It's going to happen," Trystan said, his voice dropping an octave.

"Please"—she took a shaky breath—"not right now."

"Why not? Whether we talk about it now or later, it won't change anything. We're a little over halfway through the exercises already, the date has been set, the invites sent out. I selected a dress that will look perfect on you—"

"Stop." She slammed both palms onto the table, rattling the contents. After a moment she said, "I'm not the one ruining the evening now, Trystan."

"These decisions are usually ones made by both parties."

"Yes, well, I'm sure typically both parties are also in agreement that bonding for life is what they want. Our situation is a little different. I don't want to be here. Not on Xenith. Not in Inkwell. Not—"

"With me."

At some point during her tirade, he'd rested an arm across the back of her chair. It'd brought him much closer to her, and now that she'd noticed, she could see the way his pupils had dilated. The crimson ring around his cornflower-blue eyes had thickened and darkened, a sure sign he was close to his limit.

Self-preservation kept her from outright confirming that statement, because things had been going relatively well—for them, anyway—and she didn't want to push him over the edge and have it all blow up in her face. Especially so soon after he'd let Pettus out.

"I don't know what you want me to say," she ended up admitting.

"Something I fear that's going to take you a lot longer to get to than I'd hoped," he said.

She knew she should pull away, but his expression kept her there, frozen. "We're doing this for our people."

He glanced down at her mouth, distracted. "That's how I thought it all began. Perhaps the Ander is more adept than me after all. At least in this one thing."

"What are you talking about?" And why was Ruckus involved?

"I want a partner, Delaney." He cupped the side of her face, tilting up her chin so that she was forced to stare directly into his eyes. "Someone I can confide in. Someone I can trust. I've always known I was going to rule, and I thought I'd do it alone, like my father, but . . ."

"Trystan." They were getting dangerously close to the conversation they'd had that night he'd told her about his mother. A night she'd tried really hard to forget. He'd said things that had implied he really was in it for the long haul, as he'd once claimed.

She hadn't believed him then.

She was starting to now.

And that was utterly terrifying.

"I've been distracted," he told her. "Determined not to allow myself to get tied to someone like Olena. Determined not to fail my people." His jaw clenched. "My father. When the Ander suggested it, I thought he was crazy, but now I see it."

She did not want to know what *it* was.

"We'll be good together, Delaney. With you by my side, I can achieve everything I've ever wanted. Everything my father couldn't. We'll be able to unify not only Xenith, but our two planets as well. A better race, stronger, and vastly superior."

"To who?" Had he completely lost his mind? What the hell was in that breakfast stuff?

"Everyone. We can do it. We can have everything."

"I don't want everything," she whispered, and when he stilled, she knew he'd heard her. "You were raised to be this; I wasn't. My dreams are different."

"Your dreams are of the Ander, you mean," he practically sneered.

He wasn't just saying these things to try to convince her or manipulate her. He meant them, and that was the worst thing that could happen because it meant her plan had no chance of working.

They'd made an agreement, but Ruckus had probably been right about that, too, and she couldn't cope with there being no way out of this. Couldn't lose that single shred of hope that, eventually, she'd get to go home. Back to her life.

"Let's go over everything *I've* given you," he said, his voice dipping dangerously low. "A title. Two palaces. Another planet—"

"Removal from my home." She couldn't believe they were having this conversation. "Separation from my friends and my family—"

"Choice over the next Sworn. My favorite foods. *Your* favorite foods—"

"When you've remembered to feed me!" Both of their voices continued to rise with every passing second.

"That useless Teller!"

"His name is Pettus!"

"The clothes on your back!"

"Yeah, because you took mine!"

"This!" Without letting her go, he indicated the candlelit room they were in.

"Now you're reaching," she declared without skipping a beat.

"Me!"

They both froze, equally caught off guard, so that all they could do was stare at each other for a long, breathy pause.

"Me," he finally repeated, sounding flustered by the revelation. Just as quickly he seemed to come to terms with it, so that when he spoke again, it was with conviction. "I've given you me."

Delaney's world narrowed down to a pinpoint. She wasn't even sure if she was still breathing.

"Am I interrupting?" They hadn't heard the Rex come in, but now the sound of his voice had them jumping apart like two teenagers caught reaching second base in their parents' basement.

It took her a moment to process that he was standing in the doorway, a single blond brow lifted.

"Father." Trystan cleared his throat and rose from his seat slowly. He absently smoothed down the front of his shirt, then held out his right hand to help Delaney to her feet as well.

She took it, actually grateful when he didn't immediately let go once she was standing. Her legs suddenly felt like jelly, and she wasn't sure she'd be able to remain upright on her own. In person the Rex was even more intimidating than she'd estimated he would be, especially when he was looking at them like that.

"I wasn't expecting you," Trystan continued in an even tone that Delaney was impressed with.

"That was the point," the Rex replied tersely, glancing at their clasped hands and then at the romantically lit room.

A girl stepped up behind him, not fully entering, but coming close enough for the light to illuminate her pale face and dark hair.

"What the hell is she doing here?" Trystan growled half a second before Delaney was able to.

Olena was still as a statue at the Rex's back, her face blank.

"Is that any way to treat a guest, son?" the Rex clucked his tongue.

"She's no guest of mine. The only reason you'd have to bring her along is that she's too important to leave behind."

"Caution, son," the Rex warned. "You're right about how important she is. To getting what *you* want. You'll be wise to keep that in mind before you spout more childish complaints."

Trystan clamped his mouth shut, his fingers tightening around Delaney's. If he noticed he was clinging to her, he didn't show it, which gave her the impression it was subconscious.

"It's good to meet you in person, Rex Hortan," she said, proud when her voice didn't shake and give her away.

"Likewise, Lissa Delaney." He inspected her and motioned her forward with the curve of his fingers.

She didn't want to go but was smart enough to know disobeying wasn't an option. Still, she had to practically pry her hand from Trystan's, all while keeping the fact that she was doing so from being obvious.

It was hard to find the correct balance; she didn't want to walk to him too quickly and seem eager, but she also couldn't go at a snail's pace. When she thought she was close enough, she stopped, hoping that he wouldn't find insult in the few feet she'd kept between them.

"You're taller than I thought you'd be," the Rex told her. The corner of his mouth lifted in a friendly smile.

She wasn't buying it.

"Apologies for interrupting," he added when she didn't reply fast enough for him.

"Not at all," she said.

"Are you sure?" He glanced pointedly over her shoulder at his son. "From where I'm standing, it certainly appeared as though I'd interrupted. Lovers' spat, was it?"

She caught herself from gulping, and tilted her chin up another notch instead. "You misread the situation, that's all. Things are fine between Trystan and me."

He grunted. "You'll forgive me for finding that hard to believe, Lissa. I know my son; he's almost impossible to get along with. I doubt you enjoy his company as much as you're trying to let on, but"—he held up a hand—"I commend you for that. You've certainly more skill than your predecessor."

Delaney's eyes trailed to Olena, expecting to see outrage. She was confused when she found that the other girl hadn't so much as twitched at the insult.

"Have you gotten to dessert yet?"

"We were just about to," she said, even though it was obviously a lie. How much of their argument had he heard?

"You're in for a treat then, if Trystan made it himself," he told her. "Cooking is a complete waste of time, mind you, but you know my son." He caught Trystan's gaze, held it. "Once he has an idea in his head, it's next to impossible to get him to see reason."

"I'll have rooms made up for you, Father." Trystan was suddenly at her side again, touching her elbow comfortingly.

"Already taken care of," the Rex assured him. "I've taken the East Wing and placed extra guards at Olena's room."

"You aren't placing her in a cell?"

"Not necessary." He smiled at Olena. "We have an understanding. She behaves and gets to keep her fingers and toes. Isn't that right, Ond?"

"Yes, Rex." Olena bowed her head.

Delaney had been apprehensive before, but now she was petrified. What had he done to Olena to make her so submissive?

"Perhaps it's best if the Lissa takes dessert in her chambers," the Rex suggested. "There's much for you and me to discuss. The sooner the better. You understand, Lissa Delaney, don't you?"

She stretched her mouth into her sweetest smile and nodded.

"Wait." Trystan's hand tightened around hers when she went to step away.

"It's fine." She turned back to him, settling her features into a more honest version of a smile. "Really. You two talk. I'll be fine."

"We aren't finished," he protested.

"Are you seriously willing to risk pissing off your father?" she asked, sending it through their fittings so the Rex wouldn't hear.

He paused, seeming to weigh her words before he eased his hand out of hers. "I'll come to you later."

"I'm tired," she said. "I doubt I'll even make it to dessert."

He wanted to fight with her, it was so obvious, but he practiced restraint she was certain was more for his father's benefit than hers.

"Good night, Rex." She bowed her head to him as she passed, making sure not to get too close to Olena as she did so.

"Until again, Lissa Delaney," he said, then quietly watched her go.

She managed to keep it together when the doors shut at her back, knowing they were see-through and not wanting to risk that the Rex was still looking. It wasn't until she was around the corner and definitely out of sight that she allowed herself to slump against the wall.

"Delaney." Pettus reached for her.

Her eyes were closed, but she felt his hand on her arm. "I'm fine. I just need a moment."

"The Rex has that effect on people," Sanzie told her. It was just the three of them, but it was still nice of the Sworn to try to make her feel better.

"Thanks." She took a deep breath, then straightened. She went to step away but then stopped, glancing back down the way they'd come. "Do you think—"

"The Zane will be fine," Sanzie interrupted, easily picking up on what she was getting at.

Pettus frowned and Delaney had to look away to keep him from seeing the rush of guilt. Why should it matter to her how the Rex dealt with Trystan? Shouldn't she be hoping he gave him hell, instead of worrying for his well-being like an idiot?

"Let's go." She needed this day to be over.

They escorted her the rest of the way in silence, Pettus keeping up his frown the whole way.

CHAPTER 22

A few hours later someone came to her door. The fact that they had bothered to wait after knocking gave away it wasn't Trystan, and Delaney slowed on her way toward it.

Not that her hesitation mattered. Sanzie allowed Olena to enter a second later, with Pettus close on her heels. Once the two of them were through, the Sworn returned to her post in the hall, leaving the door open.

"What are you doing here?" Delaney demanded, not bothering to mask her ire. Hadn't the Rex just got done saying she'd be heavily guarded and confined to her rooms?

Pettus kept close by, but Olena paid him no mind, traveling around the sitting area, touching things as she went. She trailed her fingers across the backing of one of the chairs on the way to the fireplace, the corner of her lush red lips turning upward in a mocking half smile. Whatever game she'd been playing in the Ice Dome, it'd clearly been for the Rex's benefit, because the meek girl was gone.

"Well, you've really gone up in the world haven't you, tiny human?" she cooed, propping an arm against the chair.

Her midnight-black hair was only a few inches longer than it had been the last time they'd seen each other. She narrowed her gold eyes, the deep purple rim around them catching the firelight and appearing darker, almost black.

"It's treason to speak to the Lissa that way," Pettus came to her defense, taking a stiff step closer to Olena, who lifted a well-manicured hand to ward him off.

"Apologies, *Lissa* Delaney," she sneered, her grin turning sharklike. "I'm impressed, that's all. Everyone seems to think you're better than me, and yet here we are, with you desperately climbing the social ladder."

Delaney opened her mouth to argue but quickly shut it. Olena didn't know that she was being blackmailed into this marriage, and with the Rex keeping her close, it wasn't worth exposing that detail.

"They let you roam the halls freely?" Delaney crossed her arms, determined to get through this—whatever *this* was.

"I'm allowed to go where I please," Olena told her arrogantly, even going so far as to lift her chin.

"So long as it's in the general vicinity of the Rex, you mean." Delaney grunted. "Our ideas of freedom are clearly very different. What are you doing here anyway, besides tainting my airspace with your presence?"

Olena scrunched up her nose, the first sign of true emotion she'd shown all night. "You're starting to sound like him. *Trystan.*"

"You say his name like he's some type of fungus."

Olena stared at her searchingly, running her gaze across her face before she blinked. "You like him."

"What?" She forced herself not to look at Pettus. "That's ridiculous."

"Yes." She nodded vigorously. "Yes, it is. But that doesn't change the fact that it's true. You've actually thawed toward the Zane. Goodness, you're naive. What did he promise you? Besides my rightful position, of course. What was it? You can tell me." Her expression turned mocking. "I'm great at keeping secrets."

"This isn't about my feelings, or non-feelings as it were, for Trystan." She kept her voice as steady as possible, though frustration caused her hands to shake slightly. "Whatever reason you're here, Olena, I don't care. I just want you to leave. Now."

"Tossing me out?" She tsk-tsked. "Where are your manners? Didn't they warn you that as Lissa you have to take council with all types of unseemly people?"

"How did she get here?" Delaney directed this to Pettus, finally giving him her attention. She was glad to find he wasn't looking at her the same way he had back in the halls earlier. There was no confusion or suspicion there, only annoyance toward Olena.

"A few of the Rex's guards escorted her," he explained tersely. "They're waiting outside with Sworn Sanzie. They insisted it was the Rex's will that she be allowed a meeting with you."

Did Trystan know? She caught herself from blatantly asking, clearing her throat at the last second.

"You have sixty seconds to say whatever it is you came here to say, and then I want you gone."

"I didn't come here to say anything," Olena said. "I was curious, that's all."

"Of?"

"My replacement," she stated matter-of-factly. "I've been told you fooled the council. How sweet."

"Leave."

Instead of listening, Olena slowly made her way around the chair, raising her hands when Pettus let out a warning growl in the back of his throat. She kept her eyes locked with his, clearly hoping to silently assure him she wasn't going to do Delaney any harm.

Oddly, Delaney believed it, and remained where she was while she approached.

"That was a lie," Olena whispered as soon as she was close enough, glancing pointedly toward the direction of the still-open door. "I came here to make you a deal. I hear those are things you tend to take an interest in."

Wow, for a supposed prisoner, she certainly heard a lot.

"I want what's mine," she continued when Delaney didn't say anything. "This is my life you're living, and I want it back. In return, I'm willing to help you reclaim yours. And I'm up for offering you the same things Trystan has. Whatever those are."

Delaney was caught off guard, and Olena must have misinterpreted that as rejection.

"Just help me, damn it," the words came out louder than the last, and Olena stomped her foot for good measure.

Sanzie peered into the room, another Kint Teller who Delaney hadn't seen before appearing directly over her left shoulder.

"Everything's fine," Delaney told them. "Olena is throwing a tantrum. I bet we're all surprised, right?"

The Kint Teller chuckled and then disappeared out of sight once more. After a moment of hesitation Sanzie did the same, leaving the three of them relatively alone again.

"How do you expect me to help you?" she demanded in a hushed whisper before Olena could voice her outrage at the insult. "It's not like I can walk up to the Rex and tell him I've changed my mind. Not to mention how Trystan would react."

"I have a plan." Olena rolled her gold-and-purple eyes skyward and heaved a dramatic sigh. "Obviously."

Yeah, because her plans always worked out so well. Delaney shouldn't even be contemplating this, shouldn't want to hear more. And yet . . . What if she really had a viable plan? Could she even be trusted long enough to consider using it?

No. No, she really couldn't.

"I have a plan of my own, thanks." Even though, after tonight, it was becoming more and more clear she'd miscalculated.

"Really?" Olena asked. "I doubt it's any good."

"Whether it is or isn't, at least I came up with it without your help."

She canted her head. "You're not sure it's going to work."

Since when had Olena been perceptive? Maybe spending all that time locked up had given her some introspection. Or, and this was the more likely option, she'd always been this way and people just hadn't realized.

"We're done here." Delaney motioned toward Pettus, hoping he'd take the hint and remove Olena before Delaney did something rash like punch the girl.

Olena allowed Pettus to take her arm and tug her back a few steps before plastering that malicious grin back on her face. "Remember, human, I tried. You're the one who turned me away."

"Take her." Pettus thrust her out into the hall and then slammed the door before Sanzie could take a step inside. He locked it with the control panel to the right and rushed back over to Delaney. "We have less than a minute. How are you, really?"

"Did that sound overly ominous to you?" She was still staring at the closed door where Olena had just been.

"She makes hollow threats all the time." He rested his hands on her shoulders, the contact forcing her to meet his gaze. "Delaney. Talk to me."

How was she? Unsettled, scared, worried, anxious . . . The list went on and on. But they didn't have time to get into any of that.

"Confused," she said. "Why do you think the Rex is here?"

"I'm not sure," he admitted. "But it can't be for anything good. You told her you had a plan. Did you mean it?"

"Yes." She frowned, shook her head. "She was right, though. I don't think it'll work anymore."

"Why not?"

"Because, Trystan—"

The door unlocked from the outside, and as if she'd conjured him, there he was, glaring. The Zane shoved the door out of his way as it swung back, his steps determined. His hair was slightly out of place, and his cheeks were flushed with anger.

"You couldn't even last a day," he growled at Pettus as he approached. "I was lenient, letting you out even though I knew it was a bad idea. And you couldn't even follow one rule. Don't touch."

His hand wrapped around Pettus's neck faster than any of them could blink. Another heartbeat later and Trystan was pressing Pettus against the window, holding him up off the ground by a good foot.

Pettus dangled there, gripping the Zane's wrist, his heels slamming against the wall. His face was already starting to turn an off-shade of purple.

"Stop it!" Delaney rushed over, shoving at Trystan's side. "What the hell are you doing? Put him down! He just wanted to make sure I was okay after Olena!"

"Olena? She was here?" His grip eased, not by much.

"Yes!"

"What did she want?"

"Put him down and I'll tell you." When he didn't budge, she shoved at him again. "Trystan! Please!"

He let Pettus go as quickly as he'd taken him up, and the Teller dropped to the ground in a heap in front of the window. Trystan took a single step away.

"Don't," he ordered when Delaney went to kneel before her friend.

"I have to check on him."

Pettus pressed his forehead to the ground, wheezing.

"He's breathing, isn't he?"

"Barely!"

"Which is more than I wanted," he snapped. "Be grateful."

She stilled, feeling a wash of cold spread through her. For weeks now he'd been subtly trying to convince her she'd be happy here, with him. Hell, earlier he'd blatantly said so. Now this?

"So," she said, hardly recognizing her own voice when she spoke, "that's how it's going to be? Your daddy shows up and you magically turn back into the asshole?"

He pulled back as if she'd slapped him.

"No, it's good that I'm finding out now, before I let myself get manipulated into believing you actually meant any of those things you said. I know"—she held up a hand despite the fact that he hadn't even made moves to interrupt—"you're laughing on the inside, right? At the naive little human. Can you believe I actually thought I was doing a good job, too? Resisting?"

She motioned toward Pettus, whose breathing had finally started to even out. "He didn't think so, but obviously his opinion doesn't mean anything to you. Guess we both had me fooled. Olena was right. I really am an idiot."

"Delaney—"

"Enough." She was so far gone, she didn't even notice that he'd actually listened, clamping his mouth shut immediately after the order was out. All she saw was red, because as she was saying the words out loud, she was realizing they were true.

How could she? It wasn't just a betrayal to Ruckus, if what he'd just done to Pettus was any indicator, but to everyone she cared about.

"I don't give a damn how badly your father just hurt your feelings, or what he said to make you go off the deep end. I don't care, Trystan. That's no excuse, and I'm done helping you make them. You're going to leave, and Pettus is going to stay so that I can make sure he's all right. That's it. You've done enough damage for one night."

"Delaney—" He tried a second time, his tone unrecognizable.

"Get. Out." She sent the words telepathically, hoping they'd have more of an impact. Talking that way had always seemed more intimate to her, proof of a stronger connection between her and Ruckus.

Clearly Trystan felt the same, because it had the desired effect. For a moment he looked incredibly sad, almost enough that she started to feel an inkling of guilt. But then he spun on his heel and disappeared without a backward glance.

Even Sanzie gave them space, slowly easing the door shut, her gaze pinned to the ground right up until the door blocked her out.

Delaney didn't know how long she stood like that, staring at the door, silently seething. Then Pettus coughed, snapping her out of it, and she dropped down in front of him, gently reaching out.

He allowed her to help him into a sitting position, using the window wall to keep him upright. There were tears in his eyes, and dark splotches on his neck in the shape of fingers. The bruises would definitely be worse in the morning. His breathing had calmed at least, though he had to suck in his breaths through his teeth.

He opened his mouth and she shook her head to stop him. Talking right now was not in the cards; it would only cause him more harm.

"I'm so sorry," she told him, deflating. All that energy she'd spent berating Trystan leeched out of her, so that it was a struggle to keep her eyes open all of sudden. "I'm so sorry."

"It's—" He had to stop, and squeezed his eyes shut against the pain.

"It is my fault, though," she picked up. "I should have left you down there, where you'd be safe. I just thought . . . I don't know. It was selfish. I wanted a friendly face around, and I didn't trust any of Trystan's men, so on a whim I asked for you. I'm no better than Olena."

His hand shot out and took hers, and he applied pressure until she lifted her gaze to his.

"I wish we'd had our frequencies linked," she said. "That would make this conversation so much easier, given the circumstances."

She hadn't realized her feelings had altered toward Trystan until tonight, before this had happened to remind her how awful he could be.

But he was also sweet, like how he treated Dominan. And devoted, because he truly cared about what was best for Kint. And attentive— he'd tried so hard to keep her engaged in this new world.

And broken.

Losing his mother had put him in the sole care of a father who was a control freak and had to rest his attentions on an entire kingdom. How much time had he had for his only son? Delaney had gotten the impression not much.

Pettus's hand tightened on hers again, pulling her from her wayward thoughts. He was watching her closely, but there wasn't any judgment in his dark eyes.

"I love Ruckus." She licked her lips, needing a second so her voice wouldn't crack when she added, "You know that, right?"

He nodded without hesitation, then reached forward and tugged her into a tight hug. Her head tucked beneath his chin, he cradled her, comforting without saying a word.

CHAPTER 23

Delaney went about her morning as if everything were normal. That meant eating breakfast in her sitting room, then being escorted to the library for tutoring. There was only one small change to her routine.

She was alone.

It wasn't like she'd expected Trystan to be there, not after how he'd reacted the last time they'd fought—avoiding her until she forced him to confront her. For the most part she was glad he wasn't around, that she didn't have to fake a smile and pretend in front of the guards and their teacher that everything was fine between them.

Things were so far from fine, and despite what she'd said to him last night, secretly she did mostly blame the Rex. His random appearance put them both on edge. Add that to the fact that she knew how Trystan got whenever his dad was so much as mentioned, let alone actually there, and she understood why he'd been so angry last night.

That didn't excuse what he'd done to Pettus, of course, and she was still pissed. Comprehending something didn't necessarily mean agreeing with it.

By the time her lessons finally ended, Delaney was about ready to jump out of her skin. She was uncomfortable and anxious, and there was only one thing she could think of doing to help spend the extra adrenaline coursing through her veins.

"We're going to the training rooms," she told Sanzie and Pettus as she exited the library, not bothering to wait for a response.

"Are you sure, Lissa?" Sanzie asked, keeping a pace back while Pettus moved ahead to lead the way. "I could have something prepared for you instead."

"Not hungry." Even the thought of eating made her stomach clench into tight knots. "Besides, why should I alter my schedule just because the Zane is off pouting somewhere?"

Pettus choked, pretending to cough in a poor attempt to cover it up. The fact that he could even get those sounds out past his bruised throat was amazing. He'd woken this morning unable to get more than a forced whisper past his lips, though his voice had greatly improved throughout the day.

Trystan was lucky; if there'd been permanent damage, Delaney would never have forgiven him.

Sanzie didn't seem to find it as funny as the Teller. Delaney could feel the Sworn bristling behind her without having to turn to verify.

"The Zane has many important things to attend to," she disagreed curtly. "More so, since the Rex has arrived."

"Sure." Delaney rolled her eyes, glad that Sanzie couldn't see her do it.

Fortunately they reached the training room shortly after, putting an end to what no doubt would have turned into an argument. Seeing as how Sanzie was loyal to Trystan, fighting with her about him seemed pointless.

Really, all she wanted was to work up a sweat and hopefully shed some of these negative emotions. Clear her head. She wasn't sure when training had turned into a form of catharsis for her, but she was grateful for it.

At least, she was right up until she entered the room and found Trystan there.

He was going through defensive moves, blocking an invisible at-tacker with his arms and legs as he swiftly shot backward across the mat. His pants were looser than his usual style, only tight around his hips and ankles. And bloodred, another instantly notable difference.

He was also shirtless.

Delaney absently tilted her head to better follow his movements, watching his muscles ripple with each arch of his back and lift of an arm.

Right before he was about to reach the end of the mat, he switched from defense to offense, lashing out with lightning strikes that were, at times, hard for her to visually follow. It certainly drove home the fact that he'd been going easy on her during their sessions.

Feeling some of her confidence drain, Delaney rested her hands on her hips. She was in the middle of debating whether she should just turn around and leave when he finished delivering a fake death-blow and looked up.

The anger and bitterness in his eyes had her heartbeat speeding, and it didn't slow even when those things cleared, leaving regret and annoyance.

Trystan casually moved across the room to a towel rack, rubbing at his face and then behind his neck. Dropping the used cloth to the ground at his feet, he lifted his gaze a second time, feigning indiffer-ence when she was still standing there.

"I didn't know you'd be here," she croaked, hating herself for it. It was hard to concentrate with him standing there all sweaty and shirt-less, looking more alone than she'd ever seen him.

More than she'd ever seen anyone, actually. Ruckus had been lonely before they'd met, but in a different way. He'd been too busy to get involved with anyone, too career oriented and distracted by handling Olena to make many friends aside from Pettus. He'd wanted people to confide in; it'd just been too hard for him to find them.

Trystan's loneliness stemmed elsewhere.

Kint loved him, but he pushed people away, using intimidation and station as weapons. He chose his sentences carefully, so that his wording could wound just as painfully as the blade of a sword. The only friend she'd ever heard him talk about had died in the war, and while he treated Dom with care and, dare she say, love, she'd yet to see him interact with the boy's mother.

He made it seem like he didn't want friends, deflecting any sense of camaraderie, putting people in their supposed places. Even she'd believed him. He was arrogant and crass and didn't care about anything but achieving his goals. What use would someone like that have for friendship?

But it was a lie. All those things he put out in the world, they were all lies. He was an asshole, there was no doubt about that, yet it was by choice, not design. Was he afraid of getting hurt? Is that why he pushed people away before they even had a chance to get to know him?

More important, why did she care?

Sanzie cleared her throat, cluing Delaney into the fact she'd been staring far longer than was socially appropriate.

Pettus shifted half an inch closer and the Zane noticed.

"How is your neck, Teller?" he asked briskly, and it was obvious he wasn't used to checking up on people.

"I'll live," Pettus managed, eyes narrowing. "Thanks to the Lissa."

Trystan clenched his jaw but took the dig. "Fair enough."

"I figured I'd get some training done," Delaney said. That seemed like a good place to end their conversation. That was more than likely the closest to an apology Pettus was going to get.

Trystan dropped his eyes to the ground and nodded. "I'll go."

Before she knew what she was doing, she moved forward, stopping him with a hand on his arm. As soon as she'd made contact, she let go. His skin was heated, and touching him while he was half naked wasn't the best plan.

"Stay," she found herself saying. "I still need work on that one move you've been showing me. I don't think I'll get it on my own."

"Pettus can help you."

The disappointment she felt should have been off-putting enough to make her drop it. It wasn't.

"Vakar martial arts is so different from Kint's," she tried, glad that it was true and something she was aware of. "If I'm going to learn it properly, I should have a Kint teacher, don't you think?"

Trystan was so still, it was hard to tell if he was breathing. They were standing close enough, though, that when she focused, she could almost catch the rise and fall of his chest.

"Delaney," he said finally, her name a mere whisper off his lips. It sounded almost pleading, desperate and full of vulnerability.

Was it because he felt bad about last night? Was there a chance he'd deliver an actual apology after all?

"What are you doing to me?" he ended up saying, only confusing her more.

"I don't . . ." She licked her lips, trying to settle her features to no avail. She couldn't stop frowning. "I don't know what you mean. I'm not doing anything."

"Don't lie to me." Again, it sounded more desperate than demanding, and again she was left with no good response. He hovered over her, the heat from his body wafting off in the slightly chilled room so that she could almost see it.

When she breathed in, the air was filled with cucumber and sweat, a clear indicator she was too close to him. She tried to get herself to move away, but it was like her legs refused to listen to reason and she was rooted to the spot.

"We're standing in the middle of the room," he told her quietly. "It's improbable for me to back you into any corners here. They're too far away. You're going to have to just give me this, this once."

"Trystan." She shook her head. "I can't give you an answer when I don't know it myself."

If he recognized the use of his own words against him, he didn't show it.

The shifting of clothing drew his gaze over her shoulder.

She'd somehow forgotten they weren't alone, and it appeared as though he'd done the same.

"You're both dismissed," he decided, raising his voice to be heard. "Wait outside."

Delaney couldn't bring herself to turn and see whether Pettus hesitated, but she heard them go.

"You're pulling away," Trystan speculated, elaborating when she glanced pointedly down at her unmoving feet. "Not physically. It's in your eyes. You're trying not to be here, not to be with me."

"I've got a lot on my mind," she said.

He paused, considering his options, then asked, "The Ander?"

"Always." She forced herself not to hesitate in admitting it. It shouldn't matter to her whether the truth bruised his ego.

"You're not with him right now."

"Since when do you want to talk about Ruckus?" she asked suspiciously. Her hands lifted instinctually to ward him off when he continued to advance, and the second they touched his bare chest, she pulled them back.

"You were the one thinking about him," he reminded her. "He'd already been brought into the room. I'm just shedding light on it. Getting it out of the way."

"Way of what?" She regretting playing into his hand, and added, "Never mind. Don't tell me. I don't care."

"The way of this"—he motioned to the small space between them—"of us. Let's be honest, Delaney: Eventually you're going to have to let him go."

"Honestly," she asserted, "I don't believe that at all."

The first sign of returning frustration flittered across his face before he got a handle on it. "Sanzie thinks she overheard that you have a plan."

"Sanzie has a big mouth."

"Care to share?"

"It's a phrase that means she talks too much."

"That I already knew." He reached for her, slowly, giving her plenty of time to move away. She allowed his fingers to twist around a lock of her hair. "You promised you'd go through with the binding, Delaney."

She didn't say anything. There wasn't any reason to.

"Having second thoughts?" he coaxed.

"Always."

Trystan dropped his hand and took a deliberate step back. "Our compatibility exercise is tomorrow."

"What?" *What just happened?* was what she wanted to ask.

"It's a test," he explained. "We'll have to work together to make it through. Prove that we make a good team." He grunted when she pursed her lips. "It's nothing to worry about."

"Is that why the Rex showed up?" she asked. "To attend this particular exercise?"

"No," he informed her, his expression darkening. "He's here so that you won't be alone."

"That's going to need some serious elaboration." She crossed her arms defensively. "Where are you going to be?" And why wasn't she going with him?

"Kilma, he hopes. I haven't decided yet." He ran a hand through his sweat-slicked hair and sighed. "It's a fairly large town off the western coast of Kint. The Tar I questioned—"

"The one your father had dropped off like delivery?" she interrupted.

"I suppose. The Tar had information of an upcoming meeting. They're trying to recruit more people. Starting a riot is the quickest way to gain attention from the public."

Seriously?

"If my father has his way, I'll take a troop into Kilma to put an end to their foolishness before it can spread any further. Right now Vakar is mostly clear; with the help of Tilda we've managed to keep their protests to a minimum. Once we wipe them out of Kint, you'll be safe. It takes place three days from now."

And he was going to kill people. That was really why she couldn't come along. That, and it'd be insanely dangerous, sure, but she could read between the lines.

"What if I don't want you to go?" she asked, and at his surprised look, she glanced away. "I don't want to be alone with your father. He makes me uncomfortable."

"As he should."

"I don't trust him."

"Want to know a secret, Delaney?" He reclaimed that step he'd put between them, lowering his head so that his mouth was a mere breath away from hers. "No one does."

"How bad is it, really?" she said, mostly to distract herself.

"I only know what I'm told," he admitted.

"That doesn't sound like you."

"It isn't," he agreed. "Usually I'm the one tracking our enemies, planning our best course of action. It comes with being the Jager."

"I've heard that before," she realized. "At the council meeting. They called you Zane Jager Trystan."

"It's similar to what one would call a secretary of defense on your planet," he told her. "I was forced to take a leave of absence during our bonding preparations."

"Let me guess," she drawled. "Your father suggested it."

"Ordered it. But yes."

"What a prick."

"Assuming that means something bad," he said, and chuckled, "I agree."

"So if you go, you won't really know what you're walking into." That didn't sound safe. What if it was a trap?

"I wouldn't be alone," he assured her. "There would be over two thousand men and women with me. We'd flood the city, cutting off all the exits to ensure none of the Tars could flee. It would also make a statement to those still questioning whether you deserve their loyalty."

"How long would you be gone?"

"I'd travel through the night," he said. "It's supposed to take place just before dawn. It'll more than likely take the day to sort through." He searched her face. "I wouldn't be able to make it back to you until the day after. I'm sorry, Delaney."

"You have to do what you have to do." She tried not to show how freaked-out the thought of him in the middle of all that made her.

"I'm not apologizing for that," he corrected. "Though I am unsettled by the thought of being away from you, even for such a short period of time. I'm talking about last night, with the Teller."

She almost wished Pettus were still there so that he could hear it himself.

"I am sorry," Trystan confessed. "I don't have any excuses, only that."

"Okay." She couldn't outright forgive him, but she could give him that much. Acceptance, knowing that apologizing at all was a huge step for him. "You can't just be sorry because it upset me, though. You have to feel bad for what you did to him."

"I know." He exhaled. "I'm not there yet."

He was implying that he was trying, which was something. Certainly more regret than he would have bothered with a month ago. Trystan stood there a moment longer, and she started to worry he was about to kiss her.

Then he pulled back and waved at the room. "We should work on perfecting that move now."

"Okay," she repeated, because there wasn't anything else she could say.

CHAPTER 24

ime." Co Gailie reached forward and plucked the shing tablet out of Delaney's fingers.

At her side, Trystan handed his over, his expression unreadable. He and Delaney were both dressed in tight black clothing, and while she kept picking at the slick and shiny material, he hardly seemed to notice that it clung like a second skin.

There were hard points at the elbows and knees, almost like small octagonal kneepads, and their sleeves stopped just above their elbows. This left plenty of room for the two bands they each wore, one on the wrist, the other just above the elbow. Their weapons had been set to stun earlier that morning, and they'd already tested their shields to ensure there weren't any glitches.

The fact that they needed them at all had Delaney on edge. She was already nervous as it was about this, and tried not to seem obvious when she glanced toward a camera hanging on the left wall.

They were on a lower level, and had been informed this was being monitored and broadcasted. She barely understood what they were about to do, and the fact the entire planet had the ability to witness it made her anxiety grow tenfold. Supposedly, the set of rooms and winding halls through the double doors in front of them were riddled with even more cameras to help capture the entire exercise.

"How does alien television work again?" she asked Trystan through their fittings.

"Try not to think about it," he suggested, and before she could counter with a snide remark about how unhelpful that was, Gailie interrupted.

"Are you ready, Lissa?" she asked softly, drawing Delaney's attention back to the matter at hand.

"We memorize the map"—she pointed to the devices in the coordinator's hands—"and then . . . make it through the maze?" That didn't seem so bad. Not that she'd been able to focus much on the actual twists and turns of the place. The map had been a confusing jumble of black lines, some of which had even curved.

"You successfully make it through," Co Gailie reiterated. "You have to reach the end in a timely fashion, and you have to arrive together, or you both fail."

"Is there a reason we'd be separated?" Because she didn't like that possibility. Not one bit.

"Relax, Delaney," Trystan said soothingly, though on the outside he didn't so much as twitch. *"You'll be fine."*

Really? Because she couldn't even recall if it was a first left or a first right at the end of the hall. Shit.

Like everyone else, the Rex was watching, and the fact that he made Trystan nervous—though he'd never admit it out loud—made concentrating on anything difficult.

Focus. That was all she had to do.

"The clock starts"—Co Gailie held up a finger—"now."

Trystan grabbed Delaney's hand and tugged her forward, sweeping open the doors in the process. They clattered against the walls, then slammed shut behind them with an audible click. Trystan was already scanning ahead, moving briskly down the wide hall.

She fell into step behind him, her finger twitching over the fritz bracelet on her left wrist. "Why do we need these again?"

In retrospect, she probably should have asked earlier, but she'd assumed someone would fill her in eventually. They hadn't, and now she was silently cursing herself. If they were going to have to defend themselves, had that been what Gailie was referring to? If one of them went down, they automatically lost?

Before she could fully wrap her head around that concept, Trystan turned them left and then sprang back, practically knocking her over. His arm reached to steady her, even as he activated his fritz and began firing around the corner.

"Do you remember the way?" he tossed at her over his shoulder, letting off a couple more shots as he waited for a response.

"No." She hated that she had to admit it. Conjuring up the image of the map, she desperately tried to recall some of the turns. There'd been colored dots as well, and even some squares, now that she was thinking about it. "Wait."

"Think quickly."

"Red squares," she blurted. "Avoid them. Follow the yellow circles. Yellow, not gold. And there may have been orange ones, too . . . ? I don't know."

"Good enough." He latched on to her wrist and dragged her out behind him, leading them down the hall he'd just been shooting up. They passed several rooms as they traveled, and there were unconscious Tellers slumped in each.

"Damn," she said breathlessly. Delaney waved her middle finger over the activation censor, her own fritz forming solidly in her hand. Gripping it tightly in her palm, she exhaled slowly to calm her racing heart.

This was just an exercise, she reminded herself. None of those Tellers were dead, only knocked out.

"Their shots will hurt," he said, as if reading her mind. "They won't knock us out unless they hit us in the head or the chest. I suggest trying to avoid getting hit anywhere, however."

"This is like paintball," she said, amazed and relieved when a shot of excitement trailed over her. She hadn't played in a long time, but back in middle school she used to go at least once a month with some of her friends.

"And that is?" Trystan asked, glancing around a corner before turning them that way.

Delaney looked at one of the walls and saw a small blue square painted there, almost too tiny to make out. Perhaps these indicated a faster way to the finish line. If he'd known, why'd he bother asking her?

"It's a game," she told him, not wanting to dwell. "You go around shooting people. Last team standing wins. Losers usually pay for dinner."

"Then yes," he concurred, "this is exactly like paintball. Only with more riding on it than pizza and sugary drinks."

She blinked at his back. "Did you just make a joke? At a time like this? Trystan." She clucked her tongue.

"I'm attempting to put you at ease." He met her gaze briefly over his shoulder. "Is it working?"

Before she could respond, the sound of footsteps echoed from around another corner. She was in the process of lifting her arm when he shoved her to the side. He'd already fired his weapon before the Teller came into view, his shot sending the guy to his knees in less than a heartbeat.

He took her hand and tugged her in the same direction, but when they took the next left, he swore viciously.

It was a dead end.

"This isn't right," he growled, low and mostly to himself, stepping closer to the wall. It was large and white and blank, so she had no clue what he was looking for.

"Nothing's going to magically appear." She turned, about to head back, when another symbol caught her attention. It was smaller even than the blue circle had been, almost the size of her thumbnail, and protruded a centimeter off the wall, barely noticeable at all. "What's this?"

Trystan came over, frustration evident in his heated gaze. When he saw the button, his mood darkened. "It's a secret door. It'll either open up a way forward, or it'll lead us farther from the end. It all depends on if we're headed in the right direction already or not."

Delaney nibbled on her lower lip, thinking it over. "You're sure that this wall shouldn't be here?"

He paused, eyes glazing slightly as he pictured the map in his head. Then he gave a single curt nod.

She reached out and pressed the button. At first nothing happened, but then there was a screeching sound behind them and the wall that'd been in their way slowly began to shift to the side, creating an opening into another corridor.

One already filled with waiting Tellers.

Trystan shoved Delaney back, hard enough that she stumbled, and activated his shield at the same time. He was so concerned with keeping her out of the line of fire, he couldn't avoid all the zees. One glowing neon-pink burst grazed the side of his left arm and he cursed, twisting them both around the corner.

He slumped against the wall, grinding his teeth. A sheen of sweat was starting to cover his forehead.

"What the hell?" Delaney snapped, instinctually moving to force his hand away from the wound so she could get a look. Because the weapons had been set to stun, there was no actual opening, but before she could feel relief, his entire limb jerked.

"Electricity," he managed between his clenched jaw. "It'll pass in a moment."

The sounds of boots hitting the ground and bodies shifting ricocheted closer. Those Tellers weren't waiting for them to make another appearance. They were heading their way.

"We don't have a moment." She shifted on her feet, preparing to round the corner and start firing back. When his fingers clamped around her wrist, keeping her from doing so, she made sure to let all her frustration show.

"Hold," he ordered, lifting himself into an upright position. The way his fingers twitched gave him away. "I'll do it."

"No." She pressed her palm flat against the center of his chest, forcing him back against the wall for support. "You need a moment, remember? I'll buy us some time."

"I said hold," he growled.

"That's what I'm doing." For emphasis, she pressed the hand she still had on him harder. "Holding you back from making another dumb-ass mistake. I don't need you to shove me out of the way. We've been training; you've seen me shoot."

They were running out of time and they both knew it. Honestly, it was amazing the Tellers hadn't already rounded the corner and taken them out.

"We're supposed to be doing this together," she urged. "As in, you protect me, and *I* protect *you*." She eased her hand away and held his gaze steady with her own. "So stop being such an alpha male and let me."

He hesitated, and she almost started in on him again, but then he nodded.

Not wanting to give him the opportunity to take it back, Delaney activated her shield band and bolted around the corner, fritz raised. She fired into the crowd, counting five Tellers as she did. Realizing she couldn't take them all out on her own, she made her way over to the other side, turning so she could use the wall as a barrier. Now she and Trystan were on either side, and she caught his eye.

He straightened and there wasn't a single tremor moving along his arm. Rotating his shoulders, he readied himself, keeping her attention all the while, silently communicating with her.

Which was funny, considering they could have actually been

communicating through their fittings. Still, she understood exactly what he intended, and took position herself. She inhaled, and then spun around the same time he did, firing into the hallway.

The remaining three Tellers went down before they could even get a shot off. In step, she and Trystan moved, weapons held aloft in front of them.

"This is stupid, right?" she said a few minutes later, after they'd taken down another group of attacking Tellers. She didn't bother glancing at the ground as she stepped over their bodies. Were they at least getting paid extra for this? "I mean, you do realize that."

Giving them sixty seconds to memorize a map of a network of hallways? Like they were in training to become spies or something. What did memorization have to do with any of this? This whole exercise felt extreme, and pretty pointless. Unless it was common for Kints to get lost . . . together . . . in mazes . . . while being shot at.

Uh-huh.

"It proves we can work together," Trystan disagreed, edging his way toward another turn. With a crook of two fingers, he motioned that it was clear. He'd taken the lead again but hadn't checked back on her nearly as many times as he had when they'd started.

"It proves neither one of us wants to get shot," she corrected him, scanning the rooms as they passed. "Or, in your case, wants to get shot again."

The corner of his mouth curled up before he got a handle on it and returned it to that damning stubborn line. "You're teasing me."

"Nothing new there."

He was silent a moment, and then: "Teasing is generally something done between friends, Delaney. Insulting is what one does with an enemy. I enjoy the idea of us being friends."

She frowned.

"But I enjoy the fact that we're bondmates more," he added privately, fortunately turned the other direction so that he missed her shiver.

Nope. She wasn't going there, not while they were currently in a high-stress environment being spied on by the coordinator, his daddy, and possibly everyone else on the planet.

"Not here," she told him aloud.

"Of course," he agreed, purposefully misinterpreting. "Here we are partners."

"Trystan." She understood that people were listening, but she also knew him well enough to know that he was still trying to mess with her. And it was working.

A hand shot out of nowhere, grabbing on to her upper arm. Her fritz was already aimed and she fired, not waiting to process the Teller who'd just leaped out of the room they'd passed. She'd glanced inside and hadn't seen anything. He must have been hiding. With a shake she turned back to Trystan, who was now facing her with an angry look on his face.

A figure appeared over his shoulder, and knowing there wasn't time to warn him, she pushed Trystan aside and shot.

The Teller at the end of the hall went down in a heap.

When she lowered her arm and glanced over, Trystan was watching her.

"What was that about shoving?" he asked, his voice little more than a purr. This time he caught her reaction, the tingle that swept down her spine. He grinned wickedly, chuckling when she quickly spun away.

Delaney continued forward, not bothering to answer him. It'd been either shove him aside or let him get shot. She just didn't want to lose, she told herself.

"Wait." She'd taken the lead and they'd come to a four-way stop. At the edge of each connecting wall there was a different-colored shape. She scanned over them, spotting the yellow circle she'd recalled from earlier. "Do you think that's it?"

He followed her line of sight, then glanced over to the blue mark they'd been following, debating.

"If you know the way," she said, and waved him forward, "let's do it. You were right before about the blue marker."

"Yellow wasn't even on my map," he disclosed. "When you mentioned it earlier, I started to wonder if we'd gotten separate ones to further throw us off. Were there any blue dots on yours?"

She hadn't been able to recall before, which probably meant no. "I don't think so."

If they'd gotten different maps, did that mean there were multiple ways out, or was one of them a false lead?

"We've been going my way," Trystan said suddenly. "Let's try it yours."

She couldn't help the surprise. "Are you sure? I feel in this particular instance we have a better chance if we continue on the path you chose. I didn't do a very good job memorizing my map, to be honest."

"But you're certain about the yellow trail leading to the exit?" he asked.

"Yeah." Only because it'd been the one path she'd latched on to and forced herself to follow all the way. It would definitely take them to the end, but whether that way was faster than the other . . . she had no clue.

It was a toss-up.

She breathed out slowly, turning back toward the hallway with the yellow circles. "Let's hope this is the right decision."

"I trust you," he said assuredly, then gently brushed past her toward their chosen exit.

"Why do we have to navigate this while simultaneously fending off attackers?" she questioned after they'd taken down another six Tellers. It showed that they could work together, sure, but the fighting? Were they meant to defend each other? Throw themselves in the way of incoming zees to prove their love or some such nonsense?

If that last part was the case, how did the coordinator actually expect both members of the party to make it all the way through to the end? Maybe that was why she'd mentioned it so firmly. What happened to regular couples if they failed this particular exercise? Were they not allowed to bond?

She didn't know why she was so curious about it—she and Trystan were *not* an actual couple. The whole thing seemed . . . sad. If you couldn't make it through a maze while being shot at you weren't allowed to marry the person you loved? Seemed like bullshit to her. Cruel, unusual bullshit.

Unbidden, she pictured Trystan doing this with Olena, and outwardly cringed at the sight. There was no way the former Lissa would be of use here, let alone defend him if need be. Hell, she'd probably be the one to shoot him in the back, and then try to claim it'd been an "accident."

Yet Trystan hadn't been expecting to use a coordinator at all, so perhaps the two of them wouldn't have even been here. The Rex would have just let Olena marry his son to get them Vakar, without bothering to test if they were a good match or not. The only reason Delaney had to go through it was because she was human. And even then, she was almost certain if the planet had miraculously rejoiced in the idea of her on the throne, Hortan End would never have suggested it.

Which was further proof he didn't care at all about his son's happiness.

"Kint respects strength and military prowess," Trystan answered. "This proves we're both good soldiers and that we can work as a team. It's also partially so that we can impress each other."

"What?" She scrunched up her nose, eyeing the muscles tensing in his back as he moved.

"Are you saying you don't appreciate watching me fight, Delaney?" There was humor in his voice, though she couldn't see his face from where she followed behind. "That you don't like the way I move?"

She tore her gaze away from his back, even though there was no way he could actually have known she'd been staring.

They took one last corner and she let out a sigh of relief. At the end of the hall was a set of massive double doors, identical to the ones they'd passed through to get into the maze.

"There," she said, despite the fact that he had to have seen it, too.

Just as they took the final turn, a half dozen Tellers stepped out from hidden rooms, effectively blocking their path. The two of them jumped back out of the way.

Delaney let out a groan, unable to keep her irritation inside any longer.

At the sound, Trystan cocked his head at her, lifting a brow. He had that deadly half smirk on his face again, and excitement flickered in his eyes.

"Come on, Delaney," he offered. "Against you and me? They don't stand a chance."

"I HATE YOU," she mumbled as he worked her palm, massaging the muscles of her hand with strong, deft fingers.

They'd come out of the maze less than ten minutes ago, and the shock waves from the zee she'd taken to the knuckles hadn't abated. She'd been so close to making it out unscathed, but no. At the last second she'd miscalculated, and one of the Tellers had shot her right where she'd been holding her fritz. The only reason she hadn't dropped her weapon to the ground was because it was attached to her wrist.

Trystan had gotten them the rest of the way out, taking down the remaining two Tellers with ease, and Gailie had been on the other side of the doors.

"This hurts way worse than you let on." She tried to flex, but all that did was cause the electric pains to flutter up to her elbow. He'd been in pain when he'd gotten hit in the arm, sure, but she was embarrassed to admit she was close to tears. Stubbornly, she tilted her head back and stared at the overhead lights until she felt the tears receding.

"Come now," he coaxed, "it isn't that bad. Give it another minute. You'll feel better then, I promise."

"If it helps," Gailie said, a huge smile on her face, "you both did spectacularly."

"We were both shot," Delaney reminded her.

"Yes, but neither of you went down." She typed something into the device she held. "You both made it to the exit, left together, and, believe it or not, getting shot only once is a record."

Her eyes widened. "No way."

"Oh yes. I'm afraid couples usually come out of the compatibility test much more bruised and broken than the two of you managed. And we got the whole thing on film. Should work wonders helping prove to the people this bond is legitimate." She said it like they should both be jumping for joy, and seeing as how she usually worked with couples who were actually together, she probably expected them to.

But Delaney just didn't have it in her. Especially now that she knew how dangerous their situation had actually been. Really, no one had even expected them to make it out of there unharmed? That should have been mentioned at the beginning. Like, a warning label or something.

"So." Gailie was back to staring down at her screen. "I've been informed the Unveiling has been moved up to the day after tomorrow. It's unconventional, but it shouldn't be a problem."

All at once, Trystan tensed, his hands, still holding hers, pausing in their ministrations.

Noticing his change in demeanor, the coordinator paled. "Apologizes, Zane, I assumed you'd been made aware."

"No," he said in a clipped tone, "I was not."

"It was the Rex's order," she told him.

"Unsurprising." He was not pleased, not even a little bit, and was doing absolutely nothing to cover that fact up.

"Well," she said, and cleared her throat. "I'm still trying to work out when exactly everything will be ready for the two of you. I'll have the reworked schedule delivered as soon as possible."

"Thank you, Co Gailie," he stated. "You're dismissed."

She was clearly taken aback by his swift command, but only froze for a split second before bowing her head and moving off. It seemed even the lady in charge of their weird exercises knew better than to mess with him in his current state.

"Trystan." Delaney forced his attention back her way, not liking how tightly he was holding his shoulders, or how loudly he was grinding his teeth. "Come now," she parroted once he was looking at her, "it isn't that bad."

"You don't even know what it is," he pointed out, but all the anger he'd been storing up seemed to drain from him at once. He sighed. "It doesn't matter. It's done. How's your hand?"

Tentatively, she wiggled her fingers, blowing out a slow breath when everything felt relatively normal again. "Better."

"Excellent." He turned his left hand around so that now their palms were pressed together, and pulled her away from the maze room. "We finished just in time."

Delaney considered taking her hand back, then opted not to bother. He'd only grab it again anyway.

"In time for what?" she asked, pressing him for answers when he didn't immediately reply. "Trystan. Come on. Finding out we were meant to get hurt back there was surprise enough for one day. Tell me where we're going."

He paused, easing himself closer as he turned, his grip on her firming. "I wouldn't have allowed anything bad to happen to you." He glanced down at her hand where she'd been hit, some of that ire from earlier returning to sweep across his expression.

"That wasn't your fault," she told him. "And I know nothing permanently awful would have happened, but still. It's unsettling hearing someone tell you that they're actually surprised you're not damaged goods. That it's normal for people to put themselves through that, knowing they're going to come out of it hurting."

"But that's part of it." He frowned. "Being willing to risk putting yourself through pain to obtain what you want the most."

"If that's the case, why didn't anyone tell me?" She pulled back slightly, inspecting him. "Did you think I wouldn't do it if I knew?" That thought bothered her more than it should.

He searched her face. "Would you have?"

"I wouldn't have had a choice."

"Which is why I didn't bother telling you," he said, weirdly unaffected by her comment. "I knew it would only make it harder on you, and for no productive reason. You were already so nervous about my father watching the broadcast."

They were alone in the hall, aside from Sanzie and Pettus, who trailed so far behind, there was no chance of them overhearing anything they said. But Delaney didn't know what to say to that.

Trystan sighed and angled his head back down the hall. "We're close."

She kept her feet rooted to the ground pointedly. "To?"

"Dinner." He grinned. "Of course."

It hit her then that she was starving. The light breakfast she'd had that morning had long since burned off, and she'd skipped lunch altogether on account of nerves.

Seeing her expression, he chuckled and began walking them forward. True to his word, less than five minutes later they entered a large room she'd never been to before.

The kitchen was massive, with counters lining the right wall. There was an island in the center big enough to be a table seating eight, and across from that another long row of counters. Delaney didn't recognize most of the devices, though the fridge looked enough like the ones back home.

Across the room, to the far left, was a dining room table, set before a wall made entirely of windows that overlooked the side of a mountain. Everything outside was white and gray and still. Like a silent winter wonderland.

Or the calm before the storm.

CHAPTER 25

Trystan began moving confidently around the kitchen, opening and closing cabinets and drawers, removing some foreign and some not-so-foreign-looking objects. His blond hair was smoothed back, the collar of his shirt straight and stiff. There wasn't so much as a wrinkle on his pants, and the deactivated metal fritz and shield bands looked like jewelry now. And not girly in the least, considering his massive height and the width of his shoulders.

No one would guess he'd just come from an exercise as physical as the compatibility test had been.

Delaney spared a glance down at herself, more baffled by their differences than anything. She still had strands of hair sticking to the side of her neck from the sweating she'd been doing earlier. They hadn't changed out of those black suits, but somehow hers looked thoroughly used. There were creases at the bends in her knees and elbows, as well as a few dust splotches, probably from those times she'd slammed up against a wall for shelter. She even saw a few scuff marks on her boots.

How the hell had Trystan managed to stay so put together? And, more important, why did he bother? Hadn't there been enough to worry about with them running through a maze and being shot at?

Distracted by her perusal, it took Delaney a lot longer than it should have to realize what was actually going on in front of her.

"Wait." She glanced between him and the island where he'd already piled a ton of different things. "Are you cooking?"

"I told you I could," he replied, rummaging through the refrigerator.

"Sure," she drawled, stalling because she couldn't quite figure out how she felt about it. "But being able to cook and cooking for me are two different things."

"I've already cooked for you," he reminded her.

Right. That was also true. The dinner his father had interrupted, Trystan had made that.

Straightening from the floor, he piled all the ingredients he'd just removed into his arms and carried them over to the island where she stood. He began organizing everything, quickly spreading it all around in a neater display.

"Do you have a problem, Delaney?" he asked, and while he kept his gaze firmly planted on what he was doing, he couldn't hide the slight edge to his words. "Would you prefer I didn't cook for you?"

Sensing that she was standing on the edge of a precipice, she was quick to shake her head. He was trying to do something nice, and she was coming off extremely ungrateful, and even somewhat rude.

"Honestly," she admitted, realizing the truth herself just in time to give it to him, "I just didn't imagine you actually doing this. It's weird, seeing you in the kitchen. Not a bad weird, just an . . . unexpected one. Is there a recipe?"

He tapped at his temple in answer, lifting a large mixing bowl and setting it before him. Next, he reached for a small pitch-black object, and a glass jar that held something grainy and magenta. After crushing the black items into the bottom of the bowl, he added about a spoonful of the powder.

When he reached silently for something that looked like a blue banana with purple spots, she sighed. He wasn't angry with her, but she'd clearly hit a nerve all the same. Whatever mood he was suddenly in, there was only one way that she knew of to crack it.

Annoy the crap out of him.

Sliding one of the glass stools from beneath the lip of the island, Delaney delicately perched on the edge and folded her hands under her chin, making sure to stare the whole time. It was childish, but the idea of getting under his skin sent a tiny thrill through her, and she began tapping the tip of her booted toe against the counter. The contact made a satisfying ringing sound, which she repeated, settling into a steady rhythm.

Trystan, pretending not to notice what she was doing, continued using the miscellaneous items between them. The way he went about it, it was obvious he'd made this dish a thousand times before.

She was momentarily distracted, curiosity getting the best of her. The closest she'd ever come to watching someone cook a meal was when she and Mariana went out for hibachi. She so didn't count those times Ruckus had attempted, or even her roommate for that matter. None of them were very prolific in the kitchen.

But Trystan wasn't worried or cautious at all in his movements. His hands worked quickly, efficiently, sometimes reaching for something without having to look first. True to his word, there wasn't any sign of a recipe anywhere, no slips of paper or the shing tablet he always carried around.

"How long did it take you to memorize this?" She wagged a finger at the stuff on the table. "Longer than sixty seconds?"

"I had to make it a few times before I could do so without the recipe," he said, "yes." Then he went quiet again.

"And your mom taught you?" She almost regretted bringing it up when his hand paused over a spoon he'd been reaching for.

His lips were pursed in concentration, and that V-shaped wrinkle between his brow was back.

She had the sudden urge to lean forward and smooth it out with her thumb, catching herself at the last second.

"You were so young. How did you manage to remember any of this?"

He'd told her before he didn't have any actual memories of his mother, just ones that bled together because they'd happened so often. Like how she'd read to him. He couldn't pinpoint an actual time and recollect it, but he recalled that it had happened a lot. Was cooking like that as well?

"My mother enjoyed being in the kitchen," he explained calmly. Too calmly. It gave him away. "When I was younger, she'd let me pretend to help. Eventually I graduated to actually helping. That's how I learned, hands-on. Most of that stuck after she was gone, and the rest I learned on my own. But the basics, the love I have for cooking—"

"That all came from her." Delaney could picture it now, a tinier, less domineering version of him, standing at his mother's hip. The image didn't match with the person he was now, and she wondered what he'd been like as a child, before he'd been left alone with the Rex. "I've never heard you use the L-word in regard to anything before." It was rare to even hear him mention that he liked something, in fact.

"I used to think love was a weakness." The corner of his mouth turned up at some private thought. "I still do. Only, now I don't wish the feeling away. Some things are worth accepting."

Delaney didn't like the secretive look he gave her then, the way he tilted his chin with that half smile still in place. Like he was toying with her, fully knowing that she wouldn't grasp the how or the why.

Trystan started moving again. He'd pushed aside the original bowl he'd been using and was now stirring a liquid concoction in a square jar. There was something that could be meat in a package on the counter, though it was green, and he tugged it closer and tore open the plastic wrap. He began shaping it into small balls, dipping them into the liquid concoction before dropping them into the original bowl with the pink-and-black mixture.

"You can help now," Trystan said suddenly, motioning to the deep triangular pan he'd pulled in front of him.

"Oh," she drawled, glad for the distraction from her darkening thoughts, "can I?"

He glanced at her, a smirk tugging at his lips. "If you'd like."

"All right." She got up and went around so she was standing next to him. "If I ruin it, though, it's really your fault for letting me near it in the first place."

"I'll be sure to keep that in mind," he said, chuckling. Then he gently took her left hand and turned it around so her palm was up. Placing one of the small green balls there, he angled his chin out toward the triangular pan.

He'd already lined the bottom with a light blue layer of dough, and had sprinkled more of that pink grainy powder over it. Now he eased her wrist toward it and helped her place the small green ball in one of the corners. Then he repeated the process.

By the third time, she finally snapped herself out of it to stop him moving her around like a marionette.

"I think I got it," she told him.

"Are you sure?" His look was teasing. "You said I'd have to take the blame if you ruined it, and it's been a long time since I screwed something up in the kitchen. I'd like to keep my record clean, you understand."

She laughed and shook her head at him, reaching for another of the green balls and pointedly placing it a half inch away from the ones already in the pan. "There, happy?"

He merely clucked his tongue and picked up the spoon he'd been using on what looked like another dish.

"What is this, anyway?" She kept placing the green balls, moving from one row to the next, all while casually trying to spy on what he was doing without seeming too eager. This was all fascinating, but she really didn't need to stroke his already massive ego by showing just how much.

"That's the main course." He pointed at what she was doing, then down at the bowl in front of him. "And this is dessert."

"There's dessert, too?" She smiled. "I should have known. This is you we're talking about. You and your huge sweet tooth."

"Perhaps you shouldn't get any," he countered. "Maybe I'll decide I want it all to myself and refuse to share."

"That . . ." She paused. "Wouldn't be very nice."

"No one's ever known me to be nice, Delaney." He frowned, looking away quickly.

"What are these specifically, though?" She brought the topic back to the green balls.

"Cish," he replied.

"Okay . . . ?"

"When someone offers you fried chicken, is your greatest desire to know exactly what the animal was prior to becoming your latest meal?"

She thought it over, then plopped another ball down. "And we're done with the questioning. Tell me about this whole process instead. What makes you like cooking so much? Aside from the control, of course."

"I don't have to do it for anyone other than myself," he confessed. "I can make whatever I like, and however I like it, without having to worry about catering to someone else's needs or desires."

"Basically," she said, downplaying it on purpose, wanting to lighten his mood again, "you can use as much sugar as you want."

Only, her comment seemed to have the opposite effect.

"Unless you're opposed to sweet things." He paused, turning toward her. "I just realized I never asked you. You do enjoy sweeter foods, correct?" He glanced at the spread on the table, that frown returning tenfold. "Or did you want something more savory? I should have—"

"Trystan." She stopped him when he went to move toward the refrigerator. "I'm sure what you're making will be great. I've liked everything else you've had me try, remember?"

Hadn't he just gotten done telling her he enjoyed cooking because he didn't have to worry about other people? Yet less than two minutes later he'd been about to scrap everything to, what? Please her? That revelation made her uncomfortable, and she pulled on the collar of her shirt, finding it suddenly too tight.

"I'm done with this," she said before he could push and ask if she was sure. She tapped the edge of the triangular pan, now layered with the small green balls, and waved at the rest of the items still there. "Show me what to do next."

He hesitated, but must have seen she was all right by the determined look on her face. "You can stir the wareni."

She glanced into the bowl he'd been working with, then took the spoon and poked at the thick mixture.

"That," he chided lightly, "is not how you stir."

She gave him a mocking salute with her free hand, then gripped the metal spoon and began swirling the contents. It was hard, and within minutes her arm started to ache. Fortunately, just as she was about to give in and complain, he stopped her, taking the bowl to add a cup of small shiny blue beads.

She assumed they were edible, and watched as he mixed them in. The result reminded her a lot of chocolate chip cookie dough.

"Tell me about the Unveiling," she said.

"It's where we exchange the gifts we selected for each other." He added something liquid to the batch. "There will be a small audience to witness it. To ensure we don't alter the results."

Because the items in the boxes were supposed to be prophetic somehow. Made sense. She understood what he was trying to say by "audience" as well, but she didn't want to think about the Rex anymore.

"What do I have to do?" She really hoped there wasn't a speech.

"Only open the gifts handed to you. Their meaning will be explained as each item is revealed. Once we've both opened all our boxes, that's it."

"That doesn't sound too bad."

"It'll go quickly," he assured her. "You won't have to be in the same room as my father for long." He'd clearly seen right through her avoidance tactic.

Knowing she wouldn't have to deal with the Rex, aside from him being there with them, was a comfort. She put the whole thing aside, focusing on the food once more. It was way more interesting than freaking out over things she couldn't control. She could see why Trystan enjoyed it. Being the Zane had to mean there were a lot of things he worried about on a daily basis.

He scooped the mixture out and filled two deep bowls, sprinkled the same grainy pink powder he'd used on the main dish, and then moved to place them in the refrigerator. When he came back, he tugged the triangular pan between them and handed her an oddly shaped utensil that reminded her of three forks melded together at their centers.

"Press the cish down," he instructed, taking her hand a second time to show her exactly what he meant, "while I make the rest of the filling."

Delaney did as she was told, too caught up in the easy rhythm the two of them had created to really even notice.

"DON'T TELL ANYONE I said this." Delaney eased closer to his side conspiratorially, and he found himself lowering his head, instinctually playing along. "But that might have been better than pumpkin pie."

Trystan laughed, the sound echoing down the long empty hallway. He was escorting her to her rooms, and was in a better mood than he could recall ever being in before. Part of him was uncomfortable about that, a sense of foreboding yawning open in the pit of his stomach. Whenever he was relaxed, something always tended to happen to take that feeling away.

"I'm going to hold a press conference," he joked, wanting to ignore that inkling of dread. "Tell the whole world."

"Then I'll have to kill you." She said it with such a straight face, he almost missed a step. But then the corner of her mouth twitched, cracking the mask to reveal she was messing with him yet again.

"You, Delaney Grace," he drawled, "are hilarious."

"Why, thank you, Trystan End." She pressed her hand against his arm and pushed lightly, not hard enough to even budge him. "I get that a lot."

"You enjoyed it then?" he couldn't help but ask, despite the fact that she'd already told him as much half a dozen times during, and then after, their meal. He hated the thread of doubt, that foreign need to please her. There'd only ever been one person he'd wanted to make happy. His mother.

When it came to the Rex, he toed the line as close as he could, making sure not to actually cross over, but coming so near to doing so, he might as well. He did what his father instructed—not to please him, but because there was no other choice.

Trystan wanted what was best for his people, that was true, but pleasing them and giving them what was best weren't necessarily the same things. Delaney was different. He wanted to charm her. Wanted to wash away all those doubts she'd had at the beginning, when she'd woken up on his ship, spitting fire, looking like she was debating the best way to remove his head from his body.

As much as he liked her angry and feisty, he found he preferred her like this. She was relaxed and content, in no rush to get anywhere. In no rush to get away from him. He was tempted to discover how long she'd remain at his side without complaining, considered leading them around the halls to test it.

But then she stifled a yawn, and he realized how late it actually was. They'd had a stressful and busy day, had both been shot with electric zees. She needed rest, which meant he had to give it to her, even if sleep was the last thing on his mind.

"I've never eaten anything that amazing in my life," she told him, glancing at him from beneath long dark red lashes. "It was like, sweet but salty, and soft but crunchy. And that *dessert*."

"You're just saying a bunch of random descriptors." A rush of pride swept through him, pushing all those disquieting thoughts out.

"That's because I've never had anything like it before," she continued. "It's impossible for me to describe it. I want it again, though. Like, all the time."

"Or," he suggested, "we can try something else. I know a lot of recipes. Perhaps even something that isn't typically served for breakfast."

"Oh no." She shook her head. "Definitely not. We're sticking with breakfast. I want to have tried every single traditional breakfast dish on this planet before we even consider moving on to lunch or dinner."

"If that's what you want," he said, chuckling, "it can certainly be arranged."

They came to her door and she spun on her heel, the move sending locks of her hair spinning around her head. She was in the process of leaning a shoulder against the wall, and he was already reaching for a strand.

He curled it around his finger, fascinated by the contrast of bright red against his tanned skin. He was careful not to tug, gently smoothing the ends between his thumb and forefinger. If he could touch her like this forever, he'd do it. Tell his father and all the other responsibilities that constantly weighed him down to go screw themselves.

Which was a dangerous thought. A deadly one. For both of them.

She'd been quietly watching him, her expression enigmatic, and he forced himself to drop her lock of hair and pull away. Distance himself before he made a mistake and voiced the way he was feeling.

If she noticed him rebuilding his walls, she didn't show it, but he wasn't foolish enough to believe she'd missed it. She was observant, smart.

Perfect.

"I have to go," he told her, inwardly cursing when his voice came out husky and low. He was giving himself away.

"All right." She nodded almost imperceptibly, her hand reaching out for the panel near her head to open the door. She kept her eyes on his, and he got the sense there was something she wanted to say but was unsure about.

The door clicked open and she moved to step through.

He resisted the urge to stop her, because it was ridiculous, misplaced, and there was no reason for it. He hadn't been lying: There were things he needed to attend to before he could even consider sleep.

"Trystan." She paused, frowning slightly. It was adorable, her struggling like that. It made him feel like he wasn't alone. "Thank you for dinner. I had . . . fun."

He fought against the satisfied grin threatening to split across his face, subduing it into an easy smile instead. Deliberately, he took a step back.

"Good night, Delaney," he said softly.

She mumbled it in return and then slipped through the doorway, shutting the door behind her. It was too late, though; he'd seen what she hadn't wanted to him see. That she was just as confused right now as he was, that there were things she suddenly wanted that were dangerous and possibly—in her mind—even wrong.

It was another minute before he was able to get his legs to work. He was halfway down the hall when his father's voice burst into his head, shattering every good thing he'd just been feeling in less than a heartbeat.

"Trystan," the Rex commanded, "you and I need to have a discussion about Kilma. You've put it off long enough."

He ground his teeth and continued walking, not bothering to

change course. *"Would you like me to meet you, Father?"* He knew the answer already. If the Rex had wanted to do this in person, he would have sent a Teller to retrieve him.

Like he was still a child, or worse, a pet.

"No, that won't be necessary. I'm sure we can work it out now. Don't you agree?"

"Is this why you've moved up the Unveiling?" He tried not to allow his ire to bleed through, but so soon after leaving Delaney, he wasn't sure he was successful. She had a way of getting into his head, messing with the cold inside he used to create the barriers to keep people out. Another reason why he should be cautious with her.

It was too late to distance himself, though. He'd already fallen.

"I've ensured you'll be available should you choose to go to Kilma with the rest. This is a serious issue, son. You don't want to see an army rise up against your human, do you?"

Trystan came to an abrupt stop in the middle of the hall, barely noticing how tightly he clenched his hands into fists at his sides.

Damn his father for being right.

"The Tars are only continuing to rebel because of your insistence to place a human on the throne," he continued, as if sensing Trystan's wavering. *"I didn't raise you to allow others to fight your battles."*

Trystan almost punched the wall. Almost.

"These are valid points, Father." He would have to be the one to lead the attack, for multiple reasons. His people needed to see he was still taking responsibility. His father needed to be shown that Delaney wouldn't get in the way of duty. And he needed to ensure firsthand the Tar threat against her was quelled.

Delaney had told him she didn't want him to go, but that was because she was afraid of the Rex. Even knowing she had Sanzie and Pettus with her wouldn't be comfort enough. Truthfully, not for either of them. If Trystan was going—and he'd just decided he was—he needed to leave more assurance behind.

"I'll consult the generals. Schedule a pickup to bring me to Kilma," he said, turning on his heel to head in the opposite direction. There was one thing he could do that might make him feel a little better. A way to leave a constant reminder to everyone here why it was best not to bother his Lissa.

"No need for the latter. I've already handled that. A ship will be here for you directly after the ceremony." His words should have bothered Trystan, but instead he was smirking, because what he was planning would undoubtedly annoy the Rex.

"Of course, Father."

CHAPTER 26

You don't have to be nervous," Sanzie said at her left. She kept her gaze on the closed double doors ahead, her hands clasped behind her back.

"Doesn't she?" Pettus mumbled from Delaney's other side.

"This is tradition." Sanzie sent him a sideways glare. "Nothing is going to go wrong. Besides, Lissa, you've met with the coordinator many times before. There's nothing to fear now."

It wasn't Gailie who Delaney was afraid of, and they well knew it. The Rex was in there, along with Olena and a handful of others. Things tended not to go well for her when she partook in alien ceremonies in the presence of royalty.

"What's with all the pomp, then?" She waved a hand at the doors. "Why can't we just go in?"

"The Rex insists this be done right," Sanzie said, a hint of apology in her tone. She'd braided her hair back, the look giving her a stronger air.

A chime sounded from within the room, and before Delaney could sigh in relief, the doors slowly eased inward. The Ice Dome had been decorated with silver, gold, and bronze streamers dripping down in curls from the curved ceiling. Where the table usually sat there were now two high-backed chairs. People were already seated in rows of stone benches that had been set to the left of the room, and a dozen or so Tellers lined the dome.

Trystan was standing in front of one of the chairs, dressed in his best Kint uniform. The dermal stone on his arm caught the sunlight from one of the glass walls, glinting at her momentarily as if in silent reminder why they were here.

"You're pale," he pointed out through their fittings as she approached, holding up a hand to take hers when she was close.

"Nerves," she admitted. Twisting so that she was positioned in front of the second chair, she looked out over the audience and felt even more anxious.

Olena was sitting next to the Rex on his right, and to his left was the Rue she'd met weeks ago, Rantan. One of the members of the high council who'd virtually attended that first meeting was there as well, but she couldn't recall her name.

"Are there usually so many people here?" she asked, schooling her features.

Gailie stepped up to them, appearing from the side somewhere. She was holding a small square tray, six boxes set on its crystal clear surface. It was placed before both chairs, in the center so that they'd have easy access, then she bowed and stepped away.

"Typically it's only our close relatives," Trystan answered as he gripped her hand tighter, signaling they could be seated. He waited until they'd both sat before adding, *"Of course, that wasn't good enough for my father. He insisted we have more witnesses."*

"Does he believe in the superstition?"

"He's always found this ceremony pointless and vastly overrated. A few years ago he actually tried to have it removed from traditional bonding preparations, but our people rejected the idea."

"Bet he loved that."

Trystan's lips curved up in a half smile, but he didn't reply. Instead he reached for one of the boxes on his side of the table and brought it to her. It was shaped like a triangle and covered in honey-toned paper.

"Pie crust," she said before she could help it, knowing exactly what had attracted him to this particular gift. She accepted it, her fingers tentatively peeling back the wrapping. The actual box beneath was white, and the top popped off easily to expose a heavy green stone.

"Growth," Gailie announced as soon as she saw it, holding her hands palm up as she spoke to the room. "This union will be blessed with ever-strengthening connection. As you each grow personally, you'll also grow together. It's a sign of deep friendship and increasing happiness."

Delaney tried not to let on how uncomfortable that prediction made her.

"Place the box at your feet," Trystan said, *"and then select one of the ones you've chosen for me."*

She did, glad to be rid of a stone that supposedly meant they'd have a long, happy life together. The squa-colored gift was the closest, and she snatched it up and held it out to him, wanting to get this whole thing over with. They'd already gotten one "good" sign via the green stone, and while she didn't necessarily want negative doomsday items to show up next, she also didn't want more indicators of a lengthy binding.

Delaney wasn't buying in to the idea that these things actually told the future, but there was part of her forced to acknowledge there was a lot she still didn't know or understand.

Inside the box with the brown paper was a small object made out of twisted silver. There was a line of bronze straight through the center, forming a *K*, and at either end was a small polished ruby. It was a bracelet, with an opening wide enough for him to easily slip it onto his left wrist, which he did as soon as Gailie got a look at it.

"Solidity," the coordinator declared brightly. "You'll have a solid bond. You'll be able to rely on each other, always."

Trystan handed her his second gift, this one purple with silver swirling patterns on it. The tips of his fingers brushed against hers as he passed it over, and his pupils dilated. She couldn't tell whether he was pleased with the items already opened.

This box was ovular, and within, nestled against black velvet, was what appeared to be a single piece of white chocolate sprinkled with silver glitter. It was in the shape of a flower, with sharp points at the ends of its rounded petals, and small enough to fit in the center of her palm.

"It's edible," Trystan informed her.

Assuming it was sweet, Delaney broke off one of the petals and offered it to him. She'd done it without thinking, but it might have been the wrong move, for the crowd gasped.

Worried she'd just messed the whole thing up, she glanced questioningly at him, only to find him smirking at her.

Without a word, he leaned over and took the piece from her fingers. With his mouth.

"Romance." Gailie clapped her hands. "Your binding will be filled with many sweet moments."

Fantastic.

Delaney set the rest of the chocolatelike thing back into the box and placed it carefully on the ground next to the green stone. She couldn't help but glare at them a little before picking up her second selection.

Trystan made quick work of the red package, smiling at her a second time as he did. Inside was a smooth reddish-orange stone in the shape of a half-moon. When he held it up to the sunlight, flecks of green sparkled like stars.

"Secrets," Gailie announced. "Those kept and held close. You'll confide in each other, shield each other."

Trystan dropped the box to the ground, but Delaney saw him discreetly slip the stone into his front pocket. She gave him a questioning look, but he was already holding out his final gift.

They were so close to being finished, she didn't bother pausing to admire the bright green wrapping, tearing through it to the brown package within. The lid on this one had a hinge, and she lifted it to find a piece of folded paper.

Frowning, she took it and unfolded it, not recognizing the bold design drawn in thick black lines.

"Our word for possibility," Gailie said, and it was clear she explained it like that for Delaney's benefit. "Written down because, like paper, possibilities are fragile. Chances don't always last."

"What does that mean for us?" Delaney asked.

Gailie wasn't annoyed by the question, her expression softening. "It means your relationship will be ever changing, with a thousand different possible outcomes. Don't worry—when added to the rest of the items already here, it leans in a good direction."

There was only the one gift left, and her hand hovered over it for a split second. It was the yellow one, the one she'd chosen with a bit of defiance in mind. With Ruckus in mind. After everything that had taken place since, it felt a little wrong, especially with all these witnesses.

She gave it to Trystan and immediately saw that even if the others didn't, he knew why she'd done it. It took all her willpower, but she didn't look away. Things were different between them, sure, but she'd made it clear the other night, and by giving him this, she was making it clear again. She loved Ruckus, and there was no reason for her to feel guilty or ashamed about that fact.

Trystan peeled the paper on this one like it was physically hot to the touch, burning him every time he made contact. He discarded it onto the ground as soon as it was off the box, flipping off the cover in the same impatient manner.

She couldn't see inside of it right away, but his stiffening spine and tight expression clued her in that whatever was there, it wasn't good.

Gailie stepped forward to see for herself when he didn't immediately offer it up for her inspection. At first her expression mirrored his, but it quickly morphed into confusion. Her gaze shot across the room toward the Rex, an indecipherable question in her eyes that had Delaney's blood chilling.

What was going on?

The look the two of them shared didn't last long, though it was apparent a silent message had been exchanged. When Gailie turned back, her face was white as a ghost, and her hands shook slightly where she had them clasped against her stomach.

"Disruption," she called, voice quavering. She had to clear her throat before she could continue. "There will be an uncompromising obstacle. Possibly a death or"—she licked her lips—"betrayal."

Whispers broke out across the room, and while she'd made a point of ignoring Olena, Delaney now found her eyes drawn to her.

Out of everyone there, she was the only person currently smirking.

Trystan shifted, finally snapping out of whatever had come over him.

The item in the box was now visible to Delaney, and when she saw it, she couldn't help but frown.

It was a golden statue of a lizard-type creature, no bigger than Trystan's pinky finger. The thing had been created with great detail, showcasing the pointed talons and long front fangs. The tail was curved slightly, the outer edge thin and sharp. A knife.

Delaney felt herself grow cold. Even though she'd just gotten done telling herself she didn't believe in any of this, a flash of fear ran through her. She'd chosen that item because of Ruckus, not Trystan. Did that mean . . . No. She refused to believe in this nonsense. A few random items wrapped in boxes did not foretell her and Ruckus's future.

Her eyes trailed over to Trystan, expecting to see satisfaction written across his face. He'd known she'd picked that box with Ruckus in mind the second he'd seen it. Initial reaction aside, he had to be feeling pretty smug right about now. And why wouldn't he?

Except that wasn't what she saw when she met his gaze. He was no longer stiff, sure, and there was a glimmer of curiosity coming off him, but he wasn't rubbing it in her face. That could be because of their audience, and yet she didn't think it was.

If he didn't feel the need to gloat, there had to be a reason. Like perhaps, the one Ruckus had presented to her himself. Trystan was never going to let her go.

And if he thought there was already no possible way she and Ruckus would end up together, then why bother rubbing the proof of that in her face when it appeared? Even as literally gift-wrapped as this particular "proof" was.

Co Gailie had grown silent, her gaze dropped to the ground, brow furrowed. The rest of the room was still filled with harsh whispers.

"Enough," Trystan's voice boomed out, instantly silencing everyone. If he noticed his father's annoyed look, he ignored it. He slammed the lid back on the box and stood, dropping it with a heavy thump to the floor in the process. "We aren't yet finished."

"That was the last gift, son," the Rex reminded him. "And I can't say any of us are pleased with the results."

"It leaves questions," Rantan chimed in, "certainly. The last time that particular item was given at a royal Unveiling, the couple met with a dastardly end."

Delaney made a sound in the back of her throat, drawing their unwanted attention. Once she had it, she was forced to voice her thoughts, hoping she didn't accidentally make things worse by doing so.

"You can't honestly believe in this stuff, right?" No one offered up a reply, and she shook her head. "Come on. It's a piece of metal in a box I randomly picked. It doesn't mean anything."

It couldn't.

"Some would argue otherwise," stated the high council member she didn't recall the name of.

"I said enough," Trystan reminded them, adjusting the cuffs of his shirt. He motioned toward the two Tellers guarding the doors, who yanked them open to admit a tall gray-haired man.

The man was carrying a navy pillow in both hands, with a pearly white box at the center. His heels clicked lightly against the stone floor as he entered, keeping his chin up and eyes lowered the entire walk over to them. He bowed and presented the pillow to the Zane, holding the position as if he'd just been turned to stone.

"What is this?" the Rex demanded, rising from his seat. His lips were pressed into a thin line, his hands clenched into tight fists.

His sudden burst of anger caught everyone else off guard, and both the Rue and the high council member stared at him in surprise.

"It's the Claiming ceremony," Trystan said in the most matter-of-fact tone imaginable. He took the offered box and turned to Delaney, pointing over her shoulder. "I had yours brought as well."

She glanced behind her and found Sanzie holding the same bowed position as the man on Trystan's other side. Slowly, she got to her feet, taking the similar box from the top of the bloodred pillow the Sworn held.

He hadn't mentioned anything about this the other night at dinner. They were only supposed to exchange gifts and then leave. The sudden change made her skin feel prickly, and that, coupled with what had just happened, made her want to throw up a little.

By the time she'd swiveled back around to him, Trystan had already opened his box, and her breath caught in her throat.

It was a necklace with a circular pendant the size of a half-dollar. The ring was a few centimeters thick, silver, with dozens of different-sized blue gems. The stones winked when he removed the necklace, letting it dangle from his curved fingers so she could get a better look.

"Allow me," he whispered, catching her gaze, silently telling her what he wanted.

She hesitated but ended up turning back around so he could link the chain around her neck. The pendant hung directly between her breasts, but it felt lighter than she'd expected.

"Trystan," the Rex growled, even more displeased now than he'd been only a moment prior. "This is not the way of things."

"It's the way I wanted it, Father," he challenged him, then caught Delaney's eye again. "I didn't want to leave without having done this first. Without making it clear to everyone that you and I are already spoken for."

Her immediate thought was that he'd done it to further tie her to him, to trap her. But despite how badly she wanted to, she couldn't hold on to that line of thinking. The truth was too obvious, aided only by how upset he'd just made the Rex.

Trystan was doing this to give her added protection. It was his weird way of keeping her safe while he was away in Kilma.

"Delaney."

She'd been standing there, staring at him, but at the sound of her name off his lips, her hands moved to open the box she held. She was so distracted by her thoughts, she barely gave the item inside a glance as she held it out to him.

Trystan lifted another necklace from the box, this one done in Earth colors, bronze with red stones. Seeing as how she'd have to stand on the chair to be able to put it on him, he didn't ask, slipping it over his head himself. The second it settled on his chest, he pressed his palm against it protectively, as if needing to feel it, ensure it was close.

Gailie, who'd been deathly quiet up until this point, suddenly shook her head, coming out of her daze, and took a shaky breath.

"Symbols exchanged, promises made." She waved at them. "From here on out, let the world know these two are set and tied."

Trystan hooked a finger gently into the loop of her necklace, curving around the ring and tugging to urge her closer.

She moved to prevent the chain from chafing the back of her neck, dread already starting to crawl up her spine.

When he took up her hand and brought it to the pendant he wore, she knew with certain clarity what was going to happen next. For some reason, the other night, even though it'd been so clear that he'd wanted to, he'd stopped himself from kissing her.

He wasn't going to stop now.

"We're going to have to—"

"Yeah," she cut him off, not wanting to hear him say the actual words.

Trystan lowered his head, and her finger tightened on the ring around his neck in preparation. His free hand went to her hip, gently resting there so he could pull her close enough that she felt his front press against her own. Once he was sure she was staying put, he brought that same hand to her face, tipping her chin back to give him better access.

She stood frozen, emotions warring with her mind over what to do, how to feel. Part of her wanted to pull away before it could go any further, the implications of doing so in front of their current audience be damned. The other part of her wouldn't budge.

They'd been doing this dance forever, far longer than just the past month. Even when she'd pretended to be Olena, there'd been this terrifying chemistry between them. It'd been purely physical, and frightening because he'd been the monstrous Zane threatening everything she cared about.

That hadn't changed, had it? It couldn't have. He was still the same person, and she was still here pretending to be someone else for his benefit.

So why did it feel different?

He'd been waiting for her to make the final move, but his patience must have run out, for in the next instant, his mouth was on hers. His lips were firm, demanding, leaving no room for rejection. His fingers slid to the back of her skull, holding her in place so he could deepen the kiss.

He didn't taste anything like he smelled, more rich with a hint of sweetness than like cucumber, though that scent surrounded her, fogging up her brain.

She tried to remind herself they weren't alone, that there were people—like Pettus—watching, but before the thoughts could fully form, he forced them away with a stroke of his tongue.

She didn't know what was going on with her, why she tilted her head to accommodate him when he changed the angle of the kiss. Why she pressed herself closer still. There was only one thing she knew with total certainty.

She did not want to feel this way. Not toward him. But she couldn't stop it.

Fortunately, Trystan finally ended the kiss, pulling back and steadying her when she would have lost her balance trying to follow. He held her like that for a moment, the two of them staring at each other while they tried to regain focus.

Delaney was out of breath and felt off-kilter, annoyed when she noticed how he still seemed so put together. Apart from the reddening of his lips, he could have just come straight from an office meeting, for all the indication he gave. She went to take a step back, needing space between them, but he took her hand, keeping her close.

"There's a ship on standby waiting to take you to Kilma." The Rex stepped forward, a mocking edge to his voice. For whatever reason, he was seriously displeased about these necklaces.

Delaney couldn't understand why, because she was pretty sure it didn't hold the same meaning as exchanging rings on Earth would.

"Of course, Father." Trystan somehow managed to sound just as flip as the Rex. Almost like he'd gotten an extra boost of arrogance. That self-satisfied half grin was once again painted across his face.

Yet when he turned back to Delaney, it vanished. It looked as though he wanted to say something specific, his gaze dropping back to their clasped hands. Whatever it was, he must have opted against it, because the smile he gave her next was forced, as was the almost chaste kiss he pressed against the space between her shoulder and neck.

"I'll walk with you," the Rex said, attempting to hurry this along. The rest of his party was crowded close behind him.

Delaney watched their exchange, absently rubbing at the nail marks she'd inadvertently made on her palm.

"Until again," Trystan told her softly, and she thought she caught a hint of sadness in his eyes before he turned from her.

And left.

CHAPTER 27

Delaney almost hadn't come for a couple of reasons. The first was guilt. She had to admit, if only to herself, that she hadn't entirely hated the kiss.

Not like she should have.

The second . . . was more guilt, but a different kind altogether. She actually felt a little bad about going behind Trystan's back. Visiting Ruckus was taking advantage of the fact that the Zane was away this morning, and even though it shouldn't, it bothered her.

She thought about it the whole way there, through the halls and down the different stairwells. She was so distracted by the confusing onslaught of mixed emotions that she hardly noticed Sanzie or Pettus following behind.

After the ceremony, everyone had simply disappeared, including Gailie, who'd mumbled something unintelligible and then bolted after the Rex.

She hadn't known what to do with the items—Trystan had taken two of his, but that was only because he'd been wearing the bracelet and sneaked the stone in his pocket—so ended up leaving them there on the floor. The whole ordeal from start to finish had been a conundrum. Especially that final item.

It'd promised betrayal, but because she'd been the one who'd chosen it, did that mean it was foreseeing she'd be the bringer, or the receiver? This alien prediction crap was confusing, and when she was feeling lost and out of sorts, she instinctually wanted to turn to one person.

Ruckus.

And that brought up the other issue. She'd been thinking about him when she'd selected that particular item. Would Ruckus want to know she'd done it with him in mind? Did he buy into the superstition? She didn't know, and that worried her when it shouldn't. She should have more faith in them than that.

There was only a single Teller at the bottom of the steps, and he was busy playing with a shing. As soon as his eyes passed over Sanzie, he quickly shoved the device into his pocket and straightened.

Delaney swept past, coming to a stop when she spotted Gibus sitting against the wall, facing the room's entrance. He perked up when she came into view, leaping to his feet.

Gibus moved closer and waved. For a guy who'd been held hostage for the past month, he looked surprisingly well and high-spirited.

Pettus stepped forward, clearly excited and relieved to see his friend. "Are you being treated well?"

Delaney looked toward Ruckus's cell to find him already waiting for her at the front. All his bruises had healed, leaving little to no sign that he'd been forced into captivity.

How could she even be remotely softening toward Trystan when he was the reason for all this?

"They told me you had your Unveiling yesterday," Ruckus said, his voice deep and rough.

"It was a real treat," she drawled, hoping he caught the note of sarcasm. "Guess whose future is filled with betrayal?"

His shoulders stiffened and she made a face at him.

"Don't tell me you believe in that junk?" Her heart clenched painfully as she waited.

"It's not me I'm concerned about," he explained. "Whether you take it seriously or not, a large enough part of the Vakar population will. This isn't good. Where's Trystan?"

She quirked a brow. "You're asking about Trystan?"

"He shouldn't be leaving you alone, not after those results."

"We get some time to talk without him," she said, moving closer to the barrier that separated them. "Let's not waste it. Besides, Trystan's not here because *he's not here*. He went on some mission to Kilma to stop the Tars."

"What?" Ruckus frowned, stilling all over again. "Why are the Tars congregating in Kilma? It's a Kint town."

"Which makes sense . . . seeing as how they're mostly made up of Kints. Right? They're trying to convince the rest of them to agree to overthrow me." She clucked her tongue. "Honestly, after how much they hated Olena, you'd think Trystan would have thought on this a little harder."

Though he was so sure of himself, positive that his world would accept her simply because he did. What he wanted, obviously, was what everyone else should as well. Yet another reason why she should have pushed him away yesterday when he'd kissed her, or at the very least, cut it short.

The initial meeting of their lips had to happen—the Rex had been right there watching—but it'd lasted way longer than a brief brushing of mouths.

"Ruckus." She had to tell him.

"Does Vakar know about this?" he asked before she had the chance to say anything else. "You," he called out to Sanzie, who glared back. "Has the Basilissa been notified about the situation in Kilma?"

"I'm not at liberty to discuss such things with you, Ander," she stated.

"If the Tars are rallying against her successor, she deserves to be alerted," he insisted. "The Vakar could help put an end to them before things get out of hand."

"Your opinion has been duly noted."

He growled and slammed his palms against the barrier, hissing and pulling back as sparks flickered off. His hands were red and he shook them as if the air would help cool the burn.

"Damn it, Ruckus," Delaney snapped. "The last thing we need right now is you losing it."

She glanced over her shoulder at Pettus and Gibus, who were still deep in conversation. They were angled toward each other, speaking in hushed whispers. That was what she and Ruckus should be doing, not debating whether Kint was keeping Vakar in the loop.

"It just doesn't make any sense, Delaney," Ruckus said.

"What doesn't?" Aside from everything, of course.

"If they really are growing their numbers in Kilma, and the Kint know about it, why send Trystan? It should be simple enough to stop them without involving the Zane, especially now, when tradition dictates he stay focused on you and the bonding steps. Why go?" He paused, caught up in his own thoughts. "Was it his decision?"

"No."

When Trystan had told her yesterday he'd decided to go after all, she'd been worried, and then annoyed because of that worry. More than that, though, she'd been frustrated, because the real reason he was going was because of the Rex.

Ruckus was staring at a spot on the floor, frowning. Being Ander meant having certain skills, certain instincts. If he was really this concerned, there had to be a legitimate reason. And if so, why hadn't Trystan seen it?

"The Rex ordered it," she shared, realizing that if there was a reason Trystan overlooked something, that would be it.

He tried so hard not to speak against his father, especially now.

She knew that it was a constant battle of wills between Trystan and his father. That keeping things on his particular track took massive amounts of effort and compromise with the Rex.

"Knowing where the Tars are going to be should make taking them out simple," Ruckus mumbled, more to himself than to her. "So sending Trystan is pretty pointless. It also still poses enough risk that you'd think the Rex would keep him away from all of it, at least until the two of you are actually—"

"Isn't this sweet," Olena's voice abruptly cut him off. She was standing in the center of the room, an arm outstretched before her with an activated fritz at the end.

Aimed at the back of Sanzie's skull.

Pettus moved to open his own, but two Tellers stepped up behind the old Lissa, weapons drawn. He held up both hands, palms out.

"This must be what it looked like," Olena continued lightly, "the two of you hanging out in dark corners, exchanging romantic quips. That's it, right?" She rested her gaze on Ruckus. "That's why you abandoned me for Earth—to be with her. It's why you helped her steal everything from me. Because the two of you *fell in love*." She stuck out her tongue in disgust.

"And all while she looked like me," she continued perkily. "Ruckus, let's pretend you have a gun to your head."

One of the Tellers at her back shifted so he was now aiming at the Ander.

"Oh." She smiled. "Now you really do. Anyway, answer this honestly." She leaned forward, pressing the barrel of her fritz against Sanzie's head in the process. "You liked her better when she was me, didn't you?"

He didn't bother acknowledging that with a response.

"Come on." She rolled her eyes. "Don't deny it. You used to watch me night and day. You can't truthfully tell me you didn't feel attraction. I'll tell you the truth. It was mutual."

"Can bullets pierce through the shield?" Delaney sent the question to Ruckus. The barrier keeping him locked up was strong; there was always the chance it could keep zees from entering, despite it not having an electrical current on the outside.

"They can through the ones in Vakar," he said.

"You think I can't tell when you two are talking behind my back?" Olena stomped her foot, the fritz in her hand letting off a rattling sound.

"Technically," Gibus spoke from within his cell, holding up a finger, "they're standing in front of you, Olena dear." He glanced pointedly at Pettus then said from the corner of his mouth, "She never was very intelligent."

"Shoot him!" she screamed, jabbing her hand in his direction. "Shoot his stupid face off!"

"But"—the Teller at her left glanced to the one on her right—"the Rex said—"

"I don't *care* what he said," she growled. "I'm saying to shoot him!"

"You might want to be more careful with your words."

Olena instantly paled at the sound of the Rex's voice.

He came up behind her, slipping through the open doorway without skipping a beat. It was impossible to tell how long he'd been out there, if he'd maybe just been on his way and she'd been unlucky, or if he'd intentionally been listening in.

"Rex." Delaney pulled back her shoulders, determined to appear in control despite how quickly this was all spiraling. "I assume you're down here to explain why Olena has been let loose in the building?"

"Happily." He adjusted the front of his jacket, the move eerily similar to Trystan's. "I'm afraid there's been a change in plans, Miss Grace. Your services will no longer be required."

"Excuse me?" It felt like a bucket of ice water had just been dropped over her head.

"What the hell are you talking about?" Ruckus demanded.

"Ander." He tsk-tsked. "You've always been so cordial. Pity to put an end to that now, don't you think? It's one thing to talk to my son like that, another to speak to a Rex. Still, I understand your ire, and can assure you that once Miss Grace has been taken care of, I'll let you out of that cell. I even have a job proposal for you. It seems Lissa Olena is quite taken with you and insists that you be reinstated as her personal bodyguard."

"That's a hard no," both Ruckus and Delaney hissed at the same time.

Olena made another face. "Earth phrases. When you're my Ander again, I'm making it a rule that they can never be used in my presence."

"Trystan will never allow this," Delaney said. Not that she thought the Rex would care about that.

"My son is not here," the Rex stated. Then he grinned, the malicious twisting of his lips and the darkening of his eyes also such familiar gestures, her breath caught. "Why do you think that is, Miss Grace?"

What? No.

No.

"He left because you made him," she reminded him, feeling another sweeping rush of doubt when that caused the Rex to laugh.

"Made him?" he said through chuckles. "Surely you're more perceptive than that? No one makes my son do anything, Delaney. He's too hardheaded. He isn't here because he wanted to go, practically ran to the ship yesterday to get away from you."

"You're lying." He had to be. Though Trystan had been in a rush to leave after they'd kissed . . .

"I may have been the one who suggested he oversee the takedown in Kilma," he confirmed, "but it certainly wasn't necessary to twist his arm about it. He leaped at the opportunity to get back out there. You see"—he took a deliberate step closer, passing Olena's left—"my son is a warrior, always has been. The best Kint has to offer, the best Xenith has, actually.

"All his life he's trained, preparing for greatness. I groomed him to not just rule one kingdom, but—"

"Three." She couldn't move as he continued to approach, but it was nothing like the paralysis Trystan caused in her. This was terror, pure and undiluted. Simple. The Rex was angry; it was so obvious now, she was actually shocked she hadn't seen it before. He was furious, and that fury wasn't directed at his son.

It was directed at her.

"Not stupid after all," the Rex said. "Trystan insisted upon that fact, but I couldn't be sure it was truth and not just a fanciful exaggeration concocted by his infatuation with you. All this hard work, years of preparation, of sacrifice, and he was willing to give it all up. For a human."

"You made him believe you were on his side," she whispered.

"My son isn't stupid, either, Miss Grace," he disagreed. "Blinded, certainly, but not stupid. He knew when he left it meant leaving you behind, and he did it anyway. He chose his future, the right future."

Delaney barely resisted the urge to reach up and touch the necklace she still wore. She'd tucked it under her shirt before coming down here, not wanting to rub it in Ruckus's face, but she hadn't taken it off.

How much of this was really a father lying to a son, and vice versa? If the Rex was to be believed, Trystan had been in on this from the get-go. But Trystan had told her he no longer intended on taking Earth, and she'd believed him. Had that just been a means of making her complacent?

"Oh, come on." Olena shook her head. "You can't honestly be debating over this, can you? This is Trystan we're talking about here." She heaved a frustrated sigh when Delaney didn't respond. "What was that thing you said to me back on the ship? Right before you stole my Ander and ran back home? 'If Trystan ever found out you'd deliberately tricked him, he'd be murderous.' That was it, wasn't it?"

Delaney had been warning Olena against spilling their secret. She'd hoped reminding her that Trystan wasn't the forgiving type would keep her from telling him the truth about where she'd been, and who'd been posing in her place.

"Trystan needs me."

"No, Miss Grace," the Rex said, and clucked his tongue, "I'm afraid he does not."

"He's got me," Olena added. Then, at Delaney's confused look, she elaborated with, "I've come around to the idea."

And all it had taken was the murder of her father and a couple of weeks in a cell. Awesome. Any other time, Delaney probably would have been relieved to hear Olena was finally willing to accept her betrothal to the Zane. Now, though? Not so much. Not if it meant what she was afraid it did.

"Think about it, Ander; you're a smart man." The Rex turned to him. "A strategist. Who's going to complain about having Olena as Basilissa/Regina when it means avoiding having a human there? No one. It's brilliant, and thanks to my son, it'll put an end to resistance. People are prone to accepting the lesser of two evils."

The Rex lifted his chin and the Tellers moved forward, one roughly spinning Pettus away from Gibus's cell and shoving him toward the door.

Half a dozen more Tellers entered, a few breaking off to surround Delaney, while the rest moved toward a panel on the side of the wall. One man clicked away at a few buttons and then waited for the barrier keeping the Sutter trapped to drop.

"Stop!" Delaney took a step forward when they yanked Gibus out of the cell.

He tripped, and the Tellers holding him yanked him back to his feet, causing him to cry out in pain.

"Careful with that one," the Rex ordered. "We need him fully functional. The only real issue I took with my son's plan was not utilizing Sutter Gibus more appropriately. He'll be tremendous help in conquering Earth."

Delaney tried to move toward them, but she was effectively blocked off by Tellers.

"I wouldn't fret about it, Miss Grace," the Rex offered. "We won't start preparations on that until well after Olena's coronation. You'll be long gone by then. Take her."

Ruckus began yelling her name, pounding against the barrier as two Tellers reached for her. No one paid him any mind, too focused on completing their tasks.

She punched the first Teller who touched her, slamming her knuckles into the center of his throat. When he went down, she elbowed him at the top of his spine, then twisted and kicked out at the next Teller.

He dropped just as quickly, and she was about to attack another when the distinct click of an opening fritz gave her pause. It wasn't aimed at her but pointed directly at Ruckus.

She met the Rex's gaze head-on, anger warring with fear.

He held up a hand to the Teller currently holding the weapon on the Ander, and gave Delaney another once-over. The look in his eyes spoke volumes of what he thought of her, that she was becoming a nuisance he couldn't wait to be rid of.

"We'll be holding the Ander there awhile longer," he said in an even tone. "I suggest you go along quietly, Miss Grace, to ensure that nothing happens to him. I can leave him in that cell to rot if I so choose."

Olena opened her mouth, and without looking, the Rex stopped her with a hand gesture.

He didn't care what Olena wanted; obviously he never had. The only thing he cared about was himself, which made him more dangerous than Delaney had initially believed.

Had she been wrong about everything? This whole time?

"You never wanted peace," Delaney stated, needing to hear him admit it himself. "This whole thing, convincing the Basileus to betroth his heir to yours; it was all a setup from the start. You never intended equal rule, did you?"

But by being the one to suggest it, he'd certainly convinced the world otherwise. Even Ruckus had bought into it.

"Send Delaney home," Ruckus suggested desperately. "Like you said, she's no longer necessary. She did her part. Let her go. You owe her that much for dragging her into this."

"Technically," he corrected, "it was you who led the initial kidnapping, Ander. Even if that weren't the case, it's out of my hands. I can't have her warning her people we're coming, now can I?"

He was going to kill her. He'd hinted as much, but this last comment made it blatantly obvious. She was going to die on Xenith, despite all the things she'd survived. This was it, and there was no one left who could help her.

"Take her and the Teller outside," the Rex ordered, pleased when Delaney didn't fight this time. "Lead them as far from the castle as possible, somewhere no one can accidentally witness the deed. After that, leave them. We'll let the elements take care of the bodies."

"I want to be the one who does it," Olena said, and he paused to think it over.

"All right. You'll need to suit up. The temperatures are already dangerously low. They'll be deadly by the time you find the right spot and are ready to head back."

Great, more to look forward to. Delaney seriously doubted they were going to stop and get her a jacket as well. She tried to keep her expression neutral, but as soon as they started dragging her from the room, she felt her mask waver.

"Delaney!" Ruckus screamed, and pounded against the barrier again.

She tried to turn, to see him, but the Tellers blocked her view and picked up the pace.

"Delaney! Delaney!" He swore, the sounds becoming more and more desperate, trailing her all the way down the hall and up the stairs.

I love you, she sent through the fitting quickly, before they'd gotten her too far away to be able to do so. There was so much more she wanted to say to him, but there wasn't any time.

Delaney had been delusional. About all of it. She'd actually convinced herself that somehow, someway everything was going to work itself out.

At least, from the sounds of it, Ruckus was still going to get out of this alive even if she wasn't.

The second she could no longer hear him, the world seemed to fuzz around the edges. She continued moving in a trancelike state, thoughts too scrambled to catch and hold for long.

They walked for a while, Olena leading the party down the twists and turns of the halls, which were emptier than usual. At one point, they stopped and the Tellers took turns holding a fritz to Delaney's head as they each attached a strange object shaped like an octagon to the center of their chests.

"D," Pettus whispered, his voice barely breaking through to her. "Delaney, you need to focus."

Why? There was literally nothing left to do, no way out. If she fought them, and by some miracle actually managed to get away, they'd kill Ruckus. She wouldn't be able to make it back inside without being caught, even with Pettus helping.

"If you can get away, do it," she said back, ignoring the slight chuckle of the Teller currently guarding them. "They want me dead. As long as that happens, it shouldn't matter if you live. They won't hurt Ruckus for it."

Knowing Olena, a girl who somehow always managed to get what she wanted despite all odds against her, she wouldn't allow it. The Rex would give in, and Ruckus would live another day. Hopefully he'd find a way to escape later on.

"Delaney." Pettus inched closer, stopping abruptly when the Teller shook his fritz in warning. "You can't give up. It's not like you."

"All right," Olena returned, a smug look painted across her

deceptively angelic face. She made a big show of swinging her hips as she approached them. "Have you ever felt true cold before, Delaney? You're about to. This is going to be so much fun."

A humorless bark of laughter slipped past Delaney's lips.

"What could you possibly find funny?" Olena demanded.

"Nothing." She let out another chuckle, cluing her in to the fact that she was definitely losing it. "Just something Trystan said to me a while back. About hypothermia."

"Well"—Olena flicked her jet-black hair over her shoulder—"you'll be dead long before you have a chance to freeze."

"Suddenly you're fine going along with whatever the Rex wants?"

"After spending a month locked in an empty room?" Olena momentarily sobered. "Yes. You heard him the other day. Keeping my appendages is a good trade-off for having to go through bonding to Trystan."

She motioned toward the doors, clearly done explaining herself. "On our way now."

Delaney noted all of them were now wearing one of those octagonal devices. She and Pettus were the only two without. She wasn't sure how they were supposed to protect against the cold, and was partially tempted to ask. It made her feel more foolish that she could still be curious at a time like this, when she should be worried about dying.

"If we can get the cilla suits off them, we might be able to get away," Pettus murmured out of the corner of his mouth. "It'll have to be quick, though. We stay out there too long without protection, despite what the oh-so-brilliant Olena thinks, we'll begin to freeze."

"Quiet!" ordered one of the Tellers at their backs. His tone was brusque, and he was tall and muscular. Like the rest of the five Tellers, Delaney had never seen him before. They must be the Rex's private stock.

"It's fine," Olena drawled. "They'll be dead soon anyway; let them have their meaningless last moments. Oh, we're here!"

Two large doors stood before them. They were traditional Kint blue with silver paint depicting falling icicles at the top. There weren't any Tellers to open the doors for them. In fact, this entire part of the castle was silent and still, their footsteps against the solid floor the only sounds.

Olena slammed a palm onto the center of the octagon on her chest. There was a slight pressure releasing sound, a hiss, and then black fabric began shooting out from all angles. It wrapped itself around her body, somewhat like a second skin. Less than a minute later she was completely covered by the cilla suit.

It was airtight, forming gloves over her hands and even encasing her boots. A collar stretched all the way up her neck and then her head, turning to clear plastic at the front so that she was wearing a helmet. A row of built-in lights lined from her shoulder to her middle finger on each side, the colors flashing from yellow to orange to red. The lights were also on the outside of each leg, from hip to ankle, a thin piece of reflective tape beneath them.

The rest of the Tellers activated their suits, so in no time at all, she and Pettus were surrounded.

Delaney looked at them, feeling more like she was on an alien planet than she had in a while. That feeling heightened when one of the Tellers shoved open the doors, exposing the outside.

The closest she'd come to seeing the landscape had been in the Ice Dome, and even then there hadn't been much to see other than never-ending white. While that was still mostly the case, they'd opted to exit near a thick forest. The trees were dark purple and stretched so high, they looked like they disappeared into thick gray clouds. The blanketing snow had the same glimmering sheen it had in the Ice Dome, rainbows sparkling with every turn of her head.

A massive gust of wind immediately assaulted them, slapping against Delaney's cheeks hard enough that she gasped and stumbled back a step. One of the Tellers shoved her from behind, and she fell to her knees. The cold of the snow she landed in seeped through the thin material of her pants faster than she could blink.

Pettus helped her up, keeping an arm around her waist as Olena began leading them into the forest. He huddled his body close to hers, turning to take the brunt of another gale, this one almost taking them both down.

It was better among the trees, but not by much. They shielded from most of the wind, but not the ice. The sky was also darkening, and it was hard to see in front of them. While the Tellers seemed to have no problem moving in their heated suits, Delaney and Pettus stumbled around like drunks, desperately trying not to nose-dive into the deadly snow.

"If we're going to attempt this," Pettus whispered to her through chattering teeth, his face beet red, lips already turning purple, "we have to d-do it qu-quick."

Delaney clutched at him as he tripped, tugging him back up before more than one of his hands could brush against the ground.

Even still, he hissed and held his hand curled close to his chest, shaking. He'd only made contact for a split second.

She caught herself against one of the trees, the prickly pine-like needles cutting through her windburned skin as if it were tissue paper.

Trystan had warned her that the temperatures were brutal out here. But this was so much worse than she'd even imagined. This was the painful kind of cold, the sort that felt more like fire licking against your skin, burning through your veins.

She realized with a sick twist in her gut that that was the point. The Rex hadn't only wanted to make getting rid of their bodies easy. He'd wanted her to feel this. He'd wanted to torture her for daring to think she could be with his son.

This had been the real plan the whole time.

CHAPTER 28

Trystan tried to focus on the voices rushing around him, on his men gathering information from the beaten Tars, but it was a struggle. Since he'd boarded the ship yesterday, one thing had constantly hounded him, fraying his thoughts whenever he so much as attempted to place them elsewhere.

Delaney was all he could think about on the way to Kilma. Even once he'd gotten there, his mind refused to let her go, distracting him when he needed to stay focused.

"You keep claiming you don't know, but someone here has to." One of Trystan's Tellers jabbed a finger against an older Tar's shoulder as he spoke. "You will tell us the truth."

Trystan was only partially listening, annoyed by the fact his men could have easily done this job without him. Which meant he'd left Delaney for no good reason, and in the company of his father, no less.

Being away from her was hard. He'd never truly missed a person before, hadn't understood what it felt like when people claimed they did. There was this strange unsettling feeling in his chest, this annoyance whenever anyone approached him because they weren't her.

"I promise," urged the Tar currently being interrogated. "I only know what we all do. The meeting was scheduled anonymously. It's usually done that way. We have a series of secure phone lines to help conceal our identities."

"Zane?" called another Teller standing in the corner of the room, momentarily snapping Trystan back to the present.

He glanced over his shoulder at the other man, silently giving him the okay to proceed. They were currently standing in a small room built inside an abandoned warehouse. Another three spaces had been set up along the hall, each containing other high-standing Tars who'd been present for the meeting.

When Trystan and his men infiltrated the building earlier, he'd been surprised to find the Tars ill equipped for battle.

After all the trouble they'd caused, he'd expected them to put up a better fight. Instead it'd taken under an hour to subdue them, and even less time to sort the leaders from the rest.

"It's the same story, sir," the Teller continued, motioning with his chin toward the Tar.

They'd seated him against the wall but hadn't bothered with restraints. Up until this point, the Tar man had actually kept himself pretty humble, bowing, answering questions without hesitation.

It was something Trystan should have noticed right away. Something he would have if he didn't have Delaney stuck in his damn head. That was also why this was the first interrogation he'd bothered making himself present for, so he unfortunately needed the Teller to elaborate further.

"About?" he asked, seeing no other way around it.

"Everyone claims someone discovered a way around the Uprising tradition and scheduled this meeting to discuss it. But that no one here knows what it is," the Teller said.

"Truly, we do not," the Tar stated, his voice almost pleading, which caught Trystan's attention.

He made himself focus on the Tar, sitting there on the filthy dirt-covered floor. A large bruise was already starting form beneath the Tar's left eye, and his shirt had been torn at the sleeve. This man was his enemy, deserved this type of treatment, and yet Trystan couldn't help but wonder what Delaney might think if she saw what he was currently looking at.

"What's your name?" Trystan asked, taking a step closer.

"Henran, Zane." He appeared to be in his early sixties, and tipped his head respectfully at the Zane's approach.

"I was told by one of your members you all planned to riot in the streets, Henran."

"The only ones mentioning riots are you and your men. We only came here for a meeting."

"About undermining my authority and the authority of the Uprising tradition? How?" There was no way around it—Trystan had been sure of that—but he couldn't help the strain caused by the possibility.

"We came to find out."

"It's the same all around, sir," the Teller repeated. "This is the sixth time I'm hearing this myself."

"How do I know this story isn't just well rehearsed?" Trystan asked. Their organization was smart; coming up with a cover story wasn't too far of a stretch.

"It's not. But that's impossible to prove, Zane, I know that," Henran said.

"Then give me something that isn't," he countered. "Tell me something that can be proven, something legitimate."

The Tar hesitated, clearly not wanting to betray his people by giving up their secrets.

"This is your one chance," Trystan warned, "and it's amazing I'm even giving it. Think about your people in here with you, not the ones out there. You could save them a lot of pain by talking to me now."

None of this felt right, and Trystan had a bad taste on his tongue.

There were less than one hundred Tars in the building, but their numbers more than tripled that. If this was meant to be an orchestrated attack, a riot, wouldn't more of them have shown up to participate?

"It's not just the one secure line that needs to be called . . . ," Henran finally began. "There are three. Each requires a password, and the last only gets you a location."

"Of?"

"A lockbox." He sighed. "That's how we schedule random meetings. Someone leaves a coded message in a lockbox. There are only five of them in Kint, and they all need a key code. That's not given over the phone; that's something we all learn when we become members."

If that was true, anyone could set up a meeting, so long as they had the codes and passwords. But that left one element out of the equation.

How had the Tar prisoner he'd tortured in Inkwell gotten the idea there was going to be a riot?

Trystan took out his shing and then opened a file, pulling up a photo of Mickan from before he'd started his interrogation of him.

"Do you recognize this man?" He turned the screen toward the other Tar, watching closely for any sign he did. Any hint to give away he might try to lie if that were the case.

It was so clear, though, that Henran didn't, Trystan didn't even wait for verbal confirmation, already turning to the other Tellers even as the Tar stated, "No."

"Show this picture around," he ordered, hitting a few buttons to send the image to everyone there. "Anyone recognizes this man, bring them to me immediately."

"Yes, Zane." Both Tellers rushed out of the room, leaving him alone with Henran.

"Here." Trystan activated a lock on the rest of his shing so no other files could be accessed and then handed the device over to the Tar. "Type down everything you know about these secure call lines. And the locations of the lockboxes. I'm going to confirm your story."

Not that he thought it was necessary. He believed him. Which meant someone else was lying. But to what end?

If someone had gone out of their way to set the Tars up, it had to have been a person who was in the know. Henran insisted the call they'd gotten was legitimate, and considering it'd worked and the Tars had gathered here, there was no reason to believe otherwise.

It was safe to assume, then, that the same person had fed the information to Mickan about a fake riot. Thinking back on it, the circumstances of his outing as a Tar were suspicious. Hadn't Trystan been told it'd been sudden? An unfortunate slip for Mickan that had exposed him.

Only, what if it hadn't been a slip at all?

If Mickan was planted, if he'd been meant to mislead them by crying riot, what was the end game? They hadn't captured enough Tars here to make any real dent in the organization, so that couldn't be it. Was there maybe someone specifically here the caller had wanted captured? Because they had to have known Trystan would be ordered to take a team and—

He came to an abrupt stop.

It was common knowledge the Zane took point in these types of missions. Always, without fail. The only reason he'd even debated not doing so this time was Delaney. In fact, being that they were in the middle of their bonding exercises, this was probably the only thing that could draw him away from her.

Before his mind could come up with all the logical reasons he was being ridiculous, Trystan found himself exiting the room. He ran through the building, ignoring all the confused calls from the Tellers he passed. He didn't have time to explain he was leaving.

He had to get to a ship.

ALL HE WANTED to do was see Delaney. The entire trip back to Inkwell was pure, undiluted torture. He'd only felt this way once before,

·

when he'd watched her board that ship, looking like Olena. Back then, it'd been a duller sensation, more frustration and doubt than what he was feeling now. He kept telling himself to calm down, that he was more than likely overreacting. That there were a million reasons other than getting him away from here to explain Mickan's false confession.

Except that was unlikely and he knew it.

The second his ship touched down, he was out, already reaching for Delaney through their fittings as he moved. When he got no response, his fear turned to full-blown panic.

He was jumping to conclusions. Maybe she was ignoring him; that wasn't completely out of the realm of possibility. Perhaps she was with the Ander right now. Another thought hit him, that maybe this had been Ruckus's plan. It was complex, and Trystan wasn't sure how he'd manage to pull it off, but it was something to consider. Wasn't it?

Who else would need Trystan away? Would go through that much trouble to ensure he left Inkwell? Having to travel back and forth from Kilma meant Trystan would be gone for a few days. If the Ander had somehow found a way to get loose, he and Delaney might be long gone by now.

Part of him didn't want to believe it, but she'd done it before. She'd gotten on that ship, looked him straight in the eye, and left.

Things had been different then, however. Now there was something between them, something real.

Or had he imagined their connection? Had he been so caught up in these new emotions, he'd only seen what he wanted to see?

Trystan ran around the next corner, and almost smacked right into his father. He was so distracted by the racing of his heart, it took him a moment to process who it was.

"Son." The Rex clapped him on the shoulder. "I heard you were back earlier than—"

"Where is she?" No matter what the truth was, whether she was simply ignoring him or she'd left with Ruckus, his father would know about it.

"I'm not sure—"

"Tell me where she is," Trystan growled low. It took all his strength not to slam him up against the wall and beat the truth out of him. Something wasn't right. He could feel it.

There was a look in his father's eyes that he recognized. It was the same sparkle he got whenever he talked about war. More aptly, winning one.

"Where she belongs." The Rex finally dropped the fake cordial act, twisting his thin lips into a sneer. "Are those emotions coming off of you? I raised you better than that. She's a human, Trystan, honestly."

He stilled. "You agreed."

"I agreed she was useful," he corrected. "And now her use has run its course."

"What are you talking about?" He couldn't let his imagination continue to get away from him, already too close to the edge as it was. Conversations with his father took presence and calculation, neither of which he was currently capable of.

"The world already expects her to be the next Regina," Trystan tried, a lifetime of knowing his father telling him it was futile. "They've accepted. The Tars have been dealt with. They hadn't been planning a riot at all."

"I know that," the Rex said, making him freeze all over again.

"It was you." Suddenly all the pieces clicked into place. Of course it was him. He'd been the one who'd delivered Mickan, the one who'd insisted that Trystan go to Kilma. If he hadn't been so caught up in getting back to Delaney, he would have seen it sooner. "Why?"

How deeply involved had his father been? He'd known how to contact the Tars, how to call a meeting. . . . Even they'd been confused by it. How long had this been in the works? Silently, he cursed himself for being so blind. He'd always known what his father was capable of, had always kept his guard up, but this had been different. He'd wanted Delaney so badly, wanted everything to work in his favor. He hadn't paid attention.

And now it was costing him. What if it cost him everything?

"Because the world needed to think there was a legitimate force against this union," the Rex told him matter-of-factly. "As a bonus, we announced the results of the Unveiling to the public this morning. They already believe the Tars oppose this, and those who've agreed to it do so only because Tilda has claimed Miss Grace as her successor. Imagine how happy they'll all be now to have Olena? At least the girl is one of them."

Trystan had been distracted when he'd opened that last gift, both annoyed and then relieved when he'd realized she'd chosen it for Ruckus. He hadn't paid attention to Co Gailie. Yet now that he was thinking back on it, she'd seemed upset, and she'd been there in the hall when he'd left, waiting to talk with the Rex.

"You planted the item, didn't you?" It wasn't a question; the second he thought of it, he knew it was what had happened. "That's why the coordinator wanted to speak with you afterward."

She was the one who would have wrapped all the items. She would have known the second it was opened that it wasn't the right thing inside. Whatever had actually been in that yellow box Delaney had selected, it hadn't been a bad omen.

"Is she all right?" he asked. If she knew his father's secret, she was a liability.

"Now you care about the coordinator as well?" The Rex shook his head. "Really, Trystan, this has gone far enough. I realize the old Olena wasn't exactly to your tastes—and who could blame you?—but she's new and improved. Willing to behave and do exactly what we tell her. We can still have everything we planned."

"And Earth?" He needed to find out where Delaney was, and fast. He couldn't even consider that it might be too late.

"We'll take it," he said. "We still have all the necessary weaponry to do so. As soon as you and Olena are bound, we'll do away with Tilda. You'll be the Basileus of Vakar, and together, you and I will invade Earth."

"Where is she?" Standing here arguing about this wasn't going to get him anywhere, and frankly, right now none of it mattered. He didn't give a damn about the future. All he cared about was getting to Delaney.

He needed her to be okay.

"Son—"

"Tell me where she is," he ordered coldly.

"You'll never make it in time anyway," his father reasoned. "I'm on my way to a meeting with the high council in Carnage. Come with me. We can discuss things on our way there."

The last thread of Trystan's control snapped. He didn't register moving, but the next instant he'd shoved his father against the wall.

"Stand down," the Rex told the smattering of Tellers at his back who made moves closer toward them.

In his fear-induced state, Trystan hadn't even noticed they were there.

"I'm not leaving here without her."

"Stubborn to the last." His father heaved a sigh and waved at the nearest window. "She's out there. Somewhere in or past the east forest. Olena—"

He didn't stay to hear the rest, bolting past them and down the hall. The ship's heating system ensured wearing a cilla suit wasn't necessary, but he and his men all carried them anyway whenever they went on mission. After his crash during the war, he'd made it a rule, which was good now, because there wasn't time for him to stop for one.

Still, he contemplated it for half a second before rejecting the idea. By now, Delaney would be in dire need of a suit, but Trystan would have to go the opposite direction to get to where they were stored.

His father had mentioned Olena was out there. She definitely wouldn't have gone outside without one.

He could always take hers and give it to Delaney.

Trystan snapped the cilla suit onto his chest and hit the release button. The material unspooled and stretched around him protectively just as he reached the doors, and he rushed out into the harsh weather.

Their initial tracks were hard to find, the wind having mostly swept them away, but once he was past the tree line he found them. Their trail led deep into the forest, and he practically ran after it, the suit making it easier for him to do so.

He didn't know the exact time frame of their departure, and without a suit, Delaney's body would have already begun to shut down. It might be too late.

It *couldn't* be too late.

His breath fogged the plastic over his face faster than it could dissipate, and he struggled to even out his breathing. Losing his head here wasn't an option; he'd been trained for situations like this. He couldn't let his emotions cloud his judgment, even if Delaney was the reason behind them.

Especially because she was.

He tracked them to the center of the forest, momentarily losing them a second time before noticing a large dip in the snow to the left. Someone had clearly fallen and been dragged to their feet. A growl escaped from the back of his throat as he pictured Delaney on the ground, frozen and in pain.

Another ten minutes passed before he shot to the rise of a small hill, heart skipping a beat when he finally spotted them at the bottom, off to the right. The wind had picked up again, tossing snow and ice into the air, and the sky had darkened, making it harder to see anything other than shadowy figures in the distance. If not for the lights on their suits, he would have overlooked them.

Turning off the lights on his own suit, Trystan hunkered lower and quickly shuffled toward the other side of the hill so he could get the drop on them. He scanned the area, counting the Tellers he could see.

One in particular stood a few feet ahead of the rest, her form slightly smaller and lithe. She held a fritz out in front of her, the flickering blue on the side showing that the weapon was at its highest setting.

Olena.

There were two people who weren't wearing suits standing a bit away from her. If that wasn't indicator enough, he caught a flash of red hair.

Delaney.

Easing himself over the side of the hill, his right hand pressed against the ground to help keep low. The second they realized he was there, they'd kill Delaney.

The closer he got, the more apparent it became that Olena was talking, though he couldn't make out any of the words over the roaring winds. Another thing he could use to his advantage.

After what felt like an eternity, he finally reached the bottom, sidling up behind two of the nearest Tellers. There were only six of them, easy pickings so long as he took them out before Olena turned around and realized what was happening.

It was difficult not to look at Delaney, not to waste time trying to see if she was all right. If he didn't hurry, she wouldn't be. Banking down all those fears and protective urges was probably the hardest thing he'd ever had to do. He inhaled deeply, then slowly exhaled out his nose, feeling that familiar calm wash over him.

He hadn't stopped to think about his fritz, which was now encased within the suit, but he didn't need it. It was easy enough for him to kill without it.

The Teller on the left, standing only a few inches ahead of him, finally seemed to notice there was someone there. He angled his head, and was in the process of turning when Trystan struck.

He had one hand under his chin, the other at the top of his head in less than a second. The Teller's neck snapped like a twig, clean and easy. He was dead before his body hit the ground, and Trystan was already in the midst of killing someone else.

The second Teller went down just as quickly, and Trystan dropped behind another, swiping his legs out from under him. His fist collided with the center of the cilla suit, smashing the device. The material of the suit began to unravel, and he took one of the long strands, wrapping it three times around the Teller's neck.

A fourth man noticed while he was strangling the third, so Trystan dropped to the ground and hooked his legs around one of this Teller's ankles. He tugged, already moving for him before his back slammed into the snow.

The Teller lifted his fritz, slipping in the snow when he attempted to right himself. The blue lights at the side of the weapon brightened, signaling a shot was about to go off.

Trystan grabbed his wrist and twisted, hard. He couldn't hear it, even as close as he was, but he felt the snapping of bone. Needing him alive for the time being, he ignored the chorusing scream, angling the fritz so that it was aimed at the back of another Teller. Slamming his finger against the man's finger, he fired.

The Teller dropped, and the last turned to find Trystan had already set the weapon on him. He didn't even have time to contemplate raising his own fritz.

That was when Olena finally noticed them. She spun quickly, clearly taking in that she was about to be the last one standing, and then swung back around to Delaney. She pulled the trigger the same instant Trystan did, but he already knew he hadn't gotten in a good shot.

His heart stopped.

CHAPTER 29

The person standing at Delaney's side grabbed her, flinging her around to shield her with his body. The zee hit right between his shoulder blades, jolting him. For a frozen moment, nothing happened, but then he wavered on his feet.

Delaney screamed something, frantically trying to catch the man as he toppled.

Trystan turned the fritz on the Teller it belonged to, shooting him once in the head. Then he dropped the now useless weapon and bounded toward Delaney.

Olena stepped in his way at the last second, momentarily catching him off guard, and aimed her fritz at his head. Blood was seeping through her left shoulder, which hung lower than her other. The zee he'd fired had gone clean through, but it wasn't a killing blow. Not if she made it out of here and back to the castle.

Which wasn't even a remote possibility.

He went to move forward, and her hand tightened on the weapon pointedly.

"You aren't going to shoot me, Olena," he growled. "No matter what kind of deal you struck with him, my father would never forgive you for killing me."

"Just let her go," she urged frantically. "Let's just leave her here, let the cold do the rest. We don't need her! She's nothing!"

"I need her." Too late, he realized how true that was.

Her eyes narrowed into thin slits. "What is it about her that has you all losing your minds?! I'll tell him it was one of them," she said, clearly to herself. "Say they killed you accidentally. He won't blame me. I'll convince him."

"You're hardly a good actress on the best of days," he reminded her. She couldn't seriously be crazy enough to shoot him, could she?

"I can do it," she insisted. "I can be free."

A figure loomed at her back suddenly, and hands clasped Olena's skull. In one swift move, he twisted it to the right.

Olena's mouth parted and her wide eyes stared at Trystan for half a second before her body collapsed in a heap.

Trystan blinked and looked up to find the Ander's favorite Teller, Pettus, standing there, a hand pressed tightly to his chest. Blood was seeping quickly through his fingers.

"You're not the only one who knows that move," the Teller volunteered before he lost his footing and dropped a second time.

Then Delaney was there, cradling his head in her lap, the tears tracking down her bright red cheeks, already starting to freeze. The wind whipped her hair around her face, making it hard to see her eyes, but she was too busy curling her body around the Teller in a poor attempt to protect him to notice she needed protection more.

"Go," Pettus heaved, drawing Trystan's attention. The Teller was staring at him. "Get her out of here. There's not much time."

The sun had practically set in the sky. He was right. As soon as darkness fully took over, the temperatures would drop to such dangerous levels that even the suits wouldn't protect them.

"No." Delaney shook her head vehemently. "No. You're going to be fine. We're getting out of here together."

"D." Pettus tried to smile but ended up coughing instead. A smear of red stained the corner of his mouth. "It's all right."

Trystan was amazed the Teller had been alive long enough to take out Olena, let alone continue to talk. He dropped down at Delaney's side, resting a hand on her shoulder, which she immediately shook off.

He bent down next to her ear and whispered, "The cold is the only thing prolonging this. He won't make it. I'm sorry, Delaney."

"Sorry?!" She let go of Pettus long enough to slam both red-stained palms against his chest. "This is your fault! You did this!"

He clenched his jaw, noting the way frost had started to form over her eyelashes. The ice crystals being flung by the wind were also cutting into her skin, leaving painful-looking scratches across her cheeks. "We can debate over blame later; right now we have to go."

She opened her mouth, closed it, then opened it again and turned to address Pettus. Whatever she'd been about to say never left her lips.

The Teller's eyes were staring up at the sky, unseeing.

Her upper body shook, but she didn't openly cry. She was still holding him in her lap, and she went to remove one of her hands, only to find it was stuck. It was too cold, and the blood had made her palm wet.

"Hold on." Trystan hit a smaller button on his suit, protracting the helmet, then brought his face down, close enough that he could blow against the spot where her hand met the Teller's cheek. A second later he yanked, hoping he didn't end up separating her own skin instead.

He did a quick check, seeing that only patches of her first layer had come off, not enough to be an immediate issue. Then he tugged her to her feet, relived when she wrapped her arms tightly around his waist and buried her face against him. Whatever anger she'd been holding on to was gone from her for now.

His relief was short-lived. As he glanced around, he realized that it was getting too dark to navigate through the storm; they'd never make it back to the castle in time, and would more than likely get lost along the way.

"We can't leave him here," she said, but it was obvious she already knew it was impossible not to, so he didn't bother wasting his breath, or more time, addressing it. Getting her out of here was his only concern.

Stealing a suit off one of the Tellers still made sense, so he reactivated his helmet and moved them toward where he thought Olena had fallen.

"Stand here for one second," he told Delaney so he could stoop down and flip Olena's body over. He swore when he saw that ice had already crawled over the surface of the device.

Any holes in the material from the fritz shots would have repaired themselves—a handy byproduct of being programmed to refit around different bodies. But they hadn't been made to withstand these types of temperatures indefinitely, especially not during an ice storm, and they'd already been out here for longer than he had.

"That's not going to work," he cursed, getting back to his feet. He brought Delaney against him again. She needed heat, fast. Checking the other suits would be a waste of time. They'd all come out together, meaning all of them would be useless by now.

He needed another plan.

"Trystan," she slurred his name when she spoke. "I can't feel my fingers."

He had to get her out of the elements. Heading back to the castle was out of the question, which meant he needed to think up another destination. There weren't any other residences nearby, and the woods would only provide so much cover. Not nearly enough to warm her.

"You're going to be fine," he promised, turning them in the opposite direction so he could try to see something that could be useful. In the distance there was a small rise, and he was hit with recognition. "This way. We've got to go this way."

It'd been a while since he'd traveled around Inkwell, but he recalled one summer a few years back right after Dominan's father had died. Trystan had taken him for a long walk to give his mother some time alone, and they'd explored the grounds. They'd ended up not too far from where he and Delaney were currently standing.

"There's a cave," he said, mostly to try to keep conversation going. By now her body was definitely starting to shut down. "Delaney, I need you to respond, all right?"

"Okay," she said breathlessly against him, barely lifting her own legs. He was practically carrying her.

"I can build a fire inside." If there was anything dry there that he could actually light. "It's going to be fine. You're going to be fine."

"You're repeating yourself," she told him, and he almost didn't hear her, she was speaking so softly.

"Stay with me," he ordered, his throat almost closing up around the words. Though his muscles were beginning to burn, he picked up the pace, hefting her into his arms so he didn't have to worry about dragging her through the snow. She felt like a bundle of ice. "We're almost there."

Hail and icy wind pounded against his suit, scraping across the material, causing pinging sounds to echo through his helmet. He could feel the pressure, and even some of the cold. Shifting her in his hold, he effectively tucked her face more protectively against the curve of his neck. If he could feel the brutality of the elements, she must be suffering.

He could make out the edge of where he believed the cave was, but it was a stretch. After that one time, he'd never come back again. For all he knew, he'd gotten the location wrong and was actually leading them in the opposite direction. It was too late to turn back or try something else, however, so he continued driving them forward, practically melting with relief when he spotted the familiar crack.

Ideally, he'd go first, make sure there was nothing lurking within, but she wasn't moving and he feared leaving her out here for even a heartbeat.

"Okay." He set her on her feet, steadying her and positioning her so her shoulder was already partially through the crack. "I need you to walk into the cave, Delaney. The opening widens farther in, but for now you'll have to go sideways."

"I don't know." Her eyes were closed and at some point she'd stopped shivering. That wasn't a good sign.

"I need you to do this," he told her. "Now, Delaney."

She mumbled something unintelligible, so he started to ease her the rest of the way himself. He pushed her as far as his arm could reach, then was forced to let her go. It was dark and hard to tell if she was still moving or not.

"Keep going." He had to squeeze himself into the crack, feeling pressure from both sides. He almost didn't fit, but this had been a problem the first time he'd been here as well. Then, Dom had raced through the gap, small enough to fit with ease, forcing Trystan to follow despite the discomfort.

Stone scraped against him, scratching at his helmet as he slowly forced his way to the left, deeper into the cave. He felt the plastic casing begin to crack, and gritted his teeth. That was one part of the suit that wouldn't be able to patch itself.

A light shone through the other side, illuminating the tight space so that he could see he was close to the end. He came through so suddenly, he stumbled, catching himself against a wall. The cavern was small; he could stretch his arms out and touch both sides, but there weren't any creatures. There wasn't much of anything at all but dirt and pebbles.

Three pieces of the stone ceiling had fallen through, exposing the sky above, a few beams of moonlight cutting across the otherwise darkness. It hadn't been there before, and he cursed, realizing it wouldn't be nearly as warm in here as he'd hoped. Heavy flakes of snow tumbled down almost lazily, piling up to the left, while the harsh wind pounded against the outside.

Delaney was sitting in the middle of the cave, in the process of peeling off her shirt. She had it halfway over her head before he could stop her.

He yanked the thin material back in place, holding on to her wrists when she struggled against him.

"I'm burning up," she told him, weakly tugging at his grasp.

"No, you're not." He needed to start a fire, but another glance around proved what he'd feared. There was nothing in here he could use as kindling. "It's hypothermia, Delaney. You only feel like you're hot, but you aren't."

He could go back out, try to find something in the woods to burn, but one look at her had him chucking that idea. She wouldn't make it another five minutes if he left her. Hell, she wouldn't make it another five minutes with him here, not in her current state of dress. The cavern was warmer than outside, sure, but with the hole in the ceiling and the snow pouring in, it wouldn't be enough to lift her temperature.

He pushed himself back toward the exit, desperately peering through the crack in the wall. All he could see through it was white. Even if she had the time, he'd never make it through that to find dry kindling. And at this point, he wouldn't even make it back to the castle before his cilla suit froze around him.

Trystan glanced down at his suit, already bringing a hand up to the controls at the center. A thin sheet of ice was starting to make its way over the surface, slipping through the buttons. If he removed it now, it might still be salvageable, at least for one more transfer. But if it wasn't, they'd both die.

He glanced at Delaney. If she was gone, his life wouldn't matter anyway, and if there was even a remote possibility this could work, he had to take it.

Not wasting any more time, Trystan deactivated his suit, waiting for it to reel itself back into the device before placing it against her chest. Icy tendrils of air bit at him immediately, and he clenched his jaw against the stings.

"Hold still," he ordered her, even though it was clear she was barely aware of what was going on.

Pressing the center button, he kept ahold of her right up until the material began to form sleeves and gloves. Then he moved back to give her space, clenching his jaw when the helmet tried forming, and he got a good look at the crack across the front. Touching another button stopped it, and the helmet receded, leaving only a covering as high as her chin.

"If I let the helmet try to reform to your specs while its damaged, it could end up shattering," he explained, even though she hadn't asked. He waited another moment and then said shakily, "How do you feel?"

Her breathing was a bit labored, but her breaths weren't coming out in thick white puffs anymore. That was something.

"Better," she said, though she didn't sound it.

Unlike her, he was at least in long sleeves. The uniform material was warm enough that he should be okay for a while, though he could already feel numbness at the tips of his fingers. It would only get colder as the night progressed. It was warmer in the cave, mostly because it kept the storm from them, but now that she was safe in the suit, he finally had time to think of himself.

And began to doubt his survival.

"How'd you find us?" she asked.

"Tracked you down."

"Aren't you a resident Boy Scout?" Delaney mumbled.

"Someday you're going to have to tell me what all these things mean." With nothing left to do, he slid back over to her. "Come here."

She peeled open her eyes and frowned at him. "Where?"

"We need to stay warm." He patted his lap and, before she could argue, swept her up.

It looked like she was going to say something, but she was still pretty weak, and she turned to putty in his arms, her body starting to thaw.

"Aren't you going to freeze without this?" she asked after a while, indicating the suit. Her eyes were closed again, her head tucked beneath his chin. She sounded sleepy and faraway, but he wasn't as worried about that as he would have been half an hour ago. The suit was working, even without the helmet.

"You need it more than I do," he said.

"Do I?"

He stared at the small opening they'd come through, tightening his arms around her. "You almost died tonight, Delaney. If I'd been even a minute later . . . I almost lost you."

"You weren't in on it." It sounded like she was confirming it for herself, not asking.

He stilled. "Is that what my father told you? That I wanted this?"

"He said you'd set me up from the start," she slurred. "That this was all a bluff to manipulate the people into accepting Olena."

"And"—he licked his lips—"did you believe him?"

It took her a while to answer, but when she did, he felt his chest constrict.

"No," she admitted.

He smiled, but he didn't get a chance to say anything to that.

She curled herself more tightly against him, then frowned suddenly. "Can we trade off?"

"What?"

"The suit." She tugged a little at the thick material encasing her body. "If we take turns, neither one of us has to be cold for long. Give me another ten minutes—I should be fine by then. Can you last that long?" Her gaze roamed over his body, seeking out the answer before he could give it.

"You would do that?" He couldn't stop himself from staring.

She was nestled against his body, clinging to him, letting him cling to her. She had her head tipped back, red hair spilling around her shoulders, and all he wanted to do was reach out and run his hand through it. Wanted to kiss her again and never stop, and before, that thought would have been more frightening than the one of him freezing to death. But not anymore.

"Are you seriously asking me that?" She managed a glare, though it was halfhearted. Keeping up this conversation was probably taking a lot out of her. "Here, do you need it now? I'm sure—"

"Don't." He stopped her with a hand on her wrist when she reached for the controls of the suit, shaking his head. "It won't work. They weren't made to operate in these types of extremes. If you take that off now, neither of us will be able to get it on again. Keep it."

"But . . ." She pursed her lips, confused. "What about you?"

"I'll be fine." He forced a half smile. "I'm the Zane, remember?"

"Somehow I don't think the weather cares about that, Trystan."

"Delaney." He held her gaze. "Trust me. I've survived worse than this."

She seemed to be thinking it over, and then: "You mean when you saved Sanzie? Was that worse? You made it through that."

He was a little surprised Sanzie had told her that story, but it didn't really matter now, especially when it could come in handy with easing Delaney's fears. So, to help make everything seem all right, he gave in, reaching out to run his fingers through the ends of her hair. He barely felt them, too numb, but the sight of him touching her was enough to calm his racing heartbeat if only a bit.

"I did," he agreed, "and it was worse."

"You also had a fire," she added, and he could see the wheels turning, "and three other bodies to help keep you warm. Trystan—"

"Please." It wasn't clear which of the two of them was more shocked by the word, yet he continued anyway. "I need you to trust me when I say everything is going to be all right. Can you do that?"

"You're going to be okay?" she persisted. "We're both going to get out of this alive, right? I need to hear you say it."

Because he didn't lie to her. With any luck, he would make it through this, and then all this guilt over lying would be for nothing. And if he didn't . . . Well, he'd be dead. So he doubted he'd care much then anyway. About anything.

But he wasn't dead yet, and he cared about Delaney, so he grinned that same cocky grin he'd given her every other time she'd come close to cracking through his defenses. "We're both going to be okay."

And it actually wasn't entirely a lie, because as long as he knew she was going to survive this, he *would* be okay.

She might have wanted to press for more, but after a lengthy pause, she let it go. "Trystan, what are we going to do about the Rex?"

There was a growing list of things he'd like to do, that was for sure. Unfortunately, most of them wouldn't be possible. At least not yet. He wouldn't know what was until they made it back to the castle. His father would be long gone by now, hopefully taking the Tellers he'd brought with him. So long as that were the case, Trystan was confident those remaining, the regulars who worked at Inkwell, would be loyal to him.

Enough so anyway, that he could trust them not to kill Delaney on sight if she ended up returning alone.

"My father has to be stopped," he said, and it wasn't the first time he'd come to that realization. But it was the first he really meant it. If he died in this cave, what would happen to her? He didn't like the thought of that uncertainty.

She snorted. "How do you propose we do that?"

"I'm not sure," he said.

"We need to get Ruckus. You know it's true," she told him. "He can help us."

As much as he hated admitting it, she had a point. Right now he didn't know who he could trust, but the Ander would never hurt

Delaney. In fact, he'd go out of his way to ensure her safety. Just like his Teller, Pettus, had.

"I'm sorry about your friend." He was surprised to find he meant it.

"Thank you." She sighed. "I'm going to miss him. Everything is going to be different now."

"I'll protect you." If his Tellers did their jobs, they would keep her safe. Technically, that was because of him, making it another half truth. He was already beginning to shake, and it was taking all his strength not to let on. If she knew he was at risk of freezing in here, she'd panic. He didn't want that.

If these were going to be his last few hours, he wanted to spend them with the hopeful version of her.

"Trystan, he's your father. You've already disobeyed him by saving me."

"I'll protect you," he repeated with more force. "I was so afraid I'd lost you."

"I'm right here."

His father had let him leave because he'd never done anything truly rebellious against him. Generally, they stayed out of each other's way, right up until the Rex ordered him to do something specific. Like let Delaney go.

He was risking everything—*had* risked everything by coming after her.

And he didn't care.

He'd spent his entire life trying to get out from under his father's thumb, and now, here with her, he finally was. It didn't matter what happened tomorrow, whether he'd wake up again in the morning. Either way, he'd defied the Rex, and if he died, he'd defy him further by taking away his heir. And if he lived? He was going to be his father's worst nightmare.

He was done playing his father's game, had been done for quite some time now. The Ander had been right; Trystan hadn't chosen Delaney for Kint. He'd chosen her for himself.

"Delaney."

She was starting to drift, the whole ordeal having taken a lot out of her. For a moment he thought she hadn't heard him, but then she mumbled something unintelligible and waved him on with a slight circling of her finger between them.

"Something happened, while I was away . . . ," he began tentatively, unsure if he really wanted to proceed. Given their current situation, however, not doing so seemed ridiculous. He needed her to know, before it was too late for him to tell her. It wouldn't change anything anymore, but at least she'd have the truth.

"Duh." She nuzzled against him, but it didn't seem like she knew she was doing it.

"Delaney." He brushed a strand of red hair off her face.

"I'm listening," she murmured, not entirely convincingly.

"I decided I love you," he told her, admitting it aloud feeling like a heavy weight being lifted. "Now you need to decide."

Though he probably wouldn't be around to hear her decision, whatever that ended up being. He planted a kiss against the space between her neck and shoulder when she stilled, silently telling her that he didn't expect a response.

"It's all right," he said quietly, cradling her close as the wind continued to howl around them and lethargy began to trickle through him.

He smiled to himself and repeated, "I love you."

CHAPTER 30

Delaney moaned, momentarily confused as to why her entire body was stiff and achy. Her joints protested when she untangled her legs, stretching them. It took a while to pry open her eyes, and when she did, the light spilling from above was blindingly bright, stinging. She shifted against the hard surface she'd been lying on, and froze as it all came rushing back to her.

The Rex had betrayed them.

Olena had been about to kill her, in the process of gloating about how she was going to be made Basilissa, but they'd been interrupted. Trystan had come rushing in like some damn knight in shining armor, taking out those Tellers, giving Delaney his cilla suit. The strings of their conversation last night were jumbled and vague, and she could only recall bits and pieces because she'd been so out of it already.

But that last thing he'd said, that she remembered vividly.

"Trystan!" She twisted onto her knees and pulled away from him, gasping.

He wasn't moving.

She'd been curled against him, his arms still around her, but now they dropped away. He still didn't stir, and he was too pale for comfort.

"No, no, no," she whispered frantically, beginning to shake him. "Trystan, damn it, wake up! Wake up!"

Her voice rose with each word, but she hardly noticed. Eventually she was screaming at him, cursing and calling him all sorts of names as if that would somehow snap him out of it. She pressed her ear against his chest, trying to hear a heartbeat, but if there was one, she couldn't find it. She tried his pulse points next, but was met with more nothing.

This couldn't be happening.

He'd come all the way out here to save her. He couldn't be . . .

She couldn't even finish that thought.

Delaney straddled his lap and took his head in her hands, futilely trying to shake him awake again. If her body heat had been enough, though, he wouldn't have gotten to this state in the first place.

Because of the pounding of her own heart rushing blood through her ears, she almost missed the yells. She stilled when one drew closer, straining to listen. At first she feared it was the Rex's men, come to ensure the job had been completed, but then she caught the familiar lilt of Sanzie's voice.

She debated for only a second whether to leave him, but realized getting help was more important than staying. It was hard to recall entering the cave last night, the whole thing blurry in her mind, but she bolted through the crack now, popping out on the other side and falling to the ground.

The sound of running came from the right as she lifted herself, and she held up both hands in warning before Sanzie could get too close.

"Wait," Delaney said, her voice sounding scratchy and raw. It hurt to speak, but that didn't matter, not when Trystan needed her. "Give me one of your fritz."

The Sworn had at least two dozen Tellers with her, and was frantically searching around, probably for signs of the Zane. She looked almost as panicked as Delaney currently felt, a far cry from the put-together woman she'd come to know.

Delaney could feel on her cheeks the temperature had finally risen, so wasn't surprised that none of them were wearing cilla suits. Probably had to do with the fact it was early in the day now. How long had they been in that cave?

"I'm not asking," she growled when Sanzie opened her mouth to argue. "For all I know, you're working with the Rex. Give me one of your weapons, Sworn. Now. Before it's too late."

Sanzie only hesitated a second more before she began to deactivate the metallic bracelet on her left wrist. She hit a few buttons, no doubt to clear its personal imprint so Delaney could actually use it, and then slowly approached with it outstretched.

Delaney took it and clicked it on, immediately activating it and holding the gun out.

"I will shoot you," she warned, and then backed up toward the crack. "Trystan's in here, and I can't tell if he's breathing. You need to help him, but if it looks like you're going to try anything other than that—"

"I would never hurt my Zane," Sanzie interrupted, and the truth of that statement was clear in her eyes. "Or"—she held out her hands palms down—"my Lissa."

Delaney swallowed the lump in her throat, the fritz wavering in her hold. There weren't many other options but to trust her, even if it meant putting both her and Trystan's lives in her hands.

She lowered the weapon and stepped aside.

As soon as she had, Sanzie ordered her men closer and they rushed into the cave. A few others tried to direct Delaney away, talking about how they needed to get her warmed up as well, but she brushed them off.

"I'm not leaving him," she told them, watching desperately as Sanzie and the others began to maneuver Trystan's body through the crack. Her breath caught in her throat when she saw he still wasn't moving.

One of the Tellers rushed forward, dropping a black square object to the snow. It expanded, turning into a stretcher within seconds. They deposited the Zane's body on it and tossed a metallic blanket over him.

"He has a pulse," Sanzie informed her. "It's faint, but we should be able to get him back in time."

"Delaney!"

Her head whipped in the direction of Ruckus's voice, just as he ran up to her. His arms banded around her almost painfully tight, and he didn't let go.

"You're shaking," Delaney pointed out a second later when he still held her. She was torn between wanting to pull back, to check on Trystan again, and wanting to stay in the safe confines of Ruckus's hold.

"I thought—" He stopped himself, swallowing audibly. "I don't know what I would have done if you weren't here right now."

She allowed herself a second of comfort, a moment where she could pretend it was just the two of them again. That nothing else mattered. But that wasn't the truth, and too soon the reality of that hit her and she sucked in a breath. His familiar scent rushed through her, burning cedar, a crackling fire, a smell usually enough to instantly relax her.

Yet, as badly as she wanted it to, it wasn't enough, not anymore. Not with everything else currently going on, falling down around them. As badly as part of her wished otherwise, there were more important things happening here than the two of them and their reunion.

"How are *you* here right now?" Finally she did move away, enough that she could glance between him and Sanzie, who was watching as a few Tellers attached devices to Trystan. She wanted to ask about them, find out what they did, presumably how they were going to help keep him alive, but she didn't.

Mostly because none of those answers mattered. All that did was that it worked.

"Sanzie let me out," Ruckus told her. "To help search for you."

"We need to get moving, Lissa," the Sworn interrupted.

Delaney moved away from Ruckus, trusting he'd stay close, and over to Trystan. He didn't look any better than he had in the cave; in fact, out here in the light he actually looked worse.

"Let's go." She hardly recognized the commanding tone as her own, but she didn't dwell on it. No one else seemed to, either, because as soon as the order was issued, they all shot into action.

The trip back to the castle felt neverending, and Delaney kept her hand on Trystan's wrist the entire time, silently willing him to wake up. She was so focused on him, in fact, there were a few times she almost walked into a tree or tripped over a snow mound.

"Tell me about the Rex," she said to Sanzie, who was at her side. She needed to know, and she could use the distraction. Staring at Trystan wasn't going to bring him back, but she could at least figure out the rest so that when he did wake up, she'd have something useful for him.

"He left almost immediately after the Zane's arrival," she said. "He took his Tellers with him, and only left us behind because he believed his son would return shortly. I was ordered to tell the Zane to meet with him in Carnage by tomorrow night at the latest."

"Bastard." He hadn't even stuck around to be sure Trystan was all right. "How do I know I can trust you, Sanzie?"

"You trusted me enough to request I be made Sworn," she told her. "Do so again now. I swear on the stars, Lissa, my loyalties lie with you." She glanced down at Trystan pointedly. "With both of you."

"The Rex doesn't recognize my claim to the Vakar throne," Delaney reminded her.

"I am not the Rex."

"Still"—she licked her lips—"doesn't that cause a conflict of interest? He's your king."

Sanzie looked away, her expression tight, determined. "Trystan will be Rex soon enough. It's all about getting there. Always has been. And I am not the only one who feels this way."

"He has many loyal followers," Ruckus joined in then, surprising her at first because she'd almost forgotten he was there. Up until this point, he'd been quiet. "Enough that this location should remain safe for the time being. But it won't be for long."

"Once the Rex realizes how badly injured the Zane is, he'll send his personal Tellers to investigate. Try to force him to Carnage when he wakes up," Sanzie told them.

"If he wakes up," Ruckus said, and Delaney couldn't help the twist in her gut.

"He will," she growled, too focused on trying to make that true to catch the Ander's shocked expression. "How much longer till we reach the castle?"

Trystan wasn't dead yet, but that didn't mean he wouldn't die on the way there. She needed him to be all right, couldn't imagine making it through the rest of this without him, and it wasn't just because the Kint were his people. It was certainly going to be useful that he had his own following separate from his father's. Having them on their side would obviously make their survival more likely.

But that wasn't what motivated her now. It was the thought of losing him that caused her chest to constrict and her hands to shake. The idea that their conversation last night had been their last.

And she hadn't even been able to tell him what he'd wanted to hear. What he'd needed to.

Had he known when he'd said it that there was a chance he wouldn't see the next day? If so, why keep that from her? Why hadn't he told her the truth? She would have . . . Done nothing, she realized. Because there'd been nothing to do. Trystan had figured that out, probably before he'd even made the decision to give her his cilla suit.

He'd fully and unequivocally risked everything for her. Including his own life.

"We're almost there," Sanzie answered, her voice sounding far off in the midst of Delaney's major revelation.

She felt the Sworn push at her arm then, steering her out of the way of yet another tree trunk. She couldn't bring herself to pay closer attention to where she was going, afraid that if she looked away from Trystan for even a second, he'd somehow disappear.

"Perhaps you should go on ahead, Lissa," Sanzie tentatively suggested. "Take care of yourself. You have cuts all over."

Her hand inadvertently tightened on Trystan's wrist, as if she thought they might try prying her away. She shook her head vehemently and said in her most authoritative voice, "I'm not leaving him."

Sanzie nodded and continued on in silence.

Ruckus didn't say anything, either.

They were close to the castle, and once they were there, everything would be fine. They'd fix Trystan, and then they would all figure something out. First things first, getting him conscious again. And he would be.

She had to believe that. Had to believe that Sanzie was right before and that they'd be able to heal Trystan. That he'd wake up.

"I'm not leaving him," Delaney repeated.

And she meant it.

EPILOGUE

He's going to be fine, Lissa," Sanzie's soft voice came from the other side of the room, but Delaney didn't bother looking up.

They were in a small room, the soft hum of beeping machines the only sound up until the Sworn had spoken. There wasn't much aside from the bed and a couple chairs, one of which Delaney was currently seated in. Everything was white, including the unconscious Zane lying before her.

It'd been over two hours since they'd made it back to the castle, one since she'd been assured by the doctors that Trystan was going to make it. Yet he still hadn't woken up, and his color was only barely better than it'd been before.

"He doesn't look fine," she said tersely, unable to keep the bitterness at bay. The worry.

"Delaney." Ruckus leaned forward from where he was standing on the opposite side of the bed. "His body just needs more time, that's all. His vitals are good, and everyone here is doing everything they can to ensure he makes it out of this."

"Are they?" She caught his gaze, held it, even knowing it wasn't fair of her, what she was asking. "Everyone?"

There was no need to elaborate; he understood what she was

implying. He glanced between her and Sanzie, contemplating. Then he ran a hand through his dark brown hair and sighed.

"We need him," he admitted, not bothering to cover up how displeased he was by that fact. "If we're going to make it home—"

"We're not going back to Earth," Delaney cut him off. "Not yet. You know we can't. The Rex is planning on taking over there, too. We go back now, it's only a matter of time before we have to deal with him all over again, and in a place where we have no power."

Ruckus was unreadable. "And you think we have that here?"

"You're an Ander," she reminded him.

"And she's the Lissa." Sanzie stepped forward, moving to the end of the bed. Her arms were crossed over her chest, her expression serious, determined. There were splotches beneath her eyes from a sleepless, worry-filled night, but she held herself tall.

"Exactly," Ruckus stated, "the Lissa. She's considered Vakar."

"That's a nonissue," Sanzie said. "We'll follow her."

"Why would you do that?"

"Because we were ordered to do so by our Zane." She turned to address Delaney. "We are yours to command, Lissa Delaney. Whatever you choose to do, we're with you, even if that choice is getting you on a ship back to Earth as soon as possible."

Delaney couldn't help it—she snorted. "Because Trystan would love that."

"The Zane is currently out of commission," Sanzie replied. "That places you in charge. We have to do what you say. If he ends up not liking that, it's his own fault. He should have been more specific with his instructions."

She eyed the Sworn, searching for some sign this was an elaborate hoax. Try as she might, however, she couldn't. Sanzie was being serious, meaning that what Trystan had told her in the cave, that his Tellers would protect her, had been the truth. Absently, she reached out and touched him, just a brush of her fingers against the side of his arm.

"Think about it." She tried to ignore the twinge of guilt when she saw the look on Ruckus's face, barreling on before she could lose her nerve. "If we go now, we'll only be delaying the inevitable. The Rex has to be stopped, before it's too late for both of our worlds."

He'd been planning this a long time, manipulating the people around him, including his own son. There was no way for peace now, not with Olena dead and Trystan against him.

And Trystan would stand against him, Delaney was sure of that. He'd told her last night his father needed to be stopped, and she believed him. Believed he meant it.

"What makes you so sure we can trust him?" Ruckus was referring to Trystan, even though he refused to look at him now. Maybe because her hand was still touching his arm. Maybe just because he'd always hated him.

"He'll help us stop his father," Delaney insisted, urging him to see the truth in that. "If you don't trust him, trust me."

For a long, painful moment, she thought he was going to turn away from her. She'd hurt him; it was obvious even if she only partially understood how. This wasn't the time to worry about them, though, not with this massive threat looming over all the people they cared about.

So she waited, holding her breath, so that once he finally did speak, the air rushed out of her lungs in a relieved whoosh.

"Always," he told her, locking her in place with his eyes. "Always, Delaney."

"What's your plan, Lissa?" Sanzie said, reminding them both of her presence.

With her overwhelming fear for Trystan, she hadn't had much time to think of what to do next, but now a thought formed and she latched on to it. It wasn't like they had many options, or many allies, even with those loyal to the Zane.

"We wait for Trystan to wake up," she told them, "and once he does, we go pay the Basilissa a visit."

She risked a glance at Ruckus, wanting his approval, his support. He knew more about all this than she did, and if they were going to succeed, they needed to be together. She turned back to Trystan. All of them.

"I'm sure she'd want to hear her about her daughter's death," Ruckus agreed in his smooth voice. "And about who is ultimately responsible."

"And then?" Sanzie asked.

Delaney thought about everything that had happened the past month, and everything that had taken place prior. She pictured Magnus Ond and Pettus, and even Olena. Stared at Trystan. The Rex was the reason for all this, and he wasn't done.

"Then"—she met their gazes head-on, hand tightening on Trystan's arm—"we do whatever it takes."

ACKNOWLEDGMENTS

BOOK TWO! I can't believe it. So many people had a hand in making this book what it is, and I'm incredibly grateful and indebted to every single one of them.

I want to start by thanking Holly, my editor, who has had so much faith in me and these characters throughout this whole process. I don't know what I did in a past life to deserve you! You always know exactly what needs to be altered, expanded, etc., and your love for Trystan always makes me really excited to write more of him. You're also an amazingly sweet human being, and I'm glad I got to finally meet you in person. Thanks again for the Funko Pop! That pretty much makes you a (much nicer) Basilissa in my mind!

Thanks to Lauren, Emily, Teresa, and all the other fantastic Swoon Reads staff members I was able to meet. I'm sorry I can't list you all! I feel so honored to have met you, and to be able to call myself a Swoon Reads author. I know many of you also had a hand in shaping this book, and I appreciate all the notes and corrections you took the time to make.

I also want to thank Liz D. for another amazing cover. I mean, seriously. I stare at it sometimes like a weirdo.

Thanks to my aunts, Grace and Irene, for supporting me by buying copies and taking the time to read the book. It means a lot that you did! And thank you to the rest of my family for standing in my corner, even on those days where I'm editing and a serious monster to be around (sorry, Daniel).

Thanks to my mom and dad especially, for still being okay with my career choice, and taking the time to read my books. Mom, I still can't believe you read the first draft of this book seven times . . . that's . . . really strange. I don't think I've even read it seven times. I don't think I ever will read it seven times. Despite the fact that I got sick of talking about it with you, I'm really glad you loved it that much. Your opinion means the world to me.

Jon and Josie, you guys are the best. I honestly couldn't ask for better best friends. Thanks to Whitney, for letting me come visit in Vermont with my laptop in the middle of a deadline, and for not caring when I spent a good chunk of my time on it. Thanks, Vicky, Kat, Genevieve, Sarah, Tracy, and all my other friends who bought the first book and sent me photos.

Thanks to some awesome people who read the first book and reached out to me, like Marissa from Burning Bright Library (I still can't get over those candles!), and Mary Ellen (that mug, though). Also, thanks to Kayleigh, who didn't help with this book, but has helped with some other projects of mine! I can always count on you to be honest!

Mary Ellen, I am so happy to have met you! Thanks for always responding to my messages about how stressed I am, or how much I like or dislike a book!

Like with everything, thanks to Matt and Lisa.

Finally, thanks to everyone who picked up a copy of this book—or one of my past books. I definitely couldn't have done any of this without readers actually wanting to get more of the story. If you've ever left a review, commented, followed me on Instagram, etc., thank you so much. You have no idea how much hearing from you all means to me.

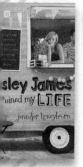

DID YOU KNOW...

READER
Swoon
READS
APPROVED

readers like you
helped to get this
book published?

Join our book-obsessed community and help us
discover awesome new writing talent.

1 Write it.

Share your original YA manuscript.

2 Read it.

Discover bright new bookish talent.

3 Share it.

Discuss, rate, and share your faves.

4 Love it.

Help us publish the books you love.

Share your own manuscript or dive between the pages
at **swoonreads.com** or by downloading the **Swoon Reads app.**